Pirvan opened one purse, pulled out a long rope of tightly wound silken cord, and checked the loop at one end. He shifted position, lowered the rope until the loop had free play, then began to swing it.

Back and forth the loop danced like a pendulum, until Pirvan judged it was moving fast enough. Then he flicked both hands, and the loop soared up to drop over one of the spikes pointing inward. A brisk tug told Pirvan that it would hold.

He pulled up most of the slack, then tied it around his waist, leaving only enough for free movement. He swung around the branch until he was hanging from it like a squirrel, found good braces for his feet, and flung himself into the air.

He flipped over as he kicked off, and landed feet first on the outer row of spikes. They bent, groaning under the impact. For a moment Pirvan feared they would bounce him on to one of the other sets of spikes, back into the branches, or off the wall entirely. But they held. It was only the first of the long night's precarious perches.

Saga

From the Creators of the
DRAGONLANCE® Saga
WARRIORS

Knights of the Crown
Roland J. Green

Maquesta Kar-Thon
Tina Daniell
(available Summer 1995)

Knights of the Sword
Roland Green
(available Winter 1995)

DragonLance® Saga

WARRIORS
Volume One

Knights of the Crown

Roland Green

DRAGONLANCE®
Warriors Series
Volume One

KNIGHTS OF THE CROWN
©1995 TSR, Inc.
All Rights Reserved.

First Printing: March 1995
Printed in the United States of America.
Library of Congress Catalog Card Number: 94-60841

9 8 7 6 5 4 3 2 1

ISBN: 0-7869-0108-X

TSR, Inc.   TSR Ltd.
201 Sheridan Springs Rd.   120 Church End, Cherry Hinton
Lake Geneva, WI 53147   Cambridge CB1 3LB
U.S.A.   United Kingdom

Prologue

Dargaard Keep rose into history and fell into ruin through Lord Soth, who could have prevented the Cataclysm but found cause to do otherwise. Its name became hardly less cursed than that of its lord.

But it was not always a ruin, haunted by evil shades and even less mentionable entities. Once it stood tall and glorious, its pink stone a beacon for anyone within three days' journeying. In the time of Istar's greatest power, it was a seat of the Knights of Solamnia, second only to Vingaard Keep itself.

The knights were not at their height in the days when Istar claimed most of the world and actually ruled a good part of it. Even in their ranks, some doubted that the knights would ever again have the high purpose that they had in the days of their founding, or more recently in the time of Huma Dragonbane. They spread their doubts, and young men eager to win honor by heroic deeds did not come forward as they once had.

Others among the knights knew better. They knew that this was one of those times when men lived so well and so much at peace that they forgot gods and warriors alike. When evil or mere folly offended the gods and sowed wars, the knights would be remembered. Men would call on them to ride out in the old way.

It was the purpose of some of those knights, in Dargaard Keep and elsewhere, to make certain preparations for that day.

Sir Marod, Knight of the Rose, had always been an early riser. On a farm, one hardly had a choice in the matter, not when the cows began lowing to be milked even before the cock's crow. In his first training at Dargaard Keep, he had been alert when too many of his comrades were still bleary-eyed and stumble-footed.

Thirty years later, he still rose early, and more so than usual on days of ceremony or battle. Today was a rite that also represented a battle won for the future of the knights, so he had been awake and praying since false dawn crept into the sky.

He had shaved his cheeks and chin and trimmed his mustache and hair, both now more silver-gray than brown, while the sky was still the color of Vingaard Keep's stone. Now he stood in white tunic and trousers, supple boots and broad belt, while his squire armed him.

Old Elius did not really deserve that traditional name, for in better days squires had been lads still in their teens, polishing their knightly skills and honor by attending their elders in chamber and on the battlefield. Elius had seen his share of battles, as a sergeant in the knights' foot scouts, and bore their marks in the form of a blind eye and a stiff knee. He deserved to be at a snug fireside, with a cup of tarberry tea and a pipe, telling of long-ago fights and frolics, rather than doing a boy's work.

But like many old warriors, Elius had neglected to provide himself with children to offer that fireside, tea, and pipe. The knights would not give the old and faithful servants to the windy road or the equally chill charity of the priests. They would provide something better.

With Elius and his like it was almost easy. Some knights needed servants, so that they could eat and sleep as well as do their duty. Others thought that their rank and state entitled them to it. If they were willing to pay for the service themselves, the leaders of the knights would look the other way.

Marod sat on a stool as Elius buckled on the leg armor and attached the spurs to the boots. Then he knelt and the two began the undignified struggle to don the heavy mail shirt. At last Marod rose, with Elius kneeling beside him to pull the shirt down to the proper level.

Now came the breastplate, the backplate, the throat protection, and the open-faced ceremonial helm with the crest of silver roses. Elius was as careful with the helmet lacings as if Marod's life would depend on them, though they were of gold-washed silk rather than robust leather and might have lasted three minutes in battle.

At last, the weapons, Marod's own choice for ceremonial occasions. He had once been chief among all the knights in the art of fighting unarmored with sword and dagger, so he wore the sword with the foxstone inlays and the dagger with the crystal pommel in the shape of a rose.

At last he looked in the mirror. It was a small one, so Elius had to move it around to give the knight a complete look at himself. Finally Marod ran a finger across his mustache and laughed softly.

"Oh, to be young again."

"Was it not you, Sir Marod, who last month left six men young enough to be your very sons, sweating and bruised when they left the training rooms?"

"I suppose it was, or someone all saw fit to confuse with me. But I was thinking of how I look in this garb. Am I only disguising myself as a warrior?"

"Eh, it's not my place to say."

"If you won't offer opinions when you have them, Elius, the knights are truly facing dire times."

"Ah, well, then I say—you don't look ready for the robe and pipe any more than I do."

Marod swallowed laughter, not too successfully, but a knock at the door drew him away.

"Who enters here?"

"Sir Lewin of Delan, attending Sir Marod."

"Enter, Sir Lewin!" Marod called. He lifted a cloak of owlbear skin, and draped it over his shoulders. Elius had just finished thrusting in a heavy gold pin when the other knight entered.

Were he a few years younger, Sir Lewin could have been the son Marod did not and now never would have. However, Marod would not have been wholly content to see any son of his loins grow to a manhood like Lewin's. The younger knight was of the second order, the Order of the Sword, so he had proved himself wise as well as formidable. But there was a brittleness in his manner and an extravagance in his dress that smelled of unhappiness—with others, with himself, with not receiving honors or attention he thought were his due?

Those were Marod's three principal guesses, but he would call them no more. Nor were any of them certain paths to dishonor or even error. Knights had fought well, lived long, and died full of years and honors with more vices than Lewin had shown so far.

"This is not an auspicious day for the knights," Lewin said briskly.

That such remarks were not an auspicious beginning for the ceremonies was on the tip of Marod's tongue. He left it there. Lewin always talked himself out of whatever temper he was in, if left alone to grumble and growl.

"Ah well, who knows what the Knights of Solamnia have admitted to their orders in days past?" Marod said, with a wry smile. "Far worse than anything we face today, I do not doubt. Yet we survive."

"We did not once survive at the mercy of Istar," Lewin said.

"I doubt that they will say much when one of their leading merchants favors today's new knight."

"Only favors? Or is he the merchant's bought man?"

That was beyond the limits that even Lewin in a temper

could be allowed.

"It is against the laws to speak against a knight's honor in that way, and very much against my wishes as well. If you hope for this day to be auspicious, consider guarding your tongue."

Lewin was not too angry to acknowledge a command from a lawful superior. He bowed his head. "Forgive me, Sir Marod."

"I do. Or rather, I will, when you have repeated your remarks to our new Knight of the Crown and begged *his* forgiveness."

"You would not—?" Lewin began, then seemed to feel the air turn chill around him from Marod's gaze alone. "You would," he finished. "Therefore, I will do as you bid. And as honor, Oath, and law require," he added, half-grudgingly.

Lewin stepped to one side, and Elius to the other, to allow Marod to precede them. The Knight of the Rose strode out, then turned to the right. As he turned, Lewin's words (and what Lewin showed on his face, which he dared not put into words) ran through his mind.

Marod had few doubts about the man who, before today's sunset, would be a Knight of the Crown. But there was even less doubt that once he had been a thief in Istar, and a prosperous one. Who would next prove worthy of the ranks of the Solamnic Knights? Kender, elves? (Full elves, that is, not half-elves, who were not unknown in the ranks of the knights and seldom much troubled if they were quiet about their ancestry.)

Two things were certain, however (at least to Sir Marod; he had doubts about other knights, beginning with Lewin). One: Almost any race could produce those who understood honor, loyalty, prowess, and statecraft. (Well, perhaps not gnomes, gully dwarves, or the majority of minotaurs.) Two: The knights could achieve little honor through their own extinction.

Content with these truths as a basis for his plans, Sir Marod quickened his pace toward the great hall.

Chapter 1

The thief crouched on the branch that reached toward the high wall of the estate. The night and the leaves concealed him for the most part, and the garb of his trade (or art, as he sometimes thought it) finished the work.

It was a summer night in Istar, so he wore shirt and trousers of light linen, dyed a soft, lustrous black and made to fit snugly, to avoid snagging on thorns or giving handholds to an enemy. His feet were shod with moccasins in the style of the Qualinesti elves' rangers, silent, supple, and also black.

He wore sailors' gloves, with strips of sharkskin woven into the palms for a better grip and light chain mail under the leather and sharkskin. He had no subtle sense of touch with these gloves, but for now he wanted his hands protected, not sensitive.

Where his shirt revealed his sinewy neck and throat, a dull glimmer of metal also revealed more light mail. A

Knight of Solamnia or a seasoned officer in Istar's army would have admired that mail—then wondered where its wearer had obtained it.

The wearer was alive and free today because he did not linger to answer such questions, even when he could not keep them from being asked in the first place.

Around his waist the thief wore a heavy belt of black leather, hung with various pouches that swayed ponderously and bulged suspiciously. They were rather an odd assortment, some bought in Pursemaker's Square, some acquired during the course of the wearer's "night work," and some made with his own hands from properly bought-and-paid-for materials to hold special tools that not one of his craft could be trusted to see.

There were more than a few of the last, for the man had been a thief for nearly fifteen years.

On his head he wore a metal cap, forged to protect the back of his head and covered with black padding both within and without to prevent chafing and soften blows. It left his ears and the whole of his face, cheeks, and throat bare—except for a carefully applied coat of blackening.

Some of the thief's comrades preferred all-encompassing combinations of hood and mask. Pirvan thought those interfered with an honest thief's hearing, might slip out of position to block his eyes, and were generally as much hazard as help.

Even among those who blackened their faces, there were differing opinions about the best material. Some favored ashes of burned Glorious Beans, others elk's-milk leaf mixed with dried bilberries, the whole burned while a Red Robe wizard cast certain minor spells over it. The thief felt that the first wore off too quickly, and that the second lasted forever—and took even longer to pay for. (Not all who lived by theft, he thought, were those who actually worked at night. There were more than a few who lived by selling to night workers that which they did not need at prices they could not truly afford.)

The crouching thief preferred a simple mixture of milk-washed hearth ashes and bear's grease, applied generously.

It had taken him some years to find a mixture that would keep anyone from gripping his face but would not shine in the moonlight, which could impartially betray thief or victim—and it did not matter which of the two bright moons cast the light. Virtuous Solinari and neutral Lunitari had at various times both helped and hindered the thief.

But he would have no more gone bare-faced to a night's work than he would have gone full-armed. The only weapon that shared space on his belt with the purses was a stout-bladed dagger, with an even stouter pommel. That pommel had much to do with the dagger's seldom having shed blood, as much as did Pirvan's distaste for violence. With the dagger reversed and the pommel applied smartly to an opponent's wrist, knee, or skull, it was a rare man who continued fight or pursuit, if he did not fall down senseless to wake later, in need of healing but not of burying or mourning.

The thief was more than a trifle proud of the fact that, though he had in his time profited enough from his night work to afford a manor (had he so chosen), no one mourned kin or swore vengeance for a life he had taken. There were those who had sworn to avenge the theft of every sort of possession, from strongboxes of golden coins to vials of alleged Qualinesti love potions. They were rare, however, folk who would avenge their goods, and less dangerous than those who sought blood.

Or so experience had taught the man who called himself Pirvan the Thief. (As with most of the brothers and sisters of the night work, he used no family name, to protect both himself and any kin.) Tonight experience would teach a different lesson, and set him on a long road away from night work. Pirvan the Thief was about to become a hero, because he could not resist the challenge of stealing the dowry jewels of Lady Eskaia of House Encuintras.

* * * * *

Pirvan was crouching by the wall around the Encuintras estate in a year when Istar ruled or at least reigned over all the human regions of Ansalon and more than a few lands held by other races. Its rule was neither as just as it had once been, nor as grasping as it later became. There were those among Istar's subjects who thought times had been better when they had ruled themselves, but in any year few went beyond muttering into their ale in the company of discreet friends.

Those mutterers, the rulers of Istar (merchants, priests, and soldiers, with occasional reluctant advice from the Towers of High Sorcery) largely left in peace. If one did not molest the various instruments of Istar's rule, one seldom suffered their attention.

It goes almost without saying that Istar's rule brought wealth to the city. Indeed, never had Krynn seen so much wealth gathered in one place. The blood of fighters in the arena flowed over gilded armor, and there was at least bread and wine, clean water, and healing for all but the poorest.

This wealth changed hands by many means, from the most lawful (purchase or tax collection) down to the work of the common cutpurses and smash-and-snatch artists. Pirvan was a thief of the highest sort, who stole more than he needed to keep food in his belly only because he enjoyed the challenge of besting someone's defenses.

Even Pirvan's kind of thievery was not a recognized profession, with a guild of its own. Both the laws of Istar and the demonstrated will of the gods limited the lawfulness of thieves. But there were those among the ranks of the wise thieves who sat in judgment on their comrades when they behaved too much like cutpurses, killing, hurting without need, stealing too much or from those whom the loss would injure, or engaging in other outrages.

Pirvan's hands had been clean these past fifteen years, and he was proud of the fact. But a man who practices both honor and theft walks a tightrope over the Abyss, and at various times good, neutral, and evil gods may give that rope a tweak, if only to see what may happen.

The idle curiosity of the gods had been the downfall of many men living less dangerously than Pirvan the Thief.

* * * * *

A light glimmered in the distance, roughly from the direction of the main house. The glow had to wriggle past too many leaf-heavy branches to tell Pirvan more. It was spring in Istar, a warm spring after a wet and mild winter, and growing things flourished exceedingly.

It was late enough in the day that Istar had fallen into slumber, and few with lawful business were abroad. The exceptions were the patrons of certain taverns and the workers at the markets and docks, unloading the night's cargoes and making them ready for the day.

Those were all a long way from the estate. Nothing except the breeze and night birds broke the silence. Pirvan lowered himself onto a branch as cautiously as a cat stalking one of those birds, to keep it from creaking. He lay motionlessly until the light went out, without any noises coming to join it.

As far as he could tell, the Encuintras estate had joined the rest of Istar in slumber.

He studied the wall. It was three times his height and half his height broad. The top flourished no fewer than three rows of silvered iron spikes, one jutting outward, one jutting inward, and one revolving in a slot in the middle.

Those spikes were encouraging. People who built such stout physical defenses seldom went to the additional expense of magical ones—at least in Istar, where a thief who wielded potent spells was apt to have the mages, the priests, *and* the sharp steel of his comrades pursuing him to the death.

Pirvan had enough magical talent that he might have earned a modest living in one of the lesser traveling shows, doing minor conjury, juggling with the aid of a levitation spell, and so on. A modest illusion caster, he had firm command of only one considerable spell, and no hope of penetrating or defending himself against serious magical defenses.

However, the physical defenses he'd seen so far were formidable enough. His mail might protect him if he drove hard against any of the spikes; better not put it to such drastic proof. Besides, his agility was his greatest pride—though "a man most often ends in the arena for what he's proudest of" was an old saying in Istar's back streets.

Pirvan opened one purse, pulled out a long rope of tightly wound silken cord, and checked the loop at one end. He shifted position, lowered the rope until the loop had free play, then began to swing it.

Back and forth the loop danced like a pendulum, until Pirvan judged it was moving fast enough. Then he flicked both hands, and the loop soared up to drop over one of the spikes pointing inward. A brisk tug told Pirvan that it would hold.

He pulled up most of the slack, then tied it around his waist, leaving only enough for free movement. He swung around the branch until he was hanging from it like a squirrel, found good braces for his feet, and flung himself into the air.

He flipped over as he kicked off, and landed feet first on the outer row of spikes. They bent, groaning under the impact. For a moment Pirvan feared they would bounce him on to one of the other sets of spikes, back into the branches, or off the wall entirely.

With another groan the spikes straightened themselves, but so slowly that Pirvan was able to step off them and onto the top of the wall in good order. He knelt and thrust several thin bronze nails firmly into the slot holding the nearest set of revolving spikes. With a few taps of a small padded hammer, he drove the nails in, until a spear's length of the revolving spikes was locked in place for the night.

Then he crossed the wall, stepping carefully and crouching low. Shards of glass and pottery were embedded edge-upward in the top of the wall, making him wish he had a layer of mail in his shoes. He was also glad he hadn't put much weight on the rope so far.

Against the background of the tree and the night he should be hard to see from almost any angle. But if he was careless, as surely as Huma slew dragons, a pair of servants would find for an exchange of affection the one place that let them see him.

Perhaps they would have their attention elsewhere—and perhaps not. Pirvan remained crouching in silence until anyone who had seen him could have given the alarm five times over. He thought briefly of clever traps, decided that that was taking too much counsel from his fears, and swung himself on his hands over the inner row of spikes.

A moment later he'd slid down to the ground, tweaked the loop's slipknot to free the rope, and gone to cover behind the nearest clump of bushes. They had the slightly sour odor of young rattlebeans, but a more pleasant scent and a few thorns told Pirvan that wood roses were twining around the rattlebean branches on their way up the inside of the wall.

Pirvan plucked a half-open rosebud and thrust it under the collar of his shirt. Then he crouched still lower and peered out from under the bush at the rest of the path to the house.

It was not a long way, perhaps fifty paces, and much of that offered cover enough for three minotaurs and a newly hatched dragonet. The nobles of House Encuintras clearly had gone right on flaunting their age-old skill at making splendid gardens, even now, when they no longer had to arrange so much as a bouquet with their own hands.

Some of the great merchant families modeled their estates on the manors, fortified or not, of the great landed lords. It was as if they wanted to suggest to the world that their ancestors had ruled broad expanses of land and armies of loyal peasants from the days of Vinas Solamnus, if not earlier.

Any self-respecting thief became something of an expert on any house that might offer worthwhile takings, and Pirvan had more curiosity than most. He knew how few of the great merchants had great-grandfathers they could present in public—and how House Encuintras was one with ancestors it could flaunt before all the world.

Indeed, the blood of Istar's old protectors ran in Lady Eskaia's veins. Yet everything between Pirvan and the house would hardly have made a decent kitchen garden on some estates. The house itself was large, but much of it unashamedly new, with no architectural fripperies to make it look ancient, and generally seemed no more than a merchant's townhouse levitated to the middle of a well-wrought garden.

House Encuintras had probably been no more honest than most merchants, in the days when it had scrabbled for every coin. Now that those days were past, it could afford only—and even practiced—*some* honesty.

Pirvan liked this among the powerful. It made it more of a pleasure to match wits with them.

For the moment, he needed less keenness of wits than fleetness of foot. He studied the grounds, calling eyes, ears, and even nose to his aid. No guard animals appeared, neither dogs, leopards, nor griffons (not that this close to the city he expected to find even the youngest and tamest of griffons).

No human guards, either, though someone had to be watching from somewhere. It was against nature for treasure to go unguarded.

Pirvan took a moment to jerk the slipknot on the loop of his rope. It hissed down into the bushes; he untangled it and rewound it about his waist. To leave one's rope ready might save a few seconds escaping, if one was lucky enough to escape the way one entered. More often, someone saw the rope, drew the appropriate conclusions, and raised the alarm at some inevitably inconvenient moment.

With the rope secured, Pirvan began his tortuous path toward the house. He had some surety about human and animal guards and magical defenses; less about mantraps and other mechanical devices. He darted from cover to cover, once using a fountain, another time a bench, but always crossing open ground as quickly as he could—which was faster than most men.

Each time he reached open ground, he faced a delicate decision, the kind he'd trained to make for half his life. Stay in the shadows, which might hide a mantrap, or cross open ground, where moonlight could reveal both traps and him? It helped that not only was he fleeter of foot than most men, but he could also see farther to either side.

His moccasins were smeared with an herbal oil that made it hard for any animal hunting by scent to track him. Every few paces he also dropped a small biscuit, baked from deergrass flour and both tempting and soporific to dogs and leopards.

Nothing lurked anywhere, nothing sprang out at him, and he reached the house without working up more sweat than the warm night had already raised under his clothing. He knew of thieves who did their night work, in spring and summer at least, in no more than a loinguard and tool belt, but that seemed an invitation to being assaulted and even repelled by common thorns.

Pirvan chose to maintain his dignity in the profession he practiced, if he could not turn to another.

From the rough plan of the house he'd obtained through devious means (including, but not limited to, indiscreet servants), he knew that the main strongroom was in the cellar, as usual. Another strongroom was off the kitchen, in the charge of the cook and holding the ceremonial tableware—doubtless valuable, but also heavy to remove and easily recognizable. (Those who melted down gold and silver articles were not above taking one bribe from a thief to hide his tracks, and another from the local watch to describe his face.)

There were also lesser strongrooms on the two family floors, and no doubt something on the upper floors for the servants who made enough (honestly or otherwise) to have possessions thieves would covet. Pirvan would not contemplate preying there; a ladies' maid might have scrimped for ten years to buy a moonstone ring.

Nor would he have time or tools to defeat the kitchen or cellar locks. For that sort of work, only the thieves willing to invest in unlawfully potent magic or hideously expensive tool kits could escape without corrupting a servant. Pirvan had numerous objections to this course of action, not least of which was that you put your future in the hands of someone who, if bribed once, might be bribed a second time. One could not corrupt others without corrupting oneself (not wise for one whose work constantly threatened to push him over into evil.)

So it had to be the two family floors. What was the best way in? All the way up to the roof would give him the best chances to spy out the ground without being seen or (if lucky) heard by wakeful spit boys in the dormitories. However, the roof was a long way up, and its edge (at least on this side) was free of protrusions on which to catch a rope. The wall was almost equally free of climbing vines, close-crowding trees, trellises, or other conveniences for the thief in a hurry.

However, that was only one of at least seven and probably more walls. The house had originally been built as a simple square. It had soon thereafter sprouted protrusions on at least three sides, designed more to increase usable space than for beauty of design or keeping out intruders.

Pirvan began his circuit of the house.

On the third side he came to that amorous couple whom he had feared. They were making enough noise that he was in no danger of stumbling over them, as he would have needed to do to attract their attention. If their enthusiasm had not already wakened the whole house, Pirvan thought, those within could hardly be alert or watchful.

The fourth side offered a two-story wing, with a balcony atop it. The balcony railing would have been easy to hook, but Pirvan preferred loops to hooks (the debate over their respective merits was loud and long among those thieves whose night work required either). Fortunately the balcony's uprights also ended in complex brass ornaments, with delicate lacing around solid cores, elven work, probably, or at least elven influenced—but stout enough to support Grimsoar One-Eye climbing a warship's anchor chain.

Pirvan briefly wished that he had Grimsoar One-Eye either ready on the balcony to haul him up or at least waiting outside to cover their retreat. Dividing the fruits of tonight's work would be no great matter with Grimsoar. Their methods for night work differed as greatly as their bodies—Grimsoar would make two of Pirvan—and they had not worked together for more than a year. Yet this had not made any great difference to their friendship.

Another brief wish: Would he ever find work where friends would be present in body instead of just his thoughts?

"He who wishes for stars will fall into ditches," was a motto the thieves had adopted for their own, even if they had not invented it.

Pirvan cleared his mind of all but attention to his work and unwound the rope from his waist.

* * * * *

Reaching the balcony was the work of moments, and retrieving his rope the work of only a few more. He studied the grounds as he coiled the rope; the amorous pair was still at *their* night work. The woman seemed to have her eyes cast upward, but whether she saw anything farther than her partner's forelock was open to doubt.

Pirvan had expected that the balcony would lead him to a corridor straight to the stairways. Instead, looking in through the metal lattices of the shutters showed him fine brocade curtains, and a gap in the curtains showed him a bedroom. A lady's, he judged—and therefore not honorable prey, only a proper passageway to such.

For a short while, Pirvan had to wonder if he would ever reach the passageway. If the shutters weren't dwarf work, they were something not much less robust. Cutting the metal without waking half of Istar would have taxed a dragon's strength and ingenuity; it blunted several of

Pirvan's tools. It was only after this that he discovered the cunning lock, working from both outside and inside but virtually invisible from the outside. He had unblunted tools enough to make short work of that, and by the favor of Reorx the hinges did not squeal when he opened the shutters.

Inside was definitely the bedchamber of a wealthy young woman, doubtless a daughter of the house, perhaps even Eskaia herself. A night lamp let Pirvan see new masonry and fresh plaster where the walls were not covered thickly with paint or tapestry. Clearly there had been some alterations made to the family quarters since he had finished assembling his map.

Staying half behind curtains, half in shadow, Pirvan studied the room. The great canopied bed stood a dagger's length off the floor and appeared to be occupied—at least the dark curls spread out over the pillow were no doll's. Pirvan listened, heard soft but even breathing, and steadied his own breath until it was inaudible.

The room displayed wealth without flaunting it, and Pirvan's opinion of the room's occupant rose. Unfortunately, everything in the room was, as prey, even worse than dishonorable. It was like the ceremonial dinnerware, either too distinctive to dispose of safely or too stout to remove at all.

The table by the wall, for example—rose marble legs, a black marble top, a screen of silver and ebony set with aquamarine, and in the screen a silvered mirror and dozens of little gilded niches holding crystal pots with gold or even jeweled lids. Exquisite work, all of it, doubtless the lady's grooming table, equally doubtless worth a good-sized farm—and so heavy that it would need two minotaurs willing to sweat to lift it!

Pirvan noted in his mind to collect one or two of the cosmetic pots if he needed to make a quick escape this way with nothing else to show for his night's work. Then he sidled toward the door—at the exact moment that a key rattled in the lock.

Pirvan's quickness knew few limits when his life or

freedom were in danger. The night lamp was beyond the reach of his hand, but not beyond the reach of his dagger's heavy pommel. It flickered out like a serpent's tongue, crushing the flame out of the wick. Acrid smoke fought with and was finally subdued by the scent of roses and delicate perfume.

The door opened moments after Pirvan had found the best if least dignified concealment in the room—under the bed. He had time to hope that the newcomer was not a lover who was about to agitate the bed in conjunction with its occupant. At least one thief Pirvan knew had been seriously hurt under such circumstances, then captured because the bed's occupants were not too besotted to notice the moans coming from under the bed!

He also had time for relief, that the newcomer was a woman. She was as tall as he and possibly as strong, judging from the solid wrists and the wide shoulders. The face was heart-shaped, however, the wide eyes an appealing green, and the hair (cut as if intended to fit under a helmet) shining and fair.

The woman wore sandals of gold-stamped leather, a robe of fine linen that clung to a figure well worth clinging to, and a broad, plain leather belt that held a purse and a dagger. Pirvan had no time to speculate what this curious combination might signify, when the woman turned and came straight for the bed.

Pirvan could not make himself invisible, but he did the next best thing. He cast the Spell of Seeing the Expected, making himself look like one of the spare quilts sprinkled with herbs and thrust under the bed in a silken bag. He was sure he only roughly matched the shape and probably did not match the color at all, but the woman was unlikely to look under the bed with a lamp in her hand, and the spell would conceal him against anything short of that.

The woman did not look under the bed. Instead she knelt beside it and reached both hands beneath without looking. If she had looked, Pirvan's luck might have been up, because her left hand passed within a finger's length of his nose. Even in the shadows and through the faint blurring of the spell, Pirvan saw that the hand was strong and shapely, with short, clean nails, weapon calluses on palms and fingers, a fresh, ridged scar across the back, and a shallower, older scar on the wrist.

Both hands gripped something in the deeper shadows just above Pirvan's head and withdrew. He heard the clink of a lock or catch, something falling, something else (heavier and wooden, he thought) also falling, and another clink. He saw the hands returning, this time clearly holding something thin, dark, and rectangular. They seemed to lay it down in thin air, then withdrew again.

Pirvan waited long after the hands withdrew, and even a good while after the hands' owner withdrew. Apart from relighting the night lamp, the warrior-lady did not linger, and Pirvan now remembered tales that one of Lady Eskaia's chief maids, being a retired mercenary, also served as her bodyguard.

Why retired? Pirvan asked the shadows. She's younger than I am, or I'm a gully dwarf.

Pirvan reached cautiously into the shadows until his fingers met something in the right place. A cautious tap said "wood." A cautious grasp brought down a wooden strongbox, as plain as any journeyman carpenter had ever made for himself, to hold the day's earnings.

Indeed, it lacked even the simplest of locks. Clearly this was something protected by secrecy rather than strength. Pirvan flipped the latch, trusting to his gloves to guard him against any spring-thrust poisoned needles.

Instead his grip slipped, and the box upended, spilling a dozen small, irregular silk packages to the floor. They were about the size of large lumps of charcoal, but from the sound they made, were a good deal heavier. They also felt heavier in Pirvan's hands, and when he opened one, he understood why.

After opening the rest, he understood much more. He held in his hand a fortune in gemstones, enough to buy this estate or dower Lady Eskaia for marriage to a prince.

Rubies, moonstones, serpent's-crowns, and more—none set, but all cut and faceted by the hand of a master. Possibly of use in magic, but one would have to deal with a mage to sell them for that. Without that dishonorable and dangerous course, they were still of use in giving one Pirvan the Thief an easy life for some time.

If Lady Eskaia and her house could spare that much. The jewels being concealed this way suggested that they were a secret between the lady and her martial maid. This suggested that they would not raise a great uproar about their disappearance.

The jewelers also would not raise an uproar. But they might ask hard questions about more than—oh, six such bags. Since each bag contained seven or eight jewels each worth a month's easy living, Pirvan decided against taking more than six. Indeed, three might be enough—but since he had never encountered such a light and valuable fruit of a night's work, why not make it four?

Four bags of jewels were in a pouch carefully left empty for just such a purpose when Pirvan crawled out from under the bed and began retracing his steps.

Chapter 2

The Willow Wand was not famous throughout Ansalon or even throughout the city of Istar. This was exactly the way the owners wanted it.

"Famous taverns go through three stages," one of them had said, some years before Pirvan had begun frequenting the place. "First, they flourish because everybody is coming and spending freely. Then the money doesn't roll in so freely, because people are coming to be seen rather than enjoy themselves. That sort drives the paying customers away, faster than a drunken minotaur.

"Finally, the 'I was at the Willow Wand last night' sort find some other place to go. They leave, all the others are gone already, and if you don't have to shut your doors, it's only because Shinare is on your side. Now, what kind of ale did you order?"

The owners carried this opinion so far that about the time Pirvan became a notable thief, the Willow Wand became a notable place if you wanted to be invisible while you amused yourself. This a man or woman could do easily enough, as the food was good, the drink better (after the owners disposed of a lot of alleged dwarf spirits, which they bought under circumstances they would never reveal), the rooms were clean, and the service as friendly as anyone might reasonably wish.

Two nights after his night work at the Encuintras estate, Pirvan was sitting at a table in a shadowy alcove, normally reserved for three or four guests. But it was a slow night; Reida had led him straight to the table and put down a mug of beer before he even had a chance to slip his boots off. She came back with bread and cheese, pickles, and word that the special stew was almost hot.

Pirvan went through two servings of the bread and cheese before the stew came (it hadn't been as far along as Reida had thought), and ordered another beer with the stew. Even a single use of his one modest spell took a good deal out of him, and he'd had to use it again on his way out, making himself look like an elaborately pruned dragon's-tongue bush for nearly ten minutes. (He'd met the lovers on their way in, with no time to hide. They were disheveled and sweaty, but not so far into passion now that they would overlook a strange man clad entirely in black wandering the grounds.)

The best way to put back into himself what the spell took out was to rest and eat well for a few days. The recovery had gone on longer than it had the last time he'd needed the spell, and he'd begun to think that the years were overtaking him. (If so, he intended to give them a long chase. He also intended to avoid having to use the Spell of Seeing the Expected more than once in any single piece of night work.)

The stew had potatoes, onions, carrots, lamb, and assorted spices. Tonight was one of the milder versions; Pirvan had encountered one batch that was potent enough to fire from siege engines, to spatter over attackers and blind them, or even blister them inside their armor. Pirvan all but inhaled the first bowl, and Reida was there with a second one before he knew that he was going to ask for it.

"Never understood how you can eat so much and stay so lean," she said, setting the bowl before him.

Pirvan smiled before he touched his spoon. Most women described him as "thin" or something even less flattering. Reida had a reputation of being the friendliest of the serving maids, though she was pleasant-looking rather than pretty. Indeed, it was said that she could be *very* friendly indeed, if she liked you—but her likes and dislikes were as random as lightning bolts (and she had a tongue that could burn anyone she disliked as thoroughly as the lightning, too).

Pirvan was nearly halfway through the second bowl of stew and beginning to think about fruit tarts when he noticed that Reida was still standing by his table. She also hadn't returned his smile. In fact, she wore a frown and the general air of one with good cause for worry.

"What is it, Reida?"

She looked around the room, then perched on the table, with her skirt hiked higher than usual. She ran the fingers of one hand through Pirvan's hair, then bent over to whisper:

"Four men, in the back room. Say they're looking for you."

"Four?" That might let out the watchmen; they seldom came to the Willow Wand at all and never more than a pair at a time. But saying that four men weren't the watch said little about what they were.

"Any of them big, black-haired, and one-eyed?" Any band that Grimsoar One-Eye had joined could hardly mean him harm.

Reida looked uncertain, whether about the men or about whether she should answer at all. Then she frowned again.

"There's one with a patch over his left eye, that much I saw," she said. "But he didn't seem all that big, and his hair was more red than—"

Pirvan held up a hand. Left eye missing and red hair meant Silgor of the Swords (he both wielded and stole them with uncommon skill). He had done little night work in the past three years, and was more likely to be found seeking thieves who had done what they shouldn't have done or left undone something that they should have done.

Pirvan wondered which group he fell into. He also wondered, very briefly, what his chances were of finding out before he joined the four men. He decided almost at once that they were small, without risking being branded a fugitive from what the elder thieves called "brothers' justice."

That was closer to outlawry than any man with wits in his head could wish for. It was apt to end with both the thieves and the watch offering rewards for a man (or his head) sufficient to make a girl like Reida turn him in before her second smile. Perhaps especially Reida, who might otherwise be suspected of having warned Pirvan. (The thieves would not shed her blood, but to end on the streets with no hopes of work in Istar might be only a slower death.)

"Tell them that I will join them—" He paused. "Are they staying here?"

"No."

"As well. I will meet them at the back gate of the timberyard across the alley when I have finished my dinner."

Reida's shoulders sagged with relief. Pirvan smiled. "Don't worry, Reida. You know what a fuss I make about not dragging the innocent—"

"What are you calling me?" Reida snapped, drawing herself up. The stance plus the low-cut blouse displayed a figure that was rather better than Pirvan had realized.

"Not what you think. You can have my company for the asking when I come back from meeting my friends."

Her eyebrows rose, and she grinned. "Break that promise, and there'll be a purgative in your next beer in this house."

Pirvan mimed horror, then addressed the rest of his

meal. The fruit tart, he decided, would take longer than was prudent.

* * * * *

The work that had expanded Lady Eskaia's bedchamber into one end of the second-floor corridor had also thickened its walls. They barred eavesdroppers almost as effectively as magic could have done.

Tonight, this was just as well.

Haimya (she could have called herself "Lady Haimya" had she thought the title a compliment) glared at her mistress. The maid wore a foot soldier's armor, except for the helmet, which she had under her arm, and lower, lighter boots. She also wore a sword as formidable as most Knights of Solamnia ever bore, though plainer and more hacked and scarred along the blade than any knight would have allowed.

The sword at Haimya's waist was hardly deadlier than the look on her face. Lady Eskaia was unaccustomed to having such looks directed at her, least of all from Haimya. In another moment Haimya would unleash her mercenary's vocabulary, and if anyone heard *that*, Haimya would be out of Eskaia's service and off the Encuintras estate before Lunitari dipped below the horizon.

"What I have done is quite lawful," Eskaia said.

Haimya shook herself, like a horse beset by flies. "It is something you will not be punished for doing," she replied. "That is not the same as lawful."

"Perhaps. But would you rather do it yourself and end in the arena?"

"Yes." That reduced Eskaia to speechlessness. Haimya went on.

"What angers me is not whether you, or I, or anybody will be punished for this. It is that you did it at all, without mentioning it to me."

"I am not at your beck and call, Haimya."

Haimya said a word that would have curdled milk if there had been any milch cows within forty paces. She took a deep breath.

"Do you remember a single word of my oath?"

"The one you swore when you entered Kingoll's Companions?"

"That one. He asked it of all women who entered his band. It was one of the things that proved him a wise man."

"I might agree, if I remembered it."

Haimya did not curse again. She sighed. "It is too long to repeat. But there is in it a promise to protect myself with my own strength and not ask for another's aid."

"Even if the alternative is death?"

"If I must win or be dishonored, I must accept whatever aid is needed for victory. But if it is not a matter of honor—"

"What makes you think this matter is anything else?" Eskaia snapped. Honor was needed, but tonight good sense as well. "Apart from the fate of your betrothed, is it honor to wink at the theft of my gift to you. You did not disdain it when I offered it.

"Of course, if you are eager to end your betrothal, you may do that with my blessing. As long as we regain the jewels—"

Eskaia stopped. Haimya wasn't crying, but her shoulders were shaking and her eyes were tightly shut. Eskaia gripped her guard-maid by both shoulders.

"Pour us both some wine, Haimya, and let me tell you *all* of what we are doing. When you learn how many lies I have told, perhaps you will not think so ill of me."

A furtive tear crept out of the corner of one of Haimya's eyes. Without opening either eyes, she wiped it away with the back of her hand. Then she forced a smile.

"Speak, Mistress. Your servant hears and obeys."

Eskaia had to stop giggling before she could begin her explanation.

* * * * *

Pirvan considered himself something of an authority on alleys. Istar had the cleanest he'd known, which meant that work gangs shoveled the refuse into carts every ten days or so. As it had been nearly that long since the last gang's visit and the weather had been hot and damp, the alley behind the Willow Wand was no flower garden.

The four men waiting for him were also not much to Pirvan's taste. He didn't recognize two at all, and he took no heart from recognizing the third. He did not know the man's name, but knew that he had seldom succeeded at night work. He was more successful as a fighter when one was needed for keeping the thieves in order.

Silgor stepped forward to greet Pirvan. He looked grim, even in the shadowed alley, but then he rarely smiled. Pirvan raised a hand in greeting.

"Hail, Brother. What is your business with me?"

"Best not spoken of here."

Custom and law allowed it. Good sense discouraged it.

"If I do not know why I must go with you, what duty do I have to go at all?"

"Duty doesn't matter," the fighter said. He stopped short of drawing his sword only because Silgor put a hand on his arm.

"Peace. I am sure that Pirvan can be brought to trust us."

Not without knowing what goes on here, Pirvan thought.

Silgor and the sell-sword were transparently playing the game of one angry, one mild, and less well than some watchmen Pirvan had encountered. He chose not to laugh.

"You do not need to take half the night explaining, Silgor. We do not have that much time, whether I go with you or not."

"Turn, fugitive," the second man growled, "and you won't see sunrise."

"Who will arrange that?" Pirvan said. "You? And which ten knights will help you?"

The sword started out again. Silgor did not try to restrain the man. Pirvan took two steps backward, made sure that he had his back to a solid wall, then did laugh.

"Silgor, I learned the angry-mild game at my mother's knee, or as close to it as matters for now. If you think you'll do anything but waste time by playing it, you're not the man you were only a month ago. That would be a sad blow to the thieves, enough to make me think of retiring."

Silgor had the grace to smile. His head jerked at the swordsman, and the blade vanished again. The other two men looked outright relieved.

"Very well. I will ask you a question. Will you answer truthfully?"

"Is the answer under bond, oath, and spell of silence?"

"Will the first two be enough?"

"From you, Silgor, I suppose so."

"Flattery also can waste time, my friend." Silgor took a breath. "Did you, two days ago, perform night work at the Encuintras estate? And was the fruit of your work—?"

"That's two questions, Silgor."

"Stop quibbling, Pirvan." Another deep breath. "Did you perform the night work of which I just spoke?"

"Yes."

"It was not work well done. Do you—oh, forgive me. One question only. But—now will you come with us?"

Pirvan nodded. He doubted that anything much would come of it, but he doubted (and regretted) more that his meeting with Reida seemed unlikely to come about.

* * * * *

Haimya was so long silent after Lady Eskaia had finished her narrative that the merchant princess felt an urge to shout in her guard's face or shake her.

She resisted both. Neither would cause Haimya to alter her judgment of what Eskaia had done. Either risked a quarrel. A quarrel with her most trusted—nay, very nearly only—friend at this, of all times, would be folly.

If the truth about the stolen jewels ever came to her father's ears, he might be angry. If he heard of her quarreling with Haimya, he would be furious. Disinheriting her as a witling not to be trusted with her share of her inheritance was not beyond probability.

Haimya at last picked up the wine jug and filled both their cups, then emptied hers with the stiff wrist and busy throat of one who badly needs a drink. The silence returned for a moment, then Haimya frowned.

"Is Tarothin a mage, foresworn to the towers?" Haimya asked.

"He is neutral," Eskaia replied.

"He says he is neutral," Haimya corrected. "That's a claim anyone can make, at least to those unable to test it."

"I have had some of the cleric's training. Or have you forgotten that?"

"Not in the least. But consider that one trained in high sorcery can conceal much from even a full cleric with many years of training."

"Very well," Eskaia said briskly. "Supposing that he cannot be completely trusted, what do you suggest? A messenger, telling him to do nothing until they have had a chance to reply to my request for the thief's name?"

"Better yet, tell him to do nothing until you explicitly command him to do so."

"He will not care for such a sign of distrust, I fear."

"If his vanity is that swollen, perhaps you need to dismiss him completely and find another to do the work."

"Haimya, what are the odds of finding another wizard willing, able, and trustworthy? Especially after word spreads of the fate of the first one?"

Haimya was silent. Eskaia decided to press whatever advantage she had.

"For that kind of message, perhaps you should be the messenger yourself. You have more authority. Also, the fewer who know of Tarothin's existence, the better."

Haimya smiled. "Go on like this, my lady, and you will be a finished intriguer before you are wed."

Eskaia was not sure that was entirely a compliment. But she would let it pass, since the danger of a quarrel with Haimya was gone.

* * * * *

The witnesses to Pirvan's description of his night work at the Encuintras estate were Silgor and three others. Pirvan knew two of these: Cresponis, a retired pirate, and

Yanitzia, one of the few women to rise high enough for such duties. The last man was a stranger to Pirvan, clearly near eighty, and with the piercing eyes of a very senior cleric of good. He almost certainly was no such thing, but his presence here made a gut-twisting occasion no easier.

Pirvan at least managed to tell his story without his voice shaking, and if his knees were shaking, his listeners had the decency not to mention it. He wished their decency had extended to at least a "Thank you" when he was done. Instead came a silence that soon had the consistency and palatability of congealed goose fat.

It was Yanitzia who broke it. "You had absolutely no knowledge of the importance of the jewels when you chose to remove some of them?" she asked.

"I have said it was work of opportunity," Pirvan replied. "Isn't that saying the same thing?"

"Perhaps I should make my question clearer," the woman said, then looked at the ceiling.

Don't take all night about it, was Pirvan's thought.

At last the woman looked down. "You had no idea these jewels were part of Lady Eskaia's dowry?"

"No, although if I had known, I might still have taken them. Encuintras can certainly afford more than a pocketful of jewels to dower their daughter."

"What did you think they were?" Silgor asked. A yawn garbled his question. Pirvan smiled thinly. Silgor might not agree with him, but at least he agreed with the idea of ending this matter before they fell asleep.

"I thought it might be gifts from friends or even lovers. Or perhaps she was saving them, to pay for her flight from a betrothal she rejected or a husband who mistreated her. Need I say that such is not unknown?"

Whatever answer might have come, Pirvan never learned. The earthquake came first.

Chapter 3

At least it felt like an earthquake while it lasted. There was only time enough for Pirvan to take a deep breath and leap for the nearest archway. From what he had learned in his travels, that was the safest place when the earth shook, if one could not reach the outdoors.

Silgor and his friends had not blindfolded Pirvan, so the thief had, as a matter of habit, memorized his route from the alley to the cellar door where he'd gone underground, then the twisting tunnels and corridors leading to this chamber. They were a long way from daylight.

Then the swaying of the walls and the thud of falling timber and stone ended as abruptly as they had begun. Pirvan pulled his neckcloth up over his mouth to keep out the dust, and realized that this had been a most peculiar earthquake. The walls had swayed, but he could recall no movement in the ground under him.

There would be time enough later (if there was a later)

to consider such mysteries of nature. Right now he was hearing through the dust and the odd rattle and crash sounds that his honor obliged him to answer. Voices were crying out not far off, men and at least one woman in fear or pain.

"We had best put this aside until we have rescued our friends," he said. He had to inhale after these words, and that brought on a coughing fit.

Yanitzia was coughing, too, but managed to squeeze out the words, "What friends?"

Pirvan's temper snapped. "The people crying out, or are you deaf from a blow on the head? I doubted that we were alone here, or that you allowed a drinking party off the streets to use these chambers. So those who cry out must be here by our permission, which makes them our friends!"

Pirvan thought he saw the old man smile, but Yanitzia was undaunted. "If so, what made you our leader?"

"Nothing," Pirvan replied. "But I have worked underground more than many, as you should know well. Perhaps I do not know these tunnels as well as one of you, but if so, then that person should lead and I will follow.

"But by all Gilean's musty scrolls, let whatever be done be done quickly!"

If any of the others had been fuddled in their wits, Pirvan's words seemed to prod them into movement. Silgor took command, and a sharp look from the old man silenced Yanitzia's protest before it left her lips.

"This way, Pirvan," Silgor said. "For common hurts we have common remedies enough. If anyone needs digging out, however, it is most likely to be along this tunnel. I would swear that some of this stonework is dwarven, old when Huma was born."

What magic might linger in such stones, Pirvan neither knew nor cared to waste his strength trying to guess. He could only hope that his supple leanness and his skill in worming himself through confined passages would be enough.

If they were, his comrades might consider whether he

deserved a lighter penalty than returning the jewels
(plainly enough what they had in mind), or at least a
fuller explanation of their reasons. Returning the fruits of
night work was a demand seldom made of a thief who
was not under some other sentence for dishonorable or
even unlawful conduct, which so far did not seem to be
true in Pirvan's case.

Quite a company of thieves and those sworn to secrecy
about thieves' lairs were now emerging from the lingering
clouds of dust. Pirvan counted at least a dozen men and
two women before Silgor started asking who was hurt
and who if anyone was missing.

"Chishun's down," one man said, "but Mara's with
him."

"She is not—" Yanitzia began.

Both Silgor and the man made rude suggestions as to
what the woman could do with her fears. "They're in the
uppermost chamber, which looks like a wine cellar until
you see the secret door, which she hasn't," the man said
irritably. "She rolled the barrel off him and is doing nice
work on his leg. Neither he nor our secrets are in any
danger."

"Excellent," the old man said. "Who else?"

One of the women shrugged. "Ghilbur, but only
Mishakal herself can help him now. A crossbeam smashed
his head like an eggshell. And Grimsoar One-Eye's
missing."

Pirvan felt as if he'd been struck hard in the stomach
with the pommel of his own dagger. For a moment it was
more than the dust that had him fighting for breath.

"Grimsoar—"

"Missing, I said," the woman repeated. "He was going
down to the weapons-practice chamber when the—when
everything shook. We think it fell in, either the chamber
or the hallway to it."

"At least we know where to start looking," Silgor said.
He wiped his face with the back of his hand, which suc-
ceeded only in transferring dust from fingers to cheeks.
He spat, which raised a puff of dust where it hit.

"Everybody able-bodied follow me and Pirvan. Everybody who needs help, up to the wine chamber and see Mara."

"Our secrets—" Yanitzia began.

The second woman made a rude gesture. "Sister, right now your tongue's the most useless part of your body. If the dust doesn't choke you—"

Silgor stepped between the two women before they could fly at each other. When he saw that peace would survive, he joined Pirvan.

"Did this feel like an earthquake to you?" he whispered.

"I'm not wagering. A quake, magic, maybe the years catching up with some fault in the construction."

"Or a spell, intended to feign some fault giving way?"

"That, too. But I'll be more apt for this sort of argument when we've found Grimsoar." Or his body.

* * * * *

Nobody else seemed concerned about the earthquake's being unnatural. They were worried more about what might have happened elsewhere in Istar. Were kinfolk and friends lying dead under rubble or trapped in the path of fires? Was the watch out and about, vigilant for looters and likely to see things the thieves would prefer to remain unseen?

One woman offered to take a look outdoors, and vanished up a debris-littered stairway. The rest of the able-bodied fell in behind Silgor and Pirvan.

They'd found Grimsoar by the time the woman returned, to report that the city was almost quiet. "A few chimneys down and some windows in the streets," she said. "People looking over their shoulders, but not our way."

Or rather, they found where Grimsoar was most likely to be, given the blood smears on the stone. It was not under a pile of rubble that must have crushed out his life, and for that everyone gave thanks, wherever they felt the thanks ought to go.

Grimsoar was at the bottom of a new hole in the floor, which had opened to swallow the big thief and then closed again. Or at least closed again, until it seemed that hardly anything larger than a dog would be able to crawl down and clear a path to bring Grimsoar out.

"If he's still alive," Yanitzia said.

"Alive or dead, we bring him—" Silgor began.

Pirvan had been crouching with his head thrust as far into the hole as he dared without a light. Now he stood, brushing gravel and splinters from his hair.

"I hear him breathing. He's alive."

"He or something," a man said. Silgor and Pirvan both glared; the man flinched.

"Whether it's Grimsoar or a dragon, the sooner we learn, the better," Pirvan said. He began uncoiling the rope from around his waist.

"Ah, I think I should go down," Yanitzia said. "I'm the smallest and—"

"I'm the next smallest," Pirvan said. "I'm also stronger and much more practiced in this sort of work. No offense, Sister, for you would doubtless look better unclad than I, but our brother needs to see help and not just a fine figure coming down to him."

The woman blushed under the dust, as Pirvan tossed the rope on the floor, unbuckled his belt, and began pulling off his clothes. The woman seemed to regard him with approval.

It occurred to Pirvan that if it hadn't been for his comrades, he might even now have been getting such approving looks from Reida, as he undressed in her bedchamber. The thought did not sweeten his temper.

"Grease," Pirvan said, when he was down to his loinguard and gloves.

"Cooking fat?" Silgor asked.

"Better than nothing."

Yanitzia darted off, apparently determined to redeem herself. Pirvan faced the old man.

"You need not answer, but a brother's life may depend

on it. Can you heal from a distance? Or perhaps levitate stones?"

"Neither," the old man said. "I have no true magic. What prayers I can utter, I will, and they may serve."

They may also be a waste of your breath, Pirvan mused.

The woman returned with the fat, somebody brought a leather pouch with a flask of some healing draft and bandages, and several men pulled out more ropes. By the time Pirvan had greased himself from crown to soles, the ropes had been tied into two longer ones. He nodded silent approval as he knotted one around his waist.

"Don't touch this unless I signal."

"The common signals?" Silgor asked.

"No, a new kind, in the tongue of the minotaurs," Pirvan snapped. "Your pardon, Brother."

"If you bring up Grimsoar, Pirvan, it will be us pardoning you, and for more than a sharp tongue," Yanitzia said.

Pirvan looked at the other faces around him and saw an encouraging lack of dissent. Perhaps this night will not be wasted after all, he thought, but losing a friend is too high a price to pay for regaining their trust.

* * * * *

Before he'd been ten minutes in the hole, Pirvan thought that he had never anticipated such a situation. He could die here, as finally as one cut down by the watch, savaged by griffons, or impaled on spikes. He could die here as slowly and perhaps more painfully, with friends above and perhaps below, no more than a spear's-length away but as unreachable as if they'd been on Nuitari.

Had anyone ever said he would be in such a situation, Pirvan would have immediately subdued and bound the speaker. Then he would have summoned a wizard or cleric, for healing a person too terribly astray in their wits to be at large on the streets without it.

Dust seemed to crawl into every orifice of his body. Sweat poured out just as eagerly, coating him with a layer of mud over the layer of grease. Stones gouged every part of his body, including some that made him wonder about his future with women. The sides of the hole quivered and occasionally dropped loose stones on him or down into the shadows.

As he widened the passage, however, he ceased to be alone. Someone lowered a lantern, which drove back the shadows. Another lowered a bottle of water, which kept the dust from clogging his throat. A third lowered a bundle of scrap lumber. This was handier for shoring up passages weakened by removing ill-placed stones, and he moved downward more swiftly after that.

It took him the best part of an hour to descend from one floor to another, a distance that on a flight of stairs he could have climbed while holding his breath. By the time he reached bottom, only his gloves kept his hands from being red ruins, and he had no doubt that Grimsoar was alive.

He could see the man, sprawled on his back, one arm apparently trapped under a tilted slab of stone overlain with some ancient mosaic. Ancient? Pirvan thought it might have been laid by beings who came before men, when Paladine and Takhisis had still been mates. The thought of such lost eons chilled him, even without the Dark Queen's name.

Grimsoar's scalp was oozing blood, and his chest was rising and falling. It appeared that once he regained his senses and the use of his arm, it would not be hard to extract him.

Oh, and once the passage is a trifle wider—say, two or three times wider, thought Pirvan.

He crept as close to his friend as he could, soaked one of the bandages in the healing potion, and started patting the blood off the man's scalp. This revealed a long but shallow gash, the sort that sheds ugly amounts of blood without doing great harm.

This healing also woke Grimsoar.

"Takhisis fly away with you!" Grimsoar said, halfway between a moan and a curse. Then he moved his head, his eyes widened, and he cursed plainly.

"Pirvan?" he said at last.

"Under the dust, the very same. And don't mention names. We're down among haunted stones, or I'm a cleric."

Grimsoar nodded, winced, and swallowed. "Any water?"

Pirvan's bottle was empty, but there was healing potion to spare. Grimsoar said that it tasted no better than it felt, but some life returned to his voice and eyes after it went down.

Meanwhile, up above they'd heard the call for more water, and two bottles came down. By the time they did, Pirvan would rather have had more grease. The stone slab had stopped its tilt short of injuring Grimsoar's arm, but not short of holding it tightly. A little grease might give the big man's largely intact strength a chance.

"As long as you hold that slab off my arm while I wriggle," Grimsoar said. "I know this is giving my proper work to you and yours to me, but we can sort it all out some better time and place. Want to try?"

"If you're ready—"

"I've been ready to be out of this place since I hit bottom, even if I didn't know it," Grimsoar said. "And you'll need me with two good arms to get us back out of here. I doubt not that the hole's cleaned out to your size, not mine."

"It would fit you like a child's loinguard on a minotaur."

"I thought as much."

"Your head—"

"—hurts like I've been drinking cheap dwarf spirits, but won't hurt less if I lie around here until another rock falls on it!"

* * * * *

It took only five minutes and two or three lesser miracles to free Grimsoar's now well-greased arm and pull him out from behind the slab. The open space was barely large enough for the two men unless they huddled close, and there was no room for Grimsoar to lift the smaller man on his shoulders as they had done in several bits of night work.

The only way out was to enlarge the hole until Grimsoar could pass outward, with as much help from above (the floor above, not necessarily the gods) as could be contrived. Pirvan called for some more shoring timbers and water, and they shared the water as Pirvan counted and judged the strength of the timbers.

After this night's work, I'll be able to take up mining in the dwarven kingdoms, if the thieving ever runs dry, Pirvan thought.

Without the help of gods or magic, getting out was going to take almost as much time as getting in. There would be two pairs of hands at work, as Grimsoar appeared remarkably fit for a man about to be rescued from burial. There would also be much more room needed, which Pirvan was making one rock at a time.

The problem was that every other rock he removed had to be replaced by a piece of timber. This could exhaust their supply of wood before the hole was safe, Pirvan realized. They might have to raid the timberyard across the alley from the Willow Wand, and though Pirvan had lost his sense of time, the night could no longer be young. It went against custom and pride among the night workers to pay for something, but these would not weigh heavily against the life of a brother.

What would weigh heavily on both men in the hole (besides a cave-in) was the matter of space. Every piece of shoring not only shrank the timber supply, it took up some of the space freed by the removal of stones. It was a question of more than philosophical interest: Could men save and doom themselves at the same time? *Much* more than philosophical interest, if you were one of the men.

"How are you coming down there?" Silgor sounded impatient.

Grimsoar grunted like a boar having a diseased tusk removed. "If we'd as much space down here as you've between your ears, we'd be long out and fondling Yanitzia on our knees."

That drew something between a gasp and a giggle from the woman. Otherwise there was silence, except for what Pirvan would have sworn was Silgor grinding his teeth.

"Truly, what do you need?" Silgor asked.

"More wood," Grimsoar replied.

"We'll have to start tearing out—"

"Do so," Pirvan said, in a commanding tone, which he realized might be unwise only after he'd spoken. "Is this hidey-hole going to be of any further use anyway?"

"Probably less than you and Grimsoar, I admit," Silgor said. "And not just to the ladies, either." They heard him ordering out another wood-gathering party. By the time they'd left, Pirvan had an idea.

"Silgor," he called. "I think that one of these big slabs is holding everything else in place. If you braced it on the top while we braced it on the bottom, we could probably clear out the rest of the passage."

"Which slab?" Silgor called. "This one?"

Pirvan heard the sound of a boot striking stone. He also heard the rubble groaning and grating as it shifted and timbers cracking from new strains. Dust filled the hole again, and a fistful of gravel rattled down and bounced off Pirvan's nose and forehead. He sneezed and thought rude things about Silgor.

Grimsoar said them aloud. He described Silgor's parents, habits, brains, and likely fate in some detail and at considerable length.

When the big man fell silent, a repentant-sounding Silgor called down, "I think we can wait for the others to come back. The more hands, the better!"

"Assuming you want us out of here alive, yes," Pirvan said. He wondered briefly if the witnesses had decided that the best way of solving the Pirvan problem was to "accidentally" bury him, even if they had to bury Grimsoar along with him.

If they do that, I will have their blood, if I have to come back from the Abyss to do it, Pirvan thought.

By the time the timber-gathering party returned, Pirvan was certain that he and Grimsoar had been down in the hole for a week. The next accident would be an underground stream breaking through into this hole, and if he and Grimsoar didn't float to the surface on the timbers, they would drown. . . .

"Many hands speed work," at least if they know how to do it. From the curses, coughs, and groans (echoed by groans from shifting rubble), Pirvan had to wonder. At least nothing serious fell.

"Almost ready," Silgor called. "At least I think so. We had to dig a trifle to clear space for the bracing."

"Just don't clear so much that the whole cursed slab shifts again," Pirvan called.

"I've learned that much," Silgor replied. "Be easy."

"Easy!" Grimsoar roared, loud enough to raise both echoes and dust. "Silgor, the next thing you learn about digging will be the first. Now are we going to climb out of here before the next coming of the dragons, or are we not?"

"Start climbing," Silgor said. "And save your breath for that. We're not going to—"

The longest groan yet came from the rubble. Grimsoar echoed the sound. He reminded Pirvan of a dying minotaur.

We're both going to be dead humans if we don't gamble that Silgor's right, Pirvan thought. He pointed upward. "You heard him."

"You should—" Grimsoar began.

"We don't have time to argue, my friend. I can slip through a smaller passage than you, and I'll be easier to pull out." Apart from the fact that I haven't come this far to have your blood on my hands!

Grimsoar's speed had surprised many men, but until tonight not his friend Pirvan. The big man seemed to fly up the tunnel, casually snapping shoring timbers as if they were dry twigs. His feet vanished above, then a roar of triumph filled the hole, along with cheers.

Pirvan wasted no more time. When the cheers began,

he was already halfway up the passage. Odd timbers clattered down and struck him on the head and shoulder. Splinters and sharp stones left sticking out added to the blood trickling across his greased skin and the smears he left behind. One large rock slid down and jammed itself under his chest; for a moment he wasn't sure if he could pry it free or save his ribs if he tried to squeeze over it.

As the rock came free and slid on down into the shadows, the loudest groan of all came. Pirvan threw caution and several pieces of wood to the winds, and flung himself at the last spear's-length of the slope. Only the grease let him slide upward until two strong hands gripped his wrists and heaved. Only the grip of those hands snatched him free of the hole, as the slab shifted and a score of stones larger than a man crashed into the hole. Before a thirsty man could have gulped a cup of water, anything bigger than a mouse would have been crushed into pulp, and the mouse stifled by the dust that poured up.

Pirvan was neither crushed nor stifled. He also drank no water. He lay on his back on the floor, and anxious hands thrust water at him. It dribbled out of the corner of his mouth, and finally someone noticed that his heart was beating but that his eyes were unseeing.

They lifted him on balks of timber and carried him out of the chamber.

Chapter 4

A rumbling, grumbling snore woke Pirvan. He sat up and tested head, ears, eyes, nose, and all his limbs. All were still attached and working.

He was sitting on a pallet in a low, whitewashed room that had the air of a recently and roughly cleaned cellar. Just beyond arm's reach was another pallet, with Grimsoar One-Eye asleep on it. The big man's head was shaved, and he wore a bandage over his scalp wound, but otherwise he looked quite healthy. His helpers had even bathed him, which was more than they had done for Pirvan. The thief stood up and prodded his comrade in the ribs with a bare toe.

"Uck," was the reply.

Pirvan prodded harder. Grimsoar rolled over, until his back was turned to Pirvan. Pirvan contemplated the other thief's back. The man had been a successful wrestler only a few years ago; his back was still slabs of rock-hard muscle.

Probably break a toe if I really kick him, the agile thief thought. Time for a bath before he wakes, I suspect.

Pirvan had no trouble arranging for a bath. The only problem was persuading Yanitzia not to attend him in it. Being in the presence of a hero seemed to have curious effects on women, which he would be glad to put to good use some other time. Unfortunately, all he wanted now, from woman or man, besides a clean body, was the full tale of what had gone awry in the matter of Lady Eskaia's jewels.

He had no aversion to seeing them returned, but beyond that, his instincts told him that he had not learned as much as was either lawful or necessary.

When Pirvan returned to the chamber, feeling fully awake at last, as well as clean, Grimsoar One-Eye was likewise awake. He was also fully clothed, except for his eye patch, and putting away a substantial breakfast.

Pirvan reached for a sausage and got a rap on the knuckles for the effort.

"There's only enough for me," Grimsoar said. "When they came with this, you were in the bath, and no one knew when you'd be out. Not with Yanitzia in there with you."

Pirvan snatched a hot roll from the wicker basket and munched on it. "Remind me not to save you, the next time you're buried alive. Whatever the lady intended, she didn't accomplish it."

"Unlike you," Grimsoar said. He gripped both of Pirvan's hands in one large, greasy one. "I don't know who sent you, or if you came by your own will. But I'm—oh, to the Abyss with all this pap. What is mine is yours, any time you ask for it."

"Except your breakfast?"

"Well, a man needs to keep a little back—"

But Pirvan had snatched up a sausage and another roll, this time without getting his knuckles rapped. By the time he'd swallowed both, he knew what he wanted.

"Find out the truth about Lady Eskaia's jewels."

"Oh, that," Grimsoar said. "Ask me something difficult."

Pirvan fought his jaw back into position. "You know?"

"Yes. I was coming to tell you. That was why I was there last night. If I hadn't thought you needed to know it, I certainly had better company in mind than a band of old thieves."

Pirvan sat back on the pallet. "I think I'm going to throw you back in that hole and then push it in on top of you. You knew and didn't tell—"

"Don't gallop without tightening your girth," Grimsoar quoted, holding up one plate-sized hand. "I only learned yesterday myself. Or perhaps I should say the night before."

"A woman?"

"A cook's maid at the Encuintras estate. I had in mind some night work there myself, and I was going to begin with her. But she was so eager to talk about the jewels that I didn't hear a word about anything else."

"Eager?"

"And frightened. Now, I don't say this is the whole story, but if the half of it's true, she has reason to be. And so do you."

After Grimsoar finished, Pirvan had to agree. It seemed that Lady Eskaia had been appropriating jewels from her dowry to make up a ransom for her guard-maid Haimya's betrothed. The gentleman was a prisoner of pirates on the Crater Gulf to the northeast, and Lady Eskaia was not going to be able to raise the ransom from her own allowance or her family's funds. They barely approved of Haimya at all; they would never approve a substantial sum of money to ransom one who was, after all, a near stranger to House Encuintras.

Clearly, Pirvan's night work had set the cat among the pigeons with a vengeance. From what Grimsoar had learned, Lady Eskaia and Haimya had covered their tracks for the moment, removing a few more jewels from the dower coffers to make it seem that these had been the thief's goal. The family had informed the watch and the priests and tightened the guard on the house, but so far there had been neither scandal nor suspicion that the maid knew about.

What she did know was a rumor that Eskaia had a mage in her pay, to find the thief or avenge the theft or punish the thieves' brotherhood or *something* portending bloodshed and dark dealings. Most likely, last night's affair was the mage's first achievement; it would not be the last.

"Even worse, one can't be sure that the mage isn't taking silver from both House Encuintras and the pirates," Grimsoar concluded. "They themselves won't come nearer Istar than Karthay, if that far, but there are always local merchants who will buy and sell for them. Merchants mentioned by name in the temples sometimes."

"That there's little justice in the world is something I've known as long as you, friend."

"Not unless you've met the kind of man who judges wrestling bouts at brass-piece fairs," Grimsoar said.

"I bow to your indescribable wisdom."

"Then don't try to describe it. What are you going to do?"

"Does your debt allow you to help me?"

"You might even say it commands me."

"As well. I mean to give the jewels back."

Pirvan had suspected for a good long while that he was going to do this, if only to keep the peace with his fellow thieves. Now that he had heard Grimsoar, suspicion became certainty.

If he did anything else, even return them by a messenger who might not hold his tongue, House Encuintras could face scandal and uproar. The thieves would face further magical retaliation.

It was against Pirvan's principles to tarnish the honor of a victim. His night work aimed at their purses, not their reputations. It was as against the customs of the brotherhood to bring other thieves into danger. Thieves older and more successful than Pirvan had ended in the arena or mysteriously dead in back alleys, the harbor, or sewers, for endangering brothers and sisters.

Prudence, honor, and his prospects for the future all

forced him in the same direction. After that easy decision, though, came the hard ones. The Encuintras estate would hardly be as open as it had been the first night. To be sure, he had only to find either Eskaia or Haimya, not open locks or penetrate strongrooms, but keeping them from betraying him (in the lady's case) or running him through (as Haimya looked fit to do) might be quite as difficult.

The thought of the sewers returned. He looked at Grimsoar One-Eye.

"Brother. How are you at deep work?"

* * * * *

"Haimya, this is the third night you have walked the halls." Eskaia emphasized her displeasure by setting down her teacup hard enough to chip the saucer and splatter the remains of the brown liquid over the bedclothes.

"You promised that you would allow me to engage the thief upon his return."

"Or her. If it is a thief."

"You have begun to doubt."

"I have always doubted that you could prowl the house like a staring cat every night with impunity."

"What punishment do you have in mind?" Haimya now looked not only tired but angry and frustrated, almost to the point of tears.

"I will give none. But the gods may make you ill, or so weak that the thief defeats you. He may return to give us back the jewels, but that does not mean he will care to be subdued and handed over to the watch. He may even have his eyes on some more lawful prey, or at least some that will cause less talk."

Haimya smiled. "Did anyone ever tell you that you talk like a counselor at law?"

"Frequently, beginning with my Uncle Petrus, who taught me that manner of speaking."

"It rings oddly on the ear, though, from one your age."

"No doubt, Grandmother."

Haimya was older than Eskaia, at least twenty-six to the lady's nineteen (twenty next month), and toughened further in several years' campaigning as a mercenary. Eskaia still refused her guard-maid the right to treat her as a child.

"Now," Eskaia said briskly, as she swung her legs out of bed. "See that the bathchamber is prepared. Meanwhile, you can sleep here in my chamber by day, once the maids have done with it. That way no one will disturb you."

Haimya frowned. "People will talk."

"They already have," Eskaia said. "I doubt that they will or even can say anything new. It was lies, it is lies, it will be lies. When we have the jewels back, you can challenge anyone whose lies have been too gross and loud. Or I can find some cause for dismissing them, even sending them to the arena."

"I will—oh, Kiri-Jolith! If I killed everyone whose tongue wagged to my annoyance, I would have been in the arena long ago."

"True. Few seem to understand that you are loyal to Gerik, and merely wait for him."

"Thank you, ma'am. I suppose gossip is less of a burden than the one you bear."

"Oh?"

"I have no father urging on me one man after another."

"No, but neither do I have old Leri. If you were not loyal to her son, what her spirit would say to you would make anything my father has ever said sound like the cooing of doves."

* * * * *

For Pirvan, deep work (as the thieves called traveling through the sewers and drains of Istar) with Grimsoar One-Eye had several advantages. The big man's bull strength combined with his shrewdness about where to push and where to pull made passages through or over cave-ins possible, if not always easy or safe. He had a sense of direction underground equal to Pirvan's above-ground. Between their combined senses it was impossible that they should get lost.

Finally, any passage wide enough for Grimsoar was more than wide enough for Pirvan, even at a dead run. He hoped tonight would demand only the Thief's Three Laws: "Silence, stealth, subtlety," but that lay with the gods. Pirvan did not intend to end in the arena for trying to make a restitution commanded by both his own honor and his fellow thieves!

The journey took longer than Pirvan had expected. Far below the ground, both his sense of direction and his sense of time weakened. He was sure that the gates were opening for the market carts of eggs and fish, vegetables and honey, when Grimsoar finally pointed up at a crack in the side of an ancient and odoriferous stretch of drain.

"There."

Pirvan looked at the crack. In the flickering light of their lanterns, it looked too narrow for an eel.

"It looks too narrow for you."

"It is," Grimsoar said.

"Then how do you know—?"

"A brother once came up here with his son, who was about your size. The lad made it up with little trouble."

"You know this—"

"I will name no names, but he took a deathbed oath."

Pirvan nodded. He trusted Grimsoar One-Eye completely, and now he had to trust the dead thief. Deathbed oaths bound thieves to be utterly truthful in what they said with their last breaths. The fate for dying liars was said to be one that might make Takhisis herself flinch away.

He still disliked that shadowy crack. At least the stone around it seemed well set, for all that it must have been laid when Huma and the first dragonlances were within living memory. Istar or some city had stood on this land for a long time.

The cities had also endured much. Pirvan remembered a chronicle he had once read, of a city here enduring a siege. A party of citizens had come down, to wait out the siege living on hoarded food.

But outside the walls, the besiegers had a wizard in their ranks. He churned up the water of the lake, and it roared through the streets of the city. Most folk were able to scramble to safety, but not those far below. When the water came down the drains, every last one of them had drowned.

Pirvan raised his lantern and studied the crack. It would be a tight fit without abandoning clothes and gear, but he'd brought a sack and a long rope to take care of that danger. He stripped, stuffing each item he took off into the bag, then tied one end of the rope to the neck of the bag and the other to his waist. The only gear with him were the jewels in a bag around his neck and the dagger in the belt at his waist.

Climbing light made it easier, and only twice was he in danger of being wedged. The crack also stank even worse than the tunnel below. Clearly a certain amount of midden waste had come down it, when servants grew lazy. He hoped none would be lazy tonight.

But Pirvan would have faced a continuous flow of filth and many tight passages to finish tonight's work. Finish tonight's work, redeem his own honor, preserve the thieves from further attacks, and be *out* of this underground warren with its stinks, shadows, and vengeful ghosts!

* * * * *

Haimya leaned back against the ancient brickwork and stretched her legs out on the bench. She laid her drawn sword across her knees and began testing the edge cautiously with the back of her thumb. It was too dark down here for even her keen night-sight to find flaws in the steel, but her skin was more sensitive anyway.

She paid a price for testing her sword thus, in small cuts and scrapes that did nothing for the appearance of hands that might have been intended for a man half a foot taller. But no friend had ever thought less of her, that her hands were not Lady Eskaia's (although those hands could wield more than an embroidery needle or a paintbrush if necessary). A good many enemies were no longer thinking at all, because of the strength and the skill in those battered hands.

She stretched her arms now, tensing, then relaxing every muscle like a cat. The sword began to slip from her lap. As she halted it, movement at the far end of the passage caught her eye.

A moment later, the movement became a kitchen boy, running with an empty slop bucket in his hand but not slowed in the least. He ran as if the Abyss were opening close at his heels, and his eyes were so wide that they were more white than not.

Haimya sprang into the boy's path. For a moment his eyes rolled, and she thought he was going to fall senseless. She gripped his shoulder, firm and friendly at the same time.

"What is it?"

"The drowned ghosts—they're coming—"

Haimya hoped her face didn't look blank or bemused as she tried to remember the boy's name and what he might be talking about. She couldn't contrive the first, but the second flashed quickly into her mind.

Except that she didn't believe in ghosts—at least not as much as she believed in live thieves.

Silence and secrecy were now as important to her as to the thief. She put a finger to her lips and shook her head. The boy nodded slowly and swallowed several times. When he spoke again, it was in a whisper.

"I heard them, Lady Haimya. Scraping, scratching, and getting louder."

She ignored the mistake about her rank. "Sure it wasn't rats?"

"I've heard rats, oh, I don't know how many times. This is different."

"Every time, I'll be bound, that you went downcellar to empty a bucket faster."

The boy could not meet her eyes. Haimya put a hand

under his chin and lifted his head.

"Come with me and be silent. If you do, I'll forget about the bucket." She thought of asking him to clean up where he'd been emptying it, but that was the cellarer's territory. The old man was also as stubborn as a badger and one of the worst gossips in the house.

"Come with me."

Haimya strode toward the cellar door, trying to remember if there was a second way out of the cellar even for a thief. Well, if there was and he used it, he would leave traces. While he was upstairs, she could place herself in the cellar to bar his outward passage, with any fresh loot he might have seen fit to gather.

The lock of the cellar door was well greased, the hinges likewise. Both made faint squeals, like kittens at the bottom of a well—an image and a memory that made Haimya flinch. Neither was as loud as the boy's quick breathing. The guard-maid would have given three good swords and her best helmet for one moment's magic, to silence the boy or at least ease his fear until he would no longer awaken sleeping drunks, let alone alert thieves.

They had just closed the door behind them when Haimya saw a faint glow of light along one wall of the cellar, between a rack of wine barrels on one hand and a rack of smoked hams on the other. She listened, the boy held his breath, and the scraping indeed sounded nothing like rats.

Then the glow died.

*   *   *   *   *

Pirvan was past the worst part of the passage when an outcropping of stone knocked the hood off his lantern. In the silence of his mind, he relieved his frustration. Shielding the lantern with his body, he learned what made him think even stronger language. A tinker would have to take hood and lantern in hand to rejoin them.

A nice dilemma now faced Pirvan. Had he been on the streets or, even better, on the rooftops, he could have gone forward as swiftly and deftly in the darkness as in the light. His agility, his night-sight, and his sense of direction kept him moving the way he wished, as long as he was in the open air.

Below ground was a different matter. He had mostly foresworn deep work for that reason, and would have done so tonight. But the open-air paths to the house would surely be guarded. The only safe way lay below, and to use that, he needed light, whether or not it gave warning to anyone waiting above.

Pirvan reminded himself that, strictly speaking, he did not have to roam the house until he found Lady Eskaia's bed and the strongbox under it. He could reach the cellar, fling the bag of jewels with its notes to Lady Eskaia attached—into the hands of any servant who might have slipped down to tap a wine barrel. Such might be indiscreet; they could even be dishonest.

Pirvan's honor and the thieves' safety demanded a complete, discreet return.

He could only hope that his mask would not go the way of the lantern shield.

Nothing more went awry in the remaining few minutes of Pirvan's underground journey. Safely far back in the passage, he blew out the lantern and drew up his sack of gear. It would be an irony to make a dozen gods laugh if he needed more tools to return stolen property than to steal it in the first place.

At last he was peering out into the cellar, the lantern behind him. All seemed as he would have expected, with no alarm given. The only light was a dim, guttering one, from a single torch or lamp high up and out of his sight to the left.

Trying to keep his head up and his eyes roaming, Pirvan slipped out of the crack in what now seemed to be a cellar wall. The dim light made the wine barrels to his right seem a solid mass, whatever was hanging to his left appear as giant bats with their wings folded.

A mouse skittering drew his eyes to the right. Then across the open space, he saw something move. A human shape, creeping on hands and knees, clearly knowing that he was not alone, thinking that he had not been seen.

Pirvan drew his dagger, tossed it so that he held it by the point, then waited until he could have a clear shot at the man's head. Man—no, a boy, more likely, or even a girl—but no one could be allowed to give warning this soon, nor would they receive more than a headache from the pommel of the dagger.

Seeking that clear line for his throw, Pirvan had taken two steps away from the wall. That was one too many. In one moment, he sensed someone approaching him from his left; in the next, the person was behind him, between him and the passage.

He whirled, angling the dagger upward to hammer the pommel up under his attacker's chin. That could kill, but he would pull his blow if he could—

The next moment, he felt as if a dragon had whipped its tail into his lower abdomen. He doubled up, all the breath going out of him in a *whuff* he was sure must be waking the house. The pain he felt was such that if he had let out the scream deserved, he would have awakened half of Istar.

But the breath for the scream would not come. He was still fighting for it when he felt the dagger plucked from his hand and a second attacker behind him. Trying to turn merely cost him what was left of his balance, and as he went down, a hard fist hammered against the side of his jaw.

Pirvan the Thief was as senseless as a log of firewood before he struck the floor.

Chapter 5

Pirvan awoke with pains lingering in both head and belly. He concluded that he must have struck his head in falling. He also discovered that his bruised temple and scraped cheek had been cleaned, salved, and lightly dressed.

He was on a pallet stuffed with fresh-smelling hay, with a clean woolen blanket over him and a wooden frame lifting the pallet off the wooden floor. Beside the pallet, on a low table, were a jug of water, a cup, and a plate of light biscuits. The water was clean and smelled of herbs, the biscuits an appealing brown, and the jug, cup, and plate good gray pewter with the Encuintras mark on it.

If he was a prisoner of Lady Eskaia's family, they were either fattening him for the slaughter or wished his goodwill.

Meanwhile, his throat tasted as if a regiment of ogres had camped in it. He washed some of the taste out with the water and cleaned the rest away with two biscuits. He was afraid that the biscuits would make him nauseated, but there was something in the water that settled his stomach enough for them to stay down.

The water also held something to make him sleep. After his second cup, he did. He awoke feeling free of pain, a bit muzzy-headed, and hungry enough to eat not only the remaining biscuits but half of a good-sized bakeshop as well.

When he'd done that, he began to study his quarters. They were well above the level of a cell, not quite a guest room. There was a private cubicle in one corner for the necessary pot, and a second pallet rolled up and leaning against one wall. The light was dim; it came from lamps set in horn-covered niches in the wall. It was enough to let him see a good deal more, once his eyes adjusted to it.

All the walls were smooth-scraped, whitewashed wood, and the other two were largely covered with racks and stands. On one wall were buckets, sponges, jugs, short robes, padded leggings, and what Pirvan recognized as exercise sticks and weights. The racks on the other wall mostly held bottles, stoppered jars, and glass vials that might have contained anything from poisons to spices. Some of them Pirvan recognized as Qualinesti work.

He stood up, realizing as he did so that someone had removed all of his garments and given him a thorough bath—which he admitted he must have needed, after his struggle up the passage into the cellar. This meant that he was neither clothed nor armed, but with the loaded racks in easy reach that hardly mattered.

He walked slowly to the rack with the exercise sticks and took down three, a pair of short ones and a long one. He tested their balance and his own, and discovered that both passed. Then he put on one of the robes, which ended the sensation of being naked and helpless.

It was odd that they would put him in a room so full of things that might be used as weapons, if in fact he was a prisoner. Perhaps they were setting a trap for him, tempting him into some bold escape attempt that would give them cause to punish him more severely.

And perhaps not. They presumably had the jewels, unless that servant had snatched them from Pirvan's prostrate form before—Haimya was her name—had been able to search him. Not that a man in a loinguard and gloves would need much searching, either . . .

The plate was empty, the jug full. Pirvan drank some more water (a thief who had traveled among the desert barbarians said that the best place for spare water was in your stomach). It seemed that someone had changed the water since the first jug; this time there was no taste or scent of herbs.

The water did nothing to ease a hunger that by now was nibbling at his stomach like rats. Much longer, and it would be tearing at him like a catamount. He also became aware of scrapes and strained muscles that no one had done anything to heal. Sleep again or remain awake, so they would not take him unawares?

Instinct told him that sleep was folly, keeping from him even a hope of going down fighting. Reason told him that House Encuintras could simply wait until exhaustion put him at their mercy, and take him then. In any event, the better rested he was, the safer. The knowledge that he should not enter a battle of wits half asleep helped soothe him.

Presently he slept again. When he awoke, Pirvan was not alone.

* * * * *

The Crater Gulf was on the eastern shore of the fat peninsula that was one of the northernmost points of the continent of Ansalon. It was not far from Istar, if one could fly. But dragons slept, pegasi were rare, kyrie the next thing to legends, and griffons so untrustworthy that no one wishing to end their journey outside their mount instead of inside cared to use one.

That left land and sea. The mountains that ran down the spine of the peninsula had many names in many tongues, but none of them sang praise. They were not high, but their upper slopes were rugged, steep, and chill; their lower slopes, overgrown with a hideous tangle of vegetation. A man could spend a whole day hacking his way through a mile of it, fall into an exhausted sleep, and never wake again as the leeches drained his blood and the insects devoured what the leeches had left.

In two days he would be unrecognizable. In five he would be bones, and before seven days ended the bone-borers would have come, and nothing of the man would be left except his metal gear, which might last as much as one season before the endless rain dissolved it with rust and corrosion.

Wise men did not seek to reach Crater Gulf by land.

By sea, one had to run the gauntlet of mist and fog, squalls and more enduring storms, reefs close to shore and reaching far out into what rash captains thought was deep water, and enough floating logs each day to build a small ship. Seafarers with no business on Crater Gulf gave it a wide berth—and they were the majority, for it offered little except timber, fruit, and fresh water, and no civilized inhabitants of any race.

It could therefore hardly have been more suitable as a refuge for pirates. Of whatever race they might be (mostly human and minotaur, with an occasional ogre; goblins seldom went to sea of their own will) they wrecked little from dangers that drove most ships well offshore. Their light, fast-sailing vessels could ride over reefs that gutted larger ships, the forest offered refuge if an enemy did contrive to land, the reefs abounded in fish, and altogether a sailor could make a dishonest living on the Crater Gulf more easily than in most other places.

In the year Pirvan the Thief did night work at the Encuintras estate, most of the pirates in the gulf gave allegiance to one Synsaga. They did not give it as readily as they had done to his sister Margiela, and some had not given it at all. But most of those had left Crater Gulf for either honest livings or piracy elsewhere, and Synsaga had needed only one pitched battle five years before to make his rule at least tolerated.

The battle had left gaps in the pirates' ranks, however, as much among Synsaga's friends as among his enemies. Thus he came to need men who owed everything to him, and began to seek them from wherever they might come. One source was captives, who might prefer liberty and loot to death, captivity while awaiting ransom, or slavery. One of those captives who swore allegiance to Synsaga, in the fourth year of the pirate chief's authority, was a young Istarian named Gerik Ginfrayson.

* * * * *

Not much to Pirvan's surprise, his visitor was Haimya.

She was sitting cross-legged on the other pallet, without armor or any more garb than a sleeveless tunic and short breeches. The attire was mannish, as was the sword across her lap. Everything else about her was nothing of the kind. Pirvan particularly noted the length and muscular curves of her half-bare legs.

"Greetings, Haimya."

Her bushy eyebrows rose. "You know my name?"

Pirvan bowed from a sitting position. "I injured the honor of your house out of ignorance, but I did not enter with no knowledge whatever." He refrained from adding that he had seen her even before their most recent encounter. A thieves' rule was: "Give nothing, for knowledge demands the highest price."

"Then I presume you know in what way you injured us?"

That was not entirely a question, but Pirvan decided to take it as such. If he appeared to know too much, Haimya (who seemed to have wits as keen as her sword's edge) might wonder how he came by it. Grimsoar One-Eye and the servant girl were entirely innocent parties; Pirvan would leave no trail leading to them.

"The rumors and certain events were enough to bring me to my decision, to undo that dishonor by further night work. But I much doubt that the rumors told everything."

"They could not have, for there is much we do not wish known."

"Altogether wise and proper. But I insist on learning one thing. Are the jewels safe?"

Haimya appeared to hesitate. Pirvan could have even sworn that she looked at the lamps, as if their flickering yellow glow might tell her yea or nay. If she sought an answer there, she did not find one.

At last she nodded.

"I am delighted. I am also free of any further obligation to House Encuintras, am I not? Your hospitality has upheld its reputation—"

"It should have. This is no discipline cell, but my exercise room."

"Ah. I thought the robes and sticks had some such purpose."

"Indeed. A warrior must have a private space, for practice."

Pirvan was of the same mind, but he could not help smiling. Into his mind strayed, not quite unbidden (those legs were still in plain view), the image of Haimya at weapons practice, in garb that would indeed require privacy.

"Such is my custom, too."

"When there is great sickness in the house, I practice elsewhere, if I have time to do so at all. This is the sick chamber, for those too ill to tend for themselves or too likely to spread their sickness to others."

The Encuintras pesthouse, to be rude about it, mused Pirvan.

Pirvan's stomach twisted. A vigorous effort kept his face from doing the same. His horror of disease went far back, to his earliest memories of his mother lying dead and covered with boils, on a pallet far dirtier than this one. But there was no need to let Haimya know how effective her threat to keep him here had been.

If it was a threat. Again Pirvan wondered what construction he should put on the curious conduct of House Encuintras.

"Well, I should not care to cause trouble for either you in health or anyone else in sickness. I should think that after the return of the jewels we have no more business, one with the other."

"That is not quite so."

"Oh. Then perhaps you should indeed explain the circumstances of your house. The rumors certainly said nothing about my having given you any further insult beyond the theft of the jewels."

To Haimya's credit, she explained quickly. The story was much as Pirvan had heard it, with certain additions that no one not of House Encuintras could have made. Pirvan also heard a certain note in Haimya's voice that made him wonder what she truly thought of her betrothed.

Oh, the words came out as propriety demanded. But behind the words Pirvan did not so much hear yearning for a beloved partner as outrage at the pirates' insult in taking him away. For the sake of Gerik Ginfrayson (and, indeed, for the sake of Haimya, on whom he did not wish unhappiness in love), Pirvan hoped he was misjudging the lady.

At last Haimya finished the narrative and looked around for something to drink. Pirvan lifted the jug; it had not been refilled this time.

"I will not dry your throat much more," he said. "You have told me all I wished to know, except one thing. That is what further service is required of me." He was able to get that far without his voice betraying him, as far as he could judge from her face.

"Oh, it is simple enough. You will sail with us to the Crater Gulf, when we ransom Gerik Ginfrayson."

When the gods wish a rare jest, they will answer a man's questions. If that was not an old saying, it ought to be.

Pirvan decided that he had nothing to lose by firmness. "That may be difficult. Or will you strike further at the thieves with your tame mage if I do not obey?"

Haimya's face said nothing one way or the other.

Pirvan decided to leave her no illusions. "I cannot be the judge of honor for all the brothers and sisters of the night work. Not even my own honor. If I were to cast it away by doing as you ask, I would not be safe in Istar. And if I were not released, your house would be in peril."

"The watch—"

"The watch can be bribed by the enemies of your house, who I am sure are numerous. Also, night work can be done so subtly that only you will know the injuries you suffer."

"What of thieves' honor, in not striking at the innocent?" Haimya snapped.

Pirvan was briefly glad to have broken through that iron mask. "I will be an innocent victim if held here after the return of the jewels."

"Your innocence will not keep you safe if you remain forever defiant."

"I will not have to remain defiant forever. I will be out of here, preferably alive but perhaps dead, before Branchala is half gone."

"Nonsense."

"If you wish to wager that it is nonsense, wager what you can afford to lose."

Haimya glared at him. One could not justly say that anger made her beautiful, but her features were certainly so arranged that anger did not mar them. Pirvan looked for his sticks, discovered that they were within easy reach (in fact, unmoved), and decided that Haimya was not planning to have at him with naked steel.

That left only three or four hundred other courses of action that she might be contemplating. Pirvan took a deep breath and lay back on the pallet, his hands in sight.

"Haimya," he said. "I do not doubt that Lady Eskaia trusts you in all things. But what you have said is so improbable that I must hear it from her. If Lady Eskaia says there is need for me to go to the Crater Gulf, I will listen. I do not promise to go, but I promise to give her the same hearing I would a blood brother or a father."

He thought he saw Haimya bite her lip, but the sound

of the door opening drew his attention. The moment it had opened wide enough, a dark-haired young woman in a simple robe with wine-hued trim at throat and wrists slipped into the room.

"Pirvan, I believe you asked for me? I am Lady Eskaia of House Encuintras."

* * * * *

It was going to blow up a storm before nightfall. Gerik Ginfrayson knew this, though he had no inborn weather sense, and his reason for being in the healer's huts had given him none. A fall into a stream while chasing a fleeing captive had twisted a leg, and swallowing the scummy water had given him both a flux and a fever. Nothing to kill a man, only to make him (for a day or two at least) wish he could die.

But he had taken oath to Synsaga a year ago, and in that much time on the Crater Gulf only a fool failed to learn storm signs. The sticky stillness in the air, the thick but high clouds, and the odd note in the birdsong all said the same thing.

It would be a storm from the west, as the mountains tore at the winds. On shore there would be no more than rain, but a few hour's rowing out to sea it would be a different and more deadly matter. Not as deadly as an easterly or northerly gale, however—there would be plenty of sea room for any ship able to run with the storm.

Gerik knew the perils of a lee shore as well as any seafarer now, though it would be years if ever before he was trusted with keeping a ship off one.

The one-armed sailor who acted as servant to the patients in the healers' huts appeared in the doorway and coughed.

"Yers, sorr?"

Whatever had taken his arm had also taken most of his wits or speech or perhaps both. There was little magical healing of such wounds here, and Gerik had heard of men so hurt that they took their own lives or begged a mercy stroke from comrades. This man had not wished to die, however, and since he had taken his wounds in avenging the death of Synsaga's sister Margiela, the pirate chief would have given him a golden throne had it been in his power.

Gerik looked at the bag, then took it from the old man and set it on the table. Everything he had brought into the huts was there, even the few brass coins and the silver tower. Of course, stealing among the pirates was punished in ways that made a sentence to the arena seem a slap on the wrist. . . .

"Naid barrers, sor?"

Gerik shook his head. He needed no one to help him navigate the path downhill to his quarters, let alone carry him. He lifted the bag and for a moment almost changed his mind; his leg was strong enough for unburdened walking, but running or carrying loads would take longer.

He rummaged out three of the brasses and handed them to the man. "More when I've made another voyage and have a share or two to spend."

"Ach. End whan thet, sor?"

"I don't know."

He'd sworn oath only to Synsaga, which protected him ashore and allowed him a place aboard *Golden Troll* or *Seacleaver*. To the other captains, he was an Istarian of uncertain skill and no loyalty they were bound to recognize. Synsaga was two days overdue already, would not be making landfall in this storm, and might take more than the usual time repairing itself before going out again.

"Warrd?"

"Word of honor," Gerik said. The man had done more for him than for the other five in the huts, though two of those were in no condition to demand much. One was dying of a gut wound from a brawl, another of some ailment doing vicious things inside his brain and requiring him to be strapped to his bed half the time. Even then, when the fits took him, his howls frightened birds and apes a league away.

Dignity forced Gerik to walk swiftly down the path

until he was out of sight of the gate to the healing huts. By then he'd drawn blood from his lips at the pain of muscles pushed beyond their limits.

Must find some way of exercising them, he thought, where no one can see or hear until I've regained the lost ground.

He had been hard and fit for a man whose work was mostly counting timber in the city dockyards. Haimya would never have looked at him otherwise. But the pirates had a standard of fitness all their own, and it had taken six months for Gerik to reach it.

In that time he had gained muscle, lost fat and sweat, and come to understand just what Haimya must put herself through to keep her warrior's body. Woman's body, too—more than woman enough to disturb his thoughts, in ways that had no place on this slippery path.

Gerik put memories of Haimya from his mind and turned his attention to descending the slope. Out of sight of the huts and everyone else, he could slow his pace to one his muscles could endure. That took him to the most thickly grown part of the path just as the first thunder rolled in the west.

He looked up, eyes rising with the birds as they flew up screaming. The zenith was darker now than it had been, but not so dark that he missed a great black-winged shape soaring into view, then vanishing in the clouds. At least he thought he saw it, and he had been at least as sure the other three times as well.

He continued his descent. What had he seen, always briefly and today for hardly more than a blink as it plunged into the clouds? Long wings, a long tail, a crested head, all a black that seemed to swallow even the dim storm light.

No bird ever took that shape or grew so large. It seemed too large and the wrong shape for a griffon. That left only one possibility.

A black dragon. A creature of evil, a minion of Takhisis— and a thought cold enough to make a man forget the jungle heat for a moment.

The chill passed. A black dragon was also impossible. All the dragons, good and evil alike, had left the world after Huma wielded the dragonlance and died bringing victory to the forces of good. All were in dragonsleep, none to be waked except by the gods.

At least that was what Gerik Ginfrayson had heard. And he had heard that this came from wise men, clerics and wizards, who knew as much about the matter as mortal men could learn.

Either such men were wrong, or what Ginfrayson had seen passing overhead four times was not a dragon.

Another chill thought struck him. Synsaga's little pirate village had no gods at its command, and was probably not even in the favor of many (save perhaps Hiddukel). But it had a renegade sorcerer, who received gold, slaves, food, and labor as though he were actually doing something useful for the pirates!

Had Fustiar the Renegade found a way to break dragonsleep?

If so, it was a secret to which Gerik would be years being admitted. But tongues wagged when the wine flowed freely, and Gerik could feign both drinking and drunkenness. The wine would flow freely when Synsaga returned, and Gerik could certainly enter *that* feast, with a sober head and receptive ears.

* * * * *

Pirvan dared not ask how he looked after Lady Eskaia's entrance. He hardly needed to.

Both women took one look at him and burst into wild laughter. There was nothing ladylike or dignified about the laughter. They looked and sounded like two streetgirls who had just played a fine, profitable jest on a man.

Pirvan waited with as much dignity as he could manage while the women laughed themselves breathless. He thought of taking advantage of the unlocked door and the women's distraction to escape. But to where? And how, seeing that he had neither decent garb nor weapons and that all in the house were likely awake and alert.

Also, if the women were not entirely out of their right senses—well, he had never wittingly struck a woman in his life, and was tolerably certain he had never gravely hurt one by chance. (Indeed, he was more sure of that than about having left behind no unlawful children.)

It was at this point that Pirvan noted that Lady Eskaia had put down on the floor—put down, the gods be praised, not dropped—a robust wooden platter loaded with cheese, bread, ham, pickles, ripe red grapes, and a bowl of something that looked appetizing even though Pirvan could not have said what it was.

For a moment he tried to maintain his dignity. Then the smell of the bread and the strong cheese reached his nostrils. It had been days since he'd eaten more than water and biscuits. He snatched up a piece of cheese in one hand, a piece of ham in the other, and crammed both of them in his mouth with neither the dignity nor even the manners of a child of five.

By the time Pirvan had started chewing, the women were no longer laughing. Their faces were an identical red, Lady Eskaia's normally carefully arranged hair was a tangled mess, and Haimya seemed to have the hiccups. But they were in a state where a man might hope to ask a question and even, if he was sufficiently lucky and made the proper prayers to the right god, have it answered.

"Lady Eskaia, I am grateful for your hospitality and your presence," Pirvan said. "As I made my promise in the hearing of you both, it will be kept. Remember, though, what I asked of you."

Eskaia touched her hair and grimaced as she realized the shambles she'd made of it. Then her jaw set. It was a well-shaped jaw, in which were set two rows of even white teeth. Had she been born a poor man's daughter, she would still have been a much-sought marriage prize.

"Very well. But I must ask one further promise—indeed, an oath by all you hold most in honor. That you will never speak of what I am about to tell you, unless Haimya, I, or my father gives you leave."

Josclyn Encuintras being suddenly brought into the matter briefly unsettled Pirvan. He sensed that what he was about to hear would unsettle him even more. But a promise was a promise; an honest thief could not live in a world where promises were not kept.

Pirvan swore himself to silence, invoking Gilean and Shinare, then looked at Eskaia. "My silver, your service."

Haimya looked shocked. Eskaia stuck out her tongue at him. Then she sobered.

"It is a matter of what the pirates of Crater Gulf may be doing. Or, rather, what they may be having done for them . . ."

By the time Eskaia had finished (with a trifle of prompting from Haimya), Pirvan understood why her father was taking a hand in this matter. What might be happening in Crater Gulf could wreak havoc on Istar's trade and even on the city itself. Josclyn was a leader of the merchants in their rivalry with the priests for supreme power in Istar.

Discovering and ending a menace to the city could bring more than honor or gold to House Encuintras. It could bring an offer of marriage to a high noble or even a royal heir for Eskaia.

Lucky man, Pirvan thought, then turned wits and tongue to more practical matters. Clearly father and daughter were speaking more openly to one another than the rumors said. Just as clearly, this was to his advantage. It endangered no secrets of the thieves, and put more of the resources of House Encuintras behind the voyage.

"I can see why you wish my company on this adventure," Pirvan said. "I can go where neither of you can. But I did not promise to face the dangers that come with being—a spy, not to make hard an easy matter. A spy, among folk who are even harsher than most in dealing with such."

"You will be paid, of course," Eskaia said. "At least the wages of a chief guard, and perhaps more."

"As well," Pirvan said. "I returned the jewels gladly, but what they would have bought me must be paid somehow."

"Why not more?" Haimya asked. "The price of one of the jewels—the full price, not what the night merchants would have given you—upon your return."

Pirvan looked at the two women with increased respect. There was no foolishness in Haimya, and under the gown and finely done hair, hardly more in Eskaia. But then, a mercenary soldier and a merchant princess should hardly feel soiled by talking of money.

"Am I allowed to pick the jewel?"

"How can you be sure we will offer you the ones you took?" Eskaia replied.

"I will ask to see all of them. Also, one hundred towers now, to be subtracted from my payment."

"Only that?" Haimya said.

Pirvan nodded. "I thought you might not care to be too generous to the thieves. I have neither wife nor children nor any living kin or sworn friends I know of, so that is all I will ask beforehand. Oh, that and my equipment."

"The bag you were going to pull up into the cellar?" Haimya asked. Her smile was almost a grin.

"You have it?"

"Yes, although not without some strong words from—a comrade, I assume—lying below to cover your retreat."

"It is well to know that he is unharmed. Had you shed his blood . . ." The grimness of his face took the smile off Haimya's.

He let them change the subject after that. He did not know when they would be sailing, but if it was not tomorrow, he had a plan.

They were taking him north to help guard their backs. Why should he not enlist someone for this curious voyage, to do the same for him?

Chapter 6

Golden Cup loomed against the cloud-hazed sky above the skiff like a castle curiously set afloat. From her massive bulk, Pirvan thought she might better deserve the name Golden Kettle.

The breeze had risen since they had left the quay. The creaking of the timbers and the rigging almost drowned out the splash of the oars as they carried the skiff the last few yards to the gangway.

Pirvan slung his new seabag over his shoulder and looked forward, counting the other crates and bags among the feet of the rowers. He didn't think they had orders to drop his gear overboard, but he intended to guard against both that and accidents as well.

The ship loomed higher in a darkness that seemed to have grown deeper. They were well out in the harbor now, where the largest ships anchored, waiting for a fair wind outbound or, if inbound, for space at the deep-water quays their draft required. The ship had no neighbors, and none of them were lit up except for the common bow, stern, and gangway lanterns.

The ship seemed all lumps and lines, and apart from its great size Pirvan could not have said much about it. He had never lived by the waterfront, where one could not take a five-minute stroll without seeing a dozen different ships. Lodgings there were apt to be cramped and noisy, and sailors and harborfolk in general not overly fond of men of his profession.

(It did not matter that they were hardly adverse to practicing it themselves, nor that Pirvan would never have stooped to robbing a working sailor. Neither would have saved him, if his luck was out, from a quick voyage to the bottom of the harbor with old shackles bound to his feet.)

"Ahoy, the boat!" split the night as someone on the gangway spotted them.

"Passenger for *Golden Cup!*" one of the rowers shouted.

"Come alongside and be recognized."

Pirvan hoped that the ship was as well kept as it was big. Poor shipkeeping, worse seamanship or navigation, drunkenness, fire—all could prematurely end this voyage (which Pirvan rather hoped would succeed) as well as Pirvan's life (which he intended to preserve for longer than House Encuintras had any use for it!)

The gangway rose as high as a two-story house, and the railing was higher than a man, solid timber, and loopholed for archers. As Pirvan climbed the last steps, a splash and a curse rose from below.

He looked down. Someone had opened a port and emptied a bucket into the harbor, without looking out first. Some of the bucket's contents had caught the boat and the second rower, who was handing cargo to the first rower and a sailor on the bottom of the gangway.

A large man was suddenly before Pirvan, but ignoring him. He leaned over the side.

"Hush your noise there, or you'll have a bath afore you're back to shore!"

The rower hushed, but the cargo came aboard remarkably

quickly afterward. The man kept looking upward, as if wondering what might fall on him next.

The big man now turned to Pirvan.

"You're Pirvan, with the Encuintras party?"

"The same." Pirvan pulled a medallion out of his purse and showed it to the man. A lantern hanging from either side of the gangway gave just enough light to examine it.

"Well and good," the man said with a grunt. "You're being the last. Follow this boy to your cabin, and stow your baggage right quick. We'll be upanchoring as soon as the last shore boat brings the drinkers."

A boy of twelve or so had apparently sprouted from the deck at the big man's wave. He looked Pirvan up and down with an unnerving maturity.

Probably wonders how much he can persuade me to give him, Pirvan thought.

"Baggage?"

"Over there," Pirvan said, pointing. "Trunk with copper bands, crate with one red side, the green bag. I'll carry this."

The boy snatched up the bag and dashed toward—the stern, Pirvan thought. He followed as fast as he could, not without barking his shins on protrusions from the deck, stumbling, and hastily leaping out of the path of parties of sailors on urgent business.

There were enough people scurrying about the ship's deck to garrison a castle. Pirvan wondered if the last few men were all that important, or if someone or something valuable was in the boat. Not greatly his to worry about, either, and if he stayed out on deck much longer, he would be as conspicuous and as unwelcome as a sober cleric at a drunkards' revel.

Pirvan caught up with the boy well inside the aftercastle, which was on the same scale as everything else about the ship. Pirvan had stayed in smaller inns, and his cabin was a more comfortable accommodation than such inns often provided to even the fat-pursed traveler.

He could touch the walls while standing in the middle of it, but every bit of space was cunningly used. One side held stout racks for baggage; a second a small table with a washbasin and pitcher and more racks, with lockers under.

The third side held a bunk, with drawers under it, and above the bunk two sets of hooks. From one of them a hammock was already slung, with a blanket roll in it.

Pirvan was no stranger to hammocks, but if someone was going to yield the bunk without a word, no thief ever refused what was freely given. (Honest men were much the same, too.) He stretched out, more to give the boy room to work than because he was tired.

Intentions were one thing, the state of his body another. He must have dozed off, because the next thing he knew, the boy was standing by the bunk, wrestling the trunk on to a rack and lashing it in place with a complicated harness of brass chain and leather thongs. It looked enough to drive an embroiderer to drink, but the boy made quick work of it.

Pirvan pulled out a copper ten-piece and tossed it to the boy. He snatched it out of the air, gaped, bit it, then grinned as his teeth told him he'd been offered genuine coin.

"Well, Master, that's a good sign for our voyage together. We'll be upanchoring before you need the head again, so snug yourself down and be easy."

He was gone without another word, though he had said enough. More than enough to make Pirvan concerned that Grimsoar One-Eye might not have made it aboard, and that he would be sailing on this voyage with no friends and indeed no one aboard who would not toss him to the fish the moment his work was done. Of all the places on Krynn where it was easy to make murder look like an accident, a ship was notoriously the best.

Snugging himself down was impossible, with that on his mind. Wandering around the ship without being noticed would be as difficult as ever. The cabin had no portholes to give Pirvan a view, either.

What it did have, he discovered quickly, was a small grating in the ceiling—no doubt the deck above. There were also places where a man as agile as Pirvan could arrange himself, to listen to anything that came through the grating.

He quickly memorized the best position, then blew out the hanging lamp to give a stronger impression of sleep. A moment later, he was half hanging, half standing, with a bit of crouch thrown in, bracing himself so that his ear was against the grating.

It was a while before he heard anything but ship's work, a confused and confusing din of shouts, grunts, creaks and groans, thumps of wood and squalling of metal, and numerous mostly irreverent remarks about gods, women, and shipmates. After one particularly loud outburst, which seemed to be connected with emptying a boat and getting it aboard, Pirvan heard that which made him listen with more attention.

"Wrung the wine out of everybody?" That was a male voice with authority in it.

"Almost everybody." That was the voice of the big man who'd met Pirvan at the gangway.

"Almost may not be good enough."

"Oh, don't fret, Captain. The lad's found a new hand, worth two of the old ones. He's that big."

"We've orders about new hands. Has he his papers?"

"Signed by Berishar, or I've forgotten my own name."

A moment's silence, then the sound of numerous booted feet, diminishing as they headed forward.

"That him, the big one?"

"Aye, Captain. The one with the red cap and the red trim on his jacket. And—you can't see it from here, but he's got the lucky eyes."

"One blue and one green?"

"The blue eye's more brown, but close enough."

"It'll be enough if he's not *unlucky*, for himself or for us. This is a canny enough voyage, with so many women passengers aboard."

"Should I make an extra offering at the temple of Habbakuk in Karthay?"

"You should get out of my sight and start lashing things

down. Including your tongue, if you can't make it wag sense!"

"Aye, aye, Captain."

Pirvan stifled laughter and let himself down on to the bunk, reassured. Grimsoar normally wore a patch over his ruined eye, but had a selection of glass and crystal ones to give him the appearance of two eyes. Also, his good eye was an unusual shade of blue with tinges of brown (or brown with tinges of blue), and he'd said that he would be wearing red headgear.

Altogether, Pirvan felt that he could sleep in peace, knowing he was not alone. That knowledge and scant sleep in the two days since he had signed on for this voyage took him down almost before he could hang up his outer clothes.

* * * * *

Pirvan awoke to the knowledge that *Golden Cup* was at sea, or at least no longer at anchor. All the movements and sounds had changed.

Less expected and much less welcome was the fact that he was no longer alone in the cabin. A man was sitting on the deck, back against the door, head sunk on his chest. It was a bald head, but the face below looked no older than Pirvan's, and the body in the sailor's clothes looked both well fed and well muscled.

Pirvan counted to ten, holding his breath while he drew his dagger from under the straw-stuffed pillow. Then he looked at the hammock above and said, very slowly:

"I seem to be in the habit lately of waking in strange places and in strange company. That you may cease to be strange, please tell me who you are and what you are doing in my cabin." Without my having to ask twice, either, or I will try the pommel of my dagger across the bridge of your nose as the next question.

The man gave a *whuff* like a dwarf with a hangover and straightened. Dark eyes opened in an amiable, round face, framed from ear to ear in a close-cut dark beard.

Cautiously, as if he had sensed Pirvan's dagger and readiness to use it, he drew from the neck of his shirt a medallion.

It was hammered red metal, with silver-filled signs etched into it. The front was the mark of the Towers of High Sorcery, the rear the open book of Gilean.

Pirvan put his feet on the deck without taking his hand off the dagger. "Ah, the mage—"

"Neutral, my friend. Neutral, in spite of what the Black and White Robes may say, does *not* mean renegade."

The man sounded as though he were wearily correcting a common mistake, rather than looking for an excuse for a fight. Since Pirvan had used much the same tone on certain persons ill-informed about the thieves, he found himself both eased and amused.

"I apologize for that error. May I ask one from you, for slipping into my cabin like—shall we say, a thief?"

The man choked down laughter. "I crave your pardon. But I am aboard this ship as a stowaway. I thought you might be the least inclined to turn me over to the captain."

"That will depend on why you are here. Please don't expect to subdue me by magic, either. I can probably knock you senseless before you can complete a major spell. Even if I couldn't, using magic would be about as prudent as setting the ship on fire. You would be lucky to be thrown overboard in one piece."

The man stood up and looked down at Pirvan. "Gilean forbid I should do any such thing," he said. "For these moments I trained by handling drunks in my father's tavern. I trained well, too, little as I knew it at the time."

Pirvan looked up at the wizard. He did resemble a smaller edition of Grimsoar One-Eye, and might be enough faster to take advantage of being a smaller target. A brawl with this man might be one-sided for a good many, even without spells thrown in.

"Very well. We neither of us throw the other overboard. With that settled, who are you?"

"Tarothin, Red Robe Wizard," the man said, and sat back down. "Stowaway aboard *Golden Cup*, as I told you.

Why I am here is a long story."

"So tell it. I haven't heard the dawn whistle yet."

"You won't for quite a while. It's still dark outside, though we've been under way for several hours."

"Then we have time for a *very* long story."

"As it may please your lordship," Tarothin said, but his grin took the edge off the words.

Tarothin must have been accustomed to remarkably laconic people, because his "long story" took less than the time from one bell to another. Luckily, Tarothin had resisted the temptation to make it complex. Pirvan began to suspect that he and Tarothin might well get along splendidly, for that virtue if none other.

" . . . So, in the end, the Towers suggested that I had gone against law, custom, and my own philosophy. Not by serving it in a way careless of the consequences to others. I admitted that I had been in haste, but they called that explanation rather than excuse, and indeed a sign that I needed discipline more rather than less."

Pirvan disagreed with nothing in this summary, but it did not quite explain why Tarothin was here. His look asked that without words, and the wizard continued.

"Now, I wished to avoid danger from the thieves and also a course of discipline in the Towers. It might have lasted years, and to be trapped in Istar that long—but I run ahead of myself."

"No harm done." At least, no harm done if he finishes the tale I hear in those words some other time, Pirvan mused.

"I disguised myself, quite naturally, and went aboard while *Golden Cup* was still alongside the quay. After we sailed, I left my hiding place and came up here, having heard that your cabin had space and that you had honor."

"As to the space, the hammock is yours—"

"I'd rather sleep on the floor."

"As you wish, but don't complain if I step on you when I visit the head."

"Never fear, as long as you go barefoot."

"Let's discuss the proper footgear for stepping on you

some other time. I do have honor, which brought me on this voyage to make recompense to House Encuintras. Now it requires me to take you to their representatives."

"Why?"

Pirvan suited bald answers to the bald question. "Because you stowed away, and a wizard aboard ship can make sailors nervous. Nervous sailors can be bad sailors, and bad sailors wreck ships."

Tarothin nodded. Pirvan had the notion that he'd just passed a test of his own knowledge, rather than adding to the wizard's. He almost hoped so. Worldly wizards and clerics were the butt of any number of rude jokes, but they were the sort you wanted to have along on a voyage like this.

"I will go gladly, though more so to Lady Eskaia. She commanded my spells, so will be the best judge of what I must do. Indeed, she commanded me without—"

"Without speaking to her guard-maid?"

Tarothin's vexed look confirmed Pirvan's suspicions. That definitely made Eskaia the better woman for this business.

"Then I suggest that we finish our night's sleep," Tarothin went on. "Haimya is about at all hours—learning her way around the ship, she says. But Eskaia takes a lady's privilege and puts in a full night. Is there any reason we shouldn't do the same?"

Pirvan saw none, and slept again soon after Tarothin started snoring.

* * * * *

"That's Freshwater Point over yonder," Mate of the Tops Kurulus said. "No matter how high the tide, the water's fresh from there on back to Istar."

"How long before we reach the Delta?" Pirvan asked.

"We'll have it in sight in another two hours," Kurulus said. "But we'll be anchoring overnight. Nobody runs the Delta by night unless he's in a smaller ship or wants to run aground—or worse."

"Worse?"

"Pirates, ogres, sea trolls, or so they say—never seen one myself, but I can swear to the others."

"This close to Istar?"

"Close is as close does," the mate said. "There's plenty of places in the Delta. Might as well be on Nuitari for all the soldiers can reach them. Then there's razorflies, strangleberries, black willows if you're foolish enough—"

He broke off and looked down. "Hoa. I think we're about to have company."

Pirvan looked down *Golden Cup*'s mainmast and saw Haimya climbing the rope ladder toward the top, where he and Kurulus stood. From fifty feet above, he could see that she wore an expression of grim determination.

Probably no worse than I had this morning, he thought.

Pirvan had first gone aloft after seeing Tarothin to Lady Eskaia's cabin and being graciously dismissed. Kurulus had said it was a good way to wake up, and would give him a better name among the crew.

About the crew, Pirvan knew nothing. As to the waking, he had to agree. There was a certain degree of fear that left no room for early morning fuzziness, only for total concentration of mind and body on a single task—in Pirvan's case, not falling out of the rigging like a ripe apple from a wind-shaken tree.

He had, in fact, been higher than the maintop, on cliffs and walls and in trees. But none of these swayed as the mast did, even in the calm waters of the Istar River. His climb was slow, though his recovery afterward was mercifully quick.

Now it was complete, his head for heights had entirely returned, and he stood with one hand on the rail of the top. Haimya was now so close that she would notice him looking at her and resent it, so Pirvan turned his eyes out over the river.

Two miles wide here, it had room for a hundred vessels between green-furred shores. These ranged from at least one ship as large as *Golden Cup* down to fishermen's rowboats. There was even one odd craft with two triangular sails, crewed by figures too short to be human.

Pirvan pointed at the strange two-master. "Dwarves, kender, or gnomes?"

"Cursed if I know," Kurulus said. "Dwarves mostly don't go on water—you know they can't swim, though some use floatbelts. Kender will go anywhere and do anything that promises an adventure, so it could be they. No gnome craft ever sailed as well as that one, and I've heard they're giving up sail anyway."

"Sailing? They're building galleys?"

"The better for them if they were. No, I've heard they're working on contraptions of levers moved by steam from giant teakettles that turn wheels either side of the hull."

"Trust a gnome to run one like that."

"Aye. Word is, so far they haven't launched one that didn't burn or sink. Us old sailorfolk have a few years yet before we need to put oars on our shoulders and walk inland to take up farming."

A big Istarian galley swept by to port as Haimya climbed over the starboard railing of the maintop. For a moment, Pirvan thought she was going to fall, and resisted the temptation to put out a hand to her. She was seldom rude, save when a man offered unsought help; then she could rattle ears or even teeth with her reply.

At last Haimya embraced the mast as if it had been a lover, and murmured, her voice half-lost in the tarred timber, "A fine day for a sail."

Pirvan nodded. "And to think we're having it all without paying a single horn for it."

The mate threw back his head and howled with laughter. "Try calling it a pleasure cruise when a southwester hits, friends. If you do it then, I'll call you madmen or sailors."

Haimya turned toward Kurulus a face that was pale with a slight tinge of green. "I have always wondered how to tell the two apart."

The mate laughed even louder. Haimya frowned. "Could you leave us, please?"

Pirvan was about to suggest a more polite way of making the request. It said much about Haimya's state of mind and body that she only pressed her face against the mast again.

"Well and good," Kurulus said cheerfully. "I won't leave two lubbers like you *alone*, unless you really need it, and the top's no place for that, let me tell you. Hitting the deck all wound together like that—"

That finally drew some barracks language from Haimya. The mate's grin widened.

"I'll see to some lashings on the mainyard. The worst storms always hit the day after you've decided everything is shipshape."

He swung himself over the railing, dropped to the yard, and strode out along it as briskly as any shepherd ever drove sheep across a level pasture. Haimya closed her eyes. Pirvan didn't altogether blame her. Sailors took being comfortable high in the air somewhat farther than he ever had.

"Lady Eskaia and Tarothin thank you for more than you know," Haimya said at last.

"Am I to learn it now?" Haimya might be both dizzy and seasick; Pirvan was weary of riddles.

"My lady has it in her—she and Tarothin think—to be a cleric. But—she has never been allowed testing or training."

"That is the Towers' decision?" If the merchant princess and the peculiar wizard were going against such, they were renegades in fact and would soon be such in law. One did not need to be a sailor to be uncomfortable with that, aboard a ship on a voyage already likely to be sufficiently perilous.

"Her father's. However closely held the secret, it would escape. Then there would be tongues wagging all over Istar, many saying Eskaia was rebelling against her house or refusing marriage."

"Is she?"

Haimya's eyes turned cold for a moment, then she swallowed. "I do not know. It is not a question one asks. If she wishes me to know, she will tell me."

The tone made the words as close to an apology as Pirvan had received from Haimya since they had set sail. "It will need to be an even more closely held secret here than in Istar. We live closer together, and the sailors mostly do not care for anything except weather magic."

"They are loyal to House Encuintras."

"Loyal servants, yes, but not slaves."

He wanted to ask aloud if her years as a mercenary had not taught her the difference, but he wanted to climb down from the top with all his teeth in his head. Haimya was no fool, nor even the first person he'd known made to sound like one by a queasy stomach.

"Will *you* keep the secret, and do whatever else may be needed to guard it?" Haimya asked.

"My oath did not—"

"Is your oath dung?"

"No," the thief said. "Nor am I a slave, either."

Pirvan hoped her temper would not flare beyond bounds. It would accomplish nothing except entertaining Kurulus, and Eskaia would have to play peacemaker.

"I will guard both your lady and her secret," Pirvan said. That seemed to ease Haimya. She turned to climb over the railing into the rigging for the descent, then gripped the polished wood until her knuckles turned white. Just as Pirvan was about to reach for her, she swung herself over, as smoothly as a girl but for the white face.

"I can descend by myself, thank you," she said to no one or everyone.

She went down considerably faster than she had come up, with Pirvan sneaking a look every few moments. As she touched the deck, Kurulus returned to the top. From his face, he might have heard nothing but seen a good deal.

"That's a fine woman, and she'll be finer when she gets her sea legs and loses that temper."

"I think some of the temper is inborn."

"Ah, that can be even better."

"Or much worse."

"A man can always hope," the mate said.

"Hope is cheap," Pirvan said. "Do you really think you've a chance with her?"

"Jealous?"

"You've no cause to insult me like that."

"Aye. Forgive me. But what are my chances?"

"About the same as mine."

"Which are?"

"None."

Chapter 7

The pleasure voyage did not last much beyond the Delta.

They passed down the Great Channel (a name that had been carried by four different passages through the Delta since Istar was founded) the next day. Once they touched ground, but lightly and on a rising tide. In an hour they were afloat and bound seaward again.

At dawn the next day they were clear of the Delta and heading north down the Bay of Istar. The southern stretch of it was hardly wider than the river, but it rapidly widened until by noon they were out of sight of land from the deck. Pirvan was willing to take the word of *The Mariner's Almanak* about the features of the shore, rather than climb up the mainmast again with a spyglass to see them for himself.

Toward nightfall they took in sail, as the wind was rising and confused, and lumpy waves were making *Golden Cup* sway clumsily, rather like an owlbear trying to do a

Plainsman fertility dance. Gusts seemed to be coming in from all directions, and Pirvan saw Kurulus frowning as he watched the sails alternately fill hard as a breastplate, then flap like empty sacks.

"Oh, it's not as bad as it could be, and it's not likely to get that bad at this time of year," the mate said. "The most of the storms come up from the southwest, and if we have the searoom we can tack right out of the gulf into the open sea faster than we could without the storm."

"What about storms from other directions?"

Pirvan had heard sailors describe "tacking" for many years, but understood it hardly better than he understood Tarothin's magic. He knew that it allowed a properly equipped ship to sail without the wind blowing from directly astern, but how it was translated into the movements of the ship's three tree-tall masts and six broad sails, Pirvan did not pretend to know.

"I'd just as soon you kept this to yourself," Kurulus said. "If we've searoom and nothing carries away, we can beat about in the middle of the gulf until the blow passes. Otherwise, we might be needing to put in at Karthay, no good thing, or face even worse."

Pirvan did not ask about the "even worse," because he suspected he knew what it was. He had never been in a shipwreck but knew some who had; he preferred not to join their ranks.

As for Karthay, the mate's expression was that of a man who can be persuaded to answer but would rather not. Again, Pirvan suspected the answer. In his profession, the affairs of the mighty were of only moderate interest, and he had little need to know where Istar's rule was real and where it sat very lightly. Karthay and its outlying ports were among those where Istarians walked softly and in pairs—and because without Istar's fleet, Karthay would command the larger city's sea routes to the rest of Krynn, it was a matter of no small moment.

Pirvan walked to the railing and made a small rite to Habbakuk to avert really dangerous weather—one did not ask him for gentle breezes and smooth seas, thereby implying that one lacked both courage and sea legs. Then he looked forward and aft along the deck, and took some consolation from the view.

Golden Cup was a hundred and forty feet from prow to stern, with the bowsprit jutting out another forty feet beyond the prow. The ship carried one sail on the bowsprit, two square sails on the foremast, two on the mainmast, and a single large triangular sail on the mizzen. Forward and aft, one deck was piled on another, like miniature castles, and even amidships, where the hull was lower, the railings ("bulwarks" was the name he'd heard) were solid wood and higher than a man, the hatchways massive structures with covers bolted on and tarred canvas lashed down.

This construction, so he'd heard, was mostly intended to make the ship proof against pirates. They could hardly climb aboard at bow and stern, and if they came over the railings and amidships, the defenders could rain arrows on them until they were as dead as the deck planking. Also, the high bow and stern would stay above the waves, which could wash over and through the bulwarks amidships without harm unless the hatch covers gave way.

This would have consoled Pirvan more if he had not talked with men who'd swum away from a ship whose hatches had caved in from the battering of a storm. They'd barely made it to shore, and seen most of their shipmates drowned or taken by something in the water they did not care to describe.

* * * * *

At dawn the next day, the sun illuminated mountain ranges of clouds to the south and west. Higher up to the south rode more clouds, as dark as a flight of black dragons. The wind had risen further, but it seemed to have steadied to almost due south. *Golden Cup* was throwing up rainbows from its bow wave and a millrace from its wake as the sails caught the wind.

Pirvan was walking back from the bow, where he'd

been talking with Grimsoar, when he encountered Haimya. She wore a mate's garb with her own boots and an expression that defied anyone to comment on the greenish pallor of her face.

The way the breeze whipped her hair about her face did more in that cause, to Pirvan's way of thinking. He knew that he could find it hard to remember that she was betrothed if he did not make the effort.

"Good day, Haimya," he said.

"To you likewise, Pirvan. I expected to find you aloft, admiring the sea."

Pirvan looked at the masthead, swaying through a moderate portion of a circle, and shuddered. "The sea will do well or ill, whether I am watching it or not."

"You don't think we are in danger?"

Asking that question was a large admission of being like other folk than he had expected to hear from the warrior-maid, this side of her deathbed. He tried to be both truthful and reassuring.

"I believe it takes much worse weather than this to affect a ship of this size."

He thought the moan of the wind and the hiss of water alongside would conceal minor flaws in his speech. A moment later, he had cause to think again.

"And how many voyages have you made, Pirvan the Sailor?" She'd mustered from somewhere the will to quirk up one corner of her mouth.

"This is my first real one."

She thrust out a hand. "Very well. Let us seal a bargain. Whichever one of us sees land first after the ship goes down, she guides the other to it."

Pirvan was torn between smiling at her determination and his distaste for words of ill omen. He wondered if Tarothin had any weather spells, and if so, whether he could be persuaded to use them.

"You can swim?"

"It's one of the few things I knew from girlhood. My father thought it doomed my hopes of marriage. My mother knew I was not much inclined that way, and said I should be good at as many things as I wished. 'Man or woman who is good at nothing,' she said, 'is hapless, hopeless, and helpless.'"

Pirvan nodded, looking upward again. His eyes were not on the rigging, however. They were looking inward, at a picture of Haimya swimming—a pleasant picture even if she garbed herself, for wet clothes clung tightly. . . .

A faint laugh broke off suddenly in a choking sound. Pirvan looked about the deck to see Haimya thrusting her head and shoulders over the railing. Her torso heaved and twisted for a moment. When she drew herself back, water dripped from her face and her hair was plastered down her cheeks and forehead.

Silently, Pirvan hoped that the weather would grow no worse, or if it did, that Haimya would have no urgent duties until it quieted.

* * * * *

Pirvan's hopes were disappointed.

Toward late afternoon, the high, dark clouds swept forward and turned black, then swelled and seemed to burst. A howling wind swept across the sea, churning up the waves into gray hillocks. Rain and spray swept across the deck, turning the planks as slick as the surface of a glacier.

The sail on the bowsprit and the triangular mizzensail had long since been taken in and the yards double-lashed. Now men struggled aloft to take in the topsails on the fore- and mainmasts. Pirvan watched from the aftercastle, though he had offered to go aloft.

"No place for even the best climber if he doesn't know the way of a wet sail," Kurulus told him firmly. "You've duties to Lady Eskaia, more, I wager, than you've told me. You splatter on the deck or go over the side, the lady'll have *my* blood."

Pirvan didn't like the hint in those words, but he also knew that the mate would have been better spoken if he'd been less worried. *Golden Cup* was in no easy circumstances; the faces of the men going aloft said as much. The fair-skinned ones were many of them as green as Haimya; the darker ones looked as if they were forcing themselves to climb the rigging rather than hang over the railings.

One man did go off the main topsail yard, and in this gale there was no hope of picking him up. But he struck the mainyard on the way down, and fell bonelessly limp and probably already dead into the sea, spared the ordeal of drowning alone as his ship sailed on.

The remaining sails kept the ship manageable until after nightfall. Pirvan had gone to his cabin and was beginning to drowse in spite of the motion of the ship and the uproar of the storm, when it happened.

A shout, then several, then a scream. Wood cracked thunderously. Another shout: "All hands on deck!" Then even more thunder, drowning out the gale and sounding like some great tree falling.

Pirvan had been out of his bunk at the cry of "All hands on deck!" As he flung open his cabin door, he felt the deck under his bare feet taking up a new motion. Then it tilted, farther than it ever had, sending him slamming backward against the wall. For a terrible moment he thought the ship would never come back, and that he and everyone belowdecks faced gurgling out their lives as the ship sank.

Then the deck began to level out, with more shouts from above, cracking and creaking of wood, and screams from the cabins. The deck tilted as far the other way as it had the first way, and this time flung Pirvan forward. He would have slammed into the opposite wall if something both soft and solid hadn't broken his fall.

He struggled clear of his companion and discovered that it was Haimya, clad in a loinguard that covered no more than his did, with a sword in her hand. He noted that she offered no unpleasant surprises unclad, then gripped the nearest handhold as the ship began another roll.

"Haimya, I think it's something in the ship, not pirates. If you go out on deck, you'll need both hands."

She looked at her sword, then at herself. "Perhaps more than that," she said, and in the dimness he could have sworn that she was blushing. Then she vanished toward her cabin as Pirvan lunged out on to the deck, lurching back and forth as the ship did the same under his feet.

He kept his balance and his sea legs alike until he reached the deck. Then two steps outside, and a foaming wall of water reached his chest and swept him off his feet. Something told him not to trust the bulwarks to catch him, and as his head went under, he spread arms and legs wide.

A foot caught on something solid enough to hold him until the wave receded. Then he found a rope almost hitting him in the face and clutched it with both hands. He didn't know whether it was a shroud, a stay, a line, or a dragon's tail; sailors' fancy terms didn't matter as long as it kept him aboard and alive.

He survived three waves before he saw the problem. The foremast had snapped off a man's height above the deck. In falling, it hadn't quite cleared the ship, but flattened a long stretch of the bulwarks to starboard. Now every time the ship rolled, waves boiled in through the gap.

Already sailors were hacking at the wreckage, some holding on with one hand and working with the other, others tied to the ship and trusting to their safety lines. Other less lucky ones were struggling on the deck, or, knocked senselsss, washing back and forth in the surge of incoming waves and the rolling of the ship.

Pirvan saw one of the unconscious men wash overboard before his eyes. He also saw that the rope he held would let him reach most of the deck. He tied it around his waist and began methodically following the senseless men. He had little knowledge of even nonmagical healing, but a man who didn't slide overboard and drown might live to be healed by someone more skilled.

One by one he overtook them. He lost count of how many, and he cursed gods and men alike when a wave snatched one of them out of his hands and overboard. Other waves slammed him against protrusions from the deck, or wreckage against him, or him and the man he was trying to save together. He knew he was bruised all over and bleeding in at least one place, but ignored that until he heard a wild cry from above.

Even then, he kept crawling about the deck in search of more men to snatch from the sea, until someone shouted in his ear.

"The mast's free. Get back below and be tended to, you fool!"

It was Grimsoar One-Eye. Pirvan looked up. His friend recognized him and shrugged, then said, "So be it. You're not a fool. You still look as if you'd been wrestling sea trolls."

By now, Pirvan's exalted mood had worn off and he'd begun to feel the same way. He gripped Grimsoar's arm, and with his help rose uncertainly to his feet.

"You said the mast's cut away?"

"Gone, and a man with it. It won't pound any holes in the hull now. We're safe until we fetch up on the Gallows Reefs. This ship's too stout to founder, but she can't survive the rocks."

"What else can we do?"

"Besides pray, you mean? I've heard a mate say we've a chance to make the Flower Rocks, but how much I don't know."

Pirvan had never heard of the Flower Rocks, but they sounded like a place where you had to work hard to be saved. This meant more wrestling with the sea in a few hours or a few days.

And that meant doing what Grimsoar suggested.

* * * * *

Prayers must have reached at least some well-disposed gods; they were still afloat and off the Flower Rocks at dawn. Or so Pirvan heard someone say.

He was on the main deck, too low to see anything more than a ship's length away through the spray and the murk. All he saw was the length of anchor chain in his hands, and the sailors of the hauling party ahead of and behind him.

The Flower Rocks, he had learned, were a series of rocky mounts with deep water close inshore on all sides, enough for the largest ship men could conceive. Prudent seafarers some centuries before had sunk stout iron and stone mooring posts ("bollards" or some such word) into the rocks on all four sides. A ship that could moor to a set of bollards could ride out most gales in the lee of the rocks. Sometimes the lee of the rocks alone cut the wind enough to let a ship anchor safely.

Anchoring was the plan for *Golden Cup*, as its captain seemed not to wish the ship too close to the rocks themselves. The main bow anchor was ready to let go, but the light chain on the stern anchor would never survive this blow.

The Mate of the Hold and her gang had broken out a heavier chain from below. Now all available hands had turned to, for hauling the chain aft and securing it to the anchor.

"We'll be letting both go together," Kurulus had told Pirvan. "Riding on one anchor in this sea, we lose chain, anchor, and most chance of staying off the rocks even if it holds for a bit."

What would happen if the anchor didn't hold, needed no explanation. The ship's motion had thrown Pirvan out of his bunk three times, until between the lingering pain from his half-healing, fresh bruises, and the heaving deck, he gave up trying to sleep.

Tarothin slept through everything, strapped into his bunk and with most of his possessions wedging him in even more tightly, with more straps around the bags and boxes. Pirvan had suggested that it might not be easy to leave his bunk quickly if it became necessary; he had not forgotten the wizard's reply.

"If we strike or founder, it's hardly going to matter how fast I go anywhere. I can't swim a stroke, and I don't command any spell that will let me breathe underwater long enough to walk to shore."

Pirvan held his tongue after that.

Now he held his tongue because he needed every breath in his body for hauling on the anchor chain. Even if he had not, the sight of the waves would have left him speechless.

The ship no longer seemed to be taking solid water over the main deck. But on either side the waves leaped up, white crested, like an endless pack of wolves howling around a great stag. The stag still stood tall, but how long could this last before the wolves dragged it down?

Pirvan shivered from more than the cold, then saw that the hauler ahead of him was now Haimya.

"Haimya!" he shouted, above the moan of the wind. "Are you a shapechanger now?"

"Eh?"

"Never mind. How fares your lady?"

"She said that one of us ought to join this work."

"You say—"

"I insisted on going instead of her."

"Your lady has more courage than sense, and more sense than strength."

He did not add that the same could be said of Haimya. Her face was no longer greenish, but it was still pale and set. It was as though a long and wasting fever had just broken, leaving her well but weak.

How long they hauled before the stern anchor was ready to lower, Pirvan never knew. He remembered only a moment when he realized that the wind had dropped, and even spray no longer blew over the deck. Then came a second moment, when he realized that Haimya had turned to Grimsoar One-Eye.

The big man was hauling with a will, but his single eye seemed aimed at the sky.

"*Now* what's wrong?"

Pirvan knew he sounded petulant, but he was tired. He found distasteful, to say the least, the possibility of safety being snatched from them at the last moment.

"I don't like this lull," Grimsoar said. The wind was so mild now that he could make Pirvan hear him without raising his voice much above a whisper.

"It could be the end of the storm," Pirvan said.

"Maybe. Maybe also just the eye, or even a sign the wind's about to shift."

Pirvan did not need to ask for the details of that last danger, or wish to contemplate them. With the wind from any direction but the south, they had rocky lee shores far too close to give them much hope of surviving if the storm lasted beyond a few more hours.

At some time while Pirvan was considering this, the trumpets blew for the anchoring party and someone led Pirvan aside. Another someone pushed a cup of hot tarberry tea laced with brandy into his hands.

It was only after the third swallow that he realized that the hands holding the tray were white, clean, and lavishly ringed.

"My lady?"

He looked up as a puff of wind blew Eskaia's hood back from her head and made her dark curls dance. So did her eyes, with both mischief and determination.

"I promised Haimya that I would not haul on the line. Nothing more."

Pirvan did not care if Eskaia had promised her guardmaid some dwarf-forged armor and a castle on Lunitari. The less time she spent on deck, the happier he and many others would be.

Before he could say anything, however, a wild cry came from aloft, and more cries from forward echoed it.

"The anchor's parted!"

* * * * *

It was the chain to the main anchor that had parted, being the only one over the side. Lowering both together, it seemed, would have taken more hands than were available for the work. So the captain had gambled on the lull in the storm holding for a few minutes longer.

The lull held for the most part. But enough wind remained blowing, and imperceptibly shifting as well, to pull the chain hard against a sharp edge of rock. As the wind rose and the anchoring party rushed aft to lower the second anchor, the rock sawed at the stout chain like a notched sword at an ogre's neck.

Moments after it parted, Pirvan felt a puff of wind that turned into a steady blowing—from the northwest. In the time since they'd sailed into the lee of the Flower Rocks, the wind had shifted around until now the rocks were themselves alee shore!

If every soul aboard *Golden Cup* had been twins, there would still have been work for them all in the next few minutes. Pirvan was caught up in it all, turning his hands to whatever work he was ordered to do or saw not being done. He could not have said from moment to moment what was going on, as the ship's people struggled to save it and themselves, but he remembered what he saw when he could at last look up from the deck.

Golden Cup's stern had turned toward the wind and was driving south, with the Flower Rocks seemingly close enough to touch. The ship also seemed to be making some way toward the east, with every scrap of sail set that its two remaining masts could carry. Somebody had even tied something to the stump of the foremast, and it was beyond there that Pirvan saw it:

Tarothin stood by the railing, both hands raised, one of them holding his staff. Tarothin, the healing-weakened wizard who could not swim a stroke, stood by the railing with neither rope around his waist, nor floatbelt around his torso, nor anybody at hand to catch him if he slipped.

Pirvan dropped some work he could not remember having picked up and sprinted for the ladder. The deck seemed to drop out from under him as he clutched the rungs and hauled himself upward more than climbed. A dash, a second ladder, the ship lurching wildly again, and he was a sword's length from Tarothin.

There he stopped. To either side, the waves surged and foamed into the shallow water and over the rocks. Over a good part of the area astern, the wind seemed to have halted. Pirvan saw spray rising farther off to the north, flung toward the ship, and caught in the air to shimmer like heat rising from a fire.

He also saw one of the men working on the foremast snatch up a short spear—a boarding pike, Pirvan had heard them called—and lift it, ready to throw.

Whatever Tarothin might have in mind, he could not be meaning to sink the ship with Lady Eskaia aboard. Not unless so many people had lied to Pirvan that *Golden Cup* was already doomed.

His dagger came out in a heartbeat and flew through the air as the sailor brought his arm back. Before the pike left his hand, the weighted pommel of Pirvan's dagger smashed into his shoulder. The spear went wild, more nearly hitting Pirvan than Tarothin. The thief lunged forward, kicked the sailor in the stomach, snatched up the dagger as the man crumpled, and made ready to hold the man's comrades at bay.

"Don't touch the staff!" someone shouted. Pirvan thought wizards couldn't talk while working a spell, then realized that it was Grimsoar who had shouted. He stormed across the deck with a coil of rope under one arm and a hefty club in the other. He looped the rope around Tarothin's waist several times, then tied it with just as many knots to the railing. By the time Grimsoar was finished, Tarothin was more firmly a part of the ship than much of the surviving deck gear.

By that time, too, the sailors had retreated and Pirvan had attention to spare for what Tarothin had been doing. There was a passage in the Flower Rocks from north to south, narrow and high-walled, more like a canyon than anything else but wide enough for the largest ships.

With the wind as it had been, even a landlubber like Pirvan could see that they would never have made it. But with Tarothin's spell shifting the wind, *Golden Cup* was making steady progress toward the passage.

It was not steady all the way; the bowsprit came to grief halfway through, as the surge of the waves overpowered both wizard and helmsman. But in time there was open water ahead, where there had been solid rock too recently for anyone's comfort, and orders being shouted that Pirvan knew he should obey.

"I'll keep any witlings off him," Grimsoar said.

"Unless they need—your strength," Tarothin said. His voice rasped as if his throat was filled with sand.

"We need you." Grimsoar said. "Either Grimsoar stays or you go below."

Tarothin seemed not to hear. He gripped the railing and stared out over the waves. Even in the lee of the Flower Rocks, they had regained their wolfish aspect—and the stag had lost several prongs from one of his antlers.

The orders came from below, louder this time, and Pirvan turned and scrambled down the ladder.

* * * * *

The work the mate of the deck had called Pirvan to do was repairing the safety lines. He knew as much about ropes and knots as some of the sailors, so his hands flew, and meanwhile he listened to the sailors talk.

They weren't out of danger yet, it seemed. If the wind backed around to the south again, they had only one anchor to keep them off the rocks. If it stayed northerly, they could still be driven south to the Finburnighu Shoals. That was another feature of the Gulf of Karthay that Pirvan had never heard of and would have been glad not to hear of now.

As he strung a safety line across a gap in the bulwarks, Pirvan saw one of those sets of bollards on a shelf in the rocks, a long bowshot away. He also saw the water boiling between the ship and the rocks, and the distance opening between it and the bollards.

"Wind's one way, current's another, tide's a third," Kurulus said. He lowered his voice. "You can ship with me any time you please, Brother Pirvan."

Pirvan nodded silently. An idea was forming in his mind.

"Do we have a boat left?"

The mate shrugged. "All smashed, but they made a raft of barrels yesterday. If it's in one piece—but now, you can't steer it through that."

"What if it was on a rope?"

"A line?"

"Whatever you call it."

Pirvan's patience with the fine points of the sailors' vocabulary threatened to run out. So did every other sort of patience. He could see the gap between the ship and the bollards opening steadily, and who knew where the next set was?

"I can swim to the bollards with a line. Then the men on the raft can pull themselves ashore. Five or six men can pull a heavier line ashore. One line and the anchor should hold us."

"Can you swim well—?"

"Well enough to reach the rocks, and then it will be more a matter of climbing. *That* I can do better than anyone aboard, I wager."

"Like I said, Brother, when I have my ship—"

"I accept the offer, if we both live long enough."

"Better if your wizard friend could throw the rope with a spell."

"I don't know if he knows levitation. Also, that wind block weakened him all over again."

Kurulus and several sailors who'd gathered just within hearing looked sour. Pirvan wanted to curse. First they'd been ready to kill Tarothin for casting a spell. Now they seemed ready to kill him because he couldn't cast the one they needed.

And who should come shouldering through the sailors but Haimya, at this moment about the last person he wanted to see. (There were a few men who'd taken his thefts as cause for blood feud, but two were dead and none of the living aboard this or any other ship.)

At least the warrior-maid might not have heard him and the mate talking—

"You'll need two of us swimming the line ashore, Kurulus. Now, don't argue," Haimya added. "I swim better than Pirvan, even if he does climb better than I do."

It did not seem like a good time to mention Haimya's

seasickness. Time was passing, the bollards were receding, the wind seemed to be rising, and possibly the prospect of action had cured Haimya's seasickness.

And possibly the three moons might do a perfect hesitation dance that very night.

Pirvan pulled off his shirt and began looking around for a suitable length of rope.

* * * * *

The wind continued to rise as Pirvan and Haimya made their preparations. As swiftly as they worked, the first bollards were out of sight by the time they were ready. By the favor of the gods and long-dead masons, a second set was coming into sight as they stepped to the bulwarks.

Pirvan wore only his loinguard and gloves, Haimya a loinguard, a sailor's shirt, and sharkskin buckskins. Both carried daggers, Haimya a beltful of wooden pegs, and Pirvan a small mallet. Both had ropes around their waists.

"Now, remember, nothing fancy, and are you sure you wouldn't have float—?" the mate of the hold said. She was short and sturdy, likewise old enough to be Pirvan's mother and right now behaving much like one.

"We'll be doing as much climbing as swimming," Pirvan said. "Ready, Haimya?"

"Haimya—" Lady Eskaia began. She'd come on deck even though she now looked as sick as Haimya had been. Then her voice failed her and she only hugged her guardmaid.

Grimsoar came up, at the head of the men assigned to the raft. "Brother, Tarothin says—"

Pirvan scrambled under the lifeline and balanced on the ragged edge of the deck. Nothing from Tarothin could be worth standing here a moment longer, listening to the wind howl and wondering how many moments he had yet to live.

A wild cry rose above the wind. Haimya soared into the air, bent double, and plunged from sight under the foam. Pirvan waited only long enough for her head to reappear, then dived after her.

* * * * *

The rope snapped tight around Pirvan's waist, burning his skin even in the chill water. It also squeezed the breath out of him, so that he had barely enough air in his lungs to reach the surface. He gulped in air, his lungs stopped burning, then a wave broke over him and he choked on the water.

A strong arm slid under him, lifting him, while an equally strong hand grabbed him by the hair and lifted his face out of the water. He churned with both arms and legs, lifting himself higher, above the next wave and the one after it. By then he could breathe normally again.

No words were needed. He just looked his thanks at Haimya and began to swim toward the rocks. So did she, but with a sureness of movement in her shapely arms and legs that proved the truth of her words. She could have covered two feet to Pirvan's one if she hadn't deliberately slowed so that they approached the rocks together.

In the lee of the Flower Rocks, the waves weren't shattering both themselves and swimmers on the outcroppings. It was still like climbing out of a boiling pot with a rim two men high. Pirvan trod water for a moment, looking for the best way up.

A crack about as wide as his head seemed the best way. As long as he wasn't washed in too far and wedged tightly underwater, or swept out and battered against the rocks—

It was then that he saw Haimya's head vanish below the surface.

He thought for a moment that she'd dived away from the rocks, or been caught in an undertow. Then he saw the men aboard *Golden Cup* waving their arms and pointing. They also seemed to be shouting, but into this wind they might have been in Qualinesti for all he could hear them.

It was Haimya's bubbling scream that brought him fully alert. That, and her head popping up suddenly, with *something* huge and shapeless in the water barely ten feet behind her.

Alertness flowed into action in the space of a single breath. Diving with a dagger in your hand was a good way to lose it; Pirvan's steel was still in his belt as he entered the water. He deliberately dived deep and rolled over on his back as he drew the dagger, looking for his enemy.

The water was murky from the storm, but he could make out Haimya, thrashing in the water with both arms and one leg. *One* leg? He looked at the other, and saw that it hung limply, as if something had broken it or even worse, shattered the hip.

No blood, though—but Pirvan sensed something large and evil, circling them just beyond the limits of vision. He even thought he heard a peeping, like a newly hatched chick but far harsher, just at the upper limits of his hearing.

Then a serpentine shape came out of the murk, and Haimya thrashed still more wildly. Pirvan had just time to see her other leg go limp, then lunged at the shape. It was gray and shaped more like a sausage than a serpent, but it had scales and a face that was a nightmarish parody of a human one.

A water naga—and an evil one, or else one that thought for some reason Haimya and Pirvan were enemies. No time to argue with it, either, even if it were intelligent enough to understand.

Pirvan's dagger skidded off scales but upward and inexorably toward the left eye. The paralysis spell struck him, but on the other arm—then the dagger drove into the naga's eye and pain erased its ability to cast spells.

Pirvan stroked toward the surface, using his one good arm and two good legs, searching for Haimya both above water and below. He saw her head in the middle of a circle of foam her arms had made, then saw it slide out of sight.

Pirvan dived after her, largely convinced that he would never surface again.

At least I won't have to explain to Gerik Ginfrayson

how she drowned before my eyes.

As he dived, he felt a tingle in his paralyzed left arm. He commanded it to move, and wanted to shout as it obeyed the command. He wanted to shout a second time as Haimya swept up past him, thrashing frantically with both arms and both *legs!*

She was on the surface waiting for him, staring all about her, eyes wide with alertness and (although Pirvan would never even think it) more than a little fear. He didn't blame her; the water seemed far colder at the mere thought of the naga's paralysis spell.

"Can you climb?" he called. "I can pull up if you want to wait in the water—"

Haimya's answer was to fling herself at the rocks.

Chapter 8

Haimya might not have the greatest head for heights or skill in climbing equal to Pirvan's, but her desire to be well clear of the water before the naga revived or summoned its friends worked well enough. She was on the first ledge before Pirvan, and reached the bollards at the same moment.

On that ledge, they at last had time to regain their wind—and discover that Pirvan's line had snapped somewhere in the fight with the naga. Pirvan looked down into a churning waterscape that had swallowed the rope like a chicken snatching a grain of barley. Diving back in would be futile; how dangerous as well depended rather on what had happened to the naga.

Haimya's face was a study—gratitude to Pirvan for saving her, fear for her lady and shipmates if the one line wasn't enough, and what seemed to be doubts about her own honor. Her sense of honor was the sort, Pirvan knew, that would make her think he should have let the naga take her if only he could have saved both lines.

Soon she would realize that this was fretting herself over an impossibility, and be calm. Meanwhile, the less Pirvan said, the better.

They tied the remaining line comprehensively around the bollards and signaled. Then they started hauling in the second line, for the raft.

They were streaming with spray, sweat, and blood by the time the second line was secure. Pirvan's hands were in better shape than his companion's, who clearly felt the salt water stinging her blisters and raw spots. She had also gotten wounded climbing up the rock.

They were wiping the spray out of their eyes for the tenth time when the raft went over the side of *Golden Cup*. Squinting, Pirvan saw it carried the promised six men and the end of the heaviest remaining chain. All six men were also armed with boarding pikes, fishing tridents, or axes, and the ship's side was lined with more spearmen and a few archers.

Pirvan doubted there was a dry bowstring within a day's sail of the Flower Rocks, but the sight was reassuring nonetheless. It might even mean something if the naga came back—it seemed to have no power to bespell more than one human at a time. Young, old, sick, or merely stupid? Tarothin would know, if they ever spoke to him again. . . .

Pirvan realized that cold and exhaustion were clouding his mind. Haimya's eyes were glassy, and she was beginning to shiver. He shook his head, thought of brandy-laced tea, and hauled in a double-sized portion of the line. Haimya tightened her grip, though even her sword-callused hands were beginning to weary, and threw her weight on the line, too.

At some moment, Pirvan became aware that he and Haimya were no longer alone on the rock. They seemed to be surrounded by sailors, all as large as heroes of legend or even Grimsoar One-Eye. One of them *was* Grimsoar, and he wrapped a blanket around Haimya. Except that there was only the one blanket, and she quickly stepped close to him and let him wrap them both up in the scant but welcome warmth of the tar-smelling wool.

They sat down, and Pirvan remembered hearing someone growl, "Lucky man, cuddling that sword-wench." He remembered somebody else suggesting that the first speaker keep his tongue between his teeth if he wished to have either.

Then, for quite a long time, there didn't seem to be anything worth remembering.

* * * * *

By the time Pirvan and Haimya were asleep, wrapped up in the blanket and each other, *Golden Cup* was safe. The heavy line came ashore with a rush, as six stout sailors heaved on it. The moment it was secured to the bollards, everyone who could lay a hand on the slack of the line did so and hauled the ship around until its bow pointed north and most of the strain was off the anchor.

In that fashion the ship rode out the rest of the storm, with no more rigging lost and no more leaking than manning the pumps every other hour could handle. The raft even made a second trip, bringing jugs of hot tea (as Pirvan had hoped, laced with brandy) and porridge loaded with raisins and salt pork.

The food was even more welcome than hot drinks; Haimya and Pirvan both awoke ready to slaughter and cook one of their comrades on the rock. By the time the pots were empty, the wind was dropping so fast that even Pirvan could notice it. Soon afterward, the flag signal for everyone to return aboard rose on the stump of the foremast.

"I wager we'll be upanchoring and heading for Karthay the moment they've rigged a foremast," Grimsoar said. He pointed at a crowd on the forecastle. "They've got a spare bowsprit already out, ready to be lashed in place."

Pirvan's curiosity about the whys and wherefores of this operation was not easily answered. Grimsoar was explaining a process that he understood tolerably well (two years at sea teaches a man much about the sailor's arts), but his listener not at all.

About Tarothin and the naga, Grimsoar was able to offer more to satisfy Pirvan's curiosity. At least he was, after he'd led the smaller man farther up the rock and out of earshot of both the wakeful Haimya and the other sailors preparing to cast off the lines.

"What he *said* he did—and all this was to the lady, and I was overhearing—"

"Without being seen?"

"Am I invisible?"

Pirvan smiled. "You will be, if you've offended either of them. I will push you off the rocks."

"You and which regiment?"

"So what did Tarothin say?"

It seemed that he had used a single spell, potent and thoroughly neutral, to reverse the paralysis of Haimya and Pirvan and inflict the same on the naga. It would not die unless something large and hungry came along before it regained its senses enough to flee.

Meanwhile, it was sending out cries of distress, inaudible to human or most other ears, but painful to its fellow water nagas. Any such who heard the cry would flee the area of the Flower Rocks as if the sea had begun to boil.

"Nagas have a place in the gods' balancing of things," Grimsoar said. "Or at least that's what neutrality makes our friend believe."

"I don't dispute that," Pirvan said. "As long as that place is some ways from where I am."

"He said that, too," Grimsoar replied. "Just before he fell to the deck."

"He is—"

"Sleeping it off, I judge. So does the ship's herbalist and the merchant princess, who know a deal more of this than I do. I reckon casting the spells left him in worse shape than you or Haimya."

There was a bright side to that, Pirvan realized. Tarothin

would be some while recovering his strength. During that time he could hardly teach Eskaia much about magic. He had won the goodwill of *Golden Cup*'s crew, but if he had the plans Haimya had mentioned, he might lose that of Josclyn Encuintras. What might come of that looked no more encouraging now than the first time Pirvan had heard of the games of the lady and the wizard.

With no fitting reply ready to hand, Pirvan scrambled down the rocks to join the raft party.

* * * * *

A slow voyage from the Flower Rocks (if one was unfortunate enough to enter those waters at all) was normally three to four days. *Golden Cup* took seven and the better part of the eighth.

It was sailing through contrary winds, with two and a half masts, rigging that was more knots and splices than rope, and sails that looked like garments a beggar would have scorned. The hull was strained, the leaks seemed to be gaining, and between repairs, pumping, and the ordinary duties of a large ship at sea, the crew got little rest and less sleep.

The one consolation was generous rations. No one could doubt they were going to have to put in at Karthay, to repair and replenish. Stores that had been intended for the whole voyage to the Crater Gulf and back were now distributed at every meal, and often at other times and less formally as well. ("It would only spoil if we don't finish it off," Grimsoar said one night, speaking of a large jar of pickled and spiced vegetables.)

The generous diet helped bring back the strength of the hurt and the weary, Tarothin among them. When he walked the deck now to take the air, men who had crossed to the other side now crowded around him, asking his advice or simply kneeling in thanks before him.

He was polite about the counsel but, to Pirvan's eye, seemed sorely tried by the worship. The thief wondered if it was genuine modesty (something not unheard of in wizards, but rare) or merely the good sense to realize that adulation could turn into blazing hostility the moment he disappointed one of his worshipers.

There was also little enough that Pirvan could do if Tarothin was wanting in judgment. Readily taking the advice of commonfolk *was* almost unheard of, even in the most moderate of magic-workers.

There was even less he could do about Haimya's moodiness, which disturbed him rather more than anything that could have come to Tarothin. The guard-maid kept her distance even more than she had before the storm, and not only from Pirvan. Any man who approached her, even to thank her for saving him, met a glare and sometimes words that nailed his feet to the deck and his tongue to the roof of his mouth.

Pirvan's only consolation was that no one thought he and Haimya were lovers, and he was not, therefore, in any measure responsible for her mood. As to learning what kept her so uneasy, he could as well have learned the landscape of the Abyss. It would not have been harder, and it might have been less perilous.

Before he forced himself to feign indifference to Haimya's mood (from which she suffered as much as anyone, he could not help noticing), Pirvan had seriously contemplated asking Lady Eskaia. But the contemplation was brief and ended in silence. The mistress was as protective of her maid's secrets as the maid was of hers; Pirvan would be on the shore in Karthay when the ship sailed if he even hinted at such a breach of confidence.

Thus matters stood, when on the eighth day, toward sunset, *Golden Cup* crept into the west harbor of Karthay.

* * * * *

Like the greater part of Ansalon, Karthay, city and surrounding lands alike, owed nominal allegiance to Istar the Mighty. Like more than a few of the more notable lands, states, and powers, the word "nominal" spoke louder and more truly than the word "allegiance."

It was a rebellion or at least a manifesto of pinpricks, rather than any overt acts of defiance. But there was a long history of fraudulent money changings, shoddy merchandise (though not where it would endanger life, merely digestion, marriage, chastity, or profit), and suspiciously well-timed tavern brawls.

"One of these days," Kurulus confided to Pirvan, "Istar's going to pull together a decent fleet of her own. Then we'll sit across the mouth of the gulf, get our own ships in and out, and lock up Karthay's like a lot of temple virgins."

"Um," Pirvan said, or something like it. This was the third day in Karthay, and apart from two visits from port officials, they'd had no contact with the shore. The harbor seemed as busy as he'd been promised it would be, even more colorful than Istar's with a good strength of sea barbarian ships, but not at all welcoming.

They hadn't even been allowed to refill their water casks, and that threatened to become serious. A number of casks in the bottom tiers had sprung leaks or been ruined by seawater. *Golden Cup* had to not only replenish the sound casks but repair the damaged ones before it was fit for the open ocean. The prospect of dying of thirst two miles from Karthay's bustling waterfront would have been ludicrous had it been less real.

Indeed, the prospect of anything unpleasant seemed absurd on a day like this, when they were snug in harbor after their ordeal in the storm. The sky was a patchwork of shimmering blue and fleecy white, a light breeze cooled the skin and filled the sails of small craft, and the white walls of the port fortresses and warehouses blazed brighter than the foam on the waves. (Farther north than Istar, Karthay was hotter and mostly whitewashed its buildings to repel the heat.)

But dark undercurrents flowed beneath the still more splendid facade of Istar the Mighty. Pirvan knew that well—and like any wise thief, knew that no one man's knowledge reached far. Doubtless the same flowed in Karthay—but here he was as ignorant as a newborn babe.

He could only wait, swallowing his frustration, until either *Golden Cup*'s folk were allowed ashore or the Karthayan axe fell.

The Karthayan axe fell two days later, after a water barge met the ship's most urgent need. The hammering of carpenters at work repairing or replacing the water casks crept even into the captain's cabin, as the Mate of the Hold (who acted as the captain's deputy in matters of business) explained the situation.

"Thirteen thousand castles!" Lady Eskaia exclaimed.

"To be precise, twelve thousand, eight hundred eighty four, seven towers, nine staves," the mate said. "This is exclusive of the cost of ship repairs."

"Be quiet," the captain said.

"No," Eskaia said. "I want to hear the worst."

"You already have," the mate said. "There's the consolation that we won't have to pay for the repairs until after we've paid for the rest. They won't allow us anywhere near the dockyards until—"

The captain muttered something rude, loudly enough for everyone to hear, not so loudly that anyone had to take notice. Eskaia's face hardened. Pirvan risked a quick look at Haimya.

The guard-maid seemed to be trying to do the same as Pirvan—imitate a statue, with neither power of movement nor any senses. The captain had not been happy about Eskaia bringing her guards to this private conference. If they called themselves to the captain's notice, they would find themselves out the door even at the price of a quarrel between Eskaia and the captain.

They had always agreed on the importance of avoiding that. Even though Haimya was still marching in silence across her private battlefield, she seemed to believe that still.

"Captain, the gold is there," Eskaia said. "Even to pay Karthayan prices for repairing Istarian ships. But it is the principle of the matter, not the price. They seek to shame Istar through shaming one of the great merchant houses.

"Allow them to do this, and who knows what they will

try next? It would be a sorry day for both cities, if Istar must subdue Karthay and garrison its lands, citadels, and ports."

"Also a costly one," the mate of the hold muttered. "The taxes we'd have to pay—"

This time the captain imposed silence with no more than a rude gesture of his left hand.

"Very well, my lady," he said. "This voyage is your conception. I but serve to execute it. If you will suffer no harm through a few days' waiting, neither will I or my men. Perhaps the Karthayans will relent."

"Perhaps sea trolls will become priests of Paladine, too," Eskaia said. "I was thinking more of finding ways to repair *Golden Cup* for the remainder of the voyage without Karthayan help."

"You ask much of me and my crew—"

Eskaia held up a small hand, which now showed a few calluses of its own. "Only patience. Not facing needless danger. Patience—oh, and any knowledge of Karthayans who may not honor their rulers' writs in such matters."

"Such wouldn't come for'ard without a pledge of secrecy," the mate said. "No sailor likes to be shipbound in a port like Karthay, for fear of a flogging or a work camp."

"No one will be leaving the ship before this matter is settled anyway," Eskaia said. She looked at the captain, and he nodded reluctantly. "So no one's secrets will reach Karthayan ears except by treachery, and I judge the sailors can deal with that themselves."

The two mates exchanged looks which Pirvan had no trouble translating: If the traitor's friends don't do the job, we will.

Chapter 9

Night over the West Port—a cloudy night, moon and stars alike invisible, and the air so still and heavy that Pirvan feared another storm. And *Golden Cup* without so much as a spare anchor—although the mates had improvised one, from old barrels filled with stone ballast and strapped with scraps of iron, rope, and leather.

Forward, the blacksmith's forge glowed and his hammer rang as he worked on more fittings bent or twisted by the force of the storm. Pirvan turned to look at the more distant, silent lights of the shore, as a familiar, massive shape loomed out of the darkness beside him.

"Come with me, Brother," Grimsoar said.

"I'm allowed here."

"I'm not, save on duty."

"Isn't this duty?"

"Some folk wouldn't call it such. Not if they heard what I want to say."

"If they're not going to hear it, is it important?"

"What's your itch, Brother? Haimya?"

Pirvan sighed. "She's eating herself alive from within over that broken rope. Does she *want* to die in the next fight?"

Grimsoar shrugged. "I've seen both men and women with that itch. But I don't think it's Haimya's problem."

"Then perhaps you should tell me what you think it is, instead of offering riddles."

"Remember, you asked."

"Remember, Brother, I also have a short temper."

"So be it. She's betrothed to one man, a gentleman who may have turned pirate. She's falling in love with another, a thief who's turned honorable comrade."

Pirvan could never afterward recall how long he was silent. Finally Grimsoar laughed softly.

"If you let your jaw drop like that again, you'll punch a hole in the deck right over Haimya's cabin. That might douse her affection for you, the next time we take green water—"

Pirvan mimed thrusting a dagger into Grimsoar's ribs. "If I go with you and listen, will you be silent on the matter of Haimya?"

"Unless I see you making a fool of yourself, yes."

This promise did not much console Pirvan. He remembered that Grimsoar One-Eye often had a rather broad definition of "fool."

* * * * *

Outside Synsaga's hut, a moderate Crater Gulf rain was falling. That was to say, it looked like a heavy rain in more civilized parts of Ansalon, instead of a waterfall.

Gerik Ginfrayson resolved that if he ever attained servants here, he would have one to do nothing but dry, scrape, and oil his possessions. Otherwise the moist heat would eat them like ogres in a pigsty, and a man could be unarmed and in rags between one voyage and the next.

"You've been asked for by name, for hard but important

work," Synsaga said.

Ginfrayson returned his attention to his chief. The pirate was as dark as most sea barbarians, but shorter, and with a black beard so splendid that it seemed to have leeched all vitality from his scalp, which was entirely bald. The beeswax candle in a polished coral holder (the one loot, the other made in the camp) set amber light dancing across Synsaga's bare skull.

"May I inquire who asked me?"

That awkward phrasing killed deader than Vinas Solamnus any hope of concealing his unease. But a summons to Synsaga at this hour of the night usually meant something worth being uneasy about. Men had been known to disappear after such meetings, if they were lucky; if they were not, they left the camp chained in a slave gang.

"You may. I do not promise to answer."

"Is it honorable work?"

"By the customs of our band, yes. Do you presume to put forward any other customs as binding you? That violates your oath, and you know the punishment for oath breaking."

It was neither a quick death nor slavery, but beyond that there were many variations, depending on the offense, the offender, and Synsaga's mood at the time he handed down the punishment. From the chief's language, Ginfrayson decided to err on the side of caution.

"I make no such presumption. If it is honorable work by our customs, then it shall be done. But if it is honorable, *my* honor demands that it be done well. The more I know, the better my work."

"You will learn soon enough." The pirate chief leaned back in his chair. It creaked under his weight, which it had not done a year ago. Good living was taking its toll of Synsaga.

"Swear to silence, even in your prayers, and I will tell you," the chief added.

Gerik swore a rolling oath on Synsaga's belaying pin, the man's favorite weapon. Then he waited.

"You will be working under Fustiar," the chief said, after an uneasily long silence. "Do not ask how," he added, "for I do not know myself."

The unwisdom of asking about Fustiar's right to keep secrets from his chief was evident. Gerik merely put his fist to his heart. "I will serve him as I have served you."

"I am glad." Synsaga seemed genuinely relieved. "I can tell you that your being Istarian, with knowledge of its great houses—that spoke in your favor."

Gerik frowned. This threatened to become embarrassing, to say the least. "My mother served as nurse and attendant to Lady Eskaia of House Encuintras until her death. I never served the house myself. Their bounty to me was sending me into the fleet."

Synsaga looked bemused. "Surely your mother must have spoken of her service in your presence?"

"Never."

"You speak the truth?"

"I do. I will swear to it, and also that *she* took a potent oath of secrecy, perhaps strengthened by magic."

Synsaga made a fly-shooing gesture, as if such details annoyed him. "Why did you not mention this before?"

"No one asked me. My oath was to answer all questions truthfully, not to tell everything I knew or thought with no regard for the honor of others or the needs of our band."

"You have the soul of a counselor at law."

"Are you sure that is so different from a pirate's?" Gerik dared to ask.

Synsaga barked laughter. "Well spoken. But further questions may come your way, and they had best be answered fully and truthfully. Fustiar has been known to punish those who disappointed him without speaking to me first, or indeed at all."

Gerik prayed for a quick end to this meeting. Synsaga was revealing much that had been suspected but little that the Istarian cared to know. Also, it would go badly if questions turned to his other kin.

Any secrets of House Encuintras his mother had

learned, she had not only carried to her grave but they would be old and dusty tales by now. Haimya was another matter. In her position as guard-maid to Lady Eskaia, she might have become a treasure of knowledge to any enemy of the house. Pirates were wont to swoop down on such treasures, and Synsaga had ships in the gulf, a mage on the mountain, and doubtless sellswords in Istar itself for such work.

In time the meeting ended; Gerik strode out into rain that was now easing into mist. He was three steps from the door when a harsh scream sounded from high overhead. He looked upward, but clouds and night hid even the treetops, let alone what had made the sound.

Not that he really had much doubt. Fustiar's pet dragon was abroad again—and within days he would be going up to serve, perhaps within a ship's length of its lair.

It was not a thought that made for easy sleep that night.

*   *   *   *   *

The bulwarks amidships had been built up again to about waist height. Leaning against them, heads over the side, Pirvan and Grimsoar could whisper with little fear of being overheard. The maintop would have been even safer, but no easy explanation for climbing to it at this hour had occurred to either man.

"Do you remember a low-built, racy-looking ship with square-rigged foremast and a lateen-rigged main?" Grimsoar asked.

Pirvan mentally translated that from Sailor into Common. "Lateen—like our third—mizzen—mast?"

Grimsoar guffawed. "We'll have you talking like a sailor yet."

"The idea of this voyage lasting that long gives me no pleasure."

Grimsoar seemed about to make another jest, then shrugged. "I'm thinking of going back to sea. Which is why I noticed that ship. She also had her sails striped in green, and a deckhouse amidships. I always thought it looked like a giant wooden chamberpot."

Pirvan swore to push his fellow thief into something worse than a chamberpot if he went on talking in riddles. "So?"

"That's the bannership of Jemar the Fair."

At least that name was no riddle. "Sea barbarian, who's done some work for the brothers?"

"The same one. He also owes me a few favors, over the matter of his factor in Istar."

Pirvan assembled clues and rummaged in his memory. "The one who was found floating in the ornamental pool outside the Temple of Shinare?"

"Nice to see that Haimya hasn't entirely addled your wits, even if you've addled hers."

"Brother, if you mention that lady again before you have finished with this matter, I shall swim to Jemar's ship and bore a hole in her bottom with an augur. Then, when I am captured, I shall say that you did it."

Grimsoar recoiled in mock horror, and nearly stumbled over a coil of rope. Pirvan laughed shortly. "Now, as you were saying . . . ?"

"I was using the factor to receive some of the fruits of my night work," Grimsoar said. "I discovered that he was cheating me. Trying to recover my work, I learned that he was cheating others. Jemar was among them. I passed the word, and Jemar carried the matter on from there."

"To the point where the man was bobbing in the pool, his throat cut from ear to ear?"

"Not that badly. Jemar hires better knifemen than that. But otherwise, yes."

"I see. So he owes you a debt, and might pay it by helping us?"

"Again, yes. If we provide the money, he will be able to go shoreside and buy everything we need to repair the ship without going in ourselves. No one will know who he's buying for, so they won't even charge him more than the lawful rate. Not that the lawful rate is cheap, mind you, but—"

"I see. What about our crew?"

"The captain may growl about dealing with sea barbarians. If he growls too loud, Lady Eskaia will growl back. If he doesn't stop then, the mate of the top will be captain. I don't think the old man wants that. This stands to be his last voyage, and he wants a few extra coins to take ashore when it's done."

Pirvan did not doubt his friend's words. Grimsoar had an uncanny knack for picking up all the rumors wandering around a tavern, a marketplace, or a ship's forecastle. Then he could sort them out into truth, or at least a useful approximation of it.

He wondered if that made Grimsoar's remarks about Haimya more plausible. Then he decided not to encourage the big man to talk about that, no matter what!

* * * * *

Gerik Ginfrayson climbed the mountain to Fustiar's tower the next night. He had not planned to go up by night, though he did not mind the darkness concealing him. More than a few of the pirates had doubts about the wisdom of dealing with a renegade mage.

Gerik shared every one of those doubts, and was not looking forward to spending an unknown time where he would have to keep those doubts even out of his thoughts, let alone off his lips.

He tried to console himself that if Fustiar valued him primarily for his knowledge of the secrets of Istar's rulers, he would be hurrying down the mountain soon after he arrived. He could not help thinking, however, that Fustiar might be disposed to send him much farther than the camp on the shore.

It was a dry night for the Crater Gulf, so the path upward was only slippery, not half awash, let alone a stream in full spate. The four chained captives had fallen only twice, and the two sailors guarding them had lashed them only once.

Gerik had no duties toward the prisoners or their guards. He was going up with the party merely because no one walked the path up to Fustiar's tower at night alone, and a wise man had company even by day.

The air grew cooler as they climbed out of the thickest jungle. Now the trees did not quite meet overhead, and Gerik saw a few stars. One of them blazed down across the sky, an omen, but of what, he could not be sure.

A little higher, and the open sky showed the constellations of Mishakal and Zeboim. The Istarian told himself that it was only his imagination, but the eyes of Zeboim seemed to be open and gazing intently downward. Was Takhisis's sea-gripping daughter taking an interest in Fustiar's work on behalf of the Dark Queen?

Now the path leveled out, and walls loomed ahead. Everyone called Fustiar's abode his "tower," but in fact it was a half ruined castle, which in its youth must have been as large as the citadel of a good-sized city. That youth was also so far in the past that no one knew who had built it, when, or why.

The tales hadn't exaggerated its size, however. The one tower still standing rose eighty feet, and the half-ruined great hall was at least half that. The hall had been roughly patched with green timber and leaf thatch, and a stairway, also new and roughly built, rose up the outside of the tower.

These signs of human handiwork reassured Ginfrayson a trifle. At least Fustiar hadn't conjured up a horde of ogres to build himself a palace, or chosen to levitate himself up and down from his tower whenever the whim took him. Perhaps all he was good for was simple tricks, fit to impress the ignorant, but quite incapable of doing real harm to a man hard to deceive or frighten. . . .

A scream struck Gerik's ears like an iron bar. No human throat, and no animal commonly known in nature, ever uttered that scream. (Although the animals *and* plants of the Crater Gulf still held surprises for pirates who had lived there ten years, let alone for newcomers like Ginfrayson). The ancient stones held the echoes and tossed them back and forth like a couple of hearty children with a ball.

There was nothing childish in that cry either. It spoke of ages beyond human knowledge or even human imagining, stretching back to the earliest time of the gods themselves, when Paladine and Takhisis were allies instead of sworn foes.

It spoke, indeed, of much that would have been chilling to think about on a sunny day in a crowded city square. High on a wilderness mountain, far from anyone to talk to, with night hiding both friends and foes, Ginfrayson found it the most terrifying sound he had ever heard in his life.

He also found that it reminded him of the cry he'd heard the night before, piercing the rainstorm just after he had left Synsaga's hut. And that wasn't even the first time he had heard a cry like that, now that he thought of it, and it was always high or far off—as though what made it wished to hide from human eyes.

At this point he realized that the four prisoners were cowering on the ground or looking about them wildly. The guards looked as if they wished to do the same, had they not feared a panic-stricken flight by their charges. Ginfrayson forced his mind to receive messages from his eyes, and in due course they found a small gate with a bell-pull beside it.

At least Gerik hoped it was a bell-pull. He realized as he approached the wall that his hand was shaking. If that scream came again in answer to his pull . . .

For all that he had to pull five times before the bell rang, when it did, it was an almost cheery and quite ordinary, brazen tinkling. The little gate opened on well-oiled hinges, and a stocky man wearing only a loincloth and a collar of brass links set with cheap glass beads stood in the way. He looked not only human, but like a slave whose master wants to impress visitors without having the money or knowledge of how to do so.

Used to the real and wisely chosen splendors of House Encuintras, Gerik wanted to laugh, but held himself back from *that* particular folly.

"You come in. These stay out," the man said, pointing

at Gerik and the guards, respectively. The prisoners apparently didn't exist. He sounded as if he had learned Common late and even then only a few words, though Gerik could not place his accent.

He could recognize an order when he heard one. The guards stepped back as Gerik drew his sword. Then he fumbled with his free hand in his purse. He didn't know if the sailors were paid extra for guard duty, but, by Majere, they deserved a little something for not noticing that he was frightened!

The sailors took the money and scurried down the path with a speed that Gerik envied. He wondered how long it would be before he descended the path, at any pace. Then he raised his sword and motioned toward the door. The prisoners stumbled forward. Under the almost reptilian eye of the mage's man, Gerik followed, and the man pulled the gate shut behind them.

The clank of the lock was a sound only a trifle less agreeable than the nightmare scream.

Inside, darkness and stenches were Gerik's first impressions of the mage's lair. The darkness gradually receded as his eyes adjusted, and he saw mounds of earth, patches of weeds and grass and other patches regular enough to be gardens, flagstones, and bits and pieces of inner walls. Some of those walls had been built of stones higher than a man and longer than two or three.

Whoever built this castle, Gerik concluded, had a quarry near at hand, unlimited slaves, or some arts more potent and less pleasant to think about than either. His pleasure at the thought of living here, perhaps among magic-twisted ghosts, shrank even further.

"Ah, welcome," a slurred voice said, apparently from all directions at once. Gerik did not jump or brandish his sword. He merely tried to glare back, also in all directions at once.

The voice's owner gave in to raucous, jeering laughter. Then he appeared out of the shadows by one wall.

"Unchain them," he said, motioning with his hand. That brought two more men out of the darkness, enough like the first one that they might have been cousins. However, they had no ears, and when they opened their mouths, one could see that they had no tongues.

What else they might be missing, Gerik did not care to think. But they had swords and daggers at their belts, spears slung across their backs, and heavy keys in their hands that made quick work of the prisoners' shackles.

While the newcomers were at work, Gerik examined the man he presumed was Fustiar. There was no reason mages had to look like anything in particular, and it was dark besides. Yet he had the distinct impression of a village drunkard, the sort who will work just enough to keep himself in wine, but not enough to buy baths or decent clothes. The mage's robe showed holes and patches. If it had once been light-colored, dirt and wine stains had long since darkened it.

Fustiar took a stumbling step forward—and one of the prisoners took a long leap backward. He nearly fell, but kept his feet under him. In a moment, he was running for the far end of the castle, where the wall over a long stretch was tumbled into climbable ruins.

Gerik wished for a bow, knew he couldn't hit the tower with it in this darkness, and began to run. He'd covered about five steps when Fustiar raised both hands, shouted one word that Gerik had never heard (it sounded vaguely obscene), then added other words Gerik heard all too clearly.

"Stop, you fool!"

Gerik stopped so quickly that he nearly lost balance, sword, and dignity. He'd just regained all three when the fleeing prisoner reached the slope of tumbled blocks. He peered through the darkness as the man scrambled up with the strength and speed of desperation.

Then, from the darkness beyond the man, monstrousness came. At least that was Gerik's first thought. It was huge and evil, but had no shape.

Closer to his doom, the man apparently saw more clearly. He screamed once, but a second scream was lost in a sound like an iron gate closing. Then a third scream floated down from the sky, and after that was silence, except for the rush of air churned by what could only be mighty wings.

Gerik realized that, after all, he did not need to see what had come forth and taken the man aloft. He had seen it that day on the path.

"So, you command a black dragon?" he said to the patch of darkness where Fustiar most likely lurked.

The slurred voice replied from it. "He keeps order among my other servants, does he not?"

"I do not doubt it."

"Do not think you—will be—spared, either, if you—rebel."

"All that is mine to give, I give freely to your service," Gerik said. He thought his voice was steady. About the words he was less sure, but they came from the oath of service to House Encuintras, and if that had been good enough for his mother, it could cursed well be good enough for a drunken renegade mage!

"All that is given, I accept." Those words seemed less slurred. They were followed by a squelching thud. Gerik stepped forward, until he nearly stubbed his toe on the mage's outflung foot.

A snore floating up from the mud. It began to seem that Gerik Ginfrayson's first service to Fustiar the Renegade would be putting the man to bed.

His first act after that would be finding a means of escape that would not end either in the dragon's belly or in the jungle or sea. That might be a long search, but it was one he was now determined to make.

He had been prepared to end his betrothal to Haimya when he sailed on the voyage that ended at Crater Gulf—no longer fearing what she might say that made it easier to swear allegiance to Synsaga. Indeed, he suspected that she also would be relieved to find herself free from a betrothal that existed mostly because neither of them had been able to find a convincing argument against it.

Haimya was an excellent woman; she would not be long in burying his memory or consoling herself with another man. He owed her nothing—except what he owed everyone, which was not to consort any longer than he had to with a renegade mage who had brought a black dragon out of dragonsleep and loosed it on the world.

* * * * *

Whatever Jemar the Fair considered that he owed Grimsoar One-Eye and the thieves of Istar, it was worth two boatloads of supplies in the first four days. One was barrel staves and hoops, as well as caulking material and several of Jemar's own coopers to help *Golden Cup*'s crew put everything together.

The other was spars and rope (the ship had plenty of spare sails). Like a tribe of apes fleeing a leopard, *Golden Cup*'s people swarmed into its battered rigging, and in a single day it began to look less battered.

Pirvan was among the climbers. His minor hurts were long healed and he could climb as well as any—better than most. That he was a sober man gave him only more opportunities. The crew was kept aboard, but no sailor with money in his pocket and small craft passing close to his anchored vessel would be without wine for long.

On the fifth day, Pirvan was in the maintop, repairing the standing rigging, when a boat slid out of the mist and alongside. He took a brief look, noted that it was a barge in harbor guard colors, and returned to filing down a block that had come out of the chandler's shop a bit oversized even for *Golden Cup*'s massive rigging.

On the other side of the maintop, Haimya was feeding freshly tarred rope from a coil to two men standing on the mainyard. As before, when she was in her cabin, Eskaia had given her guards permission—indeed, orders—to join the work of the crew. Also as before, at least since the storm, Haimya worked with speed, skill, and as many words as a statue of Mishakal.

At least she smiled from time to time, since the agreement with Jemar had been reached, and once Pirvan heard her laugh (or heard that she'd laughed, which was not quite the same thing). If he was part of her problem, of course, the less he said, the better, but if Grimsoar was wrong and she confused his silence with abandoning her now, after saving her in the storm . . .

"Ahoy, the top!" Pirvan recognized the mate of the hold.

"Maintop!"

"Our lady's people—haul your arses down here now! Jump if you can."

Pirvan looked down. The harbor guard barge was now alongside the gangway. It seemed to be fuller than the normal eight rowers could account for, and there were four or five men in the guard's wine-colored coats and blue breeches on ship's deck as well.

Pirvan flung himself into the rigging and slid down, no great matter with his gloves on and the next best thing to jumping. (He would have jumped only if he'd been sure that the harbor guard men were aboard on no good business *and* that he could land on them.)

Haimya came down the ratlines, more briskly than she had when first aboard but not even trying to match the thief's pace. He was on the deck before he realized that perhaps he should have spared her dignity a trifle, not beating her so badly.

Perhaps also the mate's order was to be obeyed whoever might be embarrassed—and why was he so concerned about embarrassing Haimya? He had little control over whether she was in love with him or not, but he'd be cursed if he would, out of sheer carelessness, slip into being in love with her!

Eskaia came onto it as Haimya reached deck, wearing a gray cloak over a cream-colored traveling gown. Red boots and the cuffs of blue trousers peeped out from under the gown—garb that would have scandalized everyone at a temple feast, but eminently practical for bobbing across Karthay's harbors in a barge that certainly had wet bilges and might take in more water on the way.

"I have been invited aboard the bannership of the harbor guard," Eskaia said. "I must have an escort. Garb and arm yourselves appropriately."

"My lady—" began Haimya, then Eskaia riveted her to the deck with a glare.

Pirvan took a deep breath. "My lady. I mean no insult to either you or the harbor guard, but your safety aboard the ship is something to think upon."

"Pirvan, are you and Haimya not fit to meet even small dangers?" Eskaia said. If she was jesting, there was nothing in her blue eyes or soft voice to tell Pirvan.

"Small dangers, yes." Emboldened by Pirvan, Haimya had found her voice. "But a shipful of Karthayans might under some circumstances not be a small danger."

"You dare—" the guard's officer began.

"Yes," Haimya said calmly, though her hand was close to the hilt of her dagger. "My mother was Karthayan. I know that any man has his price. Although, to do you justice, your price would be high, and for any great crime, you could not be bought."

The officer closed his mouth, apparently unsure whether he was being praised or not. Then he sighed. "Would it be well enough if I and a few others remained aboard here, while you saw—while you went aboard the bannership?"

"Yes," Eskaia said, before Haimya could reply again. Her tone and face dared any of Golden Cup's people to so much as think Tarothin's name. "I will arrange for proper hospitality, though our work must continue."

"We would not stop it if we could," the officer said.

That last remark had Haimya and Pirvan exchanging looks as they went below to dress and arm. They didn't dare speak, but Haimya's face showed the same question that was running through Pirvan's: The guard is blowing both fair and stormy at once, like a day in Crinispus.

Why?

Chapter 10

"A dragon," Jemar the Fair said.

Pirvan could not think of a proper description for the sea barbarian chief's tone of voice or the expression on his weathered face. Putting aside that futile enterprise, he studied the man himself.

Jemar was half a head taller than Pirvan, and broad in proportion, without any of that breadth being fat. He had gained his name reasonably enough: by sea barbarian standards his skin, the color of tarberry tea mixed with fresh cream, was much lighter than average. His beard and hair (worn in a long plait gathered with three silver rings) were dark brown, with tints that in one light seemed coppery, in another amber.

He wore a snug vest that was more openings than leather, and equally tight blue trousers, flared over the tops of soft leather boots. A belt of some leather Pirvan had never seen but would have been ready to steal without asking questions supported a curved sword and a short thrusting dagger. He wore no jewelry except the braid rings and a single earring, a golden circle holding a ruby the size of a baby's thumb.

Jemar would have made a notable standing on the block in a slave market. Garbed as he was and sitting in a chair elaborately carved with coral flowers and fish, he was dazzling. He even outshone the rack of jeweled weapons (gifts or prizes of war?) and ornaments of carved and polished coral in a dozen shades from a garish red to a lavender so subtle that it was almost white.

At least he seemed to be dazzling Haimya. She could hardly keep her eyes off him, and it seemed to Pirvan that her breathing had quickened.

Pirvan also knew that he had no right to be jealous. Gerik Ginfrayson did, perhaps, but Haimya would talk to him, so that they could settle it between them in their own good time. For himself, Pirvan could only hope that Haimya would not notice the tightness of his mouth or how his fists had clenched.

"A copper dragon," Lady Eskaia corrected. She was sitting on a folding stool, but one large enough for three people, set with ivory, and half surrounded by a folding silk screen. On the screen was one magnificent seascape and two portrayals of sea barbarian warriors in battle with creatures that Pirvan sincerely hoped were long gone from the oceans of Krynn.

"So it is a good dragon," Jemar said. "That is some consolation, if not much."

He stood up and began to pace back and forth. In three places the cabin beams were too low to let him pass without stopping, but he never hit his head. He seemed to have a spine as flexible as a cat's, or the ability to shrink his height at will, like a shapechanger.

Both women were staring at him like children at a cartload of candied fruits. Pirvan would have liked to stare at the ceiling until the women came to their senses. He preferred not to offend Jemar.

Finally Jemar stopped pacing. "Lady Eskaia, your house has always had a name for honor. This day you have added much to it. The six men of mine that the guards were holding hostage have all been returned as promised. How binding is your oath to transport this dragon out of Karthay?"

Lady Eskaia told him. She fumbled over some of the terms, and Pirvan saw Haimya fighting not to help her. He also wished Tarothin were here, even if the wizard had not been allowed aboard the guard bannership.

Jemar sat down again. "Tell me— No, wait. Let me have some wine and cakes brought in, and *then* you can tell me what happened aboard the bannership. Leave nothing out, please, because I must put this matter before my council of captains if we are to help you."

Then he laughed, because all three of his guests were staring at one another in confusion. It was a laugh without malice or cruelty, most agreeable to hear for one who had heard far too much of the other kind of laughter.

Indeed, Pirvan could not help joining in. Then Eskaia threw back her head and trilled like a bird (Pirvan felt a great desire to hear her sing).

At last, Haimya could not hold in her laughter. But she was the first to stop, and when she did, she stared at Jemar as if he'd suddenly turned into a sea dragon.

"Did you say you'd help us?" she asked.

Jemar almost choked, then nodded. "If my captains agree, and for that you must tell me of your meeting aboard the bannership."

"After the wine, Jemar," Eskaia said, wiping her eyes. "After the wine, good and fair captain, we can talk of anything you wish to hear."

Unseen by either Eskaia or Jemar, Haimya's eyes met Pirvan's.

If she thinks to charm him thus, she plays for high stakes, her gaze seemed to say.

* * * * *

"Our journey by barge from *Golden Cup* to the bannership took a while," Eskaia began. "The mist seemed to delight in thickening in front of us. Fortunately we all have our sea legs, and apart from the mist, the weather was moderate."

Pirvan wondered how long Jemar's patience would last, if Eskaia told everything so elaborately. So far he seemed intent on every word, or was it on the lady's large brown eyes? She was not exactly flirting with him, but she was certainly gazing at him as if his every feature was of profound interest to her.

Looked at in that manner, Pirvan decided that he, too, would be prepared to tolerate a long-winded story.

"Once aboard the bannership, we were taken to the captain's cabin. I do not know whether the guards with us were intended to honor, protect, or command us."

Pirvan expected that Eskaia would then go on to describe each guardsman and the details of their clothing and weapons. She controlled herself, describing in great detail only the officers. The thief saw Jemar nodding slowly; apparently he recognized some of the officers from Eskaia's description. What he would do with that knowledge, Pirvan had no idea.

"In the captain's cabin was a high officer of the guards, as well as a man in the garb of a priest of Paladine," Eskaia continued. "I will consider that he was truly as he seemed. Even the lords of Karthay are not so lost to fear of the gods that they will use false priests."

Jemar smiled thinly. "You would be surprised at what the lords of Karthay can do if they see in it profit or a chance to annoy their enemies. But I agree—neither comes from offending Paladine. Pray continue."

"Very well. The captain explained that six men from the ships of Jemar the Fair had been arrested and confined. The charge was aiding evasion of port duties, fees, fines, charges, and so on. I am sure you have learned more about the situation of the six from the men themselves, so I will not weary you with what I could only guess at the time."

"Thank you." Pirvan listened carefully, but could not detect the slightest note of sarcasm in the sea barbarian's solid bass voice.

"Then the priest spoke. He said that all might be well and everyone might be pleased if *Golden Cup* could perform a certain service, to Karthay and to all humanity. I asked him what that service was. It seemed to me that it might be carrying enemies of the rulers into exile, which would be suitable if we received provisions and were allowed time to prepare the ship for additional passengers."

"The Karthayans seldom bother with exile," Jemar said. "If one offends the lords enough to be unwelcome in the city, one is usually sent much farther than the next country."

"That I did not know, and having no idea what they wished, I decided not to guess," Eskaia said. Pirvan definitely heard a faint chiding note in her voice. Jemar barely missed being old enough to be her father—he had to be well into his thirties. But she seemed ready to address him as though he were a child who had spilled jam on his best clothes.

Pirvan hoped that Jemar would continue to be as easy of temper as he had been so far.

"He said that in the lands of Karthay there had been found a copper dragon, some time in Zeboim. They could not tell its age or sex, but it seemed injured, and it either would not or could not speak. All their knowledge of dragons told them little more than they could see with their own eyes.

"Meanwhile, rumors of the dragon were beginning to spread in the city and its lands. Some persons ill-disposed toward the lords of the city said that the dragon was a sign. A sign of the coming fall of the lords and a new rule of justice in Karthay."

"There are always fools with more wind than wits," Jemar said. "Perhaps a few more in Karthay than elsewhere, but no city is free of them."

"I know little of Karthay save what has concerned House Encuintras," Eskaia said. "I daresay you are right."

"I asked why they were telling us this. They said that they proposed a bargain. If we would take the dragon aboard *Golden Cup*, transport him to a distant land, and release him there, they would permit us to complete our repairs and replenish our supplies. They would also release Jemar's six men.

"I said that I wished proof of the dragon's existence. The priest said that it was not in the city. I said that if it was not in the city, we would need to complete repairs and so on before we sailed to take it aboard.

"The priest and the captain spoke together privately for a few moments. Then the priest said that he would show us the dragon. If that was not enough, he would take trusted persons from our ranks to see it.

"I told him to show us the dragon. He conjured up its image. I believe that it was the image of something real, for one could walk around it and view it from all sides. Also, I recognized Mount Frygol in the background.

"I said that if our captain said the ship could safely carry the dragon, we would take it aboard, after we finished our repairs. The captain said that if we waited until then, he would have to send ships of the harbor guard with us until we had the dragon aboard.

"I said that I understood his reasons. But if he wished us to sail under such a badge of his distrust, he must release the six men of Jemar the Fair at once. Nothing else would be accomplished until he had done this. It seemed to me that taking hostages from the innocent is not something that should be allowed. Istarian hands are not clean of this, but I wished that mine be—"

Jemar held up a hand, then rose, walked to Eskaia, and kissed her gently on the forehead. She trembled. For a moment Pirvan thought that she was going to raise her head, open her mouth, and return the kiss much less formally.

But Jemar was backing away and sitting down again. He now sat with one leg thrown over the other, and a distant look in his eyes. Then the distant look vanished, and both feet came down with a thump on the red and yellow Istarian carpet.

"You have done better than you know," he said. "My

lady, I am more grateful than speech allows me to express. I do not speak only of my six men, either, though I imagine every one of them will be even more ready to kiss you than I—though one of them, as I recall, is a woman."

"She may kiss me, too," Eskaia said sturdily. "But, good captain, you repay me poorly for dispelling mysteries by adding more. Do you know more of this matter of a dragon than you have hinted?"

Jemar's jaw quivered but didn't quite drop. Then he nodded.

"I ask you to believe that I have not spread the nature of your voyage abroad. But—you are sailing for the Crater Gulf, are you not?"

Eskaia was beyond speech but not beyond a jerk of the head.

"I thought as much. Then it seems to me that you have been done a great favor, or indeed done yourself one, by agreeing to take the copper dragon aboard *Golden Cup*."

"The captain still has his doubts," Eskaia pointed out.

"I will try to ease them. I will even put some of my men aboard your ship—not enough to seize it, but enough to aid you with the dragon. Also, if you are going to sail for the dragon with harbor guard galleys about you, I cannot send ships with you. The Karthayans would find ways of provoking a fight, and no good would come of that.

"But I will need trustworthy witnesses from my own men, of what happens when you take the dragon aboard. If I can send them, there is no limit on the help you may ask of me."

Eskaia's voice was brisk. "That is very generous of you, fair Jemar, but I think you still leave something unsaid. Pray say it, or you are asking me to buy a pony disguised as a horse. My house did not reach its present position by making such bargains."

Jemar held out his hands in what looked to Pirvan remarkably like supplication. "I meant neither fraud nor disrespect. It is merely that I can offer you little firm knowledge in return for your admirable account, only tales and rumors and rumors of tales."

"These often give enough warning of dangers that those who listen are better armed to face them," Eskaia said. She grinned, showing all her dimples and this time definitely making play with her eyes. "If that is not a quotation from some ancient scholar, I will claim it myself."

"One need not be a scholar to be wise," Jemar replied, returning the grin. "Now, as pleasant as it is to exchange praises until the wine runs out, let me tell you of what is about among seafarers in the matter of dragons."

It took even longer for Jemar to tell his tale than for Eskaia to tell hers. Jemar did not have so many details to put in, though. He took his time explaining how reliable each tale or rumor might be, so that his listeners could judge for themselves.

It seemed that there had been, for two years, rumors that the chief of the Crater Gulf pirates, a man named Synsaga, had a renegade mage in his service. Renegades were almost always evil, and never better than neutral. So if that was true, all by itself it was enough to cause concern.

Meanwhile, other rumors had begun to accumulate. Sailors (even other pirates) commonly gave the Crater Gulf a wide berth. But ships passing as much as fifty miles out at sea had sighted something large and black in the air, usually high up but sometimes low enough that features could be made out, features that matched the ancient descriptions of black dragons. They were creatures of evil, creatures of Takhisis, creatures no man wanted to see out and about again—for that would mean the dragonsleep was crumbling and good and evil alike would soon be unleashing their winged giants upon the world.

"It seems to me that there is a less frightening explanation," Eskaia put in. "Suppose, by some quirk of his spells, this renegade had broken the sleep of a single black dragon? Then, according to what I have learned, the balance is destroyed. A good dragon is needed to restore that balance. Suppose our copper dragon is the one, and the priest of Paladine knows it, even if he did not awaken the dragon himself?"

"You reason like a cleric yourself," Jemar said. The admiration in his voice was unconcealed.

Eskaia smiled. "Thank you. I have certainly read some of the books—the ones open to all—that form the common knowledge of clerics. The concept of the balance is in books that must be intended for children."

"Some children are wiser than others," Jemar said. "And you are no child."

Pirvan was not sure he liked Jemar's tone when he spoke those words. Haimya definitely did not; he could now read her subtler moods in her face. At least it would be Haimya who had the unpleasant task of explaining to Eskaia the folly of leading a man such as Jemar on in that fashion.

"I hope not," Eskaia said. "Then I trust that we can rely on your aid?"

"As I said, what I can promise is small, until my captains have met in council and sworn to follow me in this. But there will certainly be men of mine, good fighters all, aboard *Golden Cup* when she sails for the dragon."

After that, the rest was ceremonial chat, more wine and cakes, and a return to *Golden Cup*. With all the supplies loaded and most put to use, there was little work for now, and there had been more wine than Pirvan was accustomed to drinking with so little food at this time of day.

He lay down until the buzzing in his head faded to a distant murmur, and by then he was falling asleep.

* * * * *

He awoke with Haimya sitting beside his bunk. She was good to look at, though fatigue and perhaps more had carved lines into her face that hadn't been there before.

"Pirvan, I owe you an apology."

"I'll accept it, but I'm not sure you did anything you need to apologize for."

"I've been—uneasy—Gerik . . . More uneasy than I should have been, perhaps. I keep telling myself that he's a valuable hostage, so Synsaga isn't likely to pull out his fingernails or put out his eyes. But likelihood isn't certainty. I can't be entirely easy until I see him again."

Pirvan wanted to reach out and grip her hands, but he was afraid she'd flinch at his touch. He was more afraid that she'd read through his flesh the thought in his mind: *It isn't just harm to Gerik's body that worries you. It's what might happen to his honor. A mage who can wake a black dragon can often lead astray a man far from home and alone among strangers.*

"In your situation, I might be harder to approach than a quillpig," Pirvan said. "You don't need to around apologizing to everybody and his half-elven cousin."

"I won't. I do insist on apologizing to you. We need to work together, to . . . to . . ."

"To keep Eskaia from becoming infatuated with Jemar the Fair?"

"Is that what you call it? I would have called it wanting to lie down, lift her skirts, and raise her legs."

Pirvan looked at the ceiling. "You have a family retainer's privileges. I do not."

"And I intend to use them, too," Haimya said. "But, in all seriousness, I may be even more fearful for Gerik now if he's within bowshot of a dragon's lair. But I will try not to load those fears on you, and if I do, it will be by chance."

And if you ever come out and tell the truth, it will be a miracle, Pirvan thought sourly.

Except that it might *not* be true that she was in love with him. He was not sure whether learning this would be a relief or a disappointment.

Chapter 11

"Twelve fathoms, brown mud," the leadsman at Golden Cup's bow called.

"Shoaling fast now," the man beside Pirvan said. "If your captain doesn't anchor soon, he'll—"

Pirvan didn't hear the rest of what would happen if the captain didn't anchor. Jemar might have picked the twelve men he'd sent aboard for their fighting prowess; he certainly hadn't picked them for their polished manners.

Or perhaps it was general to sea barbarians and not particular to these twelve men. It was said that the sea barbarians were elaborately polite to one another, to avoid fights aboardship. It was also said that against outsiders they competed with one another in the arts of provocation and insult.

Certainly Jemar's men hadn't been backward in those enterprises since they had come aboard a week ago. It was a minor miracle that there hadn't been any duels or, even less formal, knifings. Or perhaps not; the word was out that anyone who killed one of Jemar's men would himself die on the spot. Nobody except the leaders knew the full tale of why *Golden Cup* needed Jemar's goodwill, but most men accepted that this was so, even if they grumbled where the mates couldn't hear them.

Pirvan had done his share of making the alliance with Jemar acceptable, using Grimsoar One-Eye to spread rumors of shares of rich treasures. Everybody knew that sea barbarians had entire shiploads of gold hidden in remote anchorages. Everybody also knew that sea barbarians usually managed to cheat honest sailors in the end.

But everybody also dreamed that, just this once, the sea barbarians might be honorable or the honest sailors quicker to snatch. After all, wasn't the man who'd swum ashore and saved them all a professional thief, shrewder and even more alert than the sea barbarians themselves?

Pirvan was willing to let the sailors believe that. He himself would be entirely happy if circumstances did not require him to match wits now or at any time with Jemar the Fair. The man so far hadn't done anything to deserve it, and Pirvan also knew who was likely to come out ahead if the matter was put to the test.

He looked over the side. They were coming up to the head of a small bay, hardly more than an inlet. A bonfire on the shore illuminated calm, almost oily water dotted with dead trees and other debris. It also lit up a handful of ramshackle huts, and beyond them a more substantial log wall with guardhouses at the gates and corners.

"Ten fathoms, gravel," the leadsman called.

Before the sea barbarian could say anything, Pirvan heard in rapid succession:

"Douse the foresail!"

"Back the mainsail!"

"Down the anchors!"

Sails flapped and anchors went away with a squeal of rope on wood and the splash of massive weights hitting water. The ship stopped almost as abruptly as if it had run aground. Then a different voice called:

"Prepare to lower boats."

They'd bought (at an only moderately outrageous price) an old harbor guard barge for bringing the dragon out to the ship, if he couldn't fly. They'd also towed it all the way across the gulf, since it was too big to hoist aboard. Pirvan had heard the mates and helmsmen cursing it for days.

It was also much too clumsy for a shoreboat. Lanterns aft showed sailors hefting the longboat out of its chocks and bending the hoisting lines to the mainmast. Pirvan grinned at the sea barbarian.

"I think our captain knows his business," he said, then scrambled down the ladder. If they were hoisting out the boats already, anyone assigned to the landing party had best be down amidships before the mates started wondering where he was.

* * * * *

The water shoaled rapidly soon after the longboat left the ship. The boat actually ran aground far enough out that the landing party had to wade through soupy water to a beach hardly firmer than the water.

Tarothin was the last one ashore, stepping as if he were walking on eggs and almost daintily trying to keep a leather bag and staff out of the water. Sailors would gladly have carried both, except that he'd warned them not to touch either.

Tarothin otherwise had been leading an easy life for the last week, and without complaint from anyone. It was known that he might be the key to fulfilling whatever bargain had been made with the Karthayans. Nobody cared to think about what might happen if Tarothin failed.

The Karthayans could certainly make themselves memorably unpleasant, Pirvan knew. From the shore he could see the blue stern lights burning aboard the two harbor guard galleys at the mouth of the inlet. Those galleys had followed *Golden Cup* all the way from Karthay, their decks crowded with guardsmen and their rowing benches creaking under free weapons-trained rowers.

No galley afloat could successfully ram *Golden Cup*, but those two alone could pour a hundred fighting men onto its decks if it's captain tried to escape without the dragon. More galleys were surely lurking offshore, and even if Jemar was with them he would hardly take on Karthay with only one ship and no support from his other captains.

Golden Cup's captain was going to bring out the dragon if he wanted to come out at all.

The path up from the beach was wide enough for wagons and almost firm enough to walk on comfortably. Crawling and flying insects, drawn by the fires, buzzed and whined. Pirvan and Haimya soon looked as if they'd been in a battle, with the slime from swatted insects on their faces and arms.

They were obviously expected; no one challenged them. No one came forward to guide them either. Pirvan wondered if the dragon's lair was halfway up Mount Frygol, the landing party was expected to find their own path up to it and then persuade the dragon to fly.

The landing party's fate was not so harsh. A dozen soldiers appeared on the path, led by three officers and a priest of Mishakal. The cleric looked as if he needed some of his lady's services; he was sallow, looked feverish, and kept wiping his face, making an even worse tangle of his scanty hair each time he did it.

"Welcome, my friends," he said. He was looking about as friendly as an innkeeper welcoming a party of nine, half of whom would flee in the night without paying. "When is the supply ship coming?"

"Supply ship?" Kurulus said. He was providing the rank on this party, while Tarothin provided the magic and Haimya, Pirvan, and the sailors provided the fighting power. Three of the men were Jemar's. Eskaia had wanted to come; the captain and Haimya between them had persuaded her otherwise.

"Oh, yes. We handle the supplies for all the posts on this shore," the cleric said. The officers threw him a look that could have cut down a tree, but said nothing.

Pirvan made mental notes on the whole matter. Karthay was allowed a few posts on the western shore of the gulf, for aiding shipwrecked sailors and keeping the wild folk of the forest from turning pirate. They were not supposed to be maintaining a string of garrisons.

There were those among the rulers of Istar who would pay well for such knowledge. Now, how was a thief to carry this knowledge to them in such a way that he would receive his payment without becoming known to the rulers?

Time enough to think about that later. The officers were beckoning them to one side, and in the shadows under the trees Pirvan saw a path leading uphill.

"Lanterns," Kurulus called, then louder, "Boat guard, is all well?"

"Fair enough."

"Good. We shouldn't be long." Pirvan thought he heard something added in a mutter, like "fools' errands always take the longest," before the mate took the lead.

* * * * *

The path was not endless. It didn't even seem that way. It was steep, however, and the thick forest clinging to its flanks didn't improve matters.

The insects retreated a bit, but there were ominous chitterings and squawkings from the trees. Once a snake thicker than Haimya's leg crawled out onto the path, then crawled on across as if it had all the time in the world. In the lantern light it was dark green with red patches, and was at least twenty feet long.

As they climbed higher, Pirvan noticed that the Karthayans were looking about more intently. One officer quickened his pace until he was well ahead of the rest, then went on in that position, with his sword drawn.

Pirvan and Haimya exchanged glances and shifted position. He took the rear, she a place beside Tarothin—the two most vulnerable spots still unguarded. Her hair

141

looked as if it had been used to scrub kitchen floors, and even Tarothin looked as if he wanted to lean on his staff more than wield it.

The Karthayans openly listened—for what, Pirvan had no idea. He also doubted anyone could hear anything over the night noises. He had heard that as long as the forest creatures kept up their din, no enemy was about.

Pirvan only hoped that bit of wisdom was the truth. He was beginning to be aware of just how much he preferred cities to jungles. About ships he would keep an open mind for now—there were things a man could do to avoid shipwreck, or even be comfortable at sea.

Someone coughed—no, something. It was not on the trail, maybe not even human. Then Pirvan heard a long, low-pitched warbling, like the world's largest songbird with a bone stuck in its beak.

The Karthayans stiffened. "That's it," the cleric said. "But he doesn't call like that unless he hears something." Then, before the officers could stop the cleric, he called:

"Anybody hear anything?"

The cleric's question and the replies lasted only a few moments before one of the officers shouted for silence. Pirvan considered that if anything had alarmed the dragon, it now knew exactly where the approaching men might be. He considered hitting the cleric with the pommel of his dagger, but decided that such an impropriety was best left to Tarothin.

This is not a trap. This is not a trap. This is not a trap. What I tell you three times is true.

That little chant seemed alone and lost in the jungle, like a child in a benighted temple crypt.

In the next moment, Pirvan knew there was a trap, but not by the Karthayans. The officer ahead shouted, and Pirvan heard a soggy sort of rumble. Then out of the shadows ahead came a massive stone, half a man high, rolling down the path.

"Jump!" the officer shouted. Some of the soldiers did so, and thick, hairy arms promptly thrust out of the bushes and gripped them. One soldier slashed frantically, drawing blood and a full-throated scream, breaking the grip. Two others, less lucky, vanished into the bushes.

"Stay on the path!" Pirvan shouted. "They're waiting for us on either side."

A stone flew from the bushes. Pirvan ducked and twisted so that it only grazed his shoulder. The next moment, the boulder was past—but another came rumbling out of the darkness.

This time the men were alert to the slowness of the stone and the menace on each side. They sought the edges of the path but faced outward, swords drawn, arrows nocked, ready to fight the whole world if it showed itself.

To Pirvan it seemed likely that the attackers were without magic and few civilized weapons, but they were shrewd enough to be formidable. Their most vulnerable point and perhaps their leader would be up ahead, where the rocks came from. At least an attack there would stop the rolling rocks from driving them off the path.

Pirvan ran straight at the next boulder, at the last moment leaping to clear it. He would have succeeded if it hadn't been for the steepness of the path. Instead he fell across the boulder, flung himself off it in time to avoid being crushed, and landed beside the path.

He had his dagger out before the arm came out of the bushes, and he stabbed for the hairy wrist, thicker than his ankle. The wrist's owner howled, and the bush shook, making Pirvan wonder if he faced humans.

Then something grabbed him by the ankle.

Two somethings, actually—for a moment he knew he was either going to be dragged into the bushes or split like a wishbone. Then another howl shattered the night, one grip on his ankle eased, he kicked free of the other, and rolled back onto the path almost at Haimya's feet.

She grinned and pulled him up as the bushes cracked and splintered in the path of more attackers. Now they were in the open and easy to recognize, even if half the lanterns were out.

They were ogres, perhaps related to the legendary dwarf ogres, as they were more human in size than most of that breed. A few humans were among them, all nearly as hairy, ill clad, and undernourished as their companions.

All of them had muscles, and clubs and daggers of bone, stone, or bronze. Pirvan knew that with the unfamiliar sword in his hand he would be a menace to friend more than foe. He preferred to fight as he did when a tavern brawl turned bloody—with the difference that this time he would have to strike to kill.

He leaped to the right, faster than even a human eye could follow, went up on his hands, then over and back on his feet. He came up behind a human armed with both club and dagger, and thrust his own weapon hard into the base of the man's spine. The man screamed, reeled, clawed at his wound, turned around to strike at Pirvan— and took the thief's dagger squarely in the throat.

Pirvan snatched his bloody weapon free from the dying man, kicked an ogre in the groin, and saw Haimya's sword come down across the back of the ogre's neck as he moaned and tried to unfold himself. Then Haimya was leaping over the ogre and standing beside Pirvan, and they began to weave steel around them so that nothing could get through.

The battle shrank down to what Pirvan could see himself or what Haimya's face and eyes warned him of. He lost the ability to tell an ogre from a human, except that now there seemed to be some full-sized ogres with their immense reach.

He saw Haimya duck away from one club's swing, lose her footing on the path, and go down. Without thinking, he straddled her, kicking and slashing. The ogre drew back, but it had a comrade on each side. They came on, and Pirvan had the sick certainty that he and his friends were disastrously outnumbered.

The warbling came again, louder than before, then a third time, so loud that the bird might have been perched on Pirvan's shoulder, crying into his ear. Then the thief heard a splintering like all the fences in Istar being torn down for firewood, and a dragon came out of the forest.

It was a copper dragon—Pirvan could see its color

plainly, even with only one lantern still lit. It was a pale copper, in parts almost white, and the scales seemed smaller than the pictures, perhaps no larger than a baby's hand. One wing flapped, the other dragged, but from nose to tail it had to be more than thirty feet long.

That dragon would be formidable if it only sneezed. Pirvan hoped it remembered that it was good, and the ogres were not.

The dragon did more than sneeze. It swung its head, its eyes closed, and its breath weapon poured out. It was green and smoky, and smelled just like something that came out of a dragon's stomach.

As it struck the ogres, they stopped moving. Those caught in midstride fell down and seemed to be struggling to regain their feet. Those swinging clubs dropped them. Pirvan saw one ogre bend over to retrieve his weapon, struggle as if he were wading against a strong current, then fall over on top of the club.

The dragon warbled again, swung its head, and poured the smoke down the other side of the path. This time it caught a soldier grappled with a human opponent. A slash at the enemy's head turned into a tap with the flat of the blade, as the sword turned in the soldier's slowed hand. The enemy tried to bring a knee up between the soldier's legs, but lost his balance and fell. The soldier tried to kick him in the head, but lost *his* balance.

When the soldier fell on top of his opponent, Pirvan heard him laugh.

There wasn't much else to laugh about for at least a few more minutes. The wind was from up the path, so that as long as the dragon breathed down either side of it, those in the middle escaped the worst of the spell. Unfortunately, they couldn't close with their opponents; if they entered the smoke, they also would be slowed.

The archers were ready to try arrows on the slowed attackers. The officers weren't ready to let them, as they might hit friends. Pirvan snatched a bow out of one archer's hand, then Haimya hit him in the stomach with the hilt of her sword. He lost interest in archery.

The lack of archery made little difference. Slowed and unslowed, ogre and human alike, the attackers started to flee downhill. At times the unslowed helped pull their slowed comrades to their feet and clear of the dragon's smoke; at other times they let them lie or struggle.

Pirvan found himself leading the pursuit downhill. Halfway to the foot of the hill, the path seemed to sprout half a dozen unslowed opponents. One of them threw a club at Pirvan and hit a soldier coming up behind him. Then Haimya was again on one flank, Kurulus on the other. There were only the three of them, but the taste of victory was in their mouths, and they moved faster than their opponents could have, even unslowed.

A moment came when Pirvan realized that they faced only one opponent, though he was fighting hard enough for three. He was also shouting to comrades carrying away the wounded and others Pirvan could not see:

"Run! Run, but not downhill! The fort has to be awake! Run, you fools, the dragon's on your heels!"

Pirvan wondered about that; he hadn't heard that weird and sinister warbling for some time. Dragons were hard to kill, but what of a wounded dragon—which should be sound asleep a mile below the earth?

Pirvan suddenly knew he would feel great sorrow at not knowing the dragon better. If there were any doubt about its being good, it had settled the matter.

The defender of the retreat lunged forward, swinging a club and thrusting a short sword. Kurulus spun clear of the sword thrust, but not of the club. It cracked across his head, and he went down. Haimya nearly went with him, but rolled and sprang up, thrusting at the enemy's chest.

The thrust never went home. The ogre toppled as Pirvan lunged in from the rear, flinging his dagger. The pommel-weight drove hard against the back of the ogre's skull, and for a second time Haimya nearly went down.

By the time she was on her feet, Pirvan had wrestled the ogre over on to his back, to keep him from suffocating in the mud. No, make that *wrestled the half-ogre*.

He was the height of a tall, muscular man, and his

body's proportions were wholly human, except for the hair. The brow ridges, the jaw line, and the shape of the skull told of the mixed blood.

Mixed in blood, perhaps, but wholly a warrior. As the half-ogre opened his eyes, Pirvan knelt beside him.

"Can you walk?"

"Unh?"

"I said, can you walk? I will let you go, but you have to walk—"

Pirvan felt warm breath on his back. "I shouldn't kill him?" came a rasping voice, too deep to have a human source.

The thief did not waste time turning around. "No," he said. "He fought too well. If he can walk—"

"I heard you the first time," the half-ogre said. He might have been a child being awakened for school. With a grip on a low branch, he heaved himself to his feet and stumbled off into the darkness.

"Good," the dragon said. "I do not like killing, though I would have killed him if I were more in your debt and you asked it of me."

Pirvan tried to translate that remark; the dragon turned its head upslope. Its body tensed, both wings twitched, and moments later a mudslide rumbled and sloshed down the path. It was not a deep mudslide, just calf-deep, but it drew a furious cry from up the hill.

"What son of fifty fathers turned those rocks to mud! I had them all locked up!"

Pirvan laughed. He recognized Tarothin's voice, which made one less thing to worry about. With Haimya, he pulled the reviving Kurulus into a sitting position, so that he could spit the mud out of his mouth and wipe it from his eyes and ears.

Then he stared at the dragon. "You *can* talk!"

"Of course," the dragon said. "My only problem, once I was fully awake, was not having anyone to talk to."

He sniffed at Pirvan and Haimya. "But before we do any more talking, I think we should all bathe."

Chapter 12

The dragon was male and gave his name as Hipparan. Either Tarothin did not have the power to counter whatever protective spells guarded the true name and discover that, or he did not care to offend the dragon.

Pirvan quickly became persuaded that it did not really matter. Hipparan seemed to feel that he had discharged most of his debts to the human race by driving off what he called "a sorry pile of sweepings and scourings of several races."

Pirvan asserted that if the victory had been so easy, then the dragon owed his rescuers even more. Hipparan replied that it was all very well to say this by human reckoning, but dragons reckoned debts otherwise. Copper dragons reckoned them the most minutely, of all good dragons. Indeed, the only dragons that reckoned profit and loss more tenaciously were the evil white dragons, and *everyone* knew that they went about feeling superior with very little to justify that opinion.

"It's useful that Hipparan knows as much about his race as this," Tarothin said. He and Pirvan were standing out of hearing of even the keenest-eared dragon. The wizard looked as if he'd bitten an unripe fig. "I had hoped I would not need to teach him as well as heal him."

"Oh, I suspect there are very few things he will need to be taught," Pirvan said. "Although I begin to wish we'd had to teach him to talk."

"Consider how much time that would have cost, in readying him to face the black dragon."

"If it exists."

"I think Eskaia is right. Both are part of the balance, and I will be surprised if there is no plan for them to meet each other. Also, remember that most human weapons are useless against dragons, and only at a greater cost in lives than we can afford. Or does *Golden Cup* have a dragonlance stowed away with all the rest of the lumber in her hold?"

Pirvan held his peace. He rather wished Hipparan would do the same. The dragon might need speech to fulfill his purpose, but one could hope that he would not also use it to deafen and madden his rescuers!

It would have averted the next argument with Hipparan if Tarothin had been able to heal his damaged wing. Not that it was a matter of Hipparan's being unwilling or Tarothin not having the appropriate spells (at least some of them, those which could not harm any living creature even if they might not do it much good).

It was a matter of Karthayan law. This inlet was Karthayan territory (a claim at which most of the Istarians politely raised eyebrows but otherwise held their peace). Therefore, any wizard not licensed in Karthay could not heal dragons or anybody else anywhere around the fort.

Tarothin pointed out with polished phrases that he was an entirely lawful neutral wizard in Istar.

Did he have papers to prove it?

No, but he could cast spells to bring the evidence from Istar.

He could *not* cast spells. No exceptions or exemptions. But he could certainly send a messenger to Istar and have the messenger bring back the necessary documents, sworn statements, and so forth. The Karthayans would even be happy to provide the messenger and a ship for him, for a suitable consideration.

The Istarians were left wondering whether the Karthayans were trying to prevent the departure of the dragon entirely, or merely make it more profitable. Some of them also said, where no Karthayans could hear it, "If the Karthayans do this when they're under our rule, how are we going to know when they rebel?"

Tarothin said that he could easily overcome that miserable excuse for a cleric, but it would be like using kittens for archery practice. Also, it would undoubtedly create more delays, more legal complications, and more excuses for the Karthayans to assess fines.

With sarcasm crackling in every word, Eskaia expressed delight that he saw matters so nearly as she did without being commanded.

While some of *Golden Cup*'s people wielded words, others wielded axes. If Hipparan could not be healed enough to fly until they got to sea, then he would have to be floated out to the ship on a raft and hoisted aboard like the longboat. This presented problems, not the least of which was the dragon's weight, which required a large raft and might overburden the ship's lifting gear.

The first notion they had for building the raft was to use the cut logs at the fort. They learned that these were the property of the lords of Karthay and not to be sold, except at a price that took even Lady Eskaia's breath away.

The next idea was cutting trees. For this, however, they would need a license, the obtaining of which seemed as complicated as obtaining Tarothin's legal documents from Istar. It also bore an impressive price, roughly equivalent to a small manor.

They next considered sending a boat down the inlet or even outside it, to cut trees and tow them back. That seemed a counsel of desperation, considering the amount of time it would take to build a raft one log at a time and the improbability of the Karthayans ignoring the undertaking for very long.

In fact, one harbor guard galley followed the boat immediately. Once the boat left the inlet, the galley was so close behind that the ram actually gouged the boat's stern a couple of times.

The hint was explicit; the Istarians took it. They also took more gold from the strongroom and bought enough timber for a raft to support six dragons.

At least that was their intention. Hipparan disagreed. It had to be at least twice its present size.

"Cut the logs for it, and we'll gladly use them!" Kurulus snarled.

It would have been a considerable understatement about him, or a good many others of the shore party, to say that they were at the end of their patience. In fact, it was so far behind them that it was barely visible on the horizon.

Hipparan stared at the trees, then at Tarothin. Something passed between dragon and wizard that made Tarothin clap his hand to his forehead and turn to speak to his companions.

The dragon made a wordless sound that conveyed indescribable vulgarity. Then he thrust his head toward the base of the nearest tree, closed his eyes, and took three deep breaths.

A glowing copper-hued circle appeared around the base of the tree. A heartbeat later, it vanished in a great gout of mud. Suddenly the tree and several of its neighbors stood in a vast waste of mud, a good spear's toss wide. Tarothin and Pirvan, closest to the dragon, had to jump back hastily not to be caught in ooze that might be of any depth.

Another heartbeat, and they knew—deep enough to topple the trees, as the weight of their trunks and crowns overbalanced the remaining efforts of their roots. The largest tree was the first to fall, snapping off branches from itself and its neighbors as it came down with a soggy crash, hurling mud and twigs in all directions.

Pirvan and Tarothin jumped back even farther, but not fast enough to keep mud and twigs from splattering them. Wizard and thief wiped mud from their eyes and plucked twigs from their hair, as the rest of the trees subsided with a formidable snapping of branches. Everyone hastily gave still more ground, as splinters the size of arrows flew in all directions.

Hipparan walked as delicately as a cat along one trunk and posed on the pile of toppled trees. "I know not from rafts, they being a human contrivance. I should think that here are at least as many as you have shown me already."

To Pirvan's eye, admittedly not that of a seasoned timber feller, Hipparan had knocked down enough trees to build a small ship.

Tarothin was the first to find words.

"Why didn't you do that before?"

"I did not owe you enough to solve your problems for you. At least not before I knew how serious they were."

"I suppose we now owe *you*," Haimya muttered.

Dragons, it appeared, had exceptionally acute hearing. Hipparan waved his one good wing, sending a storm of flying leaves into everybody's face. If dragons could grin, he would have done so as he spoke.

"Of course, fair warrior. You are swiftly learning the customs observed in dealing with copper dragons."

Haimya and Pirvan did not dare speak again, but another exchange of glances told of another common thought: *I could just as well have remained ignorant of customs and much else about copper dragons.*

Then Haimya's eyes took on a distant look. Pirvan knew she was chiding herself for such selfishness, when Gerik Ginfrayson might even now be courting death close to a black dragon.

He started looking for an axe, saw none, and for a moment was afraid they'd been lost in the bog or smashed under the falling trees. Then he saw the handles of the tools sticking out from the edge of the mud. He hurried forward to grab them, stepped into a deep hole, and went in up to his waist.

He had to count to fifty to avoid an outburst of language that would surely offend the gods and perhaps the dragon, though he was very much in a mood to offend the dragon. Then he held out an axe, handle-first, Haimya and the mate gripped it, and with all three struggling and sweating Pirvan rose from the mire like some hero of legend.

If this is heroism, give me honest night's work, he thought.

* * * * *

Their troubles were almost over when Hipparan climbed aboard the raft. It had taken all the purchased and spell-toppled logs, as well as lashings that used most of the spare cordage aboard *Golden Cup* and some scores of feet of vines as well.

"If we needed any more, we'd have to start tearing up our clothes," Kurulus said. "Although some of us might look better after such work than others," he added, with a grin at Haimya.

Pirvan kept rude words off his lips with an effort, and knew he'd lost the battle to command his face before it began. Fortunately Haimya was not looking at this display of unseemly jealousy.

She stared at the mate, then smiled. It barely missed being the smile of a cat about to take a mouse by the throat. She did not move a finger, but she somehow managed to look as formidable as if she'd already drawn her sword.

"My apologies, Ma'am," the mate said, bowing. He tried to doff his hat, but it was glued to his hair with mud. "But only a blind man could fail to notice that you're more than commonly handsome."

"I do not insist that men blind their eyes," Haimya said, with a real smile now. "Only bind their tongues, at least when there's work to be done."

"As indeed there is," the mate said. It was not quite a groan.

Once the raft was assembled, it took a further while to persuade Hipparan to board it. He was reluctant to wade, no one wanted the lashings tested by his jumping, and the raft drew too much water to let him climb aboard dryshod.

So they had to buy more logs, split them, and make a gangplank long enough to reach from reasonably firm mud to the raft. At least they had the consolation that they'd built the gangplank with steps, so Hipparan might be able to climb aboard. No one dared even think about what hoisting him aboard might do to her laboriously repaired rigging.

By now everyone aboard the ship knew that they were going to be taking a dragon aboard. The fact that it was a good dragon did not ease everyone's mind, even those who had seen Hipparan fighting ashore. Sailors were notoriously superstitious, and the only one who claimed much knowledge of dragons was Tarothin. Of course, he had saved the ship and done other marvels, but no wizard was infallible.

Most of the crew muttered, frowned, or stared. Three went farther, or at least attempted to. They tried to desert.

Two stole a boat and rowed ashore. The Karthayan soldiers promptly caught them as they blundered about in the jungle, making more noise than twice their number of ogres. The soldiers also returned them to *Golden Cup*, and the punishment they received was as much for what the Karthayans charged for this service, as it was for the act of desertion.

A third man took more thought—or at least it seemed so at first. He slipped overboard from the seaward side of the ship and swam out into the inlet. Perhaps he intended to reach the watchful galley, throwing himself on the mercy of fellow sailors. Perhaps he merely intended a landfall beyond the reach of the garrison.

Whatever he intended, he never accomplished it. The boat setting out after him by the light of Lunitari saw him swimming strongly. Then he threw up his arms, screamed once as if his soul were being torn apart along with his body, and vanished.

Cramp, current, curse, or something in the water, no one knew, and few cared to speculate aloud. The grumbling became muted, and the desertions ceased.

It did not hurt that the next day Hipparan scrambled up the gangplank from the raft onto the deck without missing a step. In language that seemed to have become more flowery in the few days since his appearance, he thanked the crew for its hospitality and swore not to abuse it. Then he slipped down into the aft hold, which had been cleared for his accommodations, at the price of a good deal of labor made more exhausting by the damp heat of the inlet.

Pirvan watched the hatch cover slide back on, then he sighed.

"It's not over yet," Haimya said. "Though I admit I've seldom seen a horse go into a strange stable with as little fuss."

"Did I say it was over?" Pirvan asked.

"That sigh expressed hope at least."

"Yes. I hope he'll consider that he now owes us something, for all the work we did. He only cast a spell and knocked down some trees. Or is casting a spell as much work for a dragon as it is for a human wizard?"

"I suppose that it's different with each dragon, as it is with each wizard."

"We can always ask Tarothin," Pirvan said.

"But will he answer?" Haimya asked. Then the sour look left her face. "Wager. Hipparan still considers us in his debt."

"Accepted. What is the forfeit?"

Haimya grinned. "The loser massages all the winner's most painful muscles."

Pirvan could not have replied except in a nod, but that seemed enough. Within, he was wondering how he could possibly lose the wager.

* * * * *

They spent another day at the inlet, loading barrels of fresh water, bundles of firewood, and baskets of fruit and salt fish. Then, that evening, the captain inspected the ship, and they sailed at dawn the next day, riding the ebb tide out past the galleys, to open water, which some had doubted they would ever see again.

Three days later, Haimya stood in a corner of the hold, holding a strip of soft metal. The hold was dimly lit with brass lanterns, and in the pallid light the metal had no sheen to tell her what it might be. She had no intention of testing it by bending or gouging with a thumbnail, even if Tarothin had not warned her firmly against any such thing.

Tarothin stood beside Hipparan, just under the dragon's hurt wing. The mage wore a loincloth and sandals and held his staff in one hand. In the other he held a brass ewer.

Straddling Hipparan's half-curled tail was Lady Eskaia. She wore a tunic that left shoulders bare, likewise her legs to past the knee, and nothing on her feet. She was squeezing a sponge on to a ragged gouge in the dragon's scales. The liquid that dribbled down was bluish and foul-smelling—or was the smell just the hold, after three days of holding a dragon under the northern sun?

Hipparan seemed clean enough in all of his habits, but he was a large animal, and large animals in confined spaces left their mark. Haimya had mucked out worse stables as a girl, however, so she had only to recall her old art of pushing the smell to the back of her mind and getting on with her work.

"Is that the last wound?" Tarothin asked.

"Why don't you ask me?" Hipparan said before Eskaia could speak.

"I was asking *both* of you," Tarothin said, his voice edged.

They were all sweating from the heat of the hold, but Tarothin seemed to have run a race or rowed all day in a galley. He had also drunk three jugs of water and one of wine, and eaten the greater share of a basket of bread, cheese, and sausage let down from the deck an hour ago.

"I've doused every wound I could see," Eskaia said. "Is that every wound you can feel, Hipparan? If not, I have the strength if Tarothin has the potion."

Eskaia's voice sounded as warm as it had when she had talked with Jemar the Fair. Then Haimya started, as Eskaia lifted the hem of her tunic to wipe her face. Mercifully, she was wearing reasonably discreet men's short-drawers in red silk under the tunic. Haimya would not have cared to wager that her mistress wore anything under the tunic above the waist.

Haimya wondered for the tenth time whether her mistress was questing for knowledge of magic and the ransoming of Gerik Ginfrayson. No, that was unjust. Say it, rather, questing *only* for those things she had admitted.

Was another, unadmitted but real, goal amusing herself as much as she could, in ways that would not be tolerated at home, for once in her life? One—in a man it would be called an escapade—one journey on her own like a kender's, to prove that she was an adult? Then back to the duties of a daughter of House Encuintras, much more than a single year wiser and more sure of herself?

"Haimya!" Tarothin sounded ready to throw something at her. "This is the third time I've asked. The metal strip, please. Hand it to me, and the gods spare you if you drop it!"

Haimya marched up to the wizard as she would have marched up to her company's commander when reporting for duty. Her hands were sweat-slick but steady as she handed the metal to Tarothin.

The wizard thrust his staff into his belt to free both hands. Then he climbed awkwardly up onto Hipparan's back and bound the metal around the wounded wing. It seemed to grow longer as Tarothin worked, until it made a dull gray ring three times around the damaged member.

"Stand well back, please," Tarothin said. "This is the simplest healing magic I think will have any effect, but Hipparan is a dragon, and I am not a god."

"We will learn how powerful you are sooner if you refrain from stating the obvious," Hipparan said. Haimya had learned enough of his nuances of speech by now to detect boredom.

Eskaia, on the other hand, was biting her lip to keep from giggling as she came over to join her maid. Both watched as Tarothin stepped back, then touched the tip of his staff to the metal band and began chanting an incantation.

It was not in a language either woman knew, and for all Haimya could have said it did not even contain words. He might have been reciting the multiplication tables in the tongue of some long-lost clan of elves, for all she knew.

Hipparan was feeling something, however. His eyes were shut, and he was stretching his neck, rather like a cat being rubbed in a particularly congenial spot. His crest quivered faintly, like the same cat's ears.

This went on for some time without any visible change, and Haimya's mind began to wander to her wager with Pirvan, which was even more of a mystery than Eskaia's reasons for this voyage.

She was not afraid that he would behave improperly. A more complete gentleman where a woman was concerned could hardly be imagined, let alone found. One might search the menfolk of a large city before finding another such as Pirvan.

No, it was that she feared she was behaving as someone in her position ought not to. She had grown to wonder if she and Gerik would be as they had been when they met again after he was ransomed. She was more than doubtful that the betrothal would survive any great changes, if they were both free to decide.

But they really were not. The line of Leri Ginfrayson (sometimes called Leri the Good) ought to continue—at least Eskaia would see it that way. There was also the matter of Haimya's position in House Encuintras if she and Gerik parted. She would forfeit the substantial dowry Eskaia's father had set aside for his daughter's maid and confidante, and have small choice but to go again for a sellsword.

It was a profession she had followed with better than average success for six years. There would be neither shame nor mystery in taking the field again. But she had seen a whole other world than one saw from a place in a marching column, half choked by dust and thinking mostly of your saddlesores and the rust spot on your sword. She wanted to stay in the new world, and Gerik Ginfrayson was an honorable means to that end.

Also, he was in many ways a better man than Pirvan. He had served Istar honorably in the fleet, if not much at sea. He was more filled out; his beard might be scant, but his hair was long and fine; and his nose was more in proportion to his face.

Pirvan was all bone and sinew, like an alley cat that has foraged for every meal. His hair was a dubious mouse color and showed signs of departing before long, and his nose would make kissing him a somewhat uncertain manner.

His eyes, though, and the way he moved, and the gentleness of his speech (except when he was angry at things that would infuriate the least worldly cleric) and those hands that had found so much unlawful employment but were so fascinating to watch in movement. Fascinating, too, when the time came for them to touch her—or her them . . .

"Done!" Tarothin said. He sagged backward, and without the help of his staff and Eskaia, he would have fallen to the deck. Instead he sat down and rummaged in the basket for a few extra crumbs.

Haimya looked at Hipparan. At first she saw no difference. His eyes were still closed, and his crest still quivered faintly. Both wings now stretched out across the straw-covered bottom of the hold, as limp as candy held over a fire and turning soft.

Then she saw that the wound on Hipparan's tail was gone. She looked for other wounds that she'd seen, and saw none of them. She turned her gaze back to the wings, saw them twitch—then Hipparan opened his eyes and let out his familiar warbling cry.

It seemed different now. The bone was out of the bird's throat. Instead the call rose like a chorus of the greatest singers of some race known to neither gods nor men. It filled the hold, and Haimya wanted to hold her hands over her ears.

She did not, partly because the others weren't, and partly because it would have seemed cowardly, even impious.

"Open the hatch," Hipparan said. He did not raise his voice, nor did it sound as different as his call. But it was clearly a command, from one who thought he had every right to give it.

Haimya was not going to argue. She scrambled up the ladder and pounded on the hatch cover.

"Open!" she shouted. "Open, for the dragon!" That was nearly a scream. She would be hoarse if she had to call again.

Chains clanked, canvas hissed, and the hatch cover slid aside, pulled by a dozen sailors. Haimya wondered how long they had been waiting there, and what they were expecting. She would be happy to tell them, if she knew herself.

Hipparan reared up on his hind legs. His forelegs caught the rim of the hatch, the claws scoring deep furrows in the wood. Splinters pattered down on Eskaia and Tarothin, and one sailor cursed briefly at the damage to the ship.

He fell silent as Hipparan turned his great, dark eyes on the man. Then the dragon warbled again, and the sailors scattered as he half sprang, half climbed out of the hold. Haimya hurled herself up the last few rungs of the ladder, stumbled, and went to her hands and knees.

She was still there when Hipparan took three steps, then flung himself over the side. He dropped from sight for a moment, but then ropes snapped and sails bellied in the blast of wind as he snapped his wings to full extension and rose into view again. Legs and belly were dripping, but he continued to rise.

Then he no longer rose, but soared. The great wings beat strongly, carrying him up to the base of the nearest cloud. He vanished into the cloud, men groaned, then he dived out of it and they groaned louder as he continued his dive straight for the sea.

Groans turned to gasps as he came out of his dive with his claws above the wave tops. Then he flew straight at the ship, wings thundering. A long bowshot from *Golden Cup*, he climbed again, turned upside down, and flew over the ship with his crest pointed down at the deck and his feet at the clouds.

The Encuintras banner stood out as rigid as a board from the wind of Hipparan's passage.

The dragon climbed again, and called. It was not his warbling cry again, but something harsher, less musical, almost a roar. It still sounded like something that one god might have used in place of words to speak to another. Haimya expected the whole world to be silent until the sea and the sky swallowed that cry.

It almost was, except for Eskaia's quiet sobbing. She and Tarothin had reached the deck and stood close together. The lady's head was not quite on the wizard's shoulder, but it would certainly be allowed there.

Tarothin looked as close as a wizard ever could to being humble, even awed. But then he had healed a creature of the race that was closer to the gods than any other created beings.

It began to seem to Haimya that frivolity and pleasure had lost any place in this quest.

* * * * *

Six days later, land was far behind *Golden Cup*. The captain had laid their course straight north out of the Gulf of Karthay, then north. They were staying well clear of North Cape, to avoid any ships of Synsaga's that might be disposed to board first and negotiate afterward.

There was also the matter of the dragon. The fewer eyes outside *Golden Cup* that saw Hipparan, the better.

Pirvan was turning to descend the ladder from the forecastle when the dragon broke out of a low-lying cloudbank far off toward the sunset. The ship was rolling gently eastward under easy sail with a steady breeze from almost dead astern.

Hipparan spread his wings and glided in for a landing before Pirvan was halfway down the ladder. As he reached the deck, the dragon folded his wings and landed on his hind legs, slipping in between the shrouds as if he'd been practicing for years.

From ports and hatches bearded faces thrust themselves forward. The sailors were now only wary of Hipparan, not frightened. He had done no harm, some of them appreciated his grace and splendor, and all appreciated a fine haul of fish to which he had guided them two days ago.

They still preferred to leave dealing with the dragon to their officers, among whom Pirvan and Haimya now ranked. As Grimsoar One-Eye put it, "The feeling is, the dragon's done no harm so far. But why risk being too close when he changes his mind?"

This, Tarothin said, denied the basic concepts of good and evil. Grimsoar replied that the wizard might know a great deal about good and evil, even if he was neutral himself, but how much did he know about dragons? Or sailors, for that matter?

Tarothin departed in something of a temper, after this setdown at the hands of someone he had to force himself to respect. When matters seemed well with Haimya, Pirvan had tried to change the wizard's mind, but lately he had no time to spare for this.

Haimya had returned to her old distance. Pirvan did not unreasonably regret the lost laying on of hands, and indeed was not sure who had won the bet. Nor did the warrior-maid return to the chilly manner that had made it hard for them to work together.

But their friendship seemed part of a distant past, like the elves' Kinslayer Wars, a thing of legend. This worried Eskaia, and Pirvan had no idea how much Haimya had told her mistress and how much the young lady had guessed. Not much and quite a lot were Pirvan's own guesses.

Unfortunately, he and Eskaia could not safely put their

heads together and combine their knowledge in the hope of finding a solution. He had no such rights over Haimya, and neither did Eskaia, even if she might think otherwise. Such a well-meant conspiracy would most likely end with Haimya sundered from her mistress and disposed to geld Pirvan with a dull blade.

"Hoha, Pirvan Thief," Hipparan said. "I have sighted a storm to the northwest. Its course seems toward this ship."

That brought one of the faces, the mate of the deck, out in plain sight. "Can you tell us more?"

Hipparan described a storm fierce enough to make everyone within hearing look dubiously at one another, then up at the rigging. *Golden Cup*'s hull and belowdecks were sound enough to weather anything short of the end of the world, but its deck gear and rigging still had scars and weaknesses from the first blow. They would not have to worry much about shoals and reefs this far north, but Pirvan had heard that the storms blew longer and harder.

"Any magic in it?" Haimya asked. Pirvan saw eyes and mouths open, wanted to snap at her for her indiscretion, then realized that such discretion would require Hipparan's cooperation. Haimya could whisper her question in the dark of the nightwatch, and still have it shouted from the masthead the next day if Hipparan was in the mood.

Besides, Pirvan wanted the question answered himself.

"How should I know?" Hipparan said. He sounded testy. "I flew along the storm front close enough to see clearly. At that distance, I sensed no spells. But if I had flown close enough to sense them, they might have caught me. Then where would we all be?"

Hipparan's strength had improved. His manners had not. But everyone seemed to know the answer to his final question, and none seemed to like it.

Hipparan left his audience standing, and scrambled down into the hold. A party of sailors began dragging the hatch cover back into place.

"I hope our scaly friend doesn't mind being a little stuffy when the gale hits," the mate of the deck said. "I won't have leaking hatches for all the dragons on Krynn."

Pirvan wondered how many they might be now. He also wondered where Jemar was. Even Jemar's own ship might make a difference to the quest; his whole squadron would almost ensure its success. Synsaga could not afford to lose the men and ships that a fight with Jemar would eat.

Haimya merely stared through him. The thief wandered to the railing and looked to the north. Faint and far off, riding high above the crimson sunset glow, he could see the wispy clouds that were so often the vanguard of a storm.

Chapter 13

Jemar the Fair kept his broad-brimmed hat on his head with one hand, but nothing could keep the breeze from making its feathers dance madly. A whitecap broke against *Windsword*'s side, and spray doused his face. He blinked his eyes clear and again counted the ships in the bay.

"I see only four ships."

The first mate shrugged. "I won't try to guess, until I see who's missing. At least nobody seems to be burdened with a prize."

"Some don't call that a burden," Jemar said. "No prizes at all can unsettle men faster than leaving ones they've taken."

The mate shrugged again. Nearing thirty, he still had a boy's love for the romance of seafaring and not much respect for anyone who merely wanted to make a living on the great waters. He was worth his rations and shares many times over for the inspiration he gave the new recruits, but he needed to be brought down from the clouds every so often.

"Ahoy, the deck!" came the hail from the foretop. "I make out Youris, Geyon, Shilriya, and Zyrub."

"Good watch," Jemar shouted. "Double wine for you tonight."

He turned to the mate. "Much as I expected. Nersha was complaining about that crack in the keel all last summer. I suspect she found she couldn't really face the open sea in *Blaze*."

"She could always have sailed and moved to another prize. A ship wouldn't have to be much to be more seaworthy than *Blaze*. Or has she gone on piling up cabin furniture the way she used to? Perhaps she couldn't find a ship large enough to carry—"

Jemar cleared his throat. "For all we know, that furniture is as precious to her as that set of jeweled earrings is to you." The mate had the grace to flush slightly. Jemar grinned.

"It hardly matters, anyway. Five ships can give Synsaga enough of a fight to make him prefer talking, unless he's lost his wits or found an entire dragonarmy."

"Who knows what's behind the rumors?" the mate said. "Besides, will all five ships be united?"

Jemar opened his mouth to rip the mate open like a reef tearing at a fishing boat for withholding information. Then he realized that the mate was merely looking on the dark side. He usually did when it came to the intrigues and schemes of a council of captains, which he hated with a holy passion.

"You don't earn a mate's rations and shares as a prophet of doom," Jemar said shortly. "Right now, you earn them by having the longboat swung out and the decks manned for signaling and hospitality."

"Aye, aye, Jemar," the mate said. He moved off fast enough to ease the sea barbarian chief's temper for the moment. However, he would have felt a trifle better if he hadn't sent the second mate off with *Golden Cup*. It never hurt a man to know that there was someone to take his place if he opened his mouth too often at the wrong times.

* * * * *

Gerik Ginfrayson was somewhere between wretchedly and horribly uncomfortable on the window ledge. But he would have clung to a branch or even hung from it by his tail (assuming he could grow one) to have as good a view of Fustiar the Renegade at work.

He had indeed seen everything clearly. Fustiar had lowered the dead (or at least senseless) prisoner into a hole in the floor of the tower's dungeon, until he was out of sight. He had placed a bronze grating over the hole. He had sprinkled the grating with something that smoked like parchment sprinkled with rock oil and set alight.

Fustiar then nearly coughed himself into a fit and drank a good deal of wine (an entire large jug, Gerik judged) to clear his throat. It could not have cleared his head, but at least it did not befuddle it. Potent mages were dangerous enough working magic while sober; Gerik's curiosity did not extend to being close to one working while manifestly drunk.

Now Fustiar was trotting industriously in circles around the grating. He held his staff crosswise in both hands and chanted as he moved. He was sober enough that the rhythm of his feet and the rhythm of his chant matched, or at least they had so far.

Meanwhile, a blue glow crept up through the grating. It brightened until it illuminated the entire dungeon, and Gerik drew back from the window for a short while. He was uneasy alike about the magic being worked here and about Fustiar's noticing him as the light increased. Even the most moderate of mages dealt harshly with one who might be called a spy.

The glow continued to brighten until Gerik had to shield his eyes with one hand when he returned to his vantage. Certainly no human eye within the dungeon could any longer spy anything outside it.

If Fustiar's eye was human. . . .

The mage was still moving, still chanting. The glow was brighter than ever. But in the middle of the glowing, something more solid, a heavy mist that seemed at once colorless and filled with every color of the rainbow, was curling up from the grating.

Gerik braced himself for the lash of heat on his skin. But as the mist rose like a snake toward the ceiling of the dungeon, he felt something quite different.

He felt as if the snow-laden winds of the southernmost Turbidus Ocean were blowing from the grating, filling the dungeon, and flogging his cheek. He shut his eyes, but the cold fire on his skin grew only more intense.

It began to seem that he had come here to witness the end of Fustiar the Renegade. If the man was still human, he had to be a stiffening corpse in the midst of that swirling ice.

* * * * *

"*Habbakuk's Gift!*" was the cry from the boat.

"Board and be welcome," was the traditional greeting from *Windsword*'s gangway.

Jemar the Fair looked around his cabin. Youris's arrival made the council of captains here in Ansenor Bay as complete as it was going to be. The five here could vote for or against their all sailing in aid of Lady Eskaia and her enterprise. They could not bind Nersha, though if she spoke well of the voyage later, Jemar would see that she had a small share of whatever gain it might bring them. He and Nersha had shared too many drinks and occasionally a bed to leave her out entirely.

Youris entered as usual, rather like a mouse visiting a houseful of elderly cats. The appearance was deceptive, also as usual. Youris was undoubtedly the best swordsman of Jemar's captains, and the most ruthless in looting prizes and ransoming captives. Honest trade came his way but rarely, and at times Jemar wondered if Youris wouldn't be happier sailing under Synsaga. Somebody was going to slit his throat sooner or later, but on the

Crater Gulf it might be later.

The five captains had each brought a servant with their stool of office. Some chiefs handed out maces, or staffs, or ornamented speaking trumpets; Jemar handed out folding stools of plain leather and even plainer wood. There was a time for display, but the serious business of a council of captains was not it.

Jemar's style of addressing a council was also plain rather than florid. This was not entirely because of his pose of simplicity, though it certainly supported that pose. The simple fact was that Jemar the Fair hated long speeches, both hearing them and giving them; they made his throat dry, his ears hurt, and his temper uncertain.

Those women who shared his bed (and over the years one could have crewed a fair-sized ship with them) knew that he could be eloquent, bawdy, even tender whenever he chose, at any length he and his partner enjoyed. Among his captains and crew, however, he had the reputation of a man who seldom used two words when one would do and often preferred silence to saying anything at all.

He wondered briefly if Lady Eskaia knew that, and that the way he'd spoken to her was a sign of his high regard. He also wondered what a merchant princess of Istar would say to being well regarded by a sea-barbarian chief.

Then he stopped wondering, because Captain Youris was putting his stool in the center of the circle, the request for permission to stand and speak. Jemar swept his eyes around the cabin; the last servants departed as if the deck had caught fire behind them.

It was unusual for a captain to request to speak to the council before hearing what Jemar had to say. It was neither unknown, nor illegal, nor even particularly suspicious. Jemar decided that *he* would be the suspect one if he insisted on Youris's silence.

Also, a man speaking often revealed what a man listening could hide.

"Shall Youris speak?" Jemar asked.

"Youris shall speak." It was a ragged quartet (Jemar

had heard better in seaside taverns with all parties three sheets to the wind), but he detected no doubt or dissent in his voice or anyone else's.

"I shall speak," Youris replied, accepting the permission as formally as it had been offered. Some sea barbarian chiefs tolerated both drunken brawls and drunken brawlers in their councils; Jemar had found neither of much use, even as entertainment.

Youris remained armed as he stepped forward, but that was his right and no one so much as blinked at it. His voice was low, rather than the squeak one might expect, and his words came out as steadily as the beat of a galley's oars at cruising speed.

"I would not care to prejudge our chief's decisions, but I would be reluctant to do anything at this season except continue our cruises. Istar's fleet grows by a ship a month, and the Karthayans and Knights of Solamnia have little love for us either. They lack seagoing ships to make their enmity effective, but—"

"Youris, your pardon," Captain Shilriya said. "But counselor's talk is not what we need. If you wish to amuse yourself, I have some wine or perhaps even stronger pleasures aboard *Winged Fox*. But if you wish to amuse us, be brief. Jemar has been courteous. Do return the favor."

Youris turned to Shilriya and let his eyes linger. Most men did that. Shilriya was a robustly built redhead with a taste for long braids and short, low-cut tunics. It was hard to look at some of her tunics without wondering when she would emerge from them, with spectacular results.

Youris did not seem to be studying Shilriya's charms, however. He seemed to be trying to silence her with the sheer intensity of his gaze. That was foolish, with Shilriya. Jemar knew her better than most women he'd bedded, and knew she had a will of iron. Youris should know that, too, unless he'd turned witling.

Or unless something had him uneasy, and this lapse of memory was a sign of it.

Jemar met Shilriya's eyes. Neither of them so much as

twitched a finger, but when he looked away, he knew that they were in agreement.

Now for Youris.

"Captain Youris, I, too, must ask you to be brief. If what you want to say bears on my proposal, perhaps it could even wait until after I have spoken. Or is it something momentous, like an apparition of dragons?"

One drop of sweat had time to break out on Youris's forehead. It had no time to start rolling down toward his nose, before Youris kicked his stool at Jemar and followed up with a furious leap, drawing his sword in midleap.

That midair draw nearly defeated Jemar, for all his speed, alertness, and longer reach. He had nothing but his dagger drawn when Youris closed with him. The stool had struck him in the jaw, tearing skin and jarring his skull.

He still had the speed to dart under Youris's second slash, but not to thrust the dagger into a vital spot. Or at least an unprotected one—the first thrust met metal. Youris's extra weight was armor under his tunic.

Not badly planned, thought Jemar, which means accomplices, even if he's taken them by surprise as well as me. Who?

Jemar abandoned subtlety and gripped Youris's sword arm. Then he thrust at the man's throat and at the same time twisted the arm. The thrust caught in the embroidery of the tunic and skittered off the armor beneath. The twist was more successful. For a moment, Youris's arm was unmoving. For another moment, struggling to free it, he was nearly so.

That was enough time for Shilriya to rise, fold her stool, and swing it hard at Youris's head. She struck below the green hat that had always reminded Jemar of a badly made pudding. Youris staggered, the hat fell off, and the improvised club descended again.

The wood of the stools being plain did not make it light. It was cut from ironwood, so dense that it would barely float. It now proved harder than Youris's head. The captain's eyes rolled up in his head, and he sprawled at Jemar's feet.

Jemar barely had time to step back when the cabin door burst open. The mate staggered through, blood streaming down one arm. His good hand held a cutlass. He slashed wildly at something Jemar could not see—then Captain Zyrub jumped up.

Zyrub was the largest of the five captains, and long-armed for his height. He didn't bother folding his stool before he flung it. It hit something with a crunch, which was followed by a thud. Then he reached over the fallen mate and heaved an unconscious man into view.

It was Youris's servant—Youris's dead servant, if they could not heal him quickly. It would do the man no good in the long run; the yardarm awaited him regardless. But both he and his captain should not die with the secrets behind their treachery unuttered.

"Keep him alive!" Jemar snapped. "And that one, too," he added, pointing at Youris. Shilriya looked at Jemar as if he'd asked her to decorate her cabin with piles of manure, then sighed.

"As you wish, O Great Captain."

Jemar ignored the sarcasm. "Zyrub, you lead a boarding party from your ship and mine to *Habbakuk's Gift*. If they resist, fight. If they try to get underway, signal and we'll pursue.

"If there's no resistance, don't hurt anyone. But search Youris's cabin thoroughly. Don't let anyone else in there, and if anyone offers information, send them to me. "There will be rumors enough running about the squadron within the hour. I want to overhaul them with the truth."

Zyrub's expression said that they would be so lucky when minotaurs played the flute. But he always had a surly way of obeying—and never left Jemar in any doubt about his loyalty when matters grew serious.

Over a time Jemar could never measure, his men came in and removed the two senseless traitors, while bringing their one healer for the mate. Jemar knelt beside the man, as the healer rose and said he could do nothing.

On Jemar's lips were witling's words, such as, "I wasn't *that* eager to save your pay and rations," or "I know prophets are seldom honored, but this is ridiculous."

Instead he held the mate's hand until it went limp, and closed the dead eyes. He still felt those eyes following him as he went out on deck, and the sense faded slowly.

He did not feel really at ease until he saw the boarding party climbing the side of *Habbakuk's Gift*, then the signal for "All well" climbing up to the ship's masthead.

This half-witted treason had been strangled almost at birth. Half-witted, because if Youris wanted the chieftainship, there was the lawful Captains' Challenge. Had he killed Jemar in that, all would have been oath-bound to follow him.

For what he had done, he would never have left the cabin alive even if he had killed Jemar. Youris had been desperate. Jemar greatly wished to know why.

* * * * *

As suddenly as it had hurled itself against Gerik Ginfrayson, the freezing mist receded the way it had come. He did not dare open his eyes to see what else it was doing, lest it leap at him again and this time blind him.

As a scream echoed around the dungeon his eyes flew open and every other sense grew as sharp as a sword's edge. Someone was giving up his life in that scream, with fear or pain or both beyond normal human experience.

Not beyond the experience of the victims of mages, however.

As Gerik clung to his perch, he saw the blue light fade. The icy mist or smoke was contracting into a ball. Fustiar still stood, and as far as Gerik could tell, still lived. There was frost on his robes and hair, but he still chanted as if had not missed a syllable even while the ice-mist had surrounded him.

Then he touched his staff to the ball of ice-mist. It shook like jelly had began to change shape, flattening out and taking on a four-sided shape with one side curved—

An axehead. And from tales that might not have been intended to frighten him but certainly had, Gerik recognized what kind of axehead: an ice barbarian's Frostreaver. It was the most terrible of all battleaxes, but equally burdensome to make, even for the most potent wizards of the ice barbarians. Therefore, mercifully rare even far to the south, on the glacier-rimmed islands where the ice barbarians squatted in their sealskin huts.

As for one being made here—never. Except that the evidence of Gerik's eyes told him otherwise. A Frostreaver forged in a land of perpetual damp heat—and not melting on the spot. As far as he could see, not melting at all.

A voice told him that he should wait and see what became of that axehead of shimmering blue ice. If in an hour it was a pallid puddle on the filthy dungeon floor, he would have seen nothing that anyone need fear. Fustiar's Frostreavers were bound by the same constraints as those of the ice barbarians.

But it was enough and too much that he had seen it made at all. Gerik dropped from his perch, careless of the noise he made, careless of bruises and cuts from stones and twigs. He half slid, half fell to the ground.

When he reached the ground, he ran.

* * * * *

Shilriya tossed back the last of her brandy and bent over Jemar's table to refill her cup. Her tunic was as low as ever, but looser, and she wore perfume, a heavier scent than Jemar liked but so rare with Shilriya that it almost deserved to be entered in the log.

"So. Are there any doubts left?"

"No, except about whether Youris is fit to be tried and hanged. Only a complete idiot would record his debts to Synsaga without using the simplest cryptograph."

"That, or one who didn't want to leave a mystery behind, to confuse and divide us. Instead, he laid it all out neatly, so that when he was gone we could answer the riddle and fear nothing."

The idea of Youris possessing that sort of nobility was alien to Jemar, but it took more than brandy to make Shilriya talk nonsense. Still, the man had to have been lacking *somewhere* to go so far in debt to Synsaga—a man who neither forgave nor forgot, without very good reason.

If he had a mage and a dragon at his command now, he would have very good reasons to collect everything that was his due. Power beyond even a king's dreams might be his for the asking, but even a mage and a dragon together could not make the gold needed to make greedy men share Synsaga's dream.

Most men were content with their own little dreams, until someone else gave them larger ones, for good or for evil.

Jemar sipped at his own brandy. There was just enough left in his glass to swirl around in his mouth, letting the fumes rise up into his nose. They seemed to fill his head, but cleared his vision rather than clouded it.

One thing he now saw clearly: Shilriya was ready to share his bed. Not insisting, as she did with men as often as not, but definitely willing to listen to his offer.

Which would have been very well, except that when he looked at Shilriya he seemed to be looking through her to see another woman, one a good ten years younger than Shilriya, maybe more. Her image was fair at first glance, more than fair at a second, longer look—and far beyond him, and with no claim on him, and about as foolish a dream as any of Youris's, for a man in Jemar's situation.

But the way Eskaia had smiled at him would make him uncomfortable in Shilriya's bed. That meant staying out of it, because the lady did not stomach insults much better than a goddess!

It also meant seeing Eskaia again, away from that cursed shield-maid of hers, and asking the lady what lay behind that smile.

Jemar drank the last drops of brandy in a silent toast to Lady Eskaia and her mysteries.

* * * * *

Gerik ran he new not where, nor for how long. He knew only that when his right senses had more or less returned, he was out of sight of the tower.

That might not mean much on a night like this. It wasn't raining, but everything else he had come to loathe about the Crater Gulf weather was present. So was the entire nighttime panoply of the jungle, including insects that whined, buzzed, whistled, shrieked, and made every other sort of unwholesome sound even when they didn't tickle, sting, or bite, which most of them did.

He had the wits to sit under a good, stout tree that at least protected his back. No doubt it would start dropping nuts on him before long—though this early in the year, few nut-bearing trees bore ripe burdens.

The rough bark soothed itches on his back even as it tangled his hair. He sighed, and stretched his legs out until they encountered a fallen log. He pushed—and the log began to move.

He watched something not quite large enough to be a dragon but larger than he was rise on four splayed, clawed legs, raise a curious, bony frill along its back, and waddle off into the darkness. He could hear bushes crunching and small creatures skittering out of its path for quite a good while.

So. Fustiar was making Frostreavers. He might be making ones that would last. If so, would he and Synsaga sell them? Or would they sell the secret of making them?

One secret. Perhaps the first, but certainly not the last. Synsaga had no scruples that gold could not overcome. Fustiar had no scruples at all. (One could not afford them if one's magic involved human sacrifice.)

Gerik had scruples, more than he had realized until now. He did not much care for letting Frostreavers and whatever else Fustiar might conjure up loose on the world, to Synsaga's profit.

What should he do about those scruples?

Something like clarity was returning to Gerik's mind. He decided that the first thing he should do was wait here under this tree, or maybe up in it, until daylight. Then he could see which way the tower lay. If he could not see the tower, he could go downhill. Downhill meant toward water, and water meant a path to the shore.

But paths were meant to be walked in daylight. A man running about on a night like this could run into something's jaws, fall over a cliff, or tumble into a pond full of leeches that would drain him in an hour.

Every one of these things had happened to men Gerik had known. He would start his rebellion by avoiding their fate.

He would continue it by returning to the tower. Fustiar might not suspect anything if he returned—particularly if he returned before Fustiar was awake and sober. Fleeing, even back to the camps on the shore, would raise suspicions.

Fustiar could not, after all, do anything worse than use him to make another Frostreaver, and that would end all dilemmas at once. Anything less, and Gerik Ginfrayson might strike a blow or two before he went down.

Chapter 14

Golden Cup had been riding out the storm for two days now. Its masts still stood, but the few sails left bent to the yards had long since blown to rags. No one dared to go aloft to replace them, so the ship drove downwind under bare poles. Eight men at a time on the wheel kept the ship under control, and its hull was still sound, but sooner or later muscles or planks would weaken.

Pirvan clutched the railing and watched the storm clouds drive by above. He would not willingly look long at the waves. Out here on the high seas they were not wolves but something for which he had no name, long and deceptively slow until they were on top of you. Then they fell like hammers of solid green water.

Two men had already gone overboard without so much as a cry, let alone any hope of rescue. Even with safety lines, it was perilous to venture on deck. Belowdecks, minor leaks kept bedding sodden, the cooks had given up trying to light the galley fire lest they burn themselves alive or set the ship alight, and seasickness, flying objects, and falls had twenty men abed.

They would live to thank Tarothin for his healings. But those healings had also drained him, until he was in hardly better case than the crewmen.

What lay out there to the northwest, except what seemed to be the source of all the winds in the world? Pirvan had heard the sailors talk, hinting of a few bold voyages that far. There were islands, possibly an entire continent, and much plant and animal life. He'd even heard of intelligent creatures, some of them no better than broad jests by the gods, if the gods had anything to do with their creation at all.

A ship's boy tugged at Pirvan's sleeve.

"Master Pirvan. The dragon wishes to speak to you."

Pirvan looked at the boy, trying to decide if he'd heard the message rightly. He also tried to decide if the boy's face was green from fear or from seasickness.

"Tell Hipparan I will come directly."

They had not yet found a proper honorific for the dragon, who was giving them no help whatever in the matter. But Tarothin, Eskaia, Haimya, and Pirvan at least were not accustomed to being at the beck and call of a being whose existence they would have doubted a year ago.

Of course, a dragon in dragonsleep existed, in the eyes of the gods. But Pirvan and his comrades of the quest were not gods. Indeed, every time he looked at the waste of water and listened to the wind-demons howling, Pirvan felt less godlike than ever.

He followed the boy down the ladder, making sure that he had a firm footing on the next rung before he moved from the previous one. A man less careful had fallen yesterday, cracking his skill. Without Tarothin's skill, he would have been the storm's third victim, and he was still in bed with a headache like nine morning-afters all at once.

* * * * *

There could be no opening the hatch on the main deck in this storm. Access to Hipparan's quarters was through a door cut in the aft bulkhead, leading by way of a flimsy catwalk to the ladder. Every time the ship rolled to port, Pirvan clung to the handholds and waited for the catwalk to collapse. Every time it rolled to starboard, he was flattened against the hull until he knew he was going through the planks into the ocean.

Somehow neither happened, and after what seemed at least half the week, he was sitting on the straw, with Haimya, Tarothin, and Eskaia. The straw had not been changed in more than a trifle too long.

Every time *Golden Cup* rolled, everybody would slide back and forth, clutching at any available handhold, including one another. Once all four of the humans ended up in a pile against Hipparan, with Lady Eskaia upside down, her head in Tarothin's lap and her legs draped over his shoulder.

She might not have laughed so long and so loudly if Tarothin hadn't turned the color of a ripe cherry.

Hipparan finally cut off the day's laughter with a cough. A dragon's cough, Pirvan decided, sounded rather like a large drain backing up, and a sound like that definitely gained one's attention.

"If this storm is going to become worse, we have little time" the dragon said. "I understand that the ransom for Gerik Ginfrayson is small and light?"

"Ah—" Haimya began.

"Yes," Eskaia said briskly. "I trust you do not need to know any more?"

"If you think I am going to betray you to add the ransom to a hoard, I do not have and do not need—" Hipparan said. He sounded half outraged, half amused.

"Peace," Pirvan said. "Do I assume that you are offering to fly the ransom to Synsaga?"

"The ransom without humans to negotiate would be useless," Hipparan snapped. "Even if Synsaga's men did not seek my life, what of that black dragon? It may be rumor, it may not be. I must carry humans to deliver the ransom if I must deal with an enemy."

The tone was supercilious, almost contemptuous of the humans' lack of insight. Pirvan did not listen to the tone, but to the offer. Hipparan was saying that he was prepared to risk his life, riding the storm, to complete the quest—if some humans were prepared to match his courage.

"I know no more about riding dragons than anyone alive today," he said. "No less, either. I do know something about negotiation, craft, and stealth. I also have a small spell at my command that may prove useful, and a dagger that I know will." He stood and braced himself against Hipparan's neck.

"No one should go barebacked into Synsaga's camp," Haimya said. She joined Pirvan, and much to his surprise slipped an arm through his. No doubt this was just to keep from being flung on her nose by the next roll.

Tarothin was rising to his feet when Hipparan coughed again. "With all due respect, good wizard, you are more needed here. Also, I fear I cannot carry more than two to shore if I am to fly back with a third. Gerik is more or less of the common size, isn't he?" he added, for Haimya.

She nodded, then started as Lady Eskaia also stood.

"I am the lightest of the four—" she began.

"Also the most valuable."

"The one Synsaga would most readily negotiate with," she replied.

"The one he would most gladly hold for ransom," Hipparan growled. Haimya looked relieved at not having to say the same; Pirvan and Tarothin kept their faces carefully masklike.

So it would be Pirvan and Haimya, with the ransom, a letter from Eskaia proving they had full power to negotiate, and everything they might need to survive the flight and the landing.

"Of course, I'll wager that the storm ends the moment you people take off," Eskaia said. Her smile seemed forced; her gaiety certainly was.

"Yes, and if we don't take off, the storm will sink the ship with all hands and the ransom, too," Tarothin grumbled. "As Hipparan said, we are not rich in time. Let us be at our work."

* * * * *

Pirvan had once or twice dreamed of dragons. They were deep in human memory and at times, in the hours of darkness, rose to the surface.

He had never so much as dreamed of the problems of riding a dragon. Particularly a dragon the size of a house, who had to fly out of the hold of a storm-tossed ship without hitting the rigging, the water, or the railing, and preferably without even opening the hatch to the hold.

There was no avoiding the last. Tarothin made that plain.

"If a dragon can't wish-fling himself from one place to another, no human wizard can safely do it for him. The spells for that are good for humans and maybe horses and riders. I do not even command those completely. To attempt wish-flinging on a dragon and two riders would be to send them to their deaths."

"It will be sending even more to their deaths if the ship floods through the open hatch," Eskaia said.

They argued various ways around this impasse and came up with a solution that had at least this virtue: it risked no one except Hipparan and his riders.

They would prepare the dragon riders' harness and gear in the hold, likewise strap it on and lash the riders in place. Then sailors would loosen the hatch, and others from the shelter of the forecastle would pull it aside quickly with strong ropes. One man would signal the direction of the wind.

The moment he knew downwind from upwind, Hipparan would leap. One leap to the deck, a second into the air, and with prayers from all and any spells Tarothin thought useful and could safely cast, the ransom flight would be aloft.

This plan's virtue was more a lack of offices than an abundance of virtues. It would need luck and good timing. It would also mean that the harness had to be made absolutely strong enough without testing and adjusting. If something snapped as the dragon leaped, one rider at least would need healing and the second be on his or her way alone and barebacked.

Pirvan decided that if this prospect did not alarm Haimya or Hipparan, he was not going to be the sole voice of caution, which in this situation might look too much like cowardice. Indeed, he wondered all over again how many heroes had arisen from men's desire not to be cowards.

* * * * *

What the dragon riders were taking with them was nearly the weight of a third rider. Some of it, such as the food and water, would be consumed. But the rest included weapons, bedding, a light tent, floatbelts, spare clothing and boots, a healing pouch, a lantern, and much else that Haimya assured him would be useful or necessary even if he didn't know what it was.

Pirvan was willing to give Haimya the benefit of the doubt. After all, she'd campaigned in the field and he was definitely a city-dweller, for all his curious mixture of skills. But he did raise the point of their carrying all of this about in the jungle.

"Oh, it's no more than seventy or eighty pounds apiece," Haimya said cheerfully, then laughed at Pirvan's expression. "Also, we will probably hide much of it before we approach the camp, then retrieve it afterward. Gerik should be able to carry his share on the way out."

This assumed that they weren't carrying Gerik, or in such haste that they could not risk leaving the way they had come. However, Pirvan saw no reason to delay departure further by what might be called quibbling. The faster they struck, the more likely they would have surprise on their side, and nothing counted for more in this kind of affair.

Sailors ransacked *Golden Cup* for leather, rope, and chain to make the saddles and harness. The sailmaker personally took command of assembling them. By the time all was ready, the harness could have supported the weight of a horse and cart, let alone two humans.

Over Haimya's objections, most of the equipment was in sacks distributed over the harness. Pirvan reminded her that they might have to be ready to fight at once, and could do so better unencumbered. He had not been planning to mention the matter of swimming if they fell off, rather than sinking like stones from the weight of their gear.

Hipparan was less discreet. Haimya turned white, Pirvan put an arm around her, she did not resist, then both of them flushed as a chorus of cheers rose around them. From the expression on his face, Hipparan was ready to join the cheering; from the expression on hers, Haimya would gladly have turned all the onlookers into frogs.

The farewells had to be said in the hold, with the gale shrieking above the closed hatch. Even with that, the straw was now sodden, and every time the ship rolled, filthy water that hadn't yet found the bilges sloshed back and forth.

"Well, Little Brother," Grimsoar One-Eye said. "This is not the farewell I had expected."

"To be sure. Silken sheets and lovely ladies make a proper deathbed. But this may not be a deathbed, and the lady is lovely enough, at any rate. Indeed, I'll wager the price of a set of silk sheets that we'll be back."

"Who pays me if you lose?"

"Ask Lady Eskaia." Pirvan jerked his head to the far side of the hold, where the two women were embracing clumsily, trying not to cry or fall.

"Aye." Grimsoar lowered his voice. "There are a few of the lads who say that they don't care if you come back, as long as we're rid of the dragon."

"Oh they do, do they?"

"No more than I can handle, to be sure."

"Tarothin—"

"Begging your pardon, Brother, but sailors are sailors. They'll take my fist in their face and call it a fair fight. With Tarothin, they'll cry out, and others might listen."

"As you wish."

They gripped shoulders, then suddenly Haimya was beside him and it was time to ride the dragon.

* * * * *

"Ready above!" someone shouted. At least it sounded like that, above the endless creaking of the ship and the howl of the storm.

"Ready below!" Pirvan replied. Haimya said nothing, merely gripped her harness with one hand and patted Hipparan with the other.

"Both hands and no sentimentality, Lady," the dragon grumbled. "You don't think I'd be doing this if I didn't think I still owed you?"

Any human reply was lost in the squeal of the hatch cover sliding free, the crash as it struck the deck, and the shriek as the storm burst into the hold. Haimya shifted to a two-handed grip and leaned back into her harness, then shut her eyes. Pirvan kept his open—until Hipparan's first leap seemed to sink them all the way to the back of his skull.

He opened them again on deck, and the wind promptly tried to blow them shut. He remembered a picture of a dragon-mounted knight of Huma's time, wearing something over his eyes. Too late to worry about that now.

The sailors were shouting and waving. Pirvan couldn't hear them. He couldn't have heard a thousand clerics chanting songs to the gods over the storm. He raised a hand to wave—and had only a one-handed grip when Hipparan leaped into the storm.

For a moment, Pirvan saw the waves above and the sky and *Golden Cup*'s masts below. He noticed that more than a few ropes had joined the scraps of canvas in flying loose on the wind. The dragon seemed to fall upward, the waves reached out, then paused—and at last began to recede.

By the time Hipparan rolled over to fly upright, Pirvan had a two-handed grip. He even had his eyes open—though the first thing he saw made him want to shut them again.

Hipparan was climbing swiftly toward the base of the clouds. They were too high for spray, but not for rain. Through the murk of rain and spray Pirvan saw *Golden Cup*, already shrunk to the size of a child's toy boat bobbing in a bath.

Except that no bathwater ever had the sinister gray hue or oddly crinkled appearance of the storm-beaten ocean. And children's toy boats were always neat and colorful, not battered and drab.

Then Hipparan plunged into the clouds. Pirvan's last glimpse was of Haimya, her eyes so tightly closed and her face so pale that he could hardly tell if she was alive. He uttered a brief prayer to Habbakuk and closed his own eyes, for now there was nothing whatever to see.

Chapter 15

The world was storm for a time no human could have measured, and the only other being in the storm was a dragon too busy staying aloft to talk to his riders. Pirvan had never heard of the Abyss being an endless storm through which you rode on the back of a dragon, and in any case it ought to be an evil dragon.

He looked down and saw Hipparan's copper scales unchanged. No, not unchanged. Brighter than they had been, as if they were wet, or had been polished, or—

The clouds turned from gray to white and then fell away as Hipparan soared into the sunlight.

Pirvan realized that he was as cold as he had ever been in his life. In the sudden silence of the high skies, he thought he heard teeth chattering.

"Haimya?"

"Y-Y-Yes?"

At least they were hers, though his own weren't quite

steady—not at all, in fact. His next words came out:

"Are you all r-r-right?"

He wasn't sure if she laughed or stammered "Yes," again.

"That's as well," Hipparan said. "I know it's cold up here for humans soaked to the skin, and none too comfortable for me. But I don't dare go back down for a while. Some of the clouds are right down to the water. I can't see in the clouds, and I can't skim the waves, not in this storm."

"We weren't asking you to do any such thing, believe me," Haimya said. Now Pirvan wanted to laugh at her fervent tone. She was probably just as glad as he to see sunlight again, but she would doubtless rather have fingernails pulled out than admit it.

Hipparan wheeled in two full circles, peering upward at the sun to establish its position and his best course to the Crater Gulf. Pirvan hoped that the dragon knew navigation but would not let a word of doubt pass his lips.

He would have called Hipparan a young dragon even if Tarothin hadn't said so. The dragon had a bright youth's common vice of claiming to know more than he actually did, then sulking when one questioned his claim.

It was a vice with which Pirvan was too familiar—and those who had cajoled, argued, or beaten it out of him even more so. He hoped that Hipparan did not have as painful a journey on the road from youth to wisdom, but that was as the gods willed.

*   *   *   *   *

"Lady, it's time to leave the deck. You'll catch your death if one of those waves breaks over you."

Lady Eskaia had to look well upward to meet Grimsoar's single eye. He grinned down at her, like an indulgent uncle with a favorite niece.

"I can't get any wetter, Grimsoar." Indeed, she felt already as if she'd jumped into a pond with all her clothes on. From the looks she was receiving, she wondered if they were clinging in interesting ways.

She gripped the safety line and continued to stare into the clouds that had swallowed Haimya and Pirvan, as well as the dragon.

"Lady, I don't want to pick you up and carry you—"

"I don't wish you to. So we agree."

"As you wish. But Tarothin's wearing himself out with the sick we already have. It might be too much for him to heal you of lung fever."

That was true. It also might be true that the lung fever would leave her weak, even with healing. Wet clothes, a wet bed in a wet ship, no hot food or even drink—it was not only the poor without healing who died of the lung fever, when it came on strongly enough.

She wanted to release Haimya to her betrothed standing and facing them both, not wheezing in a damp bed.

"Here."

Grimsoar was pulling off his hooded shirt and handing it to her. He must not have been on deck long; it was still dry.

"Now who's going to catch his death—?" she began, pointing at his massive bare chest.

Then a thunderclap hammered down from aloft. Half a dozen throats tore in shouts.

"Down!" Grimsoar roared.

Eskaia started to fling herself on the deck, then found herself flying through the air. Another sailor caught her, knocked her down, then covered her with his own body as the sky seemed to fall about everyone on *Golden Cup's* deck.

It wasn't the sky. It was only the mainmast going over the side, followed by the new foremast. The mizzenmast lasted just long enough for Eskaia to stagger to her feet, then it too joined the others in the water.

It seemed a minor eternity before the sky stopped raining ropes, blocks, spars, and all the assorted gear ships seemed to carry high in their masts. Most of it went mercifully straight over the side. Some of it came down like stones from a high roof, to hammer flat anything below.

Fortunately that included very few men. Those who'd been out to watch the dragon fly had mostly gone below, and duty kept only a handful in the open.

But some of those were down, among them Grimsoar. He lay against the bulwarks, water boiling over him as the ship rolled, more wildly than ever. A ghastly red line scored his chest. Eskaia looked for a handhold, couldn't find one, and risked stepping unsupported out onto the deck.

Two steps, and it was tilting under her. She fought for balance, lost the fight, and slid on her bottom down the tilting deck straight into Grimsoar's ribcage.

His burst of curses was a beautiful sound that she could hear even above the gale. Then he pulled himself to his feet with one arm, tucked her under the other, and lumbered back to the aftercastle.

She was too squeezed to talk for a moment after he set her on her feet. Then the ship rolled again, so far that Eskaia heard curses turn to prayer. It seemed impossible that *Golden Cup* could ever come back.

But the ship did. In the fleeting moment when they could talk without holding on for dear life, Grimsoar explained his wound.

"Just a rope that caught me across the chest on the way overboard. A beautiful rope burn and maybe a rib or two the worse for it, but nothing serious."

Eskaia struggled out of Grimsoar's shirt and handed it to him. His look told her too late that she'd also struggled out of her gown. She was standing there in two sodden shifts. They not only revealed more than she really cared to display, they were letting her freeze to death even belowdecks.

"Thank you, Grimsoar. I can find my cabin now, and some dry clothes."

If there was such a thing left aboard, and if it mattered whether you changed into dry clothes when chances were you would die in wet ones within hours. That thought came and went swiftly through Eskaia's mind. In its place stood a determination to die as befitted a daughter of House Encuintras. Their code of honor was not as rigid as that of, say, the Knights of Solamnia, but it did rule out dying in your bed, feeling too sorry for yourself to help those even worse off.

* * * * *

Hipparan rode the north wind toward Crater Gulf. He rode it faster than any ship could have, faster perhaps than the wind of the storm. Pirvan found the wind in his face so savage that most of the time he kept his eyes shut.

Both humans struggled to stay awake. They both knew that this was the sleep that comes with being chilled, the sleep from which few awake.

As the hours passed, the sun crept past the zenith and began its slide down into the west. Also with the passing hours, the canyons and hills of gray cloud below began to show patches of sea.

By sunset, they were flying low over an ocean that seemed restless rather than stormy. Although they were flying steadily south, their lower altitude made it warmer. Now they could dare to sleep, and did.

Pirvan awoke some time in the night, with a dim memory of a dream that must have been frightening at the time. Haimya was still asleep, and Hipparan's great wings had slowed to a steady, almost lethargic beat.

By moonlight the thief saw that they were back down to wave-top height, following the moon trail across the water. The air was almost warm, damp with more than the sea, and hinting of land scents. They were flying much more slowly, so that he could keep his eyes open now against what was hardly more than a stiff breeze.

"We're not far from the Crater Gulf," Hipparan said. "But we have a problem."

"Why am I not surprised?" Pirvan said. A yawn made his words almost incoherent.

Hipparan cocked his crest to one side and rumbled with mordant laughter.

"Do you really want to know? Pardon, this is not a time for jests."

If that wasn't the first apology Hipparan had made, it was close to it. Pirvan listened open-mouthed as the dragon explained.

"They do have a black dragon in the gulf. He was reaching out to see if there were other dragons about, and reached me."

"Did he learn where you were?"

Hipparan was silent for a moment. "I doubt it. But if I learned that he was evil, then he had to have learned that I was good."

Pirvan took a moment to digest this news. Before he could reply, Hipparan shivered.

"I wonder what he will make of it," the dragon said, in an oddly distant voice. "He must have thought he was alone, too, serving some purpose that he would die without knowing."

"Wouldn't—if there's a mage there—?" Haimya put in.

If dragons could spit, Hipparan would have done so. "That for mages! Even the most lawful folk haven't always told their dragons what they need to know. We all remember that, and I could tell that the black had been left ignorant."

"I feel sorry for him," Pirvan said.

The silence this time lasted so long that Pirvan wondered if he had offended by sympathy for the black dragon. Then Hipparan quivered, and for a moment the beat of his wings almost stopped. He lost enough altitude to make Pirvan nervous before he resumed steady flight.

When Hipparan finally spoke, one might have said of a human that he seemed about to weep.

"Then it's not a wonder that you have done by me as you have. You—there is nothing and nobody you will use like a tool, then throw away. What that means to me—when one is where I am—"

The dragon was silent, and in the silence Pirvan tried to make sense of what he'd just heard. It did not take him long, once he'd come to think of Hipparan as a boy sent on a man's quest, in a world he did not know, where he could not expect to find other dragons or even human friends.

But he had found them, humans who had freed him from captivity, healed him of wounds that might have led to his death, and *told him the truth.* Or at least as much of it as they knew, so he could decide for himself whether to help them learn the rest or not.

But there was no decision to make. All the while Hipparan had been muttering about the human debt to him, his debt to the humans had been growing. An honest dragon could not deny it.

Of course, a good dragon had to be honest. But this honest? Pirvan wondered if he had just learned something new about good, evil, and neutrality, and wished Tarothin were here.

"Very well," Pirvan said. "I think we'll land on the slopes of that mountain to the east of the Ewide River. Not the high one with the lake in its crater, but the lower one closer to the shore.

"We'll just untie our bags and let you fly while we hide ourselves and unpack. If anyone does strike back, we'll be hard to find and you'll be well out to sea."

"I thought I was the soldier," Haimya muttered.

"So you are. But neither of us knows much about war on dragonback, so both of us can speak."

"Quite right," Hipparan said. "Haimya?"

She laughed. "It's a good plan. I'm only worried about dragonfear. I've heard that evil dragons can use that. Do you know if the black can?"

"No, and I can't learn without his learning as much or more about me. There are times when mutual ignorance is safest."

This went against everything Pirvan had ever learned, and he suspected it raised his companion's hackles as well. But under these—call them, *peculiar*—circumstances, it seemed the best course.

* * * * *

As if the storm had exhausted even its giant strength in dismasting *Golden Cup*, the wind began dropping soon afterward. Sailors risking their lives wielded axes and knives, cutting away the wreckage of the fallen masts before they pounded holes in the hull.

Other sailors managed to set a scrap of sail on the stump of the foremast. This brought the ship's bow around enough to keep it from rolling wildly like a log, until it rolled herself under. It became possible to stand and even move about without the four limbs of an ape, and even do work without risking bone-breaking falls.

Eskaia worked until after nightfall, helping Tarothin with lesser and greater healings until she was as exhausted as she could ever remember being. But Tarothin was even more so, from working so much magic in so short a time. The mate of the tops and Grimsoar One-Eye had to carry him to his bed in Lady Eskaia's cabin.

By the time the cook had wrought, with no magic whatever, the miracle of hot tea, the wizard was just awake enough to drink it. Then he lay back on the pillows, smiling feebly up at Eskaia.

"Thank you is—inadequate," he said.

She returned his smile. "It's enough until you have the strength for more." Then she flushed as she realized what an opening she had left, for a bawdy jest.

The jest never came. Tarothin was a gentleman. Instead he beckoned to Grimsoar One-Eye.

"Friend, if you can go to my cabin and remove from the chest under my bunk the largest of the three books there, the one with the silver quatrefoil on the cover—"

"A spellbook?" Grimsoar said dubiously.

"Quite safe for picking up and carrying," Tarothin said. "I travel a good deal, and there's small point in slaughtering innkeepers and hostlers' boys by accident.

"No, the book is safe, as long as you pick it up and bring it straight here. Don't drop it, don't try to open it, and don't let it get wet in wild water. That means water falling from the sky, in case you didn't know."

"None of that belowdecks, or if there is, we've more trouble than I care to think about," Grimsoar said, and he stood with a grunt.

"Is your rib hurting?" Eskaia asked.

"A bit," Grimsoar said. "But it was good enough to carry this hulk of a wizard in here. It's certainly fit for carrying his books. Besides, even if it wasn't, right now our friend couldn't heal a sick cockroach."

Eskaia grimaced. "Who would want to?"

"A neutral . . . wizard," Tarothin said, and fell asleep again.

* * * * *

Hipparan swept in over the coast well to the north of Crater Gulf, keeping low. He could have as easily gone inland to the south of the gulf, but that would have meant a longer flight at low altitude, in darkness, over unknown terrain. More chances of accidents, and likewise more chance of giving the alarm, to human eyes, the black dragon, or even whatever odd ogres, gully dwarves, and the like might roam the jungles.

Pirvan had not seen jungle before this quest, and now that he had, he would not wish for even a gully dwarf to live in one. Anybody deserved better than an eat-or-be-eaten battle for life, in a perpetual combination of steam-bath and maze.

Hipparan seemed to hurl himself at the northern slope of the mountain, which was more heavily forested than the southern. Just at the line where the trees thinned out, he flung his wings wide and settled into a clearing as neatly as a log sliding down a greased trough into a stream.

Now Pirvan and Haimya had the trouble of getting themselves and their gear off the dragon to which all had been securely fastened for the best part of a day. For a while, it began to seem that they had defeated themselves, especially as they wanted to avoid cutting any more than necessary. If all went well, they would need three people's worth of harness when they flew out.

Pirvan was sweating and Haimya was using language eloquent even for a former mercenary by the time everything was free. He realized that sailors really did know more about knots than thieves, even thieves who prided themselves on their skilled hands.

"The next time we do this, we'll use chains and locks," Pirvan said with a grunt as the last bag came free and nearly toppled him. "Those I understand."

"Do I discern that you have everything?" Hipparan asked.

"I would say Haimya has everything," Pirvan said. "As for me—"

Haimya hooted with laughter, until night birds fell silent and Hipparan's crest stiffened.

"If you must laugh at the man's jests, my lady," he said, "aren't there better places? And times, for that matter?"

For a moment, Pirvan thought Haimya was going to kiss either him or the dragon. Hipparan forestalled any such demonstration by taking wing in a thunder of air and a spray of dust, gravel, and twigs.

"You grow stranger each day," Haimya said, punching the thief lightly in the ribs.

I grow fonder of you, Pirvan thought. He hoped the second was not leading to the first. There were better places and times for that, too.

* * * * *

Shilriya was the first to sight the abandoned merchant vessel wallowing in the choppy sea left by the dying storm. Jemar was the first to come alongside, as the wind favored his ship more than Shilriya's. Neither of them wished to break out the sweeps in this kind of sea.

That the ship had fallen to pirates was evident a hundred yards off. The deck was strewn with wreckage, every visible door and port had been forced or smashed, and sea birds were fighting over the more edible parts of half a dozen human bodies in sailor's garb.

Jemar sent a boarding party over, and it reported no surprises. At least none, save the fact that all the men were horribly wounded, and that, in spite of the damage to the cabins, nothing had been taken.

"It's as if the pirates were berserkers on a rampage," the petty officer said.

"Go back and search the ship from tops to bilges," Jemar said sharply. "See if you can find any more bodies or abandoned weapons."

"The pirates seem to have taken all theirs," the man replied. "Leastways I didn't see any more than what a ship like that might commonly have. Do you think—?"

"I will think, if there's need for it. That's part of what a chief is paid for. You save your thinking for later and go search."

It was Zygor who solved the mystery. He'd been just barely hull-up when the other two ships came alongside, and soon afterward the wind turned dead foul. He broke out the sweeps and came thrashing up, halting a hundred yards away and putting over a boat almost at once.

"We found a few bodies," he said, the moment he reached the deck.

Jemar heard more than the words. "Human?"

"All of them. But one of them had this in him."

He handed the find to Jemar. It was a dagger about as long as Jemar's hand, with an odd hilt, mostly hollow with a crossbar for gripping. Two side hilts jutted out on either side, and the thick blade tapered to a sharp point.

"A katar," Jemar said.

"Minotaurs," Zygor added.

The katar dagger was one of the weapons unique to minotaurs. Minotaur weapons common to all races could be used by humans, if they were strong enough. Weapons intended for a minotaur's towering strength turned up in human hands once in a century, and even less often in human bodies—unless minotaurs put them there.

"I wonder why they didn't retrieve that one," Jemar mused. He explained the scene aboard the abandoned ship to Zyrub.

"The poor wretch probably fell overboard after they stabbed him, before even a minotaur could jerk it free. We said rites over him and put him back in the water with his fellows."

Jemar was barely listening. Minotaurs in these waters were not unknown. Sometimes they appeared as peaceful traders. Even then they had the minotaurs' vast arrogance and ferocious temper, and there had been bloody incidents.

Not, however, the massacre of a whole merchant ship's crew. That told a tale of minotaurs on some warlike purpose, which might make less than no sense to humans.

The minotaurs did not have to make sense, however, to be dangerous. Dangerous especially to *Golden Cup*, which might not have survived the storm in a condition to either fight or run.

"We double the lookouts at once, wait until the others come up, then form a line of search with all five ships."

"The usual intervals?"

"Yes."

"It'll be a good fight, avenging these poor bastards."

"I hope that's all we have to avenge."

Chapter 16

Pirvan and Haimya were not sure precisely when dawn came to Crater Gulf. They slept long and deeply after they had hid themselves and their gear. Once Pirvan woke briefly to discover Haimya curled against him. This felt quite as pleasant as he had expected. If she had no complaints, he would make none. Also, on the hillside it was cool enough to make it worth sleeping close and sharing blankets.

The clouds also gave them an uncertain sense of time. Pirvan's first notion on waking was that he and Haimya had been buried under a vast pile of raw wool. However, there was no smell of sheep, many smells of other things (mostly less agreeable), and far too many trees and vines all around. The cloud-wool and the trees together left them in a curious sort of twilight, but there was enough light to find water and start packing.

They came to an argument when Haimya insisted that they take everything with them, even if that meant being

loaded down like pack mules. Pirvan prudently did not
treat her as if she had broken a promise, but discovered
that subtler methods were not that much more useful.

"We can't run with these loads," Pirvan began.

"We won't need to run this far from the pirates' camps,"
Haimya said. "This is what soldiers call an approach
march."

"I believe you. I also believe you have heard of armies
that were so burdened that the soldiers were exhausted
before the battle, and because of that, lost it. What about
making a sled, if you won't leave anything?"

There was nothing around with which to make a sled,
Haimya pointed out. Also, sleds left tracks.

"So will we, carrying this kind of a load."

"The only way we could avoid leaving tracks is to
approach wearing nothing but daggers and loinguards.
That would undoubtedly draw the pirates' attention.
Having come this far, I would like to ransom my betrothed
and learn a trifle about what is happening on the shores of
Crater Gulf." She added that a sled would limit them to
level and open ground, of which she did not see much
around here.

At no time could anyone who did not know Haimya
well have detected the slightest trace of sarcasm. Pirvan
was grateful enough for this to concede without further
argument.

They finally contrived to both carry and divide the
loads. In pouches across their chests they carried the ransom, food, water, flasks of Tarothin's healing potion, Lady
Eskaia's letter of introduction to Synsaga, and mirrors for
signaling to Hipparan. Everything else was on their backs,
easily dropped if they needed to run.

"If all goes well, we can load some of the burden on
Gerik." Haimya grinned. "We will not do all the work of
rescuing him if he is at all fit to march."

"What if he isn't?"

"Then we work harder than ever for a peaceful ransoming, and ask Synsaga for some hearty stretcher bearers."

"And if there is no peace?"

"Synsaga is not fool enough to mortally offend House Encuintras by treachery. An Encuintras fleet loaded with mercenaries sailing to the gulf will cost him far more than he gains by stealing the rubies."

Pirvan thought that Synsaga might be no fool, but he was a man with whole new vistas of power and wealth opening before him. Such men had been known to throw prudence to the winds as they would not have done before. Pirvan had known both thieves and lawful men who had died that way.

However, he and Haimya had their own wits, surprise, the ransom jewels, and their own dragon to set against all that might tempt Synsaga to treachery. To take counsel of fears was the way of neither thief nor soldier; he and Haimya had at least that much in common.

Pirvan was already sweating by the time he had his pack on and settled in place, but it seemed less burdensome than he had feared. Or was it Haimya's smiling back at him as she thrust her walking staff into the moss and took the lead?

* * * * *

"Deck ahoy!"

The cry penetrated Lady Eskaia's sleep-fogged ears. She had slept fitfully on a damp pallet on her cabin floor; that waking was going to be a burden.

Then wakefulness came in a rush, at the second cry:

"Two sail, dead stern."

Tarothin's sleep ended in midsnore as Eskaia prodded him in the ribs. He sat up and combed his hair with his fingers. It was abundant and a pleasant shade of brown, with a thatching of darker curls on his muscular chest.

A voice that sounded like Haimya's whispered in her head, *Enough, my lady. There is appreciating men and there is being wanton. Beware of crossing the boundary.*

At the moment, Eskaia wanted most of all to cross to her wardrobe, preferably without touching the deck. She needed a heavy gown, a cloak, and above all, shoes. Even the best woolen bedsocks did not keep out the damp chill of the deck.

Tarothin, wearing respectable short-drawers, stumbled out of bed. He looked tired now, rather than ill, and stared around for his staff.

"Under the bed, wrapped in oilskin," Eskaia said. "Are you fit to return to your cabin?"

"I'd better be if we have visitors," the wizard said, with a wry grin. He rubbed his forehead as if that would knead out a lingering headache. "My thanks for your hospitality. I will try to repay it by identifying those ships."

"We will be grateful. If they are enemies, we can only hope to fight them off. We cannot run."

"Some morning I shall wake to hear good news. But it will not be on this quest."

Tarothin rummaged his staff out from under the bed and was out the door before Eskaia had raised the hem of her outer shift.

* * * * *

Pirvan and Haimya made their way around the mountain while staying on the edge of the thick forest. The going was easier, the chances of spying out sentries or patrols from a distance better, and dragons easier to see, whether friend or foe.

Hipparan was supposed to return at night and seek them out at the head of a small gorge overlooking a ruined castle above the camps. They had so far seen and heard nothing to suggest that he was in peril, but matters might require him to come quickly, find them still more quickly, and lift them out with the speed of the wind.

A good view of the sky might not make so much difference if the black dragon came. The clouds were low, almost brushing the mountaintop, and mist dimmed vision farther down the slopes. A quick dash into the trees might save them from whatever breath weapons the dragon commanded, but he would certainly warn the camp if he saw them. He might also reach deep into the tall timber with dragonfear or whatever other spells he commanded.

Within an hour, they crossed a spring-fed stream that let them fill their canteens, then a stand of trees whose fruit Haimya said was edible.

"At least they look very much like what they call grivan's jug, in the Qualinesti borderlands," she added.

"No doubt, and I admit to being hungry," Pirvan said. "I also remember a friend who confused two very similar kinds of mushroom when he made a stew. Six people were sick, and he was never right afterward."

They munched on trail bread as they strode on.

Hipparan found them when the cloudy sky was still dark gray rather than black. It was also raining, and trees fit to make the pillars of a god's dwelling stood between them and the pirates.

"We should be hard to find without magic," Hipparan said. "I think I have remembered a spell I once knew, to fight off anyone trying to find me by magic. Of course, it may turn out to be a spell for making onion stew. But I believe I can at least confuse anyone casting a spell that needs to be accurately aimed."

"May it be so," Pirvan said.

Even the most potent wizards and mages could not just spray magic across the landscape like a gardener with a watering can. That quickly exhausted the magic-worker and reduced the effect at the other end.

"I have not found the black dragon, but I smelled the scent of at least two lairs," Hipparan went on. "I hope that does not mean two dragons. That would create a difficult situation."

"Your talent for understatement is admirable," Haimya said. "But pray, exercise it some other time. Where are these lairs?"

One was near the southern end of Crater Gulf, too far for anyone but Hipparan to reach. The other was in the ruined castle not far downhill.

"I also sensed traces of magic that wasn't a dragon's," Hipparan went on. "That is all I can say about it. But there were sentries in two camps around the ruins. The camps looked new."

Haimya and Pirvan looked at each other. The thief held his tongue, knowing that they would have as good a plan and also save Haimya's pride if he let her speak first.

Haimya frowned. "I think we should study this castle first. Someone there may know where Gerik is, or be a suitable hostage. Whatever new power Synsaga commands, he cannot afford to waste the lives of his men. That would turn them against him, and dragons and mages are small use when the knife's in your back or the poison's in your wine."

"If you take a captive, I will hide him," Hipparan said.

It seemed they had their night's work as well planned as possible. Hipparan took to the sky with a clap of wings, staying at treetop height until he vanished into the mizzling darkness.

Pirvan heaved his pack again onto his aching back and took up his staff. Matters were not going as badly as they might, which was better than they had for some time. He would not say, "If *Golden Cup* had not been dismasted . . ." for "if" was not a word he honored.

But when he and Haimya were safely away with her betrothed, he would not only be saying farewell to her. He would say farewell to any more traveling aboard ships. If the gods wanted him to change his profession and take up questing, he would do so, but only on dry land.

* * * * *

Lady Eskaia was buckling a belt on over her gown when she heard more hailing from the lookouts. The belt was a simple affair of leather and silver, intended for wear outdoors when it might be needed to support weighty purses, daggers, and the like.

It was also one she could don herself, as was everything else she wore now. Eskaia had never believed in needing maids to put on every garment from shift to gown and from sandals to hat plume. With Haimya's help, she had picked a dozen arrays, for everything from temple ceremonies to berry-picking, that she could put on by herself. Then she had packed that dozen aboard *Golden Cup*.

Some of them would never be the same again, she feared. Salt air and drenchings in seawater wrought enough havoc on the robust garb of sailors. With a respectable woman's wardrobe, they made a shambles of anything they could reach.

Perhaps she should find a good seafarer's tailor when she returned to Istar. A few gowns of heavy wool, with robust trousers to wear underneath (short-drawers let the breezes up), and some sailors' jackets, with a trifle of embroidery to set them apart . . .

Eskaia broke off her musings as she realized that the ship had fallen silent. She snatched a box of hairpins, chose a handful at random, and started putting her hair up. It would be convenient to wear it as short as Haimya's, which never needed more than a ribbon if that, but . . .

The silence ended abruptly in a din, where everyone aboardship seemed to be shouting at once. Eskaia thrust the last pin into her hair and nearly pierced her scalp as the door to her cabin flew open.

"Is knocking an art unknown to sailors?" she snapped. Then she recognized Grimsoar One-Eye.

"Your pardon, my lady." Pirvan's big friend was breathing heavily, and his good eye was twitching fiercely, something she had not seen it do since the dismasting.

"What is happening?"

"Minotaurs, my lady."

"Spare the 'my ladys' and tell me more. Those two ships?"

Grimsoar nodded. "They've the rig of minotaur ships, for certain. Nobody else uses it, or buys a minotaur ship without rerigging her. Ever seen the tackle on a minotaur ship?"

"I've seen minotaurs," Eskaia said. "I can imagine it."

"Good. Then you can imagine that we're in trouble."

"Are minotaurs always hostile? Bad-tempered, yes, but

that's not the same thing—"

Grimsoar laughed. "Glad somebody can find something funny in this. No, I think they're coming in for a fight. They don't look like merchant ships, and even one of their traders might take a chance at us, helpless as we are."

"Thank you," Eskaia said. She hooked her purse on one side of the belt and her dagger on the other. "If you will escort me on deck—"

Grimsoar used several choice phrases that indicated how extremely unlikely it was that he would do any such thing. He also mentioned several gods whose assistance Eskaia would need to get past him.

Eskaia wanted to laugh. But the big man was in a position that she owed it to him not to make more humiliating.

"Step aside, please, Grimsoar."

"Pirvan and Haimya—"

"Are not here. I am my own mistress." She cocked her head to one side, decided not to bat her eyelashes at him, but used her most winning smile.

"Have you orders to keep me below?"

"Ah—"

"No, I suppose."

"Well, put it that way . . ."

"I thought as much. Then please, step aside."

Grimsoar frowned but did not move. Eskaia sighed. She wanted to use some of the big man's words right back at him. There was, however, the dignity of House Encuintras to preserve.

"You cannot keep me below without using force," she said coolly. "If you have no orders to keep me below, then using force will be assaulting me. For that you could be hanged or thrown overboard with weights on your feet.

"Of course, they may decide to spare you until after the fight. You are a good fighting man. But they will certainly expect you to get killed in the fighting. *I* will expect.

"You may live and you will not be dishonored if you let me pass. If you hold me here against my will, you will surely die and you may be dishonored."

Grimsoar's wits were much faster than one might expect in a man of his size and appearance. He sighed and stepped away from the door.

"On your head be it, my lady. Ah—do you want a helmet, so if what's on your head is a stone—?"

"Thank you, Grimsoar."

"I'll see if there's one that fits." He went out, muttering not quite under his breath about the futility of helmets for women who didn't have anything important in their heads.

* * * * *

The two sentries both looked like men farther out in the darkness and much farther from their comrades than they cared for. They were also well armed, one with a bow as well as a sword. Both wore breastplates and low-crowned helmets with rims.

They would still have been no great matter except for one problem. Their post was astride the only route Pirvan and Haimya could take to the castle without passing close to one of the two guard camps. Each of those camps contained twenty times two soldiers, and would have sentries out as thick as bees around a rosebush.

Haimya whispered, "If those two have the wits of a hen, we can't take one without alerting the other. We don't have bows, and one of them does. So we have to be close, silent, and take both of them at once."

Her words did not say that this was impossible or at least dangerous. Her tone was eloquent.

Pirvan feared he would need eloquence, too, if he was to persuade her of the need to avoid killing.

"We also have to leave them alive," he said.

"In our rear?"

"If they are senseless—"

"They can awake and give the alarm. Even their absence from their posts might do that."

"They will be even more absent if we kill them and have to dispose of the bodies. That will cost us time, and perhaps any hope of peace with Synsaga. He may not hold his men back from vengeance for slain comrades."

"You were not so reluctant to kill the night we went to Hipparan."

"Nor will I be reluctant if such a situation comes again. It has not."

Her jaw set. He wanted to loosen it with a kiss, but knew she would in return loosen his teeth, at the very least.

"Haimya, once you spoke of doing the work we came here for. So do I."

A silence broken only by dripping from the trees and a distant rumble of thunder lasted so long that Pirvan wondered if his companion was still breathing. Then she sighed.

"Perhaps a soldier's memories are not always the best guide."

"I will say the same of a thief's. Now, let me turn a thief's eye on these gentlemen."

Pirvan studied the edges of the open ground where the sentries stood. If they had a comrade, even one, hiding under cover—

He saw no one, and his night-sight was as good in the country as in the city. He picked a tree near the left-hand sentry, one whose branches drooped with a burden of seed pods. He began the familiar exercise of committing every detail of the tree to memory, until the spell would let him appear to *be* that tree for a few minutes.

Which, with luck, would be all they needed.

"Pirvan, what—?"

Pirvan put a finger to his lips. He finished the memory work, then motioned Haimya back into the thicket, where they could whisper without fear of being overheard.

"We have to move fast, because I don't know when they relieve the sentries. If we wait, we could stumble on four men instead of two."

"A pleasure I can do without."

"Likewise. But the two—have you noticed that they've chosen places where they can watch without having to move far?"

"Places with good views, too."

"Yes, but their movements are still predictable."

"I have done sentry duty, Pirvan."

"I'm sure of it. And I'm sure you moved around unpredictably. I wasn't trying to teach my grandmother to suck eggs."

"Then what—"

"There's a part of their rounds that brings them close together, close enough that they can be taken together."

"If they weren't out in the open, able to see anyone coming . . ."

"What about trees?"

"Walking trees—?" Her face started to show scorn, then her mouth opened. "Your Spell of Seeing the Expected?"

Pirvan nodded.

* * * * *

By the time Eskaia came on deck, the two minotaur ships were close enough that she could make out details.

They were low, rakish craft, more like Jemar's ships than *Golden Cup*, though minotaur size meant they were higher out of the water. They had two masts, with square rigging on the foremast and lateen on the mainmast, a bowsprit, and what looked unpleasantly like rams at the bows.

As Eskaia watched, minotaurs swarmed into the rigging and clutched lines. Their red-and-green sails vanished, and the ships slowed until the water barely rippled over their rams.

Then white sweeps thrust out of ports set low along the waterline. It made the minotaur ships look as if they had a sea bird's wings.

Kurulus came up beside Eskaia. "Here, Ma'am. Grimsoar found it, but he had to go up forward."

Eskaia set the helmet on her head. It was heavy enough to make her arms tremble while she held it, and her neck trembled after she put it on. She had worn pageant armor for costume parties a few times, but this was very different—smelling of leather, sweat, and oil, tight on top and loose at the sides, and with a chin strap she was making a hopeless botch of tying.

"Let me help you, Ma'am."

She stood, staring at the approaching ships as the crew took battle stations. Most remained on the fore and aftercastles, where they would have the advantage of height. That would make it harder for the minotaurs to force a hand-to-hand grapple, where their superior strength and reach would give them the advantage.

Now the two minotaur ships were turning bows-on to *Golden Cup*'s port side. Smoke curled up from their low aftercastles, and Eskaia wondered if they mounted siege engines, or by some miracle had caught fire.

It was neither. Two smoking pots rose slowly up the mainmasts, until they dangled just below the tops, swaying in the slight breeze. The smoke drifted away downwind, turning from black to brown to pale gray before vanishing in the haze over the sea.

Eskaia started as the mate slammed a large fist against the bulwarks. Her mouth was too dry to let her ask what was happening. Besides, she knew she would learn in moments.

"Sorry, Ma'am," the mate said. His words came out like the last breaths of a dying man. "That's the sign for an honor fight."

"Is that—?"

"Important? Yes. Those minotaurs—they've had their honor attacked. So they're out to regain it. They'll fight hard and demand high ransoms if they win and think we've fought honorably."

"What happens if they think we haven't—?"

"Then they'll give no quarter."

No quarter. No quarter. No quarter. The words tolled in Eskaia's mind like a great bell in some distant shrine, borne down the wind.

Then foam gushed over the enemy's rams, as both teams of rowers dug in their sweeps.

* * * * *

Pirvan raised a hand, then dropped it palm down. The two sentries were both looking away from him. This wouldn't last more than a few seconds, but that would be enough for him to prepare his only spell.

Without looking behind him, he took three steps to the right and two forward, then knelt. The kneeling made him harder to see. He could not safely change position while surrounded by the spell. (That was one of the few things that made him regret not putting himself in the hands of the Towers for more formal testing or training.)

The two sentries seemed to be talking. Certainly they were close enough to do so, without Pirvan hearing. Lower down on the mountain, the jungle life was louder.

The sentry would never accept the tree sprouting from nowhere as he watched. The spell had to be done before the man turned back—

There. Everything around Pirvan took on the wavering aspect of the world seen through the veil of magic. The jungle noises were as loud as ever. So was the sound of footsteps coming up behind Pirvan.

Haimya, barefoot and lightly armed, sprinted up behind Pirvan, slapped both hands on his shoulders, vaulting over him. Her impact jarred him from teeth to knees. For a moment he feared the spell would break.

It did not. What broke was the silence, as Haimya dashed up behind the nearer sentry and punched him in the neck. Then she rammed her knee into the small of his back.

He was the archer. Haimya snatched up bow and quiver almost as the man hit the ground. The other sentry stood gaping at the spectacle of a woman apparently sprung from the earth or fallen from the tree behind her.

Pirvan heard the twang of the bowstring. The arrow skewered the second man's leg—and as he began to dance around on one leg, a third man burst out of cover to Pirvan's right. He ran toward Haimya, a foolish thing when he should have fled to give warning, but showing

211

honorable courage as well.

He also had a good chance of killing Haimya, if he closed faster than she could shoot again. For speed, she had left behind all other weapons but her knife, and he had a sword.

Pirvan's dagger was in his hand before he thought of drawing it, then in the air. The pommel cracked against the third man's temple, below the rim of his helmet. He went down in midstride, furrowing the mud with his face.

Meanwhile the crippled second man had realized it was prudent to flee. Prudence came to him too late. Haimya caught him before he reached cover and kicked him hard under the jaw. If Haimya had not been barefoot, she would have broken his neck, if not taken his head clean off his shoulders.

The Spell of Seeing the Expected had died the moment Pirvan had drawn his dagger. The thief rose to his feet. He really wanted to sit—or better, lie down, preferably with some brandy and a bowl of lamb stew. . . .

"You would make a good soldier, Pirvan," Haimya said as she came up.

Pirvan let her squeeze his shoulders until the worst of the pains were gone. Then he touched the back of his hand to her cheek. It left a muddy streak.

"You would make a good thief, I should say."

"Thank you. Shall we bind these gentlemen and be about our business?"

Chapter 17

Much of the time, Grimsoar One-Eye did not miss his lost eye. Without it he had lost some of his power to judge distances, but that was a loss a man could live with, except in a fight and sometimes even then.

Today would be a fight that everyone who survived it, human or minotaur, would retell to his grandchildren as long as he had breath in his body. A man who could not tell whether a minotaur with an axe was in striking range might have to survive in the stories other men told.

At least he would die among men who would see that his body received decent rites and his death was properly reported to the brothers. That would ensure the lawful division of what he had left behind.

Grimsoar shifted his gaze from the onrushing minotaur ships to study the decks of *Golden Cup*. Lady Eskaia lacked the wits to go entirely below, but remained on the aftercastle. She looked to be well guarded and alert, which was about as much as anyone could contrive now. Up there was a less likely victim of stray arrows or stones, and if the aftercastle fell, *Golden Cup* was doomed anyway.

Gazing forward, Grimsoar sought Tarothin. So did some of the men beside him, the largest, strongest, and most finished fighters aboard. The fore- and aftercastle *had* to be held, but the longer it took the minotaurs to fight their way onto the midships deck (the waist, as sailors called it) . . .

Grimsoar saw no wizard; neither did his comrades, and some of them cursed. Grimsoar clamped a hand on the shoulder of the loudest.

"Tarothin can't do a blessed thing except heal in this battle. Otherwise, we've gone beyond the limits of honor, and the minotaurs will fight to the death. Ours or theirs, it won't matter."

The sailor was suddenly stricken mute. In the next moment a dozen voices cried out as one. A minotaur slid down to the ram of the leading ship, guiding himself with one hand while he held a shatang—the heavy, barbed minotaur throwing spear—in the other. Balancing as if on the level sand of the arena, he raised the shatang and flung it.

"Stand!" Grimsoar bellowed, echoed by Kurulus and the captain. "Flinch, and they'll fight harder."

Nobody flinched, and mercifully the shatang flew high. It cleared the bulwarks and sank a hand's-breadth into the tough wood of the mainmast's stump. Everyone stared at the quivering shaft until Grimsoar walked over to the mast, jerked the spear free, and snapped it over his knee. Then he held up the broken pieces, and made an unmistakable gesture with them. The minotaur spearman shook both fists at Grimsoar, then scrambled back onto the deck of his ship.

No further minotaurs made any such grand gestures; the ships were too close. Indeed, the nearer ship was now within easy bowshot. *Golden Cup* archers let fly from both fore and aft, but Grimsoar saw they'd been given the right orders. None of the arrows sank into minotaur flesh; they merely sprouted from bulwarks, decks, oars, and gear. The minotaurs had been warned, not hurt, let alone enraged.

Not that it ever takes much to get a minotaur into a rage, Grimsoar reminded himself. Even the most honorable ones act like they were born in a bad mood.

The first ship was slowing now, and some of its oars were disappearing through the oar ports. Grimsoar heard someone shout a taunt, but knew that this could hardly be good news for *Golden Cup*.

The next moment proved it. The rowers below were leaving their oars, arming themselves, and swarming on deck. More spears flew, and not warnings or defiant gestures now, but aimed to kill.

Only one shatang found a mark. With its barbed head and the impetus of a minotaur's throw behind it, the spear not only pierced a sailor's throat, it nearly took his head off. His blood was the first to spread across *Golden Cup*'s deck as two of the ship's boys ran to pour sand on it.

Hope we don't run out of sand, was Grimsoar's vagrant thought.

Then the second ship swept past its comrade, oars flashing and rainbows blazing in the spray, driving straight at *Golden Cup*. Its crew seemed determined to show that no beings created by the gods could row like minotaurs.

This ship is supposed to be proof against ramming, Grimsoar reminded himself. Then somewhere in his mind something impudent added: But did anyone tell the minotaurs?

Then the show ended, as the second minotaur ship drove its ram into *Golden Cup*'s side. Grimsoar jerked his head back just as the deck quivered under him. He still needed a good grip to keep from sprawling, and he heard tortured metal screaming and overburdened wood cracking. He could not tell which ship was giving off those agonized sounds.

He could tell the minotaurs' tactics at a glance, however. With the ram wedged in *Golden Cup*'s side, the minotaur whip might not have given the enemy a mortal wound, but it was a wide, firm bridge to let the minotaur crew reach the larger vessel's side amidships.

Reach it, and perhaps swarm onto *Golden Cup*'s decks in numbers that—

Trumpets blared from both sides, drums drowned out the trumpets, and war cries fought to drown out both. The minotaurs' bellowing gave them the advantage in this war of dreadful sounds, but they weren't relying heavily on their stout lungs and deep chests.

The crew of the second ship was already swarming aboard its comrade. Meanwhile, the crew of the first was rushing forward. Some held lines ending in grappling hooks, some hooked poles, and still others light ladders (at least "light" by the measure of minotaurs).

All of them carried more than one weapon, but wore them on their belts or across chests and backs, to leave their hands free for climbing.

Grimsoar finished his previous thought: We may just have too many minotaurs coming aboard to do them much damage with a rearguard action.

Again the blare of trumpets, but this time only from *Golden Cup*, and before they died, Grimsoar heard the whine and hiss of arrows.

* * * * *

Pirvan and Haimya did their best to stay under cover, move quickly, and avoid leaving a trail as they fled the place of their battle with the sentries. The moment the men were found, the hunt would be up, perhaps less merciless because the men were not dead, perhaps not.

On this ground, it was impossible for the thief and warrior-maid to do all three tasks at once, until the rain began. By the time the rain was in full spate, they might as well have been marching under a waterfall. Their footprints vanished before they'd covered fifty paces, the rain itself was as opaque as the undergrowth and much easier to push through, and they hardly needed to move quickly.

Nobody was likely to be following them.

"Nobody may need to follow us, either, if we fall down a cliff in this murk," Haimya reminded Pirvan. She had to put her mouth close to his ear, spit rain out of her mouth, brush strands of hair from her face with her free hand, and then shout to be heard above the rain. When thunder rumbled and crashed across the land, no human voice could make itself heard.

"Are you suggesting we find shelter?" Pirvan replied, making himself understood after four tries. "Look for it, anyway. In this rain I don't know if anything but a cave will do, and somebody may have already claimed it."

"The black dragon?" Haimya asked.

"I was thinking more of sentries who don't want to face the rain. I'm sure you've known that breed."

Haimya had enough wits left to grin at Pirvan's words. "Then you suggest we go on?"

"It's the last thing anybody will be expecting us to do. That makes it the best way of keeping our surprise."

Haimya had the grace to look up at the sky and shake a fist at it before nodding. Pirvan dug in his staff and took the lead.

I hope I don't have to use the Spell of Seeing the Expected, the thief thought. How does one look like a rainstorm, anyway?

* * * * *

As the minotaurs swarmed up *Golden Cup*'s side, to Lady Eskaia they looked like a rockslide—solid brown, black, and gray masses moving in an irresistible wall. Except that this rockslide was sliding up rather than down, each "rock" a strong, seasoned, and well-armed fighter, and there was no safety out of their immediate path. This avalanche would pursue every human aboard *Golden Cup* to death or slavery, unless the humans could fight it to a standstill.

Eskaia began to wonder if she'd been wise to remain on deck. She could hardly do much up here except perhaps get useful fighters killed trying to protect her, and fighting her own fear would be harder. She wanted to put her hand in her mouth and bite down on it hard to stifle a whimper of terror.

But a look over the side told her that the archers' shafts had flown true, once they started shooting to hit live targets. At least one minotaur was sitting down, with a shaft in one arm and another in his left thigh. He was awkwardly trying to work the second arrow clear, when a human archer put a third shaft into his eye. He threw up both arms, fell over backward, and lay still except for a trickle of blood from his mouth.

He wasn't the only minotaur who needed to pluck encumbering shafts from his body, but he was the only one who fell. The rest came on, streaming blood or with rag dressings about their wounds. The first minotaur to reach the deck actually had the stub of an arrow protruding from his belly. Eskaia closed her eyes and shuddered at the thought of how the minotaur must feel.

That much pain ought to be unlawful. . . .

"Are you well?"

Eskaia opened her eyes and saw Kurulus beside her. His voice was tight, and that almost frightened her into another shudder.

"Frightened, yes. Is that a sickness?"

"Right now, it's good sense." Kurulus looked her up and down. "I take that back about the good sense. Is that helmet all the gear you have?"

Eskaia patted her dagger. "I have everything I know how to use. In a fight, anything else is just extra weight."

"You've been listening to that sellsword maid of yours—" Kurulus began.

"She is a shrewder fighter than most aboard this ship, I tell you," Eskaia snapped.

"I don't deny that," Kurulus said. "I only wish she and Pirvan were here now."

"I could wish for a pair of siege engines and fifty Qualinesti archers, too," Eskaia snapped, "but my wish would be as futile as yours."

From below, a sling stone whistled up, parting Kurulus's hair. A finger's-breadth lower and it would have split his skull. The mate drew his sword, a broadsword rather than a sailor's cutlass, and pointed toward the stern.

"Stay behind me. War luck may save you from the minotaurs, but if it doesn't, nothing will save me from Jemar."

"Jemar—?" Eskaia began, knowing she'd heard something not really intended for her ears. But Kurulus was balancing on the railing, then leaped down to the next deck, and at last vanished into the swirling chaos that was now *Golden Cup*'s deck amidships.

Another stone flew, and this one took a sailor in the arm. Before he could cry out, Eskaia was beside him, urging him to the deck while she drew clean cloth and a flask of healing potion from her purse.

With her hands busy, it became almost easy not to think of what might happen next, even not to listen to the charnel house din of what was happening now.

*   *   *   *   *

Pirvan and Haimya found their cliff only after the rain had slackened. In civilized lands, it would still have been called heavy rain, enough to break a drought or send streams out of their banks, but Crater Gulf was not a civilized land.

The thief mentally amended his resolve to avoid quests that took him to sea. He would also *try* to avoid those that took him into jungles, at least during the rainy season (though it had begun to seem doubtful that this coast had any other).

They still had ample warning of the cliff. Unfortunately, this warning did them little good. The sixty-foot drop was by far the easiest way down. Indeed, as the rain lifted more, they saw that it was virtually the only way down on their present route. Elsewhere the descents were either higher, more dangerous, or waterfalls swollen by the rain.

The only other alternative was retracing their steps and taking their chances with alerted sentries, not to mention patrols from the two camps also probably warned by now. Following this route to the castle had at least the same virtue as marching in the rain—it was something that no sane person would be expected to do.

"We'd better lower our heavy packs first," Pirvan said. "Easier and safer than pulling them after us."

At least Haimya made no protest at the idea of climbing down. Her face seemed the same hue as when she had been seasick, but she began unbuckling her pack with steady hands.

It took both ropes together to get the packs safely down, and for a while afterward Pirvan wasn't sure if the slipknot was going to slip. Finally it did its duty and he hauled the rope in hand over hand, watching carefully for places where it might snag or fray against sharp edges.

"This face seems fairly smooth," he said, as he examined the rope.

"Also fairly visible to anyone who wanders by," Haimya said. She looked down. "Oh, pardon. I see that rock spur a trifle farther down the valley. Anyone beyond it won't be able to see the cliff."

"No, and on a day like this nobody is going to be wandering about from idle curiosity," Pirvan said.

"Or perhaps even strictly ordered duty," Haimya said.

"You're the soldier," Pirvan said. She grinned. "Now I want you to move around as if you were dancing," he added. "A lively dance, like something sea barbarians would do in a tavern."

Haimya looked at the cliff. "Let me step back a few paces."

It did not surprise Pirvan to see that each one of Haimya's movements flowed naturally into the next. Had she been dancing in a tavern, she would have danced on silver by the end of the evening.

"Good." He stepped forward and began undoing the knots on one of her pouches.

She raised a hand and gently pushed his away. "Pirvan,

what *are* you doing?"

"Sorry. I should have explained." He told her briefly about the need for having all one's gear balanced while climbing.

"I balanced mine without thinking, but I nearly forgot that you don't have a thief's training."

"Perhaps I should gain it," Haimya said. This time she made no protest when he started rearranging her gear.

Pirvan shook his head. "Ten years ago I would have said that. Now—I don't know."

"Night work is hard for one who is more good than not, I suppose."

"You flatter me, Haimya. I'll go where the gods put me, when they tell me where that is. But meanwhile, I wouldn't mind work that let me sleep easier of nights. I beg your pardon," he added, realizing that his hands were roaming over parts of Haimya's body that might give offense.

"None needed," Haimya said. Her smile showed a good many teeth; also true warmth. "But do keep your thoughts on the serious work. Else we shall end up sleeping together at the bottom of this cliff never to wake."

* * * * *

Grimsoar One-Eye had fought minotaurs twice before, once in a wrestling bout that not only began friendly but remained that way, and once in a brawl that was unfriendly from beginning to end. It had taken a skilled healer to put his back and hip in order after the brawl, which had left him willing thereafter to keep his distance from minotaurs.

Now he found himself close enough to half a score of minotaurs to bite their ears or gouge their eyes if it came to that—which it might, as these minotaurs seemed to put wide limits on what was honorable in fighting humans. . . .

At least they followed minotaur tradition in not using shields. But it was hard to reach the life in those massive bodies with most human weapons without coming in reach of the deadly sweep of the minotaurs' arsenals. They were following tradition in another respect as well—most of them had foresworn shields in order to wield two weapons at once.

About all that had kept the minotaurs from sweeping the decks was the close quarters of the fight. The minotaurs could not choose their distance and chop their smaller opponents apart like a kitchen maid with a cabbage. There was simply no room for that, and many chances for humans to slip under the swing of the kausin or the clabbard and thrust or slash at a minotaur's unprotected flesh.

Grimsoar had an improvised shield, a barrel lid. In the next moment it saved him, as a minotaur thrust with a katar. Not all minotaur weapons needed room. Grimsoar caught the katar's point in the barrel lid, felt it being twisted out of his grasp by sheer brute strength, and slashed crosswise with his cutlass.

The heavy blade rode up the minotaur's chest and caught him across the throat. It drew blood but did not reach his life, as he wore a collar of bone plates. Grimsoar snatched his cutlass free and wished he were as agile as Pirvan, able to kick up under the shield and take the minotaur in a painful if not deadly spot. *That* would end the big bull's enthusiasm for hacking a reputation out of human bodies.

Instead of kicking, Grimsoar spun and rammed the edge of the barrel lid where he had planned to land his foot. The effect was similar. As the minotaur bellowed and doubled over, the big man also rammed his head up under the minotaur's jaw. He wondered if he'd cracked his skull, but knew that the minotaur was no longer in front of him.

His head aching, Grimsoar plunged through the gap left by the wounded minotaur. His shield splintered under a tessto blow, but he snatched his arm clear in time and opened the tessto wielder's arm with his cutlass. That would be the end of the tessto wielding for today;

the huge spiked club was a brutally heavy weapon even for a minotaur.

Arrows whined past, thudding into wood or flesh. Grimsoar roared a wordless protest at such wild archery from the castles, then realized he'd completely pierced the minotaurs' line. He was behind them, where the archers fore and aft had been showering arrows to keep the minotaurs on the ships from joining their comrades.

They hadn't completely succeeded, judging from the number of minotaurs fighting aboard *Golden Cup*. Grimsoar decided to help the archers, even at the risk of taking a friendly arrow between his ribs.

He whirled and slashed a minotaur across the back of both knees. The wounds weren't deep, but they maddened the opponent even more. He whirled in turn, swinging a double-bitted axe with all his unimpaired speed and strength.

Speed and strength might have been unimpaired; judgment was not. The minotaur was heedless of his comrades and only the axe turning in his hand saved two of them from serious wounds. The two minotaurs mistakenly assaulted turned on their comrade, raising their own weapons and completely ignoring Grimsoar.

The human had plenty of time to slash one minotaur's good arm (he was the tessto wielder, now without his club but with a shortened shatang that looked quite capable of killing any human who ever walked). The pain didn't make him drop his remaining weapon, but it made him thrust wildly. Grimsoar caught the shaft in his free hand and heaved. Off balance, the minotaur stumbled into his comrade, just as the other axe victim was throwing a punch at the axe wielder.

The punch connected—with the side of the tessto wielder's head. A horn snapped off nearly at the root, all three minotaurs bellowed loudly enough to drown out the rest of the battle, and Grimsoar knew that he'd pushed his luck far enough. Fighting with minotaurs front and back and friendly arrows above could have only one ending, and that soon.

A flight of arrows finished off the tessto wielder the moment Grimsoar burst through the minotaur line and rejoined the human ranks.

* * * * *

Haimya went down the cliff first.

"I can hold you if you fall, but I doubt the same is true the other way," Pirvan said.

"I was not going to argue," Haimya replied. "Really."

Pirvan raised one eyebrow. Haimya clenched a fist and mock-punched him in the jaw. Then she stepped to the edge of the cliff and looked down.

"I wouldn't do that—" Pirvan began.

This time Haimya's face was grim as she turned to him. "I have to know how much it frightens me."

What blood does flow in your veins, my lady comrade? Pirvan thought. Admitting one's fear might not everywhere and always be called the highest form of courage, but it showed loyalty to those who depended on you.

Such a woman would also demand that same high loyalty from others. Can I offer it? And even if I can, does it matter?

It was clearer than ever to Pirvan, that something good would pass out of his life when Haimya and Gerik Ginfrayson were reunited. Better that, however, than something good passing out of the world entirely by Haimya's falling down the cliff.

It would help if we don't have to do this very often, he mused. Indeed, there is much to be said for questing on level ground, if one's comrade is not a thief-trained climber.

* * * * *

Eskaia forgot how many men she'd treated when the healing potions and the clean cloths ran out. She'd barely noticed that both purse and flask were empty when a ship's boy thrust another wad of cloth at her.

"I need more potion," she snapped. "Where is Tarothin?"

"Don't know, milady. For'ard, I think. That's where the worst hurts been going, mostly."

Eskaia thought sailors' words about boys who could not tell you anything useful, then straightened up. Her head was throbbing from the sun beating on the helmet, and her back and arms ached from the bending and healing. She pressed both hands to the small of her back and gave a little sigh as the pain eased.

Standing, she had a view of the deck amidships. Humans and minotaurs now had *Golden Cup*'s waist divided between them. The minotaurs were outnumbered, thanks to hard fighting on deck and the human archery playing on their reinforcements from the ships. But they'd also strewn the deck with enough human dead that the humans below had no hope of driving the boarders back to their ships.

To Eskaia, it seemed that no one would ever again question the courage or honor of these minotaurs, through all the ages to come. She herself would not listen to a breath uttered against that courage and honor—though their judgment might be another matter.

Minotaurs on deck bellowed, and others replied from the ships. Four of the minotaurs on deck turned to face the humans. The others—Eskaia thought she counted seven—turned aft. One of them bellowed again.

Then they charged the ladder to the aftercastles.

The charge caught the men on the lowest deck by surprise, and four went down in bloody ruin almost before they knew they were in danger. One of the survivors thrust a pike wildly at a minotaur's throat, and by sheer chance drove the point home. The minotaur wrenched the weapon free, snatched it from its wielder, swung it like a club, and broke the man's skull.

Then the minotaur fell backward on to the deck, knocking down a comrade. The throat-pierced minotaur did not rise again, as his blood joined all the rest on the deck. The second minotaur gave the loudest bellow Eskaia had yet heard from any hostile throat in this ear-piercing battle, and returned to the attack.

Five men remained, two of them archers. The archers scrambled sternward, one of them nearly knocking Eskaia down as he climbed over the railing. But they had no weapons for close work other than daggers, and they began shooting again the moment they were safe.

Three men against six minotaurs was not a fight. It was a massacre. To do them justice, the minotaurs did not play with their smaller opponents, like cats with mice. They simply drove at them from three sides, wielding kausins, clabbards, and katans. One minotaur also had the hideous mandoll, with a silvered spike on the armored gauntlet— or at least Eskaia thought it was silvered under the blood.

The merchant princess did not realize how fast the minotaurs were coming until one of them reached over the railing toward her. She wanted to run, but discovered that sheer terror had joined fatigue to root her feet to the deck. The minotaur was the one with the mandoll, and now the spike looked as large as a spear as the attacker drew back his arm for a straight punch at Eskaia's head, to splatter her brains across *Golden Cup*'s deck—

Fury boiled up in Eskaia, ending the paralysis. She dived as the mandoll lunged forward, and the spike only scraped across her helmet. She landed rolling, drawing her dagger as she rolled, taking boots in the head and ribs as sailors tried to get out of her way, and ended up lying by the railing.

It took her a moment to realize that she was invisible to the minotaur, but that she could see his whole chest and stomach through the railing. His whole *unarmored* chest and stomach.

In the next moment, the minotaur discovered that Lady Eskaia knew precisely how to use her dagger. Haimya had taught her well, though she lacked the strength of wrist and arm to make a deadly thrust with those alone.

Instead, she put not just wrist and arm, but shoulders, back, and all her slight weight into the thrust. It was like carving overdried meat or piercing thick leather, but she'd done both before and she did as well now.

The minotaur did not bellow. He howled like a hundred lost souls crying out from the Abyss, and clutched at the railing. Wood cracked, and as Eskaia gripped the dagger in both hands for a second thrust, the railing suddenly vanished in front of her.

By then it was too late for her to stop her thrust. It went home, and the minotaur convulsed as she reached his life. The minotaur's death throes plucked the dagger from her hand, but not before they also pulled her through the shattered railing and onto the deck below, in the midst of the five remaining minotaurs.

* * * * *

Pirvan did not breathe easily until Haimya stood on solid ground at the foot of the cliff and raised both hands in the agreed signal for a safe landing. Indeed, he could have sworn he did not breathe at all, but knew that, as he was not a sea elf, this was impossible.

What was not impossible was his slipping and breaking his own neck or other vital parts through carelessness on his own way down. Haimya's safety was necessary for the completion of their quest; it was not by itself sufficient.

Pirvan was more careful than usual to breathe steadily and stop whenever his hands shook. He had learned these and other elementary safety precautions of climbing before he had seen his nineteenth year, but they did not seem as easy to remember now as they had before he had entered the Encuintras estate—it seemed years ago, now.

All his caution made the descent slower and noisier than it might have been. His hands were shaking harder than ever as he finally coiled up the rope, and he had a rope burn on one cheek.

But he could see (or rather hear) that no one was going to easily discover them here. A rain-swollen stream boiled past only twenty paces away, filling the valley with an endless echoing roar and hiss. A dozen hearty dwarven smiths all working hard at their forges would have been lost in the tumult of the stream. It was also the only way out of the valley—unless they felt equal to a climb back up the cliff.

Pirvan felt weary even thinking of that course. Instead he began collecting their packs and studying them for damage, while Haimya contemplated the ribbon of silver spray and churning greenness.

"I think there's a shallower spot a trifle farther downstream," she said, pointing. He noticed for the first time that part of her left forearm was scraped red, almost bloody, from some brush with the rocks.

"Shallow enough to let us cross dryshod?"

"Not unless Hipparan flies down to carry us or Paladin himself builds a bridge. But it looks as if we won't be swept away if we use the ropes. Oh, and on this passage, I think I should be the leader."

It made sense, since she swam better than he and climbing would not be needed. More sense than the other way around, and infinitely more sense than a quarrel.

None of this good sense, however, will do much for the pain of seeing her drown before my eyes, thought Pirvan.

* * * * *

Eskaia did the first thing that came to her mind, which was not screaming. Instead, it was kicking. Her first kick landed on a minotaur's ankle, and had about the same effect as kicking a mature oak tree.

The second kick, she aimed higher, aware that her gown was likely to leave her quite immodestly garbed and totally indifferent to the fact. The second kick enjoyed better luck, as it struck a minotaur who was stooping down to clutch this rare prize suddenly fallen at his feet.

Delivered by Grimsoar One-Eye or even Haimya, the kick might have done real injury to the minotaur's person. As it was, it injured his balance and self-command. He reeled backward, throwing out his arms with a bellow of rage. One arm struck a jutting splinter of railing, hard enough to drive barbed wood through hairy, leathery hide. The minotaur bellowed louder.

At this point, one of his comrades clutched at his flailing arm, to immobilize it and extract the splinter. This put two minotaurs momentarily out of the fight, leaving only three to seize Eskaia.

The two archers above promptly reduced this number by one more. At close range, both arrows pierced the minotaur's chest. He plucked one arrow out, but the other was deep in a lung. Feeling death in him, he lunged for the men above, gripping one by the ankle. He heaved, and the man flew over his head. The man's head struck the deck a hammerblow, also breaking his neck. Then the minotaur grasped the second arrow, gasped as it came free, coughed blood, and fell.

He nearly fell on Lady Eskaia, and her survival under those circumstances (and that minotaur) would have been precarious. However, he fell beside her, where the two free minotaurs had to step over or around him to be within reach of Eskaia.

Before they could do this, arrows and men hit them from above and men hit them from below. Also, Lady Eskaia hit them from within their own ranks, wielding a katar she'd snatched up. She had to use both hands for it, but the crossbar hilt gave plenty of room. She thrust into the back of a minotaur's thigh, then slashed another wound across his posterior as he whirled to skewer her with his shatang.

The spear pierced her gown without piercing her flesh. She was pinned to the deck, but the shatang's head drove so far into the planks that the minotaur had to fight to free it. This battle cost him more time than he could afford; Kurulus leaped up behind him and hamstrung him with two quick, brutal slashes of his sword.

Then Eskaia's greatest danger was being trampled to death before she could free herself. She finally rolled desperately, tearing her gown free of the shatang. As she staggered to her feet, she hoped she had not torn it entirely free of her body as well.

Then two hands large enough to belong to a minotaur

gripped Eskaia under the shoulders and heaved her upward. She flew through the air, until four smaller hands caught her and lowered her to the next deck sternward.

She gripped the nearest solid objects, not caring whether they were animate or inanimate, or even minotaur or human. She would *not* fall down in a faint over a mere narrow escape from capture or death by minotaurs. She would save that for something serious, such as a proposal of marriage or being with child.

One immodest thought led to another—how much was left of her gown? She had the undeniable sensation of breezes blowing on places that should not have been exposed to breezes. Before she could look down, someone behind her reached over her shoulder and handed her a sailor's cloak. It was large enough to make a tent for two women her size, but it certainly satisfied all possible requirements of modesty.

It did not, however, satisfy the requirements of mobility. It dragged on the deck, and on her third step Eskaia stumbled over the heavy wool. She would have fallen if one of those large hands hadn't held her up.

"Grimsoar?"

"What would Haimya and Pirvan say if you were killed? Compared to them, minotaurs are a trifle."

He tried to keep her turned away from the ship's waist, but she looked anyway. She counted more than twenty bodies, human and minotaur, and could not find a stretch of unbloodied deck larger than a man's hand. Two of the ship's boys lay dead beside their overturned sand buckets, one impaled on a shatang, the other with his head split—

"Excuse me."

Eskaia gripped her dignity for a few moments longer, then dashed for the side. She almost reached it. Grimsoar waited until her stomach was empty, then offered her a clean cloth dipped in clean water—something, she suspected, by now almost as precious as healing potion.

That brought Tarothin back to her mind.

"We have to begin the healing work. Are the minotaurs driven off? Is Tarothin safe? Where is he? Is there any more healing potion? I need a new gown before I can—"

Grimsoar pointed over the side. Both minotaur ships now rested on their oars just out of bowshot. The sides of the one that had rammed *Golden Cup* was smeared with blood and seemed to be lower in the water.

"They'll be back. They've left bodies aboard, and they can't do that without losing honor."

"Suppose we threw the bodies—?"

Grimsoar said something that shocked even Eskaia's newly hardened ears. "Then they'll fight to the death, and if they capture anybody, they'll torture him to death. Don't even think that again. They might have a mage aboard, as witness, and some minotaur mages can read thoughts."

"Then let me find Tarothin, and we can try to heal any who are still alive. After we've done the work with our own—"

"No time for that. The lookouts have sighted two more ships approaching. One's too far off to identify, but the one in the lead is minotaur-rigged."

Eskaia wished she knew all of Grimsoar's words and a few more besides, preferably in the minotaur tongue so that she could curse them and be understood by even the meanest rower among them That wish might not be granted. What could she hope for?

"Very well. If we have to treat the bodies honorably, let us drag them off the open deck. They will not be the better for being trodden on by their comrades. Nor will we be the better for stumbling over them.

"Any who survive can be healed when we have leisure. But none will survive if they must endure another battle—"

"Aye, aye, Captain Eskaia," Grimsoar said, in chorus with Kurulus. The mate had joined them during Eskaia's outburst.

"If you are mocking—" Eskaia began.

"Your pardon," Kurulus said, and his stricken tone told her that he was sincere. "You are wise and honorable, and we will do as you suggest."

"Thank you," Eskaia said. She hoped they would do it without her watching. She needed to sit down, drink something (even water), and change her gown. The dignity of House Encuintras, as well as her own, required that last measure.

Chapter 18

Haimya led Pirvan across the rain-swollen stream with the same finished skill as he had used in contriving their way down the cliff. When they finished the crossing, they were no wetter than they had been, as this was impossible. More serious, they had hardly a dry article of clothing or a bite of food that had not turned to a dog's breakfast.

"We can steal food and clothing if need be," Haimya said. "But Kiri-Jolith grant that we can see to our weapons before much longer. I do not care to approach an enemy's camp with a sword that may be rusted into its scabbard before it comes time to draw it."

Indeed, Pirvan had begun to weigh the merits of an alternative course of action: Summon Hipparan, ride him into the enemy's stronghold, snatch Gerik Ginfrayson, and fly beyond the reach of Synsaga's men, the mage's spells or the black dragon.

It was much easier—except that it offered not much

more chance of success than a stealthy approach on foot, as well as risking Hipparan's life against both magic and the brute strength of an evil dragon not improbably stronger and shrewder than he was. That was more than Pirvan could in good conscience ask of Hipparan, unless for a much better reason than letting him and Haimya cover the last few miles of their journey dryshod.

Sodden as they were, the packs weighed even more, and it was good fortune that the ground beyond the stream was all downhill and much of it easy going as well. It might prove still better fortune that the firelighters in their packs seemed uninjured. Now all they needed was something dry to burn, a safe place to light the fire, and time to use the heat to dry everything they possessed, from the skin out.

Failing all of these things, they kept marching.

The smell of woodsmoke warned them long before they saw the fire, and they saw the fire long before they saw the silhouettes around it. Creeping close, they saw that the silhouettes were human, and heard speech in Common with half a score of accents.

Creeping closer, they listened.

"—a tree spirit. Had to be," one man said. "Just the tree there one moment, the next moment the woman leaping out of it at me. No footprints either."

"An army of giant ogres wouldn't have left tracks, not in this rain," somebody else said. "Proves not a thing."

"No, it proves one thing," a third man said, in a voice that seemed to carry authority. "Synsaga's not the man he used to be. Why would he leave old hands like us out in the rain, facing who knows what, while letting people like that Istarian play lapdog to Fustiar?"

Somebody suggested that being so close to the mage was maybe not much of a privilege, and drew a chorus of agreement. Somebody else added that the Istarian had, after all, sworn the true oath to Synsaga.

"A year ago," the voice of authority said. "A year ago, and him a captive for no more than two months before that. I've served Synsaga ten years, and where am I?"

"There was the king who had a tame sea troll," another

voice put in. "After ten years he asked the king for a promotion. The king told him that after ten years, he was still a sea troll."

Pirvan expected—indeed hoped—that the next sound they heard would be a brawl, as the insulted man took his vengeance in blood. Instead he heard a stifled whimper from Haimya, and then loud, raucous laughter.

"Think you can draw me into a fight for my place, Gilsher?" he asked. "I'll play games by your rules when that Istarian lapdog rides the dragon!"

After that, everybody seemed to talk at once. Pirvan listened, trying to draw some sense out of the babble, but he heard little except tales of battles and bawdy encounters. They made enough noise that he could not have heard much from Haimya unless she had come up and spoken into his ear.

So it was a surprise, when it came time to turn and slip away, to find himself alone.

* * * * *

Jemar the Fair had been in *Windsword*'s prow since first light. He would gladly have watched from the masthead, but for knowing that he would pay the price by being too weary to fight when battle was joined.

At dawn one could have said "if." Now it was definitely "when." The minotaur ship fled before *Windsword* at a pace that had to be wearying its rowers. The ship had been moving under full sail even as *Windsword*'s crewmen had sighted it, then wheeled sharply around to the south and fled under both sail and oars.

Windsword was lighter and faster; minotaur ships had to be stoutly built simply to carry their crews. Jemar's ship had slowly gained on its quarry all morning. Meanwhile, the signal to the other four ships in the line had been to continue their search. Minotaurs seldom went to war in a single ship; the fleeing vessel might be doing so as a stratagem to draw *Windsword* away from its comrades, who even now might be closing in on *Golden Cup*.

To make his ship grow wings and fly, or even give his men the strength of ogres for a day, Jemar the Fair would have struck any bargain with any being, human or otherwise, who could grant him such gifts. As it was, he could only peer ahead across the sun-dappled sea, watching the minotaur ship grow larger with a slowness that prickled like fleas under armor.

Even if they caught the ship, he reminded himself, there would most likely still be a hard fight. He had no authority to order the minotaurs out of these waters, and even if he had, they would not go without a battle. But he was confident that his seasoned fighters could overcome any reasonable number of minotaurs without offending anybody's honor.

Then it would be time to ask a few questions about the reasons for the presence of minotaurs on this coast, their strength, any other peaceful ships that might have fallen into their net. . . .

"Deck ahoy! Three ships, two points off the port bow."

Jemar cupped his hands to reach the masthead with his reply. "Three ships, you say?"

"Aye, Captain. Can't say what kind, for now."

Jemar nibbled his lower lip. He wanted to bite hard enough to draw blood. Keep after the minotaur ship, overhaul it, and go on as he'd planned all day? Or gamble that these three ships might include *Golden Cup*, go about and head that way?

If he broke off the pursuit, the minotaur ship ahead would undoubtedly escape, to continue a career of havoc among the peaceful shipping routes. But if he allowed the ship to draw him away from the others, and one of them was *Golden Cup*, in danger . . .

In such case, Lady Eskaia's blood would be on his hands, and though she might be dead already, he would always hear her death cries at night, until his eyes closed for the last time. He might be throwing away a certain gain for only a possible one, but gambling took on a different color when the stakes were human lives.

A ship's boy ran aft, with orders to the helmsman. Sailors heaved the sails about, the beat of the oars changed, and everyone not rowing, steering, or hauling on lines began to break out the arms chests.

Jemar had armored himself with brass-studded leather jack, silvered, open-faced helm with its plume of scarlet-dyed sea gull feathers, cutlass, and dagger, when the lookout hailed the deck again.

"Captain, it's three ships, all right. Two of them look minotaur-built."

For a moment, Jemar's throat was too dry to let him speak. Before he could—

"Hoaaa!" the lookout squalled. "The third one's big, and she's dismasted. Looks like *Golden Cup*."

Jemar did not kneel in prayer. He knelt because his knees, briefly, would not support him. However, he let it be known that he had prayed to Habbakuk for an honorable victory, and no one was the wiser.

No one was the happier, either, for seeing the pursued minotaur ship turn about and become the pursuer. The wind was now on *Windsword*'s best point of sailing, however, and Jemar could rest half his rowers and still keep his distance from the minotaurs.

What might happen when all five ships were together depended very much on what had happened aboard *Golden Cup*. If it was holding strongly against the minotaur attack, Jemar's help might turn the battle.

If it was already a prize, however, Jemar knew he might have a busy time saving himself and his ship from three minotaur vessels. The odds would be long, until the rest of his own ships understood that he'd been gone to the south far too long and came in search of him—or of vengeance for both him and *Golden Cup*.

Life would be simpler and merrier, Jemar decided, if *Windsword* could reach *Golden Cup* in time to make all that extra work unnecessary.

* * * * *

Pirvan could not remember ever having been so frightened in his life as when he saw that Haimya was missing.

No, he reminded himself, you were at least as frightened when you thought the sea naga had taken her.

There would be no sea nagas in this jungle, but otherwise it was no easy guess what had become of Haimya. She might have taken a wrong turn, encountered a silent menace such as a poisonous snake, or been ambushed and captured by sentries set out beyond the circle of firelight.

Reluctantly, Pirvan also considered that she might have been tried beyond endurance by hearing of the mysterious Istarian. Or perhaps not so mysterious—if the man was not Gerik Ginfrayson, then Synsaga was holding two Istarian captives.

Two Istarian captives—one of whom had turned his coat. That could hardly be doubted, with all the men had said.

No, believing in coincidence was often soothing, but seldom wise. Haimya's betrothed had sworn oath to Synsaga, and even worse, was now in the confidence of the man's pet mage (though the mage doubtless considered Synsaga *his* "pet pirate").

At least he was alive and fit. But rescuing a man who did not care to be rescued, who might think he was better off where he was, who might betray his would-be rescuers to Synsaga . . .

Pirvan shuddered and thought that perhaps he now had sufficient cause to summon Hipparan. But the copper dragon could not aid the search for Haimya without alerting every man in Synsaga's camp and ships. So far, even the fallen sentries seemed to suspect little, except perhaps evil creatures of the jungle (and Pirvan found these easy to believe in). The advent of a dragon would be another matter.

He would wait for Haimya's return before he summoned Hipparan, and he would wait here. Even if Haimya wished to be found, they might well lose each other if he moved into the jungle. Also, if she had been captured, sooner or later she would be brought to the camp. Then Pirvan would know how matters stood, and do his best to give her a quicker and cleaner death, if nothing more.

Pirvan shifted to a tree that was thick enough to generously guard his back. There he unslung his pack, drew fallen branches under him until he was at least not sitting directly in the mud, and did his best to relax. He could see to three sides, his dagger was in his hand, and he could at least guard what little remained of his strength. . . .

Someone was approaching. Without opening his eyes, Pirvan rolled away from the footsteps, sprang to his feet, and aimed both free hand and dagger hand entirely by sound.

He halted the dagger's thrust only when he felt hair finer than any man's, as well as a smooth chin. He opened his eyes to see Haimya standing before him, arms at her sides. He stepped back, she put her hands over her face, then she crumpled like a puppet with cut strings.

Pirvan caught her so that she did not sprawl in the mud, took off her pack, then leaned her back against the tree. Soon after that, he found himself holding her hand and wrapping his free arm around her shoulders.

She did not weep loudly, from either self-command or fear of arousing the camp. But long shudders went through her, and tears streamed down her face no matter how hard she tried to squeeze her eyes shut.

Even if they'd been farther from the enemy, Pirvan had nothing to say that wouldn't sound ludicrous or insult Haimya's intelligence. If he could not lighten any of her other burdens, he could at least not add those.

They sat there under the tree until the campfire glowed more brightly, in a sinister twilight as clouds crept over the jungle. No rain fell, and Haimya finally spoke.

"Pirvan—"

"I will hear it if you must say it. You owe me nothing."

She stroked his cheek. "On the contrary. I owe you much for your silence. You—you did not judge me."

"Keeping my tongue out of other people's troubles seems to be the one lawful skill I have," Pirvan said with a shrug. "Also, we need not assume the worst about Gerik until we know the truth from his own mouth."

"How are we to do that? The dragon—"

"Hipparan or the black?"

"The black dragon—he will strike at Hipparan the moment our friend appears. But without his aid, how are we to reach Gerik and take him with us, if he has gone over to evil?"

"Synsaga may not be wholly evil—"

"Synsaga is not Gerik's new master, if the men are to be believed." Haimya realized that she'd raised her voice, took a deep breath, and continued in a whisper.

"If he follows the mage, I cannot imagine him leaving the man to return with us. Even if he wished to, the mage would not allow it. He would summon the black dragon and make an end to all three of us."

To Pirvan, this did not seem to suggest any particular course of action, other than continuing to do without Hipparan. Haimya did not seem likely to welcome a statement of the obvious, however.

After a long silence, Haimya shook her head and finger-combed her hair. That made it look more rather than less chaotic, but the gesture seemed to give her strength.

"I will not abandon Gerik over what pirates mutter around a campfire. I will trust his honor, to speak the truth and allow us to go free, insofar as that is in his power. If the mage proves treacherous, then we summon Hipparan."

"That means penetrating the mage's stronghold, I would say."

"Of course. Remember, we have the second task, of learning what powers Synsaga's mage may command."

This left unspoken the matter of living to pass on what they learned to others. However, it seemed that one had to quest as one lived—one day at a time, giving tomorrow enough thought for prudence but not forgetting the present while contemplating the future.

They were helping each other to their feet when a harsh scream rent the twilight. It seemed to come from far above, and as Pirvan listened he could hear that the screamer was moving swiftly. They listened, clasped in each other's arms, until the scream died and only the common sounds of the jungle twilight were audible.

Pirvan's feet itched with the urge to put as much distance as possible between himself and what had screamed out from the sky. He admonished himself for his lack of courage and honor and forced himself into movement. Behind him, Haimya tested the draw of her sword, lifted her staff, and followed.

* * * * *

The minotaurs took so long in rallying for their second attack that some aboard *Golden Cup* began to hope the enemy had given up the struggle. Grimsoar ruthlessly trod on those hopes, knowing that defenders unmanned by dashed hopes would not hold against minotaurs or indeed less formidable foes.

"The only way they'll not be back is if the two chiefs or captains or whatever they're calling themselves have a quarrel. Then they'll have to go off and settle it by a duel to the death, before one leader's warriors will follow the others. But even then, they'll be back. They might even be back before other minotaurs or Synsaga's pirates find us."

That was a long speech for Grimsoar, particularly when he expected to need all his breath for fighting before he was more than hours older. At least the breath he'd put into it wasn't wasted; the "Maybe it's over" mutterings fell, and the scrape of whetstones sharpening blades rose.

Kurulus was none too hopeful, either, about the minotaurs' fleeing or *Golden Cup*'s chances of meeting the next assault. "We're more than half out of arrows," he whispered, "and a good half our blades need more of an edge than we can give them aboard ship. You'd think any sailor who ever ate ship's biscuit would keep himself a blade tough enough for minotaur hide. But, no, they pay half a month's wages to some chandler who wouldn't know a good blade when it sliced off his nose!"

The mate of the top went off, muttering into his beard. A bellow from the aftercastle reminded Grimsoar of another problem—the healing potions were nearly gone, and Tarothin's strength seemed likely to be the next thing to vanish. The ship's own healer had no skills to equal Tarothin's, but was doing his best on the minotaurs and the less gravely hurt humans. Grimsoar could only hope that the man's best would be good enough, if not to save the minotaurs, then at least to meet their comrades' standards of honor.

Off to port, the minotaur ship that had rammed *Golden Cup* was now well down by the bow. At its stern, a steady stream of minotaurs was crossing a gangway to the undamaged ship. One ship going down was likely to mean bad blood between the two leaders, with the leader of the sunken ship fighting to keep his position.

It was too much to hope for that the quarrel would break out in time to save *Golden Cup*. So the big man kept his sword handy when he stretched out on the least bloody piece of deck he could find.

Some time later, Grimsoar awoke with a headache from the sun, nausea from the uncleaned-barn smell of minotaur bodies, and a thirst fit to empty a small lake. It did empty a whole jug of water—they weren't going to die of thirst today, whatever else might kill them—and after that he felt nearly recovered.

He felt still better when he saw that his sword was still fighting-fit, and best of all when Lady Eskaia came down amidships to thank him. She even kissed him, though she had to stand on tiptoe to do it, and he was greatly tempted to pick her up again and let her do the job properly—until he saw that his hands were caked halfway up his arms with dried blood.

Before he could wash them, the lookouts shouted what every man on deck could see with his own eyes, that the minotaurs were coming in again. Grimsoar pointed at the aftercastle, and to his surprise and relief a white-faced Lady Eskaia actually ran for shelter!

The only problem was, she ran toward the forecastle.

"If I'm no use on deck, I can still help the wounded," she shouted. "Most of them are still forward, aren't they?"

"Yes, but—"

"Thank you, Grimsoar. I am more grateful to you than ever!"

She vanished, leaving Grimsoar wondering if the simplest solution to his problems wouldn't be flinging himself overboard straight away. Then he decided that even if he was going to do such a thing, he should do it after the minotaurs had laid alongside again.

After all, he was heavy enough, falling from a height, to crush even the largest minotaur.

* * * * *

Night had come to the jungle and sleep to Haimya when Pirvan heard the warbling above. It seemed just above the treetops, as if whoever made it wanted to stay low. It also seemed stationary, as if the warbler had found a rock outcropping or a treetop and perched there while calling.

Pirvan looked at Haimya, whose breath rasped in a way he did not like. For all the hardiness she'd learned as a soldier, she had been out of the field for a good long while, living on the bounty of House Encuintras. She was bearing up well, but lung fever could strike down anyone after such an ordeal.

Lung fever, and the nearest healer in Synsaga's pay, and evil in his own right as well.

Pirvan had given some thought to wounds, but none to this. He was reproaching himself when branches crackled above and a lighter patch of darkness descended before him.

"Welcome, Hipparan," he said.

"I trust so," the dragon said. He looked up. "Good. No opening remains in the branches."

"I didn't know there was one at all."

"There was not, until I made it. You wish to know how, of course? I contrived to vary my spell of softening, and made the branches so flexible that I could push through them silently. This left no broken branches to mark my trail or my hide. I do not wish scars so young, when I may yet mate."

"I'm sure that you are the finest of all copper dragons, and keeping your scales unscarred will indeed win you a mate worthy of you. But what have you—?"

The sound of a dragon clearing his throat interrupts both thought and speech. Pirvan was silent, conscious of vast eyes and an equally vast intelligence behind them both regarding him with something less than favor.

"Forgive me," Hipparan said at last. "I sense that your mate sickens. Healing is not in me, or I would offer it."

"Haimya is not my mate," Pirvan said. This was not the time he would have chosen to discuss human customs, but he remembered that clearing of the dragon's throat. "She is sworn to the one we seek to ransom. If she is released from her oath and he from his, *then* each will be free to seek other mates. Only then."

"Well, then, you should certainly offer for her if she becomes free," Hipparan said, with a tone of having settled the matter.

An unlikely sound interrupted both thief and dragon— Haimya giggling. Or rather, trying unsuccessfully to stifle giggles.

"Under such circumstances," she said at last, "I might even give him permission. But we can only know my betrothed's true mind if we speak to him. Or have you found where he is and brought a message from him?"

"The best place to seek him is definitely in the mage's tower. He is more guest there than prisoner, but the mage does not seem to trust him entirely. But then, he is the sort who trusts no one. Also, he drinks." A snow-haired priestess of Mishakal could not have spoken with a tone of such complete distaste.

"As far as I can see, the better for us if he falls head-first into a wine barrel and drowns," Haimya said. There was a brittle lightness in her voice that told Pirvan she was not done with her pain, and hinted that fever had come to join it.

"Indeed. The fewer spells he casts, the better. But potent mages hurling spells while drunk . . ." Hipparan trailed off, as if the image frightened even him.

Pirvan would have gladly put an arm around Haimya, or felt hers around him. Instead, they stood carefully apart as Hipparan continued. "Without the mage—his name comes to me as Fustiar—we have less to fear from the black dragon." He was silent for a moment, and Pirvan thought he was shaking his head in weariness or sorrow.

Sorrow was in his voice. "The black—I have no name for him—he was old when he entered dragonsleep. Fustiar woke him into a world where he thought he would die alone, the last of all dragons.

"He has served Fustiar against humans and other lesser races. He will continue to serve Fustiar. But he does not want to fight another dragon, even to serve Fustiar."

Haimya's voice was very steady when she spoke.

"Are you saying you do not wish to fight him either?"

The silence was so long that, save for Hipparan's breathing, Pirvan would have thought the dragon had flown away. Finally he heard a sigh.

"That would be my wish, but Fustiar will make the final decision. Fustiar and his minions. If dragon or man comes at me—for what I owe you, I must fight."

"Can you at least carry us closer to Fustiar's tower without being seen?" Pirvan asked. He doubted Haimya would admit her sickness by making that request herself.

"As close as I can without invading the other's lair, yes. That will still leave you some distance to walk, but should keep surprise on your side. Oh, and it will be best done at night, from a larger clearing than any I have seen about here."

"Thank you," Pirvan said. The two words in Common did not do justice to what he felt; a whole scroll might have fallen short. He swayed on his feet and gripped the riding harness for support.

"You can examine the harness if you wish, but I assure you it is in good order," Hipparan said. Meanwhile, if I may offer advice, perhaps I can help you both to better sleep."

Sleeping folded in a dragon's wing was a new experience for Pirvan, but its newness did not keep him awake long. Neither did it bother Haimya, judging from the snores he heard.

* * * * *

Even Eskaia could see that the minotaurs' second attack was driven by desperation. They simply laid their ship alongside *Golden Cup*, flung grappling hooks everywhere there was a chance of them holding, then started climbing. The one strategy they used was to station slingers and shatang throwers fore and aft, to pick off archers and sailors trying to cut the lines of the grappling hooks.

Enough defenders went down to weaken the archery and leave some of the hooks in place. Some of them stayed down, skulls shattered so that the brains were pulp or shatangs driven completely through them from chest to spine, beyond healing by twelve of the most potent priests known or imagined on Krynn.

There were still plenty of defenders on their feet with weapons in hand when the minotaurs again swarmed into the waist of *Golden Cup*. This time the bull-men had come to conquer or die, and about all that kept them from swiftly doing the first was that too many had already done the second.

It was not a battle that anyone could understand even if they had leisure and a safe place to watch it. Eskaia had neither. There was no safe place aboard *Golden Cup*, and even less leisure for anyone tending the wounded.

Not that she spent all her time under cover. Within a few minutes every able-bodied man was needed for the fight. The wounded and dying, human and minotaur alike, ended in the hands of the boys, the wounded who could sit up and use both hands to aid someone less fortunate, and a staggering, gray-faced Tarothin.

Also Eskaia. She poured out drops of healing potion, applied dressings, changed dressings, held limbs straight so their bones would not heal in unnatural positions under Tarothin's spells, and wished there were three more of her.

The only respite came when the cry arose for bearers to haul some wounded sailor or prisoner from the bloody deck into shelter. Then Eskaia was among the strongest of those who went out, a pleasant change from being among the weakest.

She only wished her dagger had a weighted pommel like Pirvan's, or that she was expert with the weighted cord as Haimya was. Both were weapons suited to her stature and strength, and would have allowed her a part in the actual fighting—at least until the sailors in a body forced her back to shelter.

Men, she had long since concluded, wanted the hog's share of the fun.

Except that this was not fun. It was closer to madness, and she felt that madness plucking with bony fingers at her mind when one of the boys went down with a gaping wound in his thigh. She tore the bottom of her gown to shreds making cloths to pack and bind the wound, but too much blood was already gone.

All she could do was hold him and try to hear what he said above the screams and bellows, the shouts and curses, the thud of stones, the whine of arrows, and the mad-blacksmith din of clashing steel.

The boy stared at her for a long while in silence, then he gripped her hand. His lips writhed, and Eskaia thought she heard the word "Mother." Then lips were still, eyes empty, and the hand gripping hers relaxed and slipped to the deck.

I sometimes think I have missed so much, yet I am five, perhaps six years older than he, she thought.

She stumbled to the side of the ship, her stomach too empty to spew, but her lungs burning for fresh air. If the price was a spear in the back or a smashed skull . . .

A roar went up, both sides cheering so loudly that for a moment they lacked the breath to fight. Off to starboard, two ships were approaching, one minotaur, the other a large, swift sea barbarian craft. For moments the second vessel was bow-on, impossible to identify.

Then it swung hard about, and another roar went up, as the humans recognized Jemar's *Windsword*. The decks were bare; every fit man must be at the oars. The ship flung itself back on its own tracks, at the minotaur ship. The minotaur ship backed its oars, trying to present its own ram-armed bow to this attack.

Instead, Jemar's ship pulled in its own near side oars down the side of its enemy. Rather than sundering timbers, her ram and bow shattered every oar on the minotaurs' port side. Eskaia closed her eyes to shut out the picture of weighted oars flailing about belowdecks, dealing blows fit to crack even a minotaur's skull.

Windsword spun about in a tight circle, only one side's oars beating until it was completely turned around. Then both flailed blue ocean to white foam, as *Windsword* flung itself like a giant shatang at the minotaur vessel's crippled side.

Eskaia did not need imagination to hear the bellows of pain and terror as *Windsword*'s ram drove into the enemy's side. She did not need imagination to see the blood spreading in the water as Jemar's ship backed away from the gaping wound it had made. Eskaia turned away as the minotaur vessel began to list to port.

The battle roar was dying now as the minotaurs began their retreat. Few of *Golden Cup*'s crew were disposed to risk their own lives to interfere with that retreat. Heavy splashes came, as unwounded minotaurs leaped over the side and thrashed to their ship. Wounded minotaurs crawled or staggered, then struggled down the ropes, sometimes losing their grips and also ending with splashes. Most of the wounded who fell into the water did not come up again.

Eskaia turned from the spectacle of the minotaurs' retreat as another splash sounded behind her. She first saw Jemar's victim listing even more sharply, its deck black with minotaurs as unwounded rowers struggled up for a slim chance of safety. Axes gleamed; some wise heads were chopping up boats and ship's gear, to make planks that swimmers could cling to.

The splash sounded again, louder and closer. A vast minotaur head loomed in the gangway, one eye closed, blood streaming from the left cheek and the right ear, hands clutching with blind, desperate strength at the bulwarks.

A timber cracked like a twig. Eskaia realized that the minotaur was at the end of his strength, but might be sworn to use that last strength to take one more enemy with him. All she had to do to prevent that was lay her dagger across his knuckles, or jab him in the nose. . . .

She stepped forward, bare-handed, and gripped the minotaur by one hand and a horn. He had been delicately balanced; a slight push would have sent him over the side to drown. An equally slight pull was enough to bring him lurching aboard. He knocked another section of bulwark to splinters, then fell.

His good eye was upward as he fell, and Eskaia thought it was regarding her with bemusement. "It's all right," she said soothingly. "You have all the honor any six minotaurs can use. Just feel your wounds." She'd counted seven or eight more besides the ones to his head, and he had to feel as if he'd been wrestling dragons.

"Urrrmmm," the minotaur said. At least she thought he'd intended to speak, but then his eye drifted closed. She pressed a hand against his chest, and was obscurely relieved to feel it still rising and falling.

She could not have found enough dressings for so many wounds if she'd stripped herself to the skin. However, her gown served for the worst, then somebody brought more dressings that covered the others, and finally somebody she thought was Tarothin stood beside her and laid the end of a staff (or it might have been a boarding pike) on the minotaur's chest and chanted (or possibly muttered) something.

Whoever had done what, it seemed to ease the minotaur's breathing. It certainly eased hers. She managed to stand, with only a little help from some sailor and then from a splintered section of railing. She saw that she was only a pace from falling over the side, but right now that hardly mattered.

Then footsteps were behind her and hands on her shoulders. She let herself be turned around, then stared into the eyes of Jemar the Fair.

She gaped until she knew that he was really here, and that she was not imagining him as she might have imagined Tarothin healing the minotaur. For a moment, she felt as if she too were being healed, simply by Jemar's touch and presence—yes, and those huge, dark eyes, which seemed to caress not just her eyes and face, but all the rest of her body, even intimate places.

She wondered just how much was left of her clothes. Then all thought ceased, as her senses departed and she fell forward into Jemar's arms.

Chapter 19

Darkness had long since spread across the ocean, following on the heels of thick clouds. A fresh breeze was ruffling the long swells, but the sailors said there was no storm smell on the wind.

Habbakuk's Gift sailed sentry around *Golden Cup* and *Windsword*. Jemar's other three ships kept a discreet watch on the homeward-bound minotaurs, honor amply regained but the survivors of three crews crammed like salted fish into the one remaining ship.

Lady Eskaia thanked Habbakuk for all his favors, large and small. She knew she should be more grateful for her being alive, *Golden Cup*'s being afloat and safe, and the minotaurs' being homeward bound, but exhaustion made that much gratitude or any other strong feeling beyond her powers. She now knew how Tarothin must feel, after healing all day and half the night, and she lacked even the consolation that she had wearied herself saving lives.

At least it was still in her power to be a gracious hostess, even if she yawned between every fifth word and her muscles felt as if giant ogres had played a game of tossball with her. *Golden Cup* was not yet short of rations or wine, though that day was close at hand. Kurulus said that it might already be at hand if they wished to make port without dry throats or empty bellies.

One of the three boys who'd survived the day fit to stand and serve brought another jug of wine. Eskaia posed it over the cups. Jemar held his up, Kurulus put a hand over his, and Tarothin merely stared blankly at her as if she were performing some ritual from a cult he did not know.

The decision as to what came next lay in their hands. Kurulus now commanded the ship in deed and, if the wounded captain did not take the deck in two days, in law. Tarothin might not have another spell in him for weeks, but what he knew about magic might still save them all without that. And Jemar—

Jemar was as he had seemed, and he had seemed the stuff of champions almost from the first day Eskaia had known him. There was also a grace and even gentleness about him, which stories seldom attributed to champions and still less often to sea barbarians.

"We are safe enough from minotaurs," Jemar said, spearing a sausage out of the bowl in the middle of the table. Eskaia's cabin stores had provided the sausage, but the rest of the meal was dried potatoes and vegetables and a tart made with jam and flour that had to be used before the weevils carried them off. At least the wine was strong; Eskaia was sure she had drunk no more than two cups, but her head buzzed as if it was half again that much.

Best drink no more, at least until we have decided what next, she decided, or rather, until I can persuade the others that what I wish is what shall be done.

Kurulus grunted. He seemed to be too exhausted to use words, but his grunt was eloquent of doubt.

Tarothin shook his head. "Jemar is right, and it's mostly your doing, my lady."

"How so?"

"That minotaur you did not push overboard—he is the son of Jheegair, one of the two leaders of our honor-seeking friends. Or rather, he was one of the two leaders. His—associate—was too badly wounded to keep the deck, so Jheegair's voice is the one now obeyed by all.

"He not only owes us a debt for honorable fighting and another for defeating him. He owes us a third debt for his son. I am certain neither he nor any who follow him will be back. Furthermore, I would wager my second best spellbook that he will tell all minotaurs that no one should attack *Golden Cup* unless they wish the battle to be as hard as it would be against their own folk."

Kurulus's mutterings indicated that Tarothin might wager spellbooks, but that he and his crew would be wagering their lives if *Golden Cup* was left undefended.

Jemar frowned. "I can leave one ship with you until you are jury-rigged again and fit to return to Istar. That will leave me only three ships and they short-manned, which is slight strength for entering Synsaga's lair—"

"Slighter strength has already done so, or have you forgotten who we sent south?" Eskaia snapped. "Pirvan, Haimya, and a dragon barely out of his childhood are already facing Synsaga, mages, spells, black dragons, treachery, reefs, storms, poisonous snakes, starvation disease—" She ran out of breath before running out the list of perils her friends were facing, and drank half her cup to clear her throat.

The wine was strong indeed; it took a moment for her vision to clear after the wine seared her throat on the way to making a warm, glowing ball in her stomach. She thought Jemar looked ready to take her in his arms again—and indeed, would protest, for those arms were strong and even welcoming, or so she'd dared to think. . . .

Eskaia stood up, pressing both hands on the table until her fingernails gouged the wood. "Jemar, there is no need to divide our strength. *Golden Cup* can be left to Habbakuk's mercy—"

Kurulus rose so violently that the table rocked and his

chair crashed backward. "My lady, this ship—"

"—belongs to House Encuintras, not to you or your captain. By law, I am the senior representative of House Encuintras present here. By law and family custom, I may choose to dispose of any piece of House Encuintras property, so long as a fair price is received for it and carried to the house accounts, or the interests of the house are otherwise served. I submit that abandoning *Golden Cup* serves the interests of House Encuintras.

"Ships can be replaced, Kurulus. Good men are another matter. You and Grimsoar, the captain, the boys, the wounded—they are all good men."

Kurulus sat down again, his jaw sagging open too wide to let him even grunt. After she was certain he would remain silent, Eskaia turned to Jemar.

"I have called you, to your face and to others, a fair and gallant captain. I now swear this, by Paladine and Habbakuk, likewise by the memory of Drigan Encuintras, the first of our house, and—" she swallowed "—my own honor in every respect—"

She took a deep breath. "I swear that if you, Jemar called the Fair, take all of us aboard your ships and sail with us south to rescue our comrades, I, Eskaia of House Encuintras, will give you my hand in marriage."

* * * * *

Haimya doubted that her sickness was the lung fever. She could breathe as readily as ever; indeed, it sometimes seemed that she was taking in enough air to make her light-headed. That might be from some other sort of fever, however, and she certainly felt the aches in her joints and the queasiness within that told of some kind of sickness coming on.

She could not easily have finished the journey to Fustiar's tower on foot, or at least been fighting-fit when she reached it. She dismounted from Hipparan's back knowing that she owed the dragon as great a debt as she could conceive any human owing to a dragon. What she could not conceive was how to pay it.

"Oh, that will come to you in time, I am sure," Hipparan whispered in her ear. The dragon had learned to control his speech so that he could, if he wished, make no more noise than a purring kitten.

Haimya subdued her resentment at having her thoughts read, and replied without speech. *If you can hear my mind, then you know I was not so grateful during the flight.*

"I know that," Hipparan said. "It was all I could do to keep from laughing, though I suppose it was not at all amusing to you."

"It was not," Haimya said shortly. Hipparan had flown toward the tower by a long, meandering route that seemed to retreat two yards for every three it advanced. He flew as slowly as he could and still stay in the air, except sometimes when he dived down to treetop height and gained speed by losing altitude.

Sometimes he even dropped below the treetops, when ravines or cleared land opened before him. Haimya remembered one such passage, with night-walking apes staring glow-eyed from the trees at the dragon and his riders. The apes were mercifully silent, perhaps because they were too astonished at the madness they saw to muster speech.

At least the flight proved that Haimya's inward queasiness could not be too serious yet. She did not need to drop to her knees and empty her stomach when Hipparan had landed. She merely wished to.

Pirvan kept a respectful distance until the urge had passed, then handed her a water bottle. The last of the spring water went down, bitingly fresh and still cool, and both stomach and head cleared. She patted Hipparan's neck, then darted aside as the dragon leaped for the sky.

If you see me coming back before you meet Gerik, it is certain that something is awry. Otherwise, the best I can do is avoid provoking the black dragon.

Haimya rather wished that she and Pirvan could hope to do the same. But two humans intruding into his master's tower might not receive the same charity from the black as another dragon. Their best hope in that case was to persuade the black that Hipparan would take vengeance for harm done to them, and also that they had no designs on Fustiar or any of his work.

The first was the entire truth; the second could be made so. They did not *need* to ruin Fustiar's work if they could learn what it was and snatch Gerik free without doing so. What others might do with their knowledge of Fustiar's work was out of their hands.

Gerik would not be. He would end this night in their hands or she would know why, and from his own lips. Even if he had sworn an oath to Synsaga, it might be the sort of oath that would be considered coerced, and not valid or punishable once he was returned to Istar and free of danger and duress. . . .

"Time to be off," Pirvan said beside her.

She nodded and slung on her pack. Was it her imagination, or was some of the lightness in her head now flowing into the pack? Certainly it seemed an easier burden, and when she test drew her sword, it seemed to fly into her hand. The ground was firmer, too, or else she had learned the art of walking across mud like a water strider on a pond. . . .

*　*　*　*　*

The first reaction to Eskaia's pronouncement was Tarothin's. He rose from his chair, put a hand on the table to steady himself, then his eyes rolled up in his head and he toppled forward. His fall knocked over his wine cup, and he ended with his nose in his plate.

There followed a lively few minutes as the other three in the cabin tried to heal, or at least revive, their healer. The last thing that any of them wished was to have this fainting spell known all over *Golden Cup*, let alone Jemar's squadron.

"I can imagine my people acceding to your wish if we have a wizard to match Synsaga's mage," Jemar said. "If they think we lack such, I doubt I could persuade them if I offered every man a woman as fair as you, and every woman a man—"

"—as fine as yourself," Eskaia finished for him. This had the desired effect of rendering Jemar speechless, and even making him flush until he was almost as dark of face as was normal among sea barbarians.

Under Eskaia's and Kurulus's ministrations, Tarothin regained his senses before Jemar regained his speech. The wizard sat up, removed a piece of carrot from his beard, and contemplated the others with a not easily describable look on his round face. It seemed to mingle surprise, amusement, and dismay in roughly equal proportions.

When he spoke, his voice conveyed the same mixture. "My lady, this is not well done. Whatever will your father say?"

"My father is not here," Eskaia replied. "I am. So is Jemar. So are the ships and men who must sail south to rescue our comrades, or cra—or abandon them, without need."

"My lady, they may well prevail on their own," Jemar said. "I am not as wise about dragons as our friendly wizard here, but Pirvan and Haimya seemed folk of uncommon shrewdness and strength."

Eskaia's look made Jemar actually refuse to meet her eyes. "Good chief," she said, with ice crackling in her voice. "I hope this continuing to argue does not mean that you refuse my offer."

A long silence ensued, in which Tarothin seemed to be staring at the ceiling and moving his lips silently. Kurulus made ready to knock him down if he reached for his staff and began a spell, but no magic flowed around them.

"I have prayed," the wizard said, finally. "I have prayed more like a cleric than a wizard. I cannot find it in me to bless this—this offering of the lady's self, for such a small—"

"It is not a small purpose," Jemar said, and his voice was now as chill as Eskaia's. He held Tarothin's eyes for a moment, until the wizard looked away. "It is a perilous one, but not small, and highly honorable.

"My lady, I accept your bargain."

"But—blessing—the law—" Tarothin stammered.

"The law is satisfied by my being of age," Eskaia said. "I have been of age to be married with my father's consent since I was fifteen, and without it since last year.

"As for a blessing—I cannot imagine that among five sea barbarian ships, there are no clerics whatever. Who is your priest of Habbakuk?"

"She's actually a priestess," Jemar said. "I am sure she will not make any great objections, once we satisfy her that this is a free agreement between two lawful persons—"

"No, and by the time we rescue our friends, Tarothin may have come around to a wiser point of view," Eskaia said.

Everyone stared again. She laughed. "Jemar—we wed after our friends are rescued, or I know their fate. I will not demand that we succeed, only that we try."

Jemar once again seemed deprived of speech.

"Jemar, I would not tempt you to steal my—to steal the bait without springing the trap. And as for fearing treachery—whatever you are, it is not the kind of fool who would do something that surely would bring the wrath of House Encuintras, all its friends, and perhaps even Synsaga himself on you. Your own people would have long since dropped you overboard with shackles at your feet, were you such a fool. So I trust you."

Jemar's first sound was laughter. When he regained his breath, he shook his head.

"My lady. Is there perhaps sea barbarian blood in House Encuintras? You know us as if you had been reared among us from a babe."

"It is only three generations since we sailed our own ships," Eskaia said. "Even today, some of our highest officers began in the forecastle. So the sea and those who voyage upon it are not a bound and sealed scroll to us. Far from it."

They summoned Grimsoar One-Eye to put Tarothin to bed, relying alike on his strength and his discretion. Jemar gave Eskaia the betrothal gift of a single black pearl from the band that circled his left forearm.

Then they settled down to finish the wine and the plans for the voyage south.

* * * * *

From where Hipparan had landed them, Pirvan and Haimya had an easy route to the ruined castle. Two visible moons rode the night, and the patchwork of clouds let much of their light through. Also, the tower rose high, and last of all, a blue glow from its base made a mark that a one-eyed man could have followed.

Pirvan thought he felt a trickle of breeze colder than any jungle ought to spawn, blowing from the tower. Of course, they were climbing up out of the rank, steaming lowlands as they approached the castle. Perhaps he only felt a mountain breeze, after so long in the jungle that he had forgotten what coolness felt like.

And perhaps not.

It also eased their way that the girdle of outposts around the castle seemed slighter than they had expected. One camp appeared all but abandoned, and there were gaps in the sentry line wide enough to allow a troop of mounted knights to ride through.

The guards' sloth was no small relief to Pirvan. He had it in him to cast the Spell of Seeing the Expected perhaps once more, and that not for long. If they could reach the tower without exhausting that resource, he would be grateful.

"We could have used a little more such sloth this morning," Haimya whispered.

"Let's not rejoice until we know the reason for the sloth," Pirvan reminded her.

"Fear of the mage?"

Pirvan shrugged.

"Then I will not rejoice. I will not halt either."

The thief touched her cheek. It seemed hotter than usual, but not hot enough to account for such a witling's remark. He hoped it was only some sickness that responded to healing, not some living creature of the jungle devouring her from within.

Hoping was as futile as halting. They moved on. Presently they were at the base of the castle's wall.

"There are ruined portions farther around to the right," Pirvan said, "but they are most likely to be guarded. Also, from unruined battlements, we can see the whole inside at a glance."

"Why not just ask if I'm fit to climb?" Haimya snapped.

"I assumed you were," Pirvan said. "If you are not—"

Haimya shook her head. "I think so."

"If you fall because you've overtaxed your strength, I'll spit on your grave," Pirvan said, with a light punch to her shoulder. "Ho, for a little healthy night work."

Haimya sounded other than healthy by the time they were on the battlements, but her breathing had eased and her pallor likewise before Pirvan finished hauling up their gear. Then they turned to study the castle.

The blue glow no longer flickered from the base of the tower, but a campfire showed one band of sentries at a gate on the far side of the courtyard. Much of the wall to their right was ruined, and at the far end was a dim, hulking shape.

"The dragon?" Haimya whispered.

Pirvan's night-sight groped through the darkness, and he shook his head. "Too big. More likely his northern lair. Remember, Hipparan said he had two."

The next moment, a shift of the night breeze made the identification certain. "Either a dragon's lair or a slaughterhouse," Pirvan added, after he was done gagging. "But no dragon, or I think Hipparan would have mentioned him."

"Unless he was as frightened as I am now, and forgot," Haimya said.

"I hope you and Gerik have a swarm of children, and you teach true courage to them all," Pirvan said.

She seemed bemused.

"True courage," he added, "is going on when you know

all the dangers. The other is ignorance or folly. Teach them or breed it into them. The world needs it."

He had meant to ease her mind with an assurance that he would not stand between her and Gerik if they wished to remain betrothed. Now he wondered if he had chosen the right time, place, or words. Perhaps this eerie place was unsettling his wits, or at least tangling his tongue.

"I will fret myself about children when I know who their father will be," Haimya replied, and now it was Pirvan's turn to stand mute. Before he regained speech, Haimya had pulled up the rope and lowered herself over the inner side of the wall.

* * * * *

Gerik Ginfrayson enjoyed sitting by the fire for more than its warmth. Half of the others seated around it were the muted slave-soldiers of Fustiar's guard. They might not like him, but they would not mutter sly asides or open insults in hopes of provoking him to draw steel. They could only kill him and, so far, they seemed to fear their mage master too much to do that.

Furthermore, the fire kept the darkness at bay, and the smoke of the half-sodden wood did the same to the insects. It even fought a rearguard action against the reek of the seldom-cleaned midden pits and the dragon's lair— tonight, mercifully without its occupant.

Best of all, the fire was a good long way from the entrance to the tower, which was now guarded by a creature who might be kin to half a score of races but seemed to belong to none of them. Nor was his creation, perhaps in defiance of the gods, the most disquieting thing about him.

He went about armed with a Frostreaver. As far as Gerik knew, Fustiar had made two that endured, a trifle smaller perhaps than the true Frostreavers but otherwise altogether as potent. They seemed immune to even the heat of a fire, let alone the heat of the jungle, and he had personally seen each of them sever a man's body at a single blow.

He would be prepared to bet on the guard creature and his Frostreaver against anything short of a dragon. He would even be prepared to watch that bout, from a safe distance. He was not prepared to calmly approach the seven-foot-tall sentry with his six-foot-high axe except on Fustiar's direct command—and for some nights past, the mage had been far too flown with wine to command Gerik or anybody else to do anything.

Gerik hoped the mage would end his bout of wine guzzling tonight, if not before the black dragon returned, then before the dragon awoke and required orders. Something was troubling the beast, putting him out of temper, enough that he'd already killed one of the mutes and crippled another in a burst of wordless rage. The black seemed to have ample command of human speech, but not a word had he spoken to explain what was troubling him.

Which made matters no easier for Gerik. He no longer cared much what he learned about anything here on the Crater Gulf. He wanted to flee with what he had already learned, and a dragon turning rogue, uncontrolled even by an evil mage, was a potent barrier to flight.

It was then that the minotaurlike bellow of the guard creature echoed around the walls, bringing everyone to his feet, most weapons to the ready.

* * * * *

Haimya was as surprised as Pirvan to see the stairs up into the tower apparently unguarded. Nor did they encounter any magical protections as they approached the base of the eighty feet of ancient stone. The shadows hid them from casual glances, and almost from each other.

The guard-maid now felt as if a hot stone were lodged in her throat. She could breathe well enough, but swallow only with difficulty. Also, the aches were growing; joints muttered dark protests with each step. Much worse, and she would be more hindrance than help to Pirvan, and she would have to trust him to deal fairly with Gerik—

No, she *did* trust him. Pirvan was not the problem. Her own doubts and Gerik's were the problem. So she had to go on, and if it was her last breath that she used to settle matters with her betrothed, then so be it. Her spirit would rest in peace, and his conscience would be clear, and Pirvan—

It was then that the man-shape stepped out from under the stairs, rising to its full height. Seven feet or more, with the stature and shape of an ogre, but a beard more like a dwarf's, clothing that was of all races and none, and in its hands—

Haimya swallowed. She had never seen one, but no sellsword of her experience failed to study tales of every weapon she might face. Sellsword work sometimes lay far to the south, so there was no dearth of accounts of Frost-reavers.

The head was smaller than she had expected, but the bluish sheen was precisely right, and the handle was longer than she was tall. In the hands of that—of Fustiar's creation, or else of some god so mad that his or her name was never spoken, even by the servants of the Dark Queen—in those vast four-fingered hands, it would be a terrible weapon.

Which made it all the more important to deal with this guard, apparently the only one on the tower, before he could alert the camp. That might bring Gerik; it would certainly bring armed men of whose allegiance there could be no doubt.

"One of us up the stairs, the other wait until our friend follows?" Pirvan suggested. "If the one on top doesn't go too high, jumping's safe. Our friend doesn't look like he can stand much of a fall."

That meant putting the creature between them, but unless he had eyes in the back of his head or a second weapon, such a situation had its advantages. She prayed briefly that whoever had contrived this being had left out intelligence, then drew her sword.

"Chance for who goes up?" She put her hand around the blade halfway up, Pirvan put his hand above hers, and so they continued. It was Pirvan whose hand ended up, waving in the air.

"Sorry. Always use your own sword for this."

The bow they'd captured from the first sentry post had an almost dry string and six arrows that probably would fly true, at least to a target the size of the axe wielder. Haimya took those as well as her sword, and whispered a final suggestion to Pirvan.

"If Gerik comes out before me, don't wait. From on top, I can discourage pursuers with the last arrows, then get out of the tower on the other side."

This made a number of assumptions that Pirvan did not share, about the likely quality of their opposition. However, this was the wrong time to argue the philosophy of combat.

Haimya slung the bow, crouched like a runner, then sprinted for the stairs. Pirvan was only two paces behind her at first, then let the distance open.

As Haimya's boots struck the stairs, the creature threw back its head and cried out. The sound seemed flung toward the moons themselves, and echoed around the courtyard and from the stones like the cry of a minotaur impaled or burned alive.

Then Pirvan fell back, drawing his dagger as the creature lumbered around to the base of the stairs. The Frostreaver shimmered—or was it glowing with a light of its own?—then the creature raised it over its head and charged at Pirvan.

Chapter 20

Haimya ran up the stairs as fast as Pirvan ran on level ground. This was not quite as remarkable a feat as it might seem, as Pirvan was not running as fast as he could. A few steps were enough to tell him that the axe wielder was somewhat ponderous in its movements. If Pirvan ran full out, he would quickly leave the creature so far behind that it might give up chasing him and follow Haimya up the stairs.

The plan of catching it between the two of them would then become precarious. Their best chance of eliminating it before the rest of the guards rallied to the tower or Fustiar awoke from besotted slumber to blast them with magic depended on that plan; its going awry would be no small matter.

Pirvan ran around under the stairs and ducked through the uprights. He hoped the creature would run full-tilt into the uprights, which were roughly dressed tree trunks, hard enough to knock itself senseless, without knocking down the stairs.

The creature was neither that swift nor that witless. It stopped well short of the collision, turned back to the stairs, and began to climb.

Fortunately the risers of the stairs left plenty of gaps for a shrewd dagger thrust. Pirvan did not even have to stretch far to thrust his steel into the creature's foot.

His problem lay in doing enough damage to draw its attention. He had to strike three times before the creature even broke stride. Only the fourth thrust, which nearly cut off a toe, inflicted a noticeable injury. The creature leaped off the stairs, brandishing the Frostreaver. It went to its knees, nearly dropping its weapon. It tightened its grip before Pirvan could close and try to snatch up the Frostreaver, however, then lurched to its feet, spun ponderously about, and struck wildly at the thief.

The blow missed Pirvan by the width of a fingernail; he felt the puff of air on his cheek. He leaped aside and backward in one movement, slashing hard at the nearer arm. Only the tip connected, but the creature halted for a moment to shift its grip.

In that moment an arrow sliced down from above and struck the creature in the neck. The arrow hit harder than Pirvan's dagger, against thinner skin than the creature's leather-tough soles. It pierced the hairy hide, to reach important blood.

The creature waved the Frostreaver wildly with one hand and clutched at its neck with the other. It weaved and lurched, but did not fall. Instead it flung itself once again at the stairs, taking them two at a time. Now it climbed too fast for Pirvan to run under the stairs and discourage it. After letting it get a few steps ahead of him, beyond the swing of the great axe, he followed it.

He tried to keep that safe distance and at the same time be close enough to strike if the creature faltered. It had to be in pain and weakening, but it showed no signs of faltering or even slowing. Nor did it seem to remember that there might be something dangerous behind it. All its bloodlust was turned entirely on Haimya, who had wounded it. It would let the rest of the world go by until it had settled with her.

Pirvan's experience was that fighters who forgot to watch their backs frequently did not last very long against skilled opponents. However, there was always such a thing as brute strength and speed doing the work of shrewdness and vigilance. This guard creature with the Frostreaver was one such.

Pirvan had wondered why Fustiar had put the Frostreaver in the hands of such a powerful but unskilled fighter. He now understood that the creature had perhaps been bred with some inborn skills.

This gave Pirvan a higher opinion of the mage's powers, which was not a pleasant thought. It also solved no part of the fight at hand.

Haimya was near the top of the stairs. She faced the creature, with that bent-knee stance that said she was ready to jump. Her sickness seemed to have taken little of her speed. He hoped her agility had likewise survived. She would be coming down on rough ground, from far too high to have a good chance of landing unhurt. Nor would it take a grave injury to make her easy prey for either the creature or the human guards who would soon be rallying to the tower.

It occurred to Pirvan that, in trying to do perhaps too many things at once, he and Haimya had contrived to finally lose the advantage of surprise, about all that would let two people confront a small army and live. Had they marched in with trumpets and drums, they might have learned nothing about Fustiar, but they might have had more success in encountering Gerik Ginfrayson and speaking with him.

The good will of the lords of Istar toward the brothers and sisters of the night work was not worth Haimya's life—and Pirvan had more than a few doubts that the blood would end with her (or even with him).

The creature lurched two steps upward. It seemed unsteady on its massive legs, and Pirvan saw that the stairs behind it were red and glistening. At least it shed something that looked like blood, rather than some vitalizing fluid conjured out of Fustiar's evil learning.

Then it seemed that everything happened at once. The creature took another step, then swung the axe. Haimya leaped to one side, thrusting upward with her sword. The axe smashed into the door, tearing through the ironbound portal as if it were silk. Pirvan did not see where the sword went.

He did see Haimya hanging by one arm from the stairs. He saw the creature whirl, heard it let out a terrible, half-choked, bubbling scream, and saw that it no longer wielded the Frostreaver. One empty hand lashed out for Haimya, she slashed at it, and the fingers closed on the sword blade. A jerk, and the creature held Haimya's sword in a bloody hand.

Then it hissed like a caveful of serpents, threw up its hands, and toppled backward, so swiftly that Pirvan could not clear the way in time. He was lucky enough not to be caught, borne down to the ground, and crushed to pulp under the creature's massive weight. But it flailed about as it fell, and one of those flailing hands crashed into Pirvan's left arm. He felt the bone snap; he thought he would have *heard* it go if the creature hadn't screamed again.

Then the creature struck the ground with a thud that jarred the stairs and sent pain shooting up Pirvan's broken arm. He ignored it, covering the last few steps to Haimya at a run. One arm was enough to grip her free hand and help her swing up to the temporary safety of the stairs.

Much too temporary for comfort. She'd lost her sword, he'd lost the use of one arm, and they had between them four arrows, three arms, two daggers, and one bow.

They also had the Frostreaver, at least in the sense that no one else could wield it against them. Whether its possession made any other difference remained to be seen, but to Pirvan seemed unlikely.

"Good company to die in" was an old adage, and it was

true here. Truer still, to Pirvan, was his opinion that Haimya would be good company to live in.

He had to drag the Frostreaver with his good arm, but it went inside with them as they staggered through the ruins of the door into the lowest accessible chamber of Fustiar's tower. It scraped and squealed on the floor, and Pirvan had a nightmare conceit that it was alive and protesting the change of ownership.

Which, given Fustiar's evident powers, was not altogether impossible.

* * * * *

Gerik led the six guards rallying to the tower. They didn't really have enough intact humans to guard the place if neither Fustiar nor the black dragon were battle-worthy. Even taking six such to the tower would leave the gate and the ruins close to the dragon's lair scantily protected, and that by mutes.

Gerik quickly saw that six at the tower might be too few. The guard creature lay sprawled on the ground, its sightless eyes fixed on the clouds, two ghastly wounds in its neck besides the injuries it had taken in falling. Also, the Frostreaver was nowhere in sight.

What was in sight was the door at the top of the stairs, splintered as if by a giant fist—or perhaps a Frostreaver. Gerik turned to the nearest man with a torch.

"Give me your torch. I'm going up alone."

The man gaped. So did most of his comrades, particularly the man who'd fought the tree spirit up in the hills.

"Ah—one's not enough—"

"If Fustiar is awake, he can deal with them. If he sleeps as usual, one is enough to keep any human foes busy until he does wake. If the foes aren't human, one is enough to die learning that. If I don't come out, no heroic rescues. Do you swear that?"

The men straightened. "No, we won't. We'll at least try to learn what befell you, *then* take word to Synsaga."

Gerik threw up his hands. "Kiri-Jolith watch over you

all." They might be pirates, but there was some good and more than a little honor in anyone who would face unknown menaces for an almost equally unknown leader.

The gods have a most peculiar sense of humor, to make me a respected leader of fighting men under these circumstances, he thought.

Gerik strode forward, sword in hand, passing the dead creature and slowing as he reached the slippery stairs. He would have thought better of his courage had he not gained a detailed description of the "tree spirit" from her victim. It could be a description of many women, but few of these were accomplished fighters, and only one accomplished female fighter was likely to be roaming the Crater Gulf shore at this time.

A reunion with Haimya under these circumstances suggested that the gods' sense of humor was worse than peculiar. One might say bizarre or even cruel, not without impiety but also not without truth.

* * * * *

For the first time since she'd been aware of her sickness, Haimya wanted to curl up in a corner and lie there until death or healing came. She had poured her remaining strength into that fight on the stairs, and though the creature was dead, she wondered how long she and Pirvan would outlive it.

Pirvan let the Frostreaver fall with a final clatter and looked about the chamber. It had clearly been a hall of some sort, in the castle's youth. Then it had been cut up into cells or small chambers by wooden partitions, but even the inhabitants of those chambers were long dead and the wood long rotted. The hall was ankle deep in dust and rotten fragments, which would make for treacherous footing when it came to the final fight.

Haimya did not seek a corner, but she did sit cross-legged in the debris and put her head down, until she felt her wits and breath return. Pirvan had unslung his pack and was rummaging bandages, salves, and healing potion out of it.

Or rather, he rummaged out the flask that had held healing potion. A large crack across its base told them where the contents had gone.

"Have you any?" he asked.

"Less we need for both of us. I have taken some, or I might not be here." She wished she had taken either more or less.

"I wish you weren't, Haimya. I wish you were in a warm bed a long way from here, with a jug of wine and a plate of cakes on the table beside the bed. I wish you wore a silk bedrobe and perfume. I wish—"

His voice sounded ready to break, and she felt her face going red. Then footsteps sounded on the stairs, a shadow loomed in the doorway, and another voice spoke. She knew it well, knew but did not care for the gentle mockery it held, and felt herself going even redder.

"Friend, who are you to conjure up such pictures of my betrothed? Or were you wishing that I was beside her in the bed?"

"Gerik," Haimya said. She tried to rise, then realized that one leg had cramped under her. She tried to straighten it, but before she could Gerik had come over to her and was helping her to her feet.

She wanted to brush off both his aid and the dust from the floor, but that would have taken three hands. She contented herself with stepping away from him and brushing herself.

"You do not look well, Haimya," he said.

"Nothing you have done lately has made my life easier," she said. At the back of her mind, a small voice whispered that he probably had no more idea of what to do now than she did. A little kindness would not come amiss.

She took a deep breath. "Gerik. It has come to my ears—I have heard—that you swore true oath to Synsaga."

She looked at him then, and although he was silent, his eyes spoke loudly enough. She wanted to turn away, or slap him, or do something to mark this moment and her disapproval. (She could not call it by any stronger word. He might have been threatened, and their betrothal would not stand or fall on that oath if he foreswore it and fled.)

"Everyone on the Crater Gulf knows that," Gerik said. "It is hardly a secret."

"Except to those who have come to Crater Gulf to—to discuss your future with you," Pirvan put in.

Haimya shook her head at her comrade. The less he drew Gerik's attention to himself, the better. Gerik had never seemed like a man who would send an imagined rival to his doom, but then he had never seemed like a man who would join the ranks of Synsaga's pirates.

"We cannot talk of this at any length in this tower, without Fustiar's consent," Gerik said.

"Then you do serve him, rather than Synsaga?" Haimya snapped.

"Be easy, Haimya. There is no conflict, for Fustiar also serves Synsaga, and does not go beyond the bounds the pirate sets for him." His voice and eyes held a plea, for her to believe him and not question him. Not here.

She began to believe that there had been duress a year ago, or at least second thoughts now. He *would* go with them, and once he was safely free of the Crater Gulf they might speak freely, learn more of Fustiar, even—

"Hup!" Pirvan shouted.

Gerik whirled. Other pirates were pushing through the ruined door. One of them stared at Haimya. She recognized the sentry she'd stunned, after leaping out of Pirvan's illusory tree.

"The tree spirit!" the man screamed. Then he snatched his cutlass from his belt and hurled himself forward, straight at Haimya.

*   *   *   *   *

If Pirvan had enjoyed his normal swiftness, he might have halted Haimya's attacker without killing him. Between the pain of his broken arm and the darkness of the chamber, he had no chance to do anything useful.

This left only two possible outcomes. Gerik Ginfrayson could resist the man, or Haimya could die on the pirate's sword.

Gerik whirled, his sword in his hand. As the man passed him, he laid the flat of the blade across the man's head. Instead of stunning him, it further enraged him. He turned on Gerik, and only a remarkably agile parry kept the man's cutlass from splitting Gerik's head.

"Stop it, you fool!" Gerik shouted. "These are my prisoners. You can die for attacking another's prisoners."

"Evil spirit!" the man screamed. There was no reason in his cry, nor any reasoning with him. Haimya stepped forward to help Gerik disarm the man and salvage some remote chance of peace.

Instead, the man drew his dagger and struck at Haimya. She was a trifle slower than usual; the point entered her left shoulder. Pain flared, and she felt blood trickling. She thought of the last drops of healing potion and how much they would have to heal.

Gerik did not think at all. His sword flashed three times, and the last time he drew it back dripping blood as the man crumpled to the floor. He stepped back, the pleading look on his face even stronger. Haimya didn't know who was supposed to honor the plea now—her, or the pirates by the door, seeing a comrade struck down.

She knew then that she had only one hope left. She poured most of the remaining healing potion on her wounded shoulder, then shook the last few drops onto her tongue. Without waiting for it to take effect, she strode over to the Frostreaver and picked it up.

She didn't know what she'd expected to happen. Would it strike her dead for stealing it, or would all the pirates discover that they had someplace else to go, and that urgently?

Neither happened. What she held in her hand was a fine two-handed, single-bitted battleaxe. It was heavy, but well balanced; clearly the guard creature's strength had not been needed. Fustiar must know more than a trifle about weapons; a pity he was entirely given to evil—

"Kill the witch!" someone shouted. He was loud enough to raise not only echoes but dust. He raised more dust as he charged forward, cutlass raised.

Haimya's arms and shoulders fought the first encounter before her thoughts could catch up with them. She held the axe with her hands wide apart and the head to the left, then shifted her grip to swing hard from left to right. The axehead smashed into the down-swinging cutlass and sent it flying out of the man's hands.

The impact hardly slowed the axe's deadly arc. It still had enough force to bite deeply into the man's torso. He stared down at the gaping red ruin where his stomach had been, then clasped his arms futilely over the wound and went to his knees. He had time only to begin a scream before blood came out of his mouth and he fell, choking and writhing.

Before he was still, Pirvan had rushed in and picked up the fallen cutlass. He brandished it in his good hand, though Haimya saw him wince as the movement shook his broken and still unbound arm.

"They are my prisoners," Gerik said, his voice tight. "Haimya, Haimya's friend, you can disarm. I promise you—"

"I promise death to traitors!" another man shouted. "The witch killed my brother. She's no prisoner!"

Gerik, Pirvan, and Haimya had just time to form a rough line before the general rush came. Then, for a minute or more, the fight became the lightning-quick clash of steel (and ice) that left Haimya no awareness of anything more than a foot beyond the reach of her Frost-reaver.

She took down two men with it, one of them dead, and remembered too late that a two-handed weapon is not ideal in a melee against enemies who can get inside its swing. But Gerik seemed to have learned more swordsmanship in the last year than in all his previous years combined, and Pirvan was as quick as an eel and as welcoming as a poisonous serpent. Each of them took a man, and Haimya began to hope.

Hope ended when the door was suddenly filled with more men. The battle must have attracted them, and these newcomers were hideous beyond belief, earless, silent, scarred, and frenzied. Even if they'd had ears, Haimya could not conceive of their listening.

She and Pirvan paired off and kept the newcomers at a distance. They were both fighting with strange weapons, she was sick, and he was wounded, but one mind seemed to move both their limbs and take knowledge from both their senses.

The newcomers seemed reluctant to attack Gerik, and Haimya wondered if this was because of his service to Fustiar, who had to be their master. The pirates seemed to have no reluctance to attack anyone, but they divided their forces so that no one was overmatched.

How long the fight might have gone on, only the gods could say. Its end came in one frightful moment, as Haimya relied on Pirvan's protecting her front to launch a full overhead swing at a pirate wearing a helmet.

The Frostreaver flashed down, it smote the helmet and pierced iron and bone to the man's nose—then it shattered like a glass globe flung on a stone floor. Except that the shattering did not strew mere fragments of glass far and wide.

Instead, pieces of mage-wrought ice flew in all directions, sharper than razors, as heavy as stones, and as deadly as the claws of a dragon. Haimya saw blood on her leg, saw two men go down, and saw the mutes drag one of their number out the door with his belly laid open as they fled from something that overmatched their mindless courage—

And she saw Gerik Ginfrayson collapse, holding a hand already red over an ice-torn wound in his thigh, over his death wound, until his strength left him and his hand fell, leaving the wound to finish its work.

Haimya knelt beside him until the light went out of his eyes. She remembered kissing his lips before they were cold, then again afterward. She remembered muttering that she had been faithful to him, until this last betrayal, and other things that it was probably as well he could no longer hear. The gods' hearing them would be enough.

She did not remember if he said anything. Probably he was silent, and even the smile on his face was almost certainly her imagination. But she held the picture of that smile in her mind, even when she felt Pirvan's hand on her shoulder and allowed him to pull her to her feet.

"We have to move."

"Where?"

"Up or down. It doesn't matter. We have to be outside the tower where Hipparan can find us—before Fustiar awakes or the black dragon returns."

"I—I took the piece—Gerik should have had it, and I his."

He looked down at her leg. "You can't climb?"

"Perhaps. I—" She forced the words out, even as she uttered them knowing that he would ignore them, that if he had to find a way of carrying her out under one arm, he would do so.

"Leave me here."

"Haimya, this is the first and probably the last time I will ever give you a command. Come, freely or against your will, but come."

A lingering remnant of dignity forced her to put one foot in front of another. Surprisingly, the wounded leg could take some weight, even as she felt the bleeding worsen.

Kicking the useless handle of the Frostreaver out of the way, they stepped over the bodies and ice fragments to the door.

Chapter 21

Hipparan was not one of those dragons with the inborn gift of sensing magic worked in a cave deep under a mountain halfway across the world. Nor had he, in his few decades in the world before entering dragonsleep, found time to learn that art—if it could be learned, as some elder dragons doubted.

But the magic he sensed now blazed like fires in dry grass. Or at least one source did—neutral he thought, but with an aura about it of danger. Evil flickered, like a campfire in yesterday's downpour, close to the neutral source.

And far away but drawing closer was the black dragon, a familiar sensation and at any other time not an unwelcome one. He had never heard of a dragon turning from evil to good, or even neutral, but it seemed likely that the black would not *do* anything evil unless Fustiar compelled him.

As he took wing, Hipparan hoped Fustiar had no spells to compel any dragon except the aged black. But a mage who could break dragonsleep, even with the aid of the Dark Queen, was too potent for the comfort of anyone except his sinister mistress.

Hipparan was of one mind with Pirvan and Haimya. He would not sorrow if Fustiar fell into a wine barrel and drowned. For now, he could only hope that at least the mage's ability to work spells was drowned in the wine he'd drunk, and would stay that way until Pirvan and Haimya were safely out of his reach.

Hipparan slanted down to just about the treetops, gaining speed as he did so. The wind of his passage blew birds' nests out of the trees, and nesting mothers squalled protest as their fledglings toppled into space.

Hipparan felt the mothers' sorrow but could do nothing about it. He owed them nothing; he owed Haimya and Pirvan (and all their friends, might Paladine protect them) a great deal.

His wings quickened their beat until he was flying faster than he ever had, even in the high skies.

* * * * *

Pirvan's arm was throbbing as if it had been held over a fire, by the time he and Haimya reached the roof of the tower. They met no one on the stairs, either friendly or hostile, though the crumbling steps, cobwebs, and reek of mold and still more unwholesome life were menaces enough to the two battered questers. Several times Haimya had to stop—for breath, she said—but Pirvan saw blood soaking through her breeches and even the rough dressing she'd torn from the clothing of a dead pirate.

When they reached the roof, they were still alone, and Pirvan quickly saw why. The roof was more holes than either stone or timber. A misstep could send them plummeting to death in the shadows.

At least it would be a quicker death than the pirates

now surrounding the tower would mete out to them. Pirvan hoped he and his companion could at least force the pirates to kill them, but with his arm and her leg and fever, he was making no large wagers. The last strength she'd gained from the healing potion had gone into wielding the Frostreaver with a skill that an ice barbarian warrior would have envied—and what had it brought her?

Gerik Ginfrayson's death, and that had taken from her something that she might never gain back, not if she survived tonight and another fifty years as well. He had thrown away his oath to Synsaga to save her, and she had repaid him with death.

Pirvan could see in Haimya's eyes that in her mind she would look upon Gerik's dying face a thousand times over, until either her mind could endure it no more or she could make her peace with what was not her fault and in any case past all altering.

He had firmly put the thought out of his mind that she was now free. She would welcome no man's approach for years, if ever. Now all he could do for her was be silent and if it came to that, keep her from dying alone.

More torches were coming across the courtyard toward the foot of the tower. Pirvan looked down, and an arrow whistled up toward him, striking the stone a good ten feet below him. Chips of stone and large chunks of mortar showered from where it had struck, however. This whole tower had to be on the verge of coming down of its own weight; how it had survived Fustiar's residence, let alone his magic, was something to marvel at.

Haimya was sitting slumped against the remnants of the battlement, her eyes as blank as if she were senseless. Only the slow rise and fall of her shoulders and the slow trickle of blood from her wound told Pirvan that she was still alive.

With every step and every movement, his arm now flung pain up and down until every part of his body seemed to hurt. It would be easy to sit down beside Haimya, take her hand, and wait until Fustiar awoke or the men below gathered their courage and came up with steel in hand.

It would also shame the brothers and sisters of the night work. Thieves either escaped or died on their feet, like badgers defending their burrows.

The torches wavered. Several arrows flew, but none of them anywhere near the castle. They seemed loosed straight up into the sky. Pirvan's ears seemed stuffed with wool, but he heard cries of alarm.

The black dragon was returning, of course. The men would retreat, but that made no difference. Between them, the black dragon and his mage master would finish the night's work—

It was not the black dragon that swooped out of the night, but Hipparan. He seemed to have grown to twice his previous size since they last had seen him, his wings blotting out the sky and his body longer than the tower's width.

Magic, natural growth, or illusion? Illusion, Pirvan realized, as Hipparan flung out his wings to stop himself in midair, then settled cautiously onto the roof. Not all the stones under him could bear even his carefully placed weight; some gave way and rattled and crashed down into blackness.

"Come and ride," Hipparan whispered. "This roof may fall or Fustiar awake, and the black dragon is coming."

Haimya stared in silence for a moment, until Pirvan thought he would have to slap or drag her. He wondered which god he should pray to, to avert this.

Then speculation ended as Haimya pulled herself painfully upright. "I must tie Pirvan in place," she said. Her voice might have been that of a swathed corpse in a tomb a thousand years old. "He has broken his arm."

"Then be quick about it," Hipparan said.

Haimya's first movements were corpselike as well, but her hands were no less deft than before. In moments, Pirvan was as snugly bound as a barbarian's infant on a woman's backboard. He did not see Haimya tie herself into her harness, but he did feel the lurch and stomach-dropping effect as Hipparan took wing.

The last thing he saw was the tower, now encircled by torches, dropping away beneath them.

* * * * *

Hipparan knew less than he wished to about human injuries and sickness. He knew even less than that about healing them, though he had once commanded some healing spells and also read more than a trifle in Tarothin's least secret spellbook.

This modest knowledge was sufficient to tell him one thing: Pirvan and Haimya would not survive their present hurts without healing. They might not need more than rest and good food brought by helpful hands every day for a few weeks, if they were aboard *Golden Cup* or guests at some castle such as this one had been long ago.

Alone in a wilderness, barely able to tend each other, though, they were doomed. Even if he remained with them and guarded them from enemies, he could not attend them as they needed.

Nor could he be sure of remaining with them. The black dragon was closer yet, and asking querulously what was amiss. So far Hipparan had not heard Fustiar reply.

May this continue, he prayed.

Hipparan had flown as high as he could without chilling his passengers, to see far and wide and be out of arrowshot or even siege engine range from the ground. Seeing no immediate danger from human weapons, dragon's claws, or mage's magic, he descended in wide circles to a landing place on a hill opposite the ancient volcano.

He had thought of landing on that weathered summit, for the lake would offer unlimited fresh water and the forests rose high and were rich with game and fruit. But the rock was crumbling and treacherous, and above the forest line there was little cover for two humans who could not move swiftly and would surely be hunted on the ground and perhaps from the air.

Hipparan had also sensed a trace of ancient magic deep

within the mountain. He could not recognize anything about it, but it seemed to him that his friends would best be well clear of the mountain when Fustiar awoke in fury, like the ancient volcano in eruption.

The clouds were low and the mist rising as Hipparan descended. He had to slow his flight until he was almost hanging in the air, at a height at which a small boy with a slingshot could strike easily. He reached out with all his awareness, searching the land about for any signs of life.

He found nothing except the life of the jungle, sleeping if it was day-living, awake and feeding if it was night-walking. None of it was human, magical, or evil, and none of it seemed in any way concerned with the odd dragon or the odd pair of humans.

That was as Hipparan wished it. He landed, then twisted his neck to examine his riders. Haimya was asleep or senseless. Pirvan was awake but flushed with the beginning of a fever and biting his lip with the pain of his arm.

Gently, Hipparan sliced through the thief's harness with two claws, wielded as delicately as embroidery needles for all that they were larger than Pirvan's daggers. Pirvan gripped the base of Hipparan's wing with his good hand and gently lowered himself to the ground.

It was not gently enough to keep him from gasping with pain. He sat down, holding his broken arm and staring up at Hipparan.

"Thank you. I wish I had the wits to say more, but you have repaid all debts—"

"Now, now, let us not argue about that," Hipparan chided. "If we survive, time enough to dispute it. If we do not, the dead owe nothing, or at least nothing that they can pay the living."

"Cheerful, aren't you?"

"I can count claws held up in front of my face," Hipparan said with dignity. "Being young does not make me foolish."

"I never—ech! Can you help me bind this arm?"

"I can do better than that," Hipparan said with more

confidence than he felt. That drew Pirvan's undivided
attention, and Hipparan did not lose it while he explained
his intention of healing the humans.

"At least enough to let you find your own food and
make your own shelter," he added. "I am not Tarothin,
and I suspect that even he is not a finished healer."

"That," Pirvan said, "is the shark calling the walrus a
glutton."

"No doubt," Hipparan said. "Now, if you will stretch
out your arm as best you can—"

"No," Pirvan said. "You heal—the lady—first. She had
both wounds and sickness, and no healing potion
remains."

Hipparan shook his head. "My friend, I said I was not
Tarothin. This means I could make a mistake. If you seek
Haimya's safety, should you not offer yourself as my first
patient?"

"As a healer, you have a wonderful way of inspiring
confidence," Pirvan said. "Very well, do your worst."

Hipparan tried to drag up from his memory and hold
in front of his eyes the words of Tarothin's most elementary healing spell. It might have no power to cure more
than blisters and dandruff, but a modest start should
avoid killing even if it could not cure.

* * * * *

The black dragon knew that his master was awake
when he returned to his lair at the far end of the castle
courtyard. He carried in his claws a small deer, and his
arrival, followed by his devouring the unfortunate creature, kept the humans at their distance. Even the ones
without speech seemed more uneasy than usual, and
none of them would approach closely enough to tell him
what might have happened in his absence.

He had to finish his meal, fly over the tower, and see that
Fustiar's living creation lay dead and the axe that it had car-
ried was gone. The dragon could sense vaguely where the
Frostreaver had been, but it now seemed shattered, even

melted.

So it is, Fustiar's thought came.

Mage, how did this happen?

The black dragon listened in growing amazement and unease as Fustiar told the tale of how badly the night had gone so far.

Is that all? he asked, finally.

The mage's fury burned into the black dragon's thoughts. *Is that not enough?*

Are you sure they told you the truth?

Fustiar made no reply to that. In the innermost parts of his mind, where the mage could not reach, the black dragon wondered if the mage's fury had not finished the work of making the guards witless with fear. They had failed, but turning them into simpletons would not mend matters.

It does not matter, Fustiar said, more calmly. *Their failure cannot be endured. They must be punished.*

Is it Synsaga's right—

"Synsaga has no rights against me!" Fustiar screamed. The black dragon heard that both in his mind and with what remained of his bodily hearing. He hoped none of the humans heard those words, foreseeing much trouble coming of them if they reached Synsaga. He had slain prisoners and slaves, at Fustiar's command or from hunger. He had yet to shed the blood of a free man sworn to the pirate chief.

What is your wish, then? the dragon asked.

Kill them, you overgrown lizard! was the not unexpected reply.

All of them?

Yes. Either they die now, or you die alone and without purpose! Is that your wish?

The black dragon threw back his head and howled his anguish at the night sky. The sky swallowed the cry and gave back no answers to his problem.

Not quite. He saw that he'd started every man around the tower into movement. Some of them were running, and some of the runners were on their way toward the gate or the climbable portions of the ruins.

The dragon picked one of the deer's ribs out from between his teeth, reared up, and took wing. If the men ran fast enough, he would have every excuse for not chasing them down. Fustiar could hardly wish open war with Synsaga through a public slaughter of pirates. If those mutes did not run, the dragon would have no qualms about strewing them all about the castle; he had never liked them anyway.

The black dragon soared over the walls and circled back past the tower, glancing at the roof to see if anyone was still up there. It was empty and even more ruined than before.

He banked, feeling stronger than he had most of the time since Fustiar had awakened him. Life was precious; he would not give it up easily, even if the price was the lives of a few humans.

But the next time you are too drunk to do your own killing, do not ask me to do it! he snarled at his master.

* * * * *

Haimya awoke so free from pain that she knew she had to be dead. Either that, or a prisoner, and Fustiar had healed her for the purpose of meting out a fate far more lingering and dreadful than dying of fever and loss of blood.

Then she realized that she was not only free from pain but that she was hungry. Hungry, nearly without clothing, but wrapped in a blanket and lying on a bed of leaves and branches.

This was a possible condition for a captive, particularly the hunger. However, she seemed to be outdoors, from the smell of the forest all around her and the sky above. Someone was moving about, close to her, and she turned her head to see.

As she did, the someone knelt beside her. She recognized Pirvan, holding out to her a bowl that was half of a gigantic nut, roughly split.

She was so surprised that she gagged and nearly

choked on the first mouthful of water. Pirvan pounded her on the back—with his *left* hand, she could not help noticing—and held the bowl out.

This time she finished it without mishap, though without really paying attention to what she was doing. She could not take her eyes off Pirvan's using both hands as if he had never been wounded.

No, that wasn't quite right. He was still favoring his left arm, using his right arm even more than a right-handed person did normally. Once she saw him rub his left arm lightly, and heard him sigh.

But he had two arms again. She sat up, holding the blanket around her, and shook her head. She felt as if she'd awakened from a long, deep sleep after a banquet of fine food and excellent wine in the best of company. No, that also was not quite right. Her stomach was rumbling too loudly for it to have been filled any time in the last— how long? She felt as if she had not eaten for a month.

But the muzzy-headedness and aches from the fever were gone. Her leg was still stiff, but when she felt it, there was no blood, little pain, and, instead of a gaping wound, only a ridged, puckered scar.

It would not be her first, and in any case she no longer needed to worry much about her appearance. As long as it did not slow her, she could return to the field, perhaps not with her old rank among the sellswords, but with every prospect of living well enough until her luck ran out.

"Pirvan, I thought you had no magic except the one spell and no strength left to cast that—" she began.

Pirvan laughed. So, in the darkness behind her, did someone much larger.

"Hipparan?"

"If I put you and Pirvan in danger, I am sorry. But it seems that the healing has been good enough that the danger was—"

Haimya sat up, not caring about the blanket, and stared at Hipparan. All she could make out were his eyes, but at her gaze he seemed to lower them.

"You healed us?" She felt her wits had shrunk to those

of a child, likewise her command of Common.

"It seemed the least dangerous course," Pirvan began, but Hipparan interrupted.

"Let me tell this story myself, if you please. We do not have much time, and I may not be with you much longer."

What those last words meant, Haimya badly wanted to know. She took Hipparan's advice and listened in silence. At some point in the story, Pirvan sat down beside her and she put her head on his shoulder, where it felt quite natural.

"Now I must fly," Hipparan concluded. "The black dragon has gone to work among the guards at his tower."

Haimya stiffened. "Killing them?"

"That is what I sense," Hipparan said. "Perhaps he only seeks to frighten them, but I must go see for myself."

Pirvan asked the question Haimya could not shape her tongue to utter. "And fight him?"

"If there is killing, and no other way to stop it . . ." Hipparan said.

Haimya did not reply in words. She leaped up, felt her leg hold up as if it had never been hurt, and ran to embrace Hipparan. She knew it was ridiculous to cry into a dragon's scales when a decent man was there with a shoulder, but she could not help herself.

Also, she realized as her sobs diminished, it was just. Pirvan was here, would be here. Hipparan was going to battle—for good, for his friends and what he owed them, for perhaps no more than being able to sleep soundly at night.

"Paladine, Kiri-Jolith—may they keep you, friend," she said at last.

Pirvan looked as if she'd stolen the words he wanted to say, then smiled. He put an arm around her, she did not resist, and they stood that way as Hipparan spread his wings, stepped into the open, and sprang into the night sky.

* * * * *

Hipparan climbed as high as he could without flying

into the clouds. He wanted to be clear of the mountaintops, able to use all his senses, with the advantage of height if matters came to a fight.

He hoped they would not. The pleasure he had found in healing Pirvan and Haimya made him realize that he was not a warrior in his soul. He could fight, and would, with the strength of his youth, which should give him the edge even though little experience seasoned that strength.

But if the black dragon continued to give him no cause for battle, there would be none.

Hipparan stationed himself high over the tower, where he could see the black dragon climbing up to him before the elder dragon's vision could reach him. This put him in reach of Fustiar's spells, but he thought he had the strength to deal with the mage.

It would be spells against the tower. The healing had been a venture into the unknown, but not physically demanding; work on humans without magical defenses did not take much strength for a full-grown dragon.

Spells. Perhaps turning the tower solid, so that Fustiar was entombed within it. Perhaps softening stones at the base, so the tower's own weight brought the rest of it tumbling down on its master.

Perhaps—

Even at Hipparan's altitude, the screams of dying men reached his ears.

* * * * *

The black dragon dived at a man clinging desperately to the steep side of a tumbled block. Instead of using breath weapon or spell, he merely flicked his tail at the man in passing.

The tail came down across the man's spine like a falling roof beam. He convulsed, bending practically double backward, his eyes wide, his mouth open but no sound coming. Then, as boneless as porridge, he slid down off the rock and lay still.

The black dragon soared and made a tight circle around

the tower, his wings almost vertical. Ancient battle joy flowed through him for the first time since waking, giving him strength he could not remember since his youth. So it had been when he had flown in the dragonarmies of the Dark Queen. So it could be again, if he served Fustiar.

He had a stray thought or two, that this state of mind was too useful to the mage to be natural. But the thoughts departed as quickly as they had come. The black dragon gave his war cry as he saw the ruined bodies strewn across the courtyard. Hardly one of the mutes had escaped, and when the battle joy had entered him he had killed even the pirates with less reluctance than before.

He circled twice for the sheer joy of being able to fly to battle again. On the third circle, he saw a man standing at the head of the stairs to the tower. He broke out of his circle and made ready to use his breath weapon against a man standing where none ought to.

Just in time, he recognized Fustiar.

With great care, one step at a time, the mage came down the stairs. Over his shoulder he carried a second Frostreaver. The dragon tried to remember if there were more, but thought Fustiar had said once (as usual, while drunk and not speaking too clearly) that he had made only two of full power, with all the magic he had used bound into them.

One of those now seemed to lie shattered in a tower that might soon fall and bury the fragments in the stones. Fustiar must be seeking to flee the Crater Gulf coast for another refuge where he could find a new ally and resources to perfect the making of Frostreavers.

If he was not doing that, the black dragon intended to persuade the mage otherwise. If Fustiar did not flee, either the dragon must remain and face Synsaga's wrath with him, or flee and leave a sworn master behind. The Dragon Queen did not look kindly on the second course of action.

Or perhaps Fustiar could be persuaded to turn his dragon loose on Synsaga's entire company. That was a pleasant thought, and the black dragon felt his blood rush and his eyes bulge with excitement. His battle fury was not yet spent, and if the battle was only begun . . .

The dragon landed at the foot of the stairs just as Fustiar reached them. Then he held out a foreclaw to keep his master from falling under the weight of years, wine, weariness, and the Frostreaver. With the other foreclaw he picked up the dead guard creature by one foot and flung it like a dead rat far into the shadows.

"Welcome, friend," Fustiar said, aloud and in Common. He had never inquired the black dragon's name. The black dragon had enough dignity that he would not offer such knowledge, even to a sworn mage master.

"Do we voyage tonight?" the dragon asked. "The castle is yours, and all who betrayed their trust are slain or fled beyond my reach. Should I pursue them?"

"Unnnnh," Fustiar said, which was not a word the dragon recognized and which he had long suspected was not a word at all. "We go south. The Frostreaver, my books, and I."

For the first time, the black dragon saw that Fustiar had a leather sack slung across his back. From the way it bulged, it must be filled, and if it held books, it must be heavy.

"I have no saddle or harness," the dragon said. "Perhaps I should drive our enemies back still farther, even raid the camp itself. Then you can make a proper harness to be ready upon my return."

It was a polite but foredoomed suggestion; the dragon knew it at once. Fustiar fell to his hands and knees and spewed up a great deal of matter that smelled worse than the corpses. It would be a gift from Takhisis if he could as much as lace up a pair of sandals.

"Very well," the dragon said. "Stand still. I will carry the Frostreaver in one claw, you and your sack in the other. But we shall not go far to the—"

"South," Fustiar said. "S-South."

That made as much sense as anything that the black dragon had heard tonight. It would also make sense to halt as soon as they were clear of Crater Gulf, to make that harness and allowed Fustiar to clear the rest of the wine from his body.

He would, however, say nothing about that plan to Fustiar.

* * * * *

The last thunder of dragon wings had long faded into the night. The night sounds of the jungle were returning. Pirvan slapped at an insect whining in his ear, taking pleasure all over again in being able to slap with his left hand.

Then he began going through their packs to see what was left, with their quest so nearly at an end. Not the danger—the black dragon or Synsaga's men might yet make an end of them—but any need to do more than stay alive had passed. Gerik Ginfrayson was beyond ransoming, they knew as much about Fustiar as they were likely to learn, and life suddenly seemed considerably simpler.

Pirvan knew that was more seeming than otherwise. What Haimya saw when she looked within herself, he did not wish even to try guessing, lest he guess wrongly and give mortal offense.

Also, healing would not be enough to keep them alive even if unpursued. They would have to make a secret camp, or even better, several, set snares for small game and lines for fish in the hill streams, find edible fruits and roots, and otherwise prepare to wait out the arrival of friends, who might then take a good long while *finding* them in this wilderness forsaken by all gods anyone ever cared to pray to.

"Pirvan," Haimya said. "Are you as healed as you seem?"

"I could ask you the same."

She stood on one foot—the foot of her wounded leg. Pirvan reached out and took the free foot with his left hand. Then Haimya twisted, throwing them both off balance. They fell beside each other on the muddy ground, then burst into laughter.

"I did not—I had not thought to laugh again," she said. "Not this soon. Gerik, forgive me."

Asking for his forgiveness every time you sneeze will not heal you, was what Pirvan wished to say. Instead, he shaped on his lips, "Haimya, I will stand far off or close by as you wish. But you need fear nothing from me if you allow me to stand close."

Haimya blinked tears out of her eyes and wiped her nose with the back of her hand, which left her as black-snouted as any pig. "What you have not said is that we had best stand close together until we leave the Crater Gulf. This is true. Likewise it is true that I am the soldier, who should know better how to live here than a city-born thief."

"I was not city-born, but as for the rest—"

Haimya rose, with much of her old grace and assurance. "Then the first thing we do is gather up all loose gear, and the second is hide ourselves."

* * * * *

Hipparan saw the black dragon climbing away from the tower long before he saw that the dragon was burdened. He saw that the other was encumbered long before he saw that his teeth and claws were bloody. And he saw the blood long before he recognized the scent of human gore, and realized that the burden was Fustiar in one claw and a Frostreaver in the other.

"Do we have a quarrel?" the black dragon called. If it was a challenge, it was phrased so politely that Hipparan knew he had the freedom to refuse it.

If he did so, the only two dragons awake in all the world would not fight each other.

Not now, at least. But what about later? The black dragon was sworn to an evil mage, and the mage was not going to abandon his perverted work. Filling the world with Frostreavers might be only the first of his works.

"I have a quarrel with Fustiar the Mage," Hipparan said. "I owe that much to my friends, who have suffered at Fustiar's hands."

"Argggh!" Fustiar snarled. His words were barely coherent, but the venom in them made Hipparan want to flinch away. "It was good work, freeing the woman of that lout! She wrought better than she knew, even if she ruined my Frostreaver. "Now she can seek a proper mate. Show me where she is, little copper dragon, and I will offer for her. She can stand beside me—"

Hipparan screamed. The black dragon flinched. So did Fustiar.

"Only one man has any claim on Haimya now, and you can never be he!" Hipparan roared. It seemed that his fury echoed from the clouds to the mountains and back again.

He lunged at Fustiar, before the black dragon could lower his head to use either his fangs or his breath weapon—not that a stream of acid was all that useful, this high in the air. Fustiar not only flinched, he writhed, screamed—and tore himself loose from the black dragon's claws.

Both dragons dived after the falling man. Hipparan was lower, and the black dragon had to stoop before he could see his master vanishing into the darkness.

Hipparan was the first to reach Fustiar, and after that it no longer mattered what the black dragon might do. The copper dragon's jaws closed on Fustiar's skull, and his teeth pierced to the man's brain. Hipparan opened his mouth, and a corpse weighted with spellbooks tumbled away out of sight.

Then Hipparan had to swerve sharply to avoid colliding with the plummeting black dragon. He opened the distance and called, "Remember, my quarrel is with one who is about to make a hole in the mud, not with you, flying strong and free."

The black dragon replied with his breath weapon. The acid sprayed wide on the wind, but even the few drops that struck Hipparan's right wing burned as though he had thrust the wing into a fire. He changed from a right turn to a left turn, as the other would most likely expect him to turn into the damaged wing.

Such ruses kept the fight between the two dragons going so long that Hipparan lost all sense of time or place. He had to look down once, to find that they were almost directly over the lake in the summit crater of the extinct volcano.

That look reassured him, and also nearly ended the fight with the black dragon's victory. The elder dragon lunged, teeth scraping across Hipparan's neck, nearly piercing scales into flesh. Hipparan folded his wings, and his dead weight tore him free; he kept them folded until he had dived clear.

That gave the other the advantage of altitude, which Hipparan realized might not have been the safest gift. The black dragon was remarkably fit for his age, skilled in battle, and actually seemed to be enjoying the fight. Perhaps he had some thought of avenging his master, but even more of simply proving himself against a younger dragon.

Hipparan had nothing to prove, and no wish to kill the other if he had any choice—which it seemed he did not. That and fear of leading the other dragon to Pirvan and Haimya was all that kept Hipparan in the fight.

He tried twice to use his breath weapon, but the slowness gas blew away even more thoroughly than the acid stream. The black dragon did not miss a single beat of his vast wings, or strike less surely with teeth and claws.

Which of them would overreach himself first, only the gods could know. Hipparan dimly remembered the dangerous art of the wing-bite, which would cripple but not kill. The black dragon remembered that he had another weapon, a legacy from his dead master. Hipparan would display his skill; the black dragon his loyalty.

So Hipparan dived upon the black dragon, striking at a wing, and the other rolled on his back and swung the Frostreaver in both foreclaws. Hipparan's teeth sank into the black dragon's left wing as the Frostreaver's edge sank into Hipparan's skull.

Hipparan died without knowing that he was in danger, the Frostreaver's embodied spells pierced all his own magic as easily as its physical being pierced his skull. The black dragon lived a trifle longer—long enough to realize that his dead foe's teeth were locked in his wing, and that both of them were falling out of the sky into the lake.

The black dragon's last sensation was of striking what had to be water but felt like stone—cold stone, as repulsive as it was painful to a creature of wet, warm forests.

*   *   *   *   *

Pirvan and Haimya had used most of their strength finding a hiding place. They had not realized that it gave them a good view across the river toward the extinct volcano. At least not until the aerial duel of dragons began, when they saw it clearly, then hurried out of cover to where they could watch.

Pirvan would have given an empire for Hipparan's victory, a kingdom to be able to help their friend, and a respectable barony to spare Haimya the sight of the dragon's death. The one person he loved ought to be spared more pain tonight.

The one person I love.

He repeated that in his mind so often that he began to fear he would say it out loud, which would break his promise to stand just where Haimya wished him. He had just clamped his lips shut when the battle reached its grisly climax.

Both dragons glowed in their death fall, so the watchers saw them plunge all the way down from the sky into the lake. Then they saw a glow from the lake that made the last light from the dragons seem as pitiful as a firefly's. An eye-searing blue glare poured over the rim of the crater, and blue mist rose from it as if the crater were boiling. Then Pirvan felt a chill breeze that had not been there a heartbeat earlier, and he knew what was happening.

The lake was not boiling, but freezing. One of the dragons must have been carrying a Frostreaver, or perhaps Fustiar had cast a spell, and the crater lake was turning to ice.

Ice expanded. Expanding, the lake would push the crater walls outward. Pushed far enough—

Haimya threw back her head and hurled a death keen at the sky, the mountain, the jungle, perhaps the gods. A goddess mourning the death of a mortal lover might have uttered such a cry.

Pirvan stood silently and still. He could no more have touched or spoken to her now than he could have molested that goddess.

She nocked an arrow to her bow and shot it at the stars. To Pirvan's eyes it seemed to rise out of sight before it began to fall—if it fell.

Haimya keened again—and this time she went on keening, until her last breath wheezed out of her throat and he finally had to hold her upright.

They were turning away from the volcano when they heard the mad god's thunder of a mountain splitting apart and falling.

Chapter 22

Pirvan climbed out of the stream and pulled on his rawhide loinguard.

"I need to splice the lines before I set them out," he called to Haimya. "So you can bathe as long as you wish."

"Thank you," she called over her shoulder. "Do you think we can try making soap, after we finish the fish trap?"

Not waiting for an answer, she removed her clothing, which consisted of a loinguard similar to Pirvan's and a rawhide strip tied around her torso, and ran down to the stream. Her hair was a chopped and raddled mess, her skin was nearly as dark as Jemar the Fair's with sun, dirt, and grease, she was more thin-flanked than Pirvan had ever seen her, and he thought she as the most beautiful woman in the world.

As for himself, Pirvan had begun with darker skin and hair, so the near month they'd spent in the wilderness had not changed his looks as much. He had lost weight, though not having much to lose, his arm still ached in wet weather (which meant a good part of the time), and he had never felt better in his life.

He turned away from the stream as Haimya dived in, a graceful pale arc against the green water, ending in a silvery splash. Neither of them was self-conscious about "standing close" as they had to do to survive, but at times a veil would come down over Haimya's eyes or even her whole face. Pirvan respected those moments and kept his eyes and thoughts in order.

Gerik had left a vacant spot in Haimya. It could well be that it would never be filled. This was because there had been a great and undying love between them, but because Haimya could not forgive herself for killing Gerik through carelessness. Gerik's death had taken something from her sense of honor, and only time (if that) could put it back.

Pirvan, on the other hand, knew exactly what he wanted out of life. There was a place within *him* that would never be filled if Haimya did not fill it—whether she came back to do so next year, or fifty years from now, when all that would be left for them was to nurse each other.

The path up from the stream forked. Pirvan realized that he'd taken the right fork only when he saw the sundered mountain, half the cone now gone. He paused to see how the vegetation was recovering from the wave that had roared down the river, to drown most of Synsaga's men and smash most of the ships to kindling wood.

Much of the ground along the river was still bare and gray. The wave must have scoured a good part of the banks down to bare rock. That kind of power probably also explained why Pirvan and Haimya had neither seen nor heard another human soul since the night the mountain had fallen.

It was the left-hand path Pirvan really wanted, leading up to the hollow tree where they had their fire. Cooking as much as they could eat and smoking the rest had given them more meat and fish in their diet, though nuts, roots, fruits, and even edible grubs also played their part. (Pirvan had not thought that some kind of nut, a sweet root, and smoked grubs could make a fine meal, but Haimya had taught him otherwise.)

He was turning back toward the fork, when a man stepped out onto the path.

Pirvan had a spear (the bow was with Haimya, in case she needed to defend herself or pick off some fresh fish). It whipped up, ready to throw, before he knew more than the man's being where no man ought to be.

Then the man laughed, and Pirvan recognized him.

"Brother Grimsoar! You've learned a good deal about silent movement since we last met. I didn't hear a single footfall."

"You've forgotten a good deal about listening, Brother Pirvan," the big man replied. He looked more weathered and even hairier than usual, but well fed and clad in sea barbarian garb and armor. His sword, however, was his old familiar blade.

"Well met, regardless," Pirvan said. "I suppose it's too much to hope for that you are here alone?"

"Here, on this path, yes, I am, but the rest of my party is down at the foot of the hill. Once we'd cleaned out the rest of Synsaga's pirates, the ones who hadn't died in the flood or fled in the surviving ships, we divided our landing party and began seriously searching—"

"When did you come?"

"Why don't we go back to camp, you tell your tale from the beginning, and then I will tell mine?"

That made sense, eager as Pirvan was to find out how it had fared with *Golden Cup*. The sea barbarian garb spoke of further dealings with Jemar the Fair, and Grimsoar would have been downcast if Eskaia or Tarothin were dead, but otherwise Pirvan could only guess.

The two men reached the fork again just as Haimya came up the slope. She was clad in sunlight and drops of water, and Grimsoar actually flushed and turned his head.

He also muttered, "Sorry to have to drag you back to

the world," loud enough for Haimya to hear him. She promptly snatched up a stick and flung it, so that it clanged off his helmet.

"What the—?" he growled.

"It's not as you think," Pirvan said. "Now apologize to the lady, or she will hit you with a bigger stick in a more important spot than your head."

"I crave your forgiveness," Grimsoar said, not quite keeping a straight face but at least looking elsewhere while Haimya resumed her garb.

"Granted." She ran her fingers through her hair, which only rearranged the disorder. "If we are leaving here, there is no reason to stint the hospitality. We have food for all your comrades and even you, unless you eat even more than I remember."

"Thank you, but we've been living off the land since we came ashore. I'm beginning to crave some honest salt meat and ship's biscuit again."

Pirvan and Haimya exchanged looks that suggested Grimsoar was mad, and went to gather the little that they did not care to leave behind.

* * * * *

Only the ruined mountain where the two dragons had died now rose above the mists of Crater Gulf. Jemar turned away from the shore and studied his squadron.

They were coming out of the gulf in battle formation, under sail to take advantage of the offshore breeze and save the men's strength for any fighting yet to come. Jemar did not think there was much danger of that. Minotaurs would be giving these waters a wide berth, and so would the three of Synsaga's ships that survived the wave roaring down the river after the mountain had fallen. Some of the starving survivors rounded up by Jemar's landing parties spoke of a fourth ship, and doubtless some bold souls were heading for their deaths in small craft.

Both the quest and the fighting were over. What

remained was mostly matters better left to clerks, and Jemar could do very little about much of the rest. (Well, he could pray for Pirvan and Haimya, if he could be sure where to direct the prayers!)

One matter was very close to him, and therefore in his hands to settle. He had his command chair brought on deck, and then sent a messenger, saying that he wished to speak to Lady Eskaia, and would wait for her at her convenience.

Instead, the next thing he saw was Eskaia coming toward him. She wore sea barbarian garb, with a light jacket over her shirt. Jemar wondered if she had donned one of the low-cut tunics she had favored for a day or two, until sunburn had taught her otherwise.

He would miss her in a way he had never expected he would miss a woman, and Shilriya would tease him about it even if she accepted the offer he would soon be making. But he had not taken his betrothal rights, so there was no impediment to setting her free from a promise that did her honor but which he could not in good conscience accept.

"I wished to see you, I think, as much as you wished to see me," she said. As there was only one chair, she sat on the deck, cross-legged and as much at ease in the pose as if she'd been a sailor for years. Jemar had to look away briefly in order to compose himself enough to speak.

"My lady—no, let me call you by that title until I have finished what I wish to say—you made a most generous offer, if I would lead my ships south to rescue your friends. This I have done. They are as safe as they can be, at least in their bodies. Their spirits—that is in the gods' gift. But I have kept my bargain. What I want to say— what I must say—"

He took a deep breath. "I will not hold you to your part of the bargain. You are free to return to Istar, with no duties to me now or ever again."

A silence came down upon the sea, in which it seemed that even the creak of timber and the soft whine of the breeze in the rigging were hushed and listening. Eskaia looked up, and Jemar saw that she had tears in her eyes.

"Is this a . . . command?" The last word was almost a sob.

"No. It is—a gift, one might say—if you wish to accept it."

She rose, came over to him, and sat down on his lap. Instead of embracing him, she crossed her arms on her breast.

"Well, I do not accept that gift. What I wish is that we complete the bargain. Jemar, do I have to go down on my knees and beg you to marry me?"

It took some while for Jemar to convince her otherwise, with hands and lips, since the words would not come. He was rising from the third kiss when he saw that they had an audience.

"Tarothin! Wizard, what do you here?"

"Ah—I came on deck and—" He took a deep breath. "I thought I might be needed, to keep one of you from throwing the other overboard."

"If anybody is going to be thrown overboard, Tarothin, it is you," Eskaia said firmly.

"I forbid that," Jemar said.

"Who are you to forbid—?" Eskaia began, then laughed. "It seems we are already having our first quarrel." The men joined the laughter.

"I believe I can now bless this wedding," Tarothin said. "Eskaia, I will have to regret the loss of a good cleric, as you might have been. But I suppose you will be even more adept as a pirate's woman—"

"Sea barbarian's lady," the couple said, in unison.

"Sea barbarian's lady," Tarothin corrected himself, "than you would have been as a cleric. Although whether your father's blessing will be on this wedding, I am less sure."

"He will surely bless it if we have a second ceremony in Istar or some other place where he can attend it," Eskaia said. "And he will bless it several times over when Jemar's ships protect those of House Encuintras from pirates and minotaur raiders."

"And when will that start?" Jemar asked, eyebrows rising as he fought to keep more laughter inside.

"As soon as the marriage is consummated," Eskaia said primly, "and thereafter as long as we both shall live."

"I had not thought to receive your dowry," Jemar said. "But neither had I thought to pay bride-price."

"You did not think about many things," Eskaia said, "but I understand that is common when a man is hot for a woman."

Jemar kissed her lightly on the forehead, then stroked both her cheeks with the tips of his fingers. "Was it that plain?"

"Even a green maiden like myself could tell, my love," she said softly.

Then they both laughed, because Tarothin was turning red. The laughter died as they looked beyond him toward the prow, where the slim figure of Haimya stood, the golden cap of her hair ruffled in the wind.

An even slimmer, darker figure was making its way toward her. Jemar and Eskaia looked at each other again, then both stepped to Tarothin, spun him around, and marched him off toward the cabin amidships.

* * * * *

Pirvan slipped up beside Haimya and looked out past the bow wave curling over the ram, to the endless sea horizon beyond. Perhaps the ocean was not so bad, in such a benign mood. But the memory of its other moods would be with him every time he smelled saltwater.

"That did not look like a farewell," Haimya said, in a distant voice.

Pirvan wondered briefly what she meant, then looked back, as Jemar and Eskaia wrapped themselves around one another.

"It looks even less like one now."

"So I expected. So I hoped."

"What will you do now?" Pirvan asked.

Haimya shrugged. "I could doubtless enlist under Jemar. To be a sea barbarian warrior in his service is better than many other fates that might be mine. He might even consider it part of his gift to Eskaia, to find me a dowry and a husband."

Several questions came to Pirvan's mind; he kept them all off his lips.

"I fear I cannot accept such a gift," Haimya said. "I have won most of what I have fairly. It is no great matter to do that again. Are you returning to Istar?"

"Perhaps, but not for long if I do. I have said I might be giving up night work. Also, I may have no choice. I am now known to many in Istar, who cannot afford to tolerate even the most moderate of thieves."

"I was asking, because Gerik has kin. A sister, at least, wed to a merchant's heir, and I believe they have children."

"House Encuintras can do more for them than I," Pirvan reminded her.

"If they so wish. Eskaia would make sure that they wished it, if she were returning to Istar. But the city may never see her again. Nor was any of House Encuintras there when Gerik died."

Pirvan understood where this was leading. Haimya was afraid to face Gerik's kin, when she saw herself with his blood on her hands. It was the first time he had seen her run away from a battle—and, in her position, he would have done the same.

"What I can do shall be done," he said. He put his hand over hers. "I also fear that the time has come for us to stand apart."

She lifted a hand and put it over his. When she turned to him, her face was a mask—except for the eyes.

"Yes, for now it is best if you stand far away. But not so far, my friend, that I cannot find you if I wish to see you again."

Chapter 23

Rumor ran that there was wailing and gnashing of teeth in high places in House Encuintras when Eskaia's "mad fling" (as one woman was said to have called it) became open knowledge.

Rumor also ran that Eskaia's father watched the wailers and gnashers run about, rather like a cat watching mice at play, then brought his paw down firmly on "this pestilential nonsense" (as it was said he called it). He had been waiting for an excuse to remove certain persons, as they had been waiting for an excuse to remove him. Now their conduct let him strike first.

However much truth there was to these tales, it was certainly some while before the matter of Eskaia's dowry and rewards for the other questers could be settled. When it was, the terms were more than generous.

An amount equivalent to Eskaia's dowry was paid out, but not as a single sum into Jemar's hands. He received some, Eskaia received more (with strong legal barriers to Jemar's ever taking it), a new ship was built to replace *Golden Cup* and Kurulus appointed its captain, and much generosity was recorded in the chronicles of the city, or at least in those of House Encuintras.

Pirvan received a generous sum, more money than he would likely have received from the factor over the sale of all the rubies. He gave part of it to Gerik's sister, using his thief's skills to make sure her husband did not know of it, for he was too respectable to take such "tainted silver."

Then he left Istar, even before Jemar and his bride sailed up to the city's piers and had a grand second wedding with a longer guest list than any wedding in the city that year. He regretted missing the occasion, but he had received warnings that his becoming well known would indeed mean exile from Istar.

Five years, at least, he was warned, and at the end of that time perhaps a full pardon. Otherwise, he might end in the arena or even on the scaffold, and at best could buy his freedom only by revealing the secrets of the thieves.

Pirvan was on the road from Istar that night, to guard against this being treachery intended to provoke him into some crime. He resolved also to yield without a fight if he could not outrun pursuit, rather than besmirch the quest's reputation down the years.

There had to be some in Istar who would count his and Haimya's eliminating Synsaga's pirates—in Istar and in every other trading city—in his favor. But they seemed to be outnumbered by those who could see no farther than ending the career of one thief and perhaps learning the secrets of his brothers and sisters in night work.

House Encuintras was powerful, but it could not do everything. So Pirvan did the one most necessary thing remaining, which was to leave Istar for the safety that lay only a few days' ride from the city.

He left so swiftly that he could not learn what had become of Haimya, and he regretted missing the wedding mostly for missing the chance to do that. It did not ease his spirits that autumn, when Grimsoar One-Eye found his way to the village where Pirvan was living and said that Haimya had not been at the wedding.

"Or at least if she was, she was so well disguised that even a man who'd seen all of her—"

"My hospitality is not without limits, Brother Grimsoar."

"Oh, sorry. But you've let a good one get away, I say that—"

"I say that you ought to keep your tongue off Haimya, if you cannot talk sense about her."

After that it was a while before a sullen Grimsoar would talk, but good wine and a better stew at the local inn brought him into a better humor. As he watched the grooms finishing work on the horse that would take him back to Istar and his ship, he clapped Pirvan on the back.

"Brother, Istar may be closed to you for five years, but that's no cause to spend them all here in this fleabite of a town. Or are you casting eyes on the maid at the tavern? I wouldn't say that red hair is all real, but—"

Pirvan punched his old comrade lightly in the ribs. "See a healer when you return to town, my friend. Even about other women, your tongue runs away with you."

"Then you are waiting for Haimya?"

"Yes, curse you! But if you spread that tale all over the land and sea, I will hunt you down and cut out your tongue and other parts, then burn them in front of your eyes."

"I shall be the soul of discretion."

"It's not your soul that I worry about, Grimsoar." Pirvan hesitated, remembering Haimya's admonition that she should be able to find him if she wished. He had hoped that "if" meant "when;" that hope was fast diminishing.

But perhaps it should not be lost.

"I still fear treachery from Istar," he said, "but if the sea barbarians—at least those friendly to Jemar—and the brothers and sisters know where I am—it should do no harm."

"Maybe even some good," Grimsoar said softly, then broke off to shout at the groom's boy for not heating the horse's drinking water.

* * * * *

Pirvan had bought a yeoman's cottage just outside the village, not cut off from it except in the worst weather. It had some fields and a large kitchen garden attached, and come spring he would hire labor, plant, and plough. He had not spent so freely thus far that anyone suspected him of hidden wealth; that would change if he did nothing to bring in silver for another year.

Meanwhile, he did well enough for himself, with an elderly manservant who slept in the barn except when he drank so much he could not walk that far. Pirvan had grown used to cleaning up after the old man; when sober, he worked well enough, and he did not deserve to end facedown in a mud puddle. One could not imagine him unleashing evil dragons and twisted Frostreavers on the world, no matter how much he drank.

Autumn had turned into winter, and the roads had turned to icy ooze, when they were not iron-hard ruts. The wind now blew against the shutters without the skitter and crackle of dead leaves driven before it. Pirvan and his servant had patched enough of the cracks so that no cold air trickled in to chill the stew or awake Pirvan even before the neighbors' cocks crowed.

The servant was gone, carrying his blankets and a kerchief full of bread, hard cheese, and a leg of chicken left over from dinner. Pirvan sat on the bench opposite the fireplace, a cup of wine nestled in his lap.

It was good wine (this village lived by coopering barrels for the winegrowers of the area), but it might have been vinegar for all the pleasure it gave Pirvan. He was tempted to toss it into the fire, but feared that would put out the flames and condemn him to sleeping cold or relighting the damp wood.

Best count the kindling and the firewood tomorrow, he

thought.

He rather hoped they would come up short, even if it might be thanks to the neighbors' boys stealing again. A good day chopping wood was as much exercise as he had these days, always leaving him able to eat well, sleep soundly, and forget how alone he was.

He set the cup on the rough-hewn table that was the only piece of furniture in the cottage when he had moved in. It might be a pleasant change to sleep in the hall tonight, in front of the fire. The bedchamber was smaller and easier for its own fireplace to heat, but he'd grown weary of falling asleep and waking up with the same pattern of cracks in the plaster before his eyes.

He had finished distributing the pallet, blankets, and furs on the hall floor when he heard the knocker clatter. Probably the old man coming back, with an eye to raiding the wine cellar—and every cup he drank was one less that Pirvan could not be tempted to toss down.

The figure in the door was not the old man. It was taller, less stooped, and showed a youthful face and figure almost lost in a hooded gray cloak of fine wool that must have cost more than the old man's wages for a year—and Pirvan was not holding back on those wages.

"Good evening, traveler," Pirvan said. "If you are lost, I can show you the way to the village. The inn there is more comfortable than anything I can offer, though on a night like this I would not turn anyone away."

"Good," the traveler said, and threw back the hood of the cloak.

"Haimya!"

Pirvan's arms rose of their own will, but he forced them down. The woman stepped forward.

"Aren't you glad to see me?" It was a question as artless as a child's, but Pirvan heard depths that no child could have learned.

At least his arms knew the answer. He embraced her, feeling the chill dampness of her cloak but with her warmth inside it, glowing like a coal in a snowdrift.

He did not trust himself to speak. He did not quite trust

his own senses. This could not be happening, or if it was, it would end suddenly and he would be standing there in the wind from the open door, embracing nothing, and looking like an idiot.

Without breaking the embrace, Haimya reached back with a foot and kicked the door shut. When she regained her balance, she tightened the hold, then kissed him.

"Pirvan, you—we have stood apart as long as we need to. Unless you think otherwise."

Pirvan did not. Both his body and mind were now sending him the message that this moment was real; he should seize it and make it last, even for a whole lifetime.

He hoped it would be that long. Also, he would not have sent Haimya away even if he had doubted what they might have after tonight. A look into her eyes, the same clear blue, told him that it would be better to die himself than to inflict such a wound.

"No, Haimya. Let us stand close."

She swallowed. "Then help me off with my . . . cloak."

The help did not end with her cloak, or his tunic, and before long they were not standing at all.

*   *   *   *   *

"Why weren't you at Eskaia's wedding?" Pirvan asked. He had to pose the question three times, because his mouth was partly muffled in Haimya's hair. She had grown it longer than he had ever seen it, and running his hands through it gave all sorts of new and exquisite sensations.

"I was, but not at the public ceremony. Eskaia understood."

"I hope so. May I ask where you've been since then?"

"Several places. Mostly Karthay. Remember, my mother was Karthayan. There were family matters I had put off too long, for all that Eskaia would have been glad to send an Encuintras factor to settle it. I suppose I was too proud to accept her aid. So I ended by doing most of the work myself, and spending a good part of my pay for the quest on the way."

Pirvan tightened his grip. She laid a hand over his eyes.

"No, Pirvan. I am not poor, not yet. If-If I live here, I can pay my own way."

The thought of having Haimya in his arms every night made Pirvan's blood race. She sensed it, and rolled over on top of him, brushing her hair across his face as her hands roamed.

It was a long while before they spoke again, at least in words, and then it was only to say good-night as they plunged down into sleep.

* * * * *

They woke before dawn, bathed in a bucket of water heated on a revived hearth fire, lay down again, and in due course slept. The sun was high when they woke, and they had barely broken their fast and garbed themselves when the knocker clattered again.

The man who stood against a harsh blue sky was almost as tall as Grimsoar One-Eye, but leaner and lighter on his feet. His long face showed breeding as well as an imposing mustache, and his hands showed Pirvan the same sort of marks left by years of work with steel.

"Warrior, what brings you here?" Pirvan asked. Behind his back, he signaled Haimya to arm herself.

"A matter of interest to all of us. May I enter?"

"If you keep the peace, you may enter and we will hear you out."

"Paladine and Kiri-Jolith hear me, that I swear to do you no harm. Whether I do you good is for you to judge, but I trust the judgment of both of you."

The man entered, looking even taller under the low ceiling and formidable even when he sat. The scabbard of a broadsword showed under his riding cloak, and Pirvan caught the glint of mail at his throat.

"I am known as Niebar the Tall—"

"*Sir* Niebar, by any chance?" Haimya asked.

"You see clearly. Sir Niebar, Knight of the Sword, here on a matter of concern to the Knights of Solamnia."

"Very well," Pirvan said. "But it will go ill with you if you lie."

"Lies do harm—at least here and now," the knight added with a wry little smile. "Therefore I shall tell none."

The knight might have been telling no lies, but his recital of Pirvan's history seemed to take forever. Pirvan half expected the shadows to be lengthening before the tall warrior was done.

"All this praise of my skill, honor, virtue, and the rest make pleasant listening," Pirvan said. "But some of it is only known to my brothers and sisters. On your oath, answer—have you spies among them?"

"Yes," Sir Niebar said blandly. "We have spies in many places, seeking folk worthy of entering the ranks of the knights."

When those words sank into Pirvan's brain, he gritted his teeth to keep his jaw from hitting his knees. Or at least that was one possible interpretation of those words, even if it might be a dream.

"If you had spies, then you knew where he was," Haimya said. If the wine in her cup had been any closer to her, it would have frozen as solid as the crater lake. "Do you know how long it took me to find him, after I knew I wished to do so?"

"Yes," Sir Niebar said again, as blandly as before. Pirvan reflected that the knight's manner of tossing off these stunning answers might one day get him killed. Not today, by Pirvan. Haimya might prove another matter.

She was quivering, and her hand was not far from the hilt of her sword, as she spoke again. "Then—may I assume that you followed me?"

Sir Niebar seemed to realize the possible consequences of another bland yes. Instead he nodded. "Forgive me, but we trusted your judgment once again, for it has never led us false. You are your grandfather's blood, as true as a sword blade and as sharp in destroying evil."

Under all this poetry, Pirvan detected another astonishing truth. Haimya's grandfather had been a Knight of Solamnia.

It's always nice to know about your wife's ancestry before the wedding, he mused.

"We followed you," Niebar went on, "because your coming to Pirvan was the final test. If he was worth seeking out, then he was worthy of the knights."

Pirvan looked at the ceiling. "That is not one of the lawful tests I have heard of, in the tales of the knights choosing men."

"Hard times strain the best laws," Niebar said. "Now—I assume that you know what I wish to know. When may I have your answer?"

"In an hour," Haimya said.

"I asked—I think it is not impious to call him 'Sir Pirvan,' among us three."

"An hour will be enough," Pirvan said.

Sir Niebar rose and bowed himself out, without taking his eyes off Haimya. Pirvan doubted he appreciated her beauty. More likely watching her sword hand.

Then Haimya fell down on the furs, biting one of them to keep from howling with laughter.

"What is so amusing?"

She strangled a last few giggles and sat up. "Pirvan, are you going to enter the knights?"

"I have left the thieves and Istar. The knights are a place where I can do some of what I do well, that others will be the better for it. If that is not enough reason for them to accept me, on their heads be it."

"Very good. All the more reason for Niebar to wait the full hour. That much time standing in the cold will let him practice austerity or some other such knightly virtue."

"Oh?"

She put a hand to the laces of her tunic. "Pirvan, the training of a knight keeps a man celibate for a year at least."

This time when Pirvan said "Oh," it was in a very different tone.

Epilogue

From the courtyard Pirvan heard the clatter of horses as the last visitors rode away from the house where Sir Marod maintained his quarters.

The older knight ushered him in, dismissed his squire with a glance, and pulled up two chairs. Pirvan chose one, but refused to sit until the other was seated.

That brought a smile to Sir Marod's face. "You bore up under the day better than I did, and I was ten years younger than you are now. My legs refused their office, and I more fell than sat on the first chair I thought would not collapse under me."

Sir Marod went on for some time in this vein, jumbling together anecdotes of his own career, that of other knights he knew, and that of knights who were history or even legend. At least he thought it was Sir Marod doing the jumbling; it might be his own wits. Fasting was only the least of the demands on a knight, on the day when he could lawfully call himself one.

"But I ramble, without enough years to be explanation or excuse," Sir Marod said. "Have you guessed what your purpose shall be as a Knight of the Crown?"

Pirvan ran past his inward vision all those anecdotes he remembered, and nodded slowly. "I think you wish me to seek out people worthy to be knights, or at least to aid them. This will mean living in the world, and moving about, using much of what I learned as a thief."

"Exactly so. Much of that can be taught in no keep, nor in twenty years of knighthood. Many knights would refuse to learn it even if they had the chance. Yet much of it is good."

"You ask a great deal of me."

"I ask no more than you just swore to give us, Sir Pirvan. Nor is it more than you did for ten years without any bond except your own honor and whatever oaths you took to your brothers and sisters."

"I think it is with honor as it is with courage. Half of both is wishing to sleep well at nights," Pirvan said. He had thought Sir Marod might take offense, but instead the other knight nodded slowly.

"Often thought by wise men, seldom uttered out loud," he said. "Also, what you do not know of such work, you can learn from your lady."

"I thought Haimya might have been doing such work. How many knights has she found?"

"That is her secret," Sir Marod said severely.

"Very true," came a voice from behind Pirvan. He whirled. Haimya was standing in the doorway. She wore a plain gown of dark green with silvery trim, not immodestly cut in any way, but still making a man vowed to celibacy regret his condition—and a man just released from such vows rejoice.

Presently, Pirvan became aware of a voice behind him. Sir Marod was saying, "Perhaps I should order wine and cakes, to sustain me until you have time to listen to me again. We old folk need our meals.

"Of course," he added, "I could just leave the wine and

cakes for you and depart. You young folk also need strength, and perhaps privacy."

Haimya unclasped one arm from around Pirvan and over his shoulder made a rude gesture at Sir Marod. The knight made a noise that reminded Pirvan so much of Hipparan that he held his breath for a moment.

"You, my lady, are not going to send me out of my own quarters into the wild and the wind as you did Sir Niebar. There is a chamber reserved for the two of you for this and several more nights. My squire awaits to lead you to it.

"Now go, Sir Pirvan, Lady Haimya!"

Obedience to the lawful orders of a superior being part of a knight's duty, Pirvan obeyed.